Marilyn Bowering

What it Takes to be Human

ALSO BY MARILYN BOWERING

TO ALL APPEARANCES A LADY

VISIBLE WORLDS

Marilyn Bowering

What it Takes to be Human

MAIA

Published in 2007 by
The Maia Press Limited
82 Forest Road
London E8 3BH
www.maiapress.com

ISBN 978 1 904559 26 9

A CIP catalogue record for this book is available
from the British Library

Printed and bound in Great Britain

The Maia Press is indebted to Arts Council England
for financial support

In memory of Elnora and Herb Bowering

What it Takes to be Human

Alexander (Sandy) Grey

'Understand that thou hast within thyself herds of cattle . . . flocks of sheep and flocks of goats . . . understand that the fowls of the air are also within thee.

'Understand that thou thyself art another world in little, and hast within thee the sun and the moon, and also the stars.

'Thou seest that thou hast all those things which the world hath.'

— Origen, *Alchemical Writings*

'I never was a Communist. I never played cards or pool. I never murdered or raped anybody; have never given anyone pornographic literature or drugs and never drowned anyone or put anybody to death. I do not smoke or drink or take drugs.

'Do not black out any of my words or say I am a liar or discredit any sentences lest God cause worms to eat your tongue until you repent.'

— Alexander (Sandy) Grey

'For when she passeth by,
She casteth from the heart all sinfull love,
Each villain thought she freezes, and lays low:
And those Love suffers in her presence, lo!
They are ennobled, or thereof must die:
And when he finds one worthy to draw nigh,
Such one full quickly doth her virtue prove,
Her greeting can his sinfulness remove,
So humble he becomes all vices fly,
And God hath lent her grace, e'en greater still
Who hath had speech with her can ne'er end ill.'

— Dante, *Vita Nuova*

'An ocean without its unnamed monsters would be
like a completely dreamless sleep.'

— John Steinbeck, *The Log from the Sea of Cortez*

'Any fool can disbelieve in sea serpents . . .'

— Archie Willis (editor, *Victoria Daily Times*), 1933

ONE
12 September 1939

The trees whoosh in the wind, their leaves are green and black in the Ford headlights that bounce up and down through the grey dust of the road. Up for heaven, down for hell. Orange circles of light that send signals, maybe, to enemy planes gliding down the dark arm of the inlet to spy on the airport at Patricia Bay. My hand is caught like a flipper in the window strap, my other hand is cuffed to the constable sitting beside me in the back. He is fatter than me. He smells like wet wool. We bump past a small cemetery – the graves are rows of pincushions stuck with white crosses; one tall white cross stands firm against the black glitter of the sea where the fishermen can see it – then the driver puts in the clutch and lets the police car run down the last few ruts of the dirt road to the ferry dock.

'Hey, Sandy,' the constable says, 'maybe we'll catch a glimpse of Caddy tonight. Heh heh.' He jabs me in the ribs with his elbow. The driver also laughs. They know, everybody who has listened to my father preach knows, that the sea serpent, Cadborosaurus, will rise out of the sea in the Last Days. My father says the Last Days are now, since war was declared on Sunday. He says I'm needed more than ever at home, we must stay together to fight Satan. I do not believe what my father believes, but nobody knows this yet but me.

The fat constable has released himself and huffed down to the dock to see if the *Brentwood* is coming. The other policeman, the driver, the young one chewing gum, has opened my door. He pulls me out and locks both my hands together in front of me. When I raise my hands to wipe the sweat from my forehead, he steps back.

I smell seaweed and smoke.

'Please take my hat off,' I say to the young policeman. 'My head is itchy.'

'Bugger off,' he says. He takes a drag on his cigarette. His free hand drifts to the gun holstered to his Sam Browne but he lets it fall when we hear the drone of an airplane. We both look up.

'It's an Avro 626,' I say. I can see the plane's double wings against the puffs of clouds. The moon is rising like the bubble in a barometer from behind the hills.

'Is it, now?' the policeman says.

'Yes. You can tell from the sound of the Armstrong-Siddeley Lynx engine.'

'You planning on joining up?' he asks me. 'When this' – he gestures to my handcuffs – 'is over?' He takes my hat off for me and spins it through the open window of the car so it lands on the back seat.

'I'm nineteen years old,' I say.

'You mean your old man won't let you,' he says.

'He can't stop me.'

'I bet he wanted to. Say, is that why you tried to . . .?'

I turn away to watch the plane begin its lowering circuits over the airport. By the time I've lost sight of it, the *Brentwood* is nearing the dock, pushing the stink of burning diesel across the pier and up the roadway. This will be the last run of the evening.

'She's running late,' I say.

'Get in quick, the both of you!' says the fat constable who has panted back to the car. 'Hurry up!' He looks around anxiously. They had to send to Victoria for the car to get me. They don't have one of their own. They aren't used to this. They're used to the village and one telephone and laughing behind our backs at my father. They're not used to my father with blood on his face, turning me in.

I wait for the driver to open my door. He steps in front of me to do so. He's a slender man, and I'm tall, and every day for the past year, while I was away at college, I exercised with Indian clubs. It would be simple to raise my cuffed fists and bring them down on the back of his neck. I could make my escape, but then what?

The door is open. I get in beside the constable. We drive up the gangway and on to the car deck, the last of the half-dozen or so cars to load.

You can tell how people are with boats right away: the driver is fine, he's made himself comfortable with his cigarettes, over by the wheelhouse, talking to a seaman winding ropes. But even before we've reached our full speed the constable sitting beside me has turned green.

'You'll feel better outside,' I tell him. 'Take deep breaths, go to the bow, away from the exhaust.' Beads of sweat stand on his forehead. 'Go on,' I say, 'you don't want to be sick in here.'

Five minutes later I'm out in the wind, too. They've left my door unlocked, because they know me, they know what Sandy Grey will do, so I've eased the handle down with my elbow. Salt spray cools my face as I thread through the vehicles to the guardrail. The other passengers have left their cars and climbed the steps to the superstructure, out of the elements. The wheelhouse is dark to protect the steersman's eyesight. There is only a slit of light seepage from the canvas over the lounge windows. The waves glow where the hull parts them, but the rest of the water as far as I can see, north towards the inlet opening, and southeast to Brentwood pier, where we'll land in half an hour, is black, trembling, shining.

'You wouldn't have a light on you, would you?' A woman slips in beside me to lean against the bulkhead. Her raincoat is open and flaps in the wind. Her long legs shimmer in their silk stockings. A hat with a velvet band holds most of her hair away from her face, but a few blonde strands blow across her forehead.

'No, sorry.' I raise my hands so she can see the cuffs on them.

'Oh my, you're worse off than I am.' She fumbles through her handbag and comes up with a single match. She has to turn her back to me to light the cigarette. When she's done, and the tip is red and glowing, she bends towards me and places it between my lips. Her breath is sweet and astringent with gin. 'Any last words from the condemned man?' she says. She has perfect skin and deep shadows below made-up eyes.

'No, none,' I say through the cigarette.

'That's too bad. I was hoping for some excitement. Isn't it too goddamn boring here?'

'What? Not for me.' The cigarette wobbles on my lips.

She laughs. 'I don't suppose.' She takes the cigarette. 'What's your name?' she asks, scrunching her eyes up against the smoke.

'I'm Sandy. Sandy Grey.'

'Well, Sandy Grey, my name is Georgina, and you know what? You're the only man worth talking to on this bolt-bucket.' She flicks the cigarette butt over the side. The spark as it arcs to the water sends a tremor through my knees. 'What did you do, Sandy Grey, to get yourself into this mess, whatever it is? Don't you know there's a war on?'

'I know. I wanted to enlist but my father wouldn't let me.'

'Wouldn't let you? Hey, how old are you?'

'Nineteen.'

'Nineteen! You're younger than my son! Well, you know what, Mr Sandy Grey, you're old enough to do what you want.'

She's noticed that I'm shaking, so she puts her arm through mine. 'It's going to be all right. I know it.' She squeezes my elbow. 'Just pretend I'm your mother . . . Talk to me, and I'll give you some advice.'

'I don't have a mother any more.'

'Well, pretend, anyway, and I'll pretend you're my son. Tell me what happened.'

So I tell her, and she doesn't make me feel ashamed or guilty and she doesn't say anything about my crying.

'I'd have done the same in your place, in the circumstances,' she says, 'but it does look bad, doesn't it. What do you think they'll do with you?'

'Take me to jail. Put me on trial.'

'And you'll tell them what you've just told me?'

'Yes. I'll have to. I'll have to tell the truth.'

'Jesus,' she says. 'I really don't think you should do that, Sandy. A lot of people aren't going to understand.' Georgina chews at a painted lip.

'What do you think I should do, Georgina?'

'Get the hell out of here, of course!' she says sharply. Then she smiles up into my eyes.

'Thank you, Georgina,' I say. 'I'll always remember you.'

When you exercise with Indian clubs, you build up your wrists, the chest is expanded, the muscles of the legs and arms are greatly improved. If you persevere in their use you become ambidextrous, the grasp of the hands is made firmer. I step close to her and slowly, so that she can move away if she wants to, I place my lips on hers. I can taste her lipstick. Her mouth moves like soft pillows under mine.

'Goodbye,' I say. I place my joined hands on the rail and I swing myself up and over. In the air I find my form and dive like an angel.

When I strike the surface of the water I cut straight through; the cold strips me of breath, and I plummet towards the bottomless trench of the inlet. Green and yellow eyes track me in the blackness – *'The great dragon which deceiveth the whole world; she was cast out into the sea.'*

By the time I surface I have kicked off my shoes. I can do nothing about the jacket that drags at my shoulders, but although I'm not a good swimmer I can float and I have endurance. The inlet is sheltered and it has warmed all summer. Perhaps I could stay here for hours. The stern of the *Brentwood* is a considerable distance away. There are no spotlights, no whistles, no shouts of 'Man overboard!'

Soon the ferry vanishes into the mist as it passes a small island. I turn on my back and kick my feet and head back the way we've come.

The biggest tides in the world flow in and out of the Bay of Fundy. As a girl, my mother stood on the dykes and watched them. The tides here are not great ones like those, but I'm no fool, not me, Sandy Grey, and I know what has happened. I can no longer make progress towards the shore. No matter how hard I try, the tide and currents take me where they will. Now, when I twist my head to check, the dock lights are not closer, as they should be, but more distant, and falling behind. A cool ripple slides beneath me, water splashes in my mouth, then there's a sweep of warmth along my back and the water turns to black oil. I glide effortlessly farther and farther towards the mouth of the inlet.

If you look on a map, you'll see that the coastline of the peninsula on the inlet's eastern shore takes the shape of a crow. Low on its breast is the dock to where the *Brentwood* crosses. Tucked under its chin is Patricia Bay, and reaching inland, from the beak towards the eye, is the airport runway. Its end lights are brilliant now as I rise and fall on the smoothly rolling waters. I am so near the point of land where the airstrip begins that I'm sure I can swim to it. It is less than fifty yards away. I turn on my side and sweep my arms up and down, as if pumping a speed car, and I scissor with my legs: I won't have to cross mountains and return to the prairie, I won't have to run away, I'll be right here at head-quarters, in the thick of things. But the cold water returns just when I start to get somewhere, and tugs me backwards.

The landing lights fade.

This time I ride a current down the east side of the inlet in a swirl of white water that frills submerged foothills. To the west are the lights of little towns, and pale scree and gravel beaches, and the occasional thrum of a fishing boat grinding from port into the night towards its catch. On the nearer shore, lights in cabins and in the high windows of large estate houses blink off. I am too tired to swim.

Call for help, Sandy, whispers the voice of the mother I had lost as a boy, *where there's life, there's hope.* I open my mouth to cry out, and a small wave fills it; then another and another. The sea boils and blackens; something long and humped rises beside me, water streams from its back. It turns its snakelike head and examines me with the flame of its eyes, then it undulates and rolls, the muscles of its body ripple, it flips its tail and propels itself forward, and I'm caught and lifted in the surge of its wake.

My father is right, we are in the Last Days.

'Jesus, Sandy Grey, you gave me a fright. Take hold of the paddle. I'll haul you in.' Georgina leans over from a rowboat and slips an oar under the chain linking my hands. 'If you hadn't started splashing, I'd never have found you. Damn you, I'd have blamed myself, too. I should know better than to give advice. Do you always take people so literally?'

'Sorry, Georgina.'

My teeth chatter as she grabs me by the belt and does her best to heave me over the stern. 'You didn't give me away?'

'No, I damn well didn't, and I'm not going to now, so lie down in the bottom and be quiet. Those goddamn cops are all over the place.'

'You're my angel, Georgina.'

'I'm no angel, Sandy. Just ask my father. The son of a bitch has been trying to get rid of me for years.' She lifts and lowers the oars and sets us moving.

'Where are we going?'

'To a safe place.'

'How did you find me?'

'Shush,' she says, but she points and whispers. 'My father's house is just over there. I grew up here – I know the inlet and I had a good idea where you'd be. You can't always let the bastards win.'

I'm quiet then. I hear the soft puffs of Georgina's breath and the hush of the blades as she slips them in and out of the sea. She stops rowing, and I hear a man's voice call out over the putt-putt of a two-stroke engine. 'Oh, shit,' she says quietly.

She dips the oars carefully into the water and pulls us, almost silently, through gentle swells until, only a few minutes later, I can sense we are nearing land. The bow scrapes on sand. 'You get out here. There's a duck blind just in those trees. I'll be back as soon as I can. I'll figure something out.' She helps me ashore, throws her coat after me, and has rowed out and is rounding the point towards her father's house before I understand I'm on an island, the little one at the foot of the inlet, where the crow's claw of the peninsula coastline would be.

I find the duck blind, struggle out of my soaking trousers and underwear, and wrap the coat around me. I wait, and listen, crouched down, and when I next rise up to look a searcher's boat is a stone's throw from the shoreline.

I climb some rocks, scramble through a stand of arbutus, jump down, in the dark, on to the beach, and fall over what I take at first to be a log. But it isn't. It moans and shifts, its skin is cold and rubbery, breath snuffles from its nose and mouth. It has swum itself on to the sand. Small waves cool its tail and lap at its forelimbs, but the head and long neck are sheltered in a cave opening. The body trembles, and it sighs, and as I watch beside it, my skin on fire with mystery, a long slithery wet miniature of itself drops from the vent in its underside into the shallow water. The baby lies grounded, then a wave washes over it and it tries to swim. It – this newborn survivor of the world before the Flood – flails its limbs, opens its eyes, turns its head and sees me. What I cannot explain is how this makes me feel. I'm no longer the last sane person in a mad world. I'm Sandy Grey all right, but I'm happy.

My father is a preacher, but only on Sundays and holidays. On weekdays, he's a plasterer. The material he uses in his trade is made of the skeletons and shells of small marine animals – the kind of creatures that thrive below me as I swim, as fast as I can, away from the island; their bones and shells break down and fall to the ocean floor where the weight of the sea crushes them to stone. You have to 'burn' limestone – heat the marine animals' remains to a high temperature – to yield lime. Once, when I was small, and I went too near the bucket when he was working, my father told me that lime dissolves human bones. I lifted the lid and stuck in my fingers. My skin burned, but my bones were fine. I knew then that my father *might* be a liar, and the things in my life that had started to worry me began to ease their pressure. But I had to be sure, I had to take my time.

I kick and glide, kick and glide, and when I think I'm far enough away, I stop, let my feet swing down, glance back and see lights begin to approach the spot where the sea serpents rest.

This is it.

'Help! Save me!' I scream. Men run, their lanterns swinging, and drag the boat from the beach; other vessels speed my way from up the inlet. An Avro 626 slips out suddenly from behind a cloud; the moon slides out, too. The beam of a pit-lamp strikes me full in the face, a rescuer dives overboard, the hum of the Armstrong-Siddeley Lynx engine reaches my ears through the crest of a wave, and suddenly, although I wasn't before, I'm drowning.

TWO

13 April and following, 1941

There are good people everywhere, Georgina says, wringing out a wet hankie and placing it over my bruised eye. I tell her I'll remember that, and I do. My father stands in the corner of the dank jail cell, his arms folded across his chest, but not so much that I can't see his watch-chain or hear his watch tick. He wears his good suit. He keeps his hat on to cover the bandages. I can smell my own must, spores itch my crotch and armpits, but I do not scratch. My father speaks several words, Georgina replies, and then a long empty darkness cleaves my life.

From out of it I can recall two winters of the smell of cabbage, the occasional scent of Georgina's perfume, and the idea that there was a trial, and with this second spring, when I awaken from my season of shock and slumber, my understanding that I've been assigned to the asylum at the end of a lane that winds from Victoria towards the inlet.

Dr Frank, the director, says when I ask him if this can ever truly be my home, 'If not here, where, Sandy?' I sit in his office and look around as I consider the question. A vase of variegated pheasant feathers has been set on a small table next to a silver tea service. On top of a hutch to the left of Dr Frank's desk perches a model of a two-masted schooner. Below it, on a shelf, propping up books, are several silver trophies.

'Are those yours, sir?' I say. Some of the items could belong in a home of mine. I have many books, I've built models, I've won prizes.

'What?' He cranes his neck around from where he stands adjusting the cord of the venetian blinds to admit more sunlight. Through the open slats I see lawns and hedges and shapely trees. A soldier carrying an army jacket hung casually over his shoulder swings a croquet mallet loosely in his hand.

I turn my eyes back to the trophies and read aloud from the engravings: 'First Prize, 1935, Pacific National Exhibition' and 'Second Prize, 1937, Canadian National Exhibition'.

'You've good eyes if you can read that.' He gazes at me thoughtfully. 'The cups aren't mine, personally. We've a herd of prize Holsteins, here on the farm. You'll see for yourself, once we put you to work.' He lowers himself into his chair. Dr Frank is a big man, well over six feet tall and, I estimate, three hundred pounds. An oval has been cut from the front of his desk to take his bulk, so that he may reach his inkwell and write. He pulls a notepad towards himself, picks up a pen, dips it in ink, bends his head and writes my name. His hair springs, thick and brown, from his scalp, but at the crown it is thinning. He looks up.

'Tell me, Grey, what did you want to do before this trouble of yours began?'

'I wanted to be a pilot in the air force, sir.'

His gaze softens with pity. 'Ah, I see, just like all the other young men.'

'I'd had some training. I'd joined the flying club.'

'But you were attending college – Damascus Road, I think your father said – where they teach the Treasures of Truth?'

'I began at Damascus Road, then the university took me in.'

'Took you in?'

'I won scholarships, I made a change.'

'I've spoken to your father. He doesn't know about the university.'

I say nothing. What is there to say?

He leans back and the coils of his chair creak, and the castors roll him backwards an inch or two. Silently I read the titles on the spines of some of the books – *Revised Statutes of British Columbia, Emotional Hygiene, Sex Life of the Unmarried Adult* – and of a number of journals – *Hospital Review, The American Journal of Orthopsychiatry*, and so on. I am interested to see *The War Neuroses* and a collection of the works of Sigmund Freud.

'I've noticed the soldiers outside, sir,' I say when I can bear the silence no longer. Several more of these men have passed by the window, accompanied by attendants. 'I was just wondering . . .'

'You were wondering why they are here?'

'Yes, sir, I was.'

'Soldiers, and airmen too, Grey, some of them badly burned. Most suffer from battle fatigue. It happens to the very best.' He sighs. 'They come here to recover. During the last war . . .' He trails off. 'Well, the less said about the evils of the past the better. Fortunately, young Sandy, we live in more enlightened times.'

He rolls his chair forward and flips open a file folder on his desk. He reads for several minutes while I watch a fly circle the yellow glass flutes of the light fixture that hangs from the ceiling. Two of the bulbs have burned out. Once more Dr Frank leans back, this time making a temple of his fingertips and resting them on the bluish pulp of his lips.

'The monsters lie inside us, Sandy, not outside, but we don't have to make things hard for ourselves as we work to defeat them. I'm here to help you.' His eyes are a pale sea green. They lounge, kindly lizards, in his long fleshy face and hold my own.

'What's going to happen to me, sir?' I say, unable to stop myself from asking. I'd been brought to the asylum by a policeman who had said, as we'd passed between flanking carved lions at the bottom of the steps, 'You know you'll never get out.' I'd glanced up at the face of the stone edifice I was entering. Bars striped every window. After the policeman had rung the bell at the inner steel door and passed me through it, he'd made a show of dusting his hands. I'd looked behind me at the outdoors, for what I feared might be the last time – at a workman cleaning the stone fountain after the long winter.

'You'll have heard stories about this place,' Dr Frank says. 'I want to set your fears at rest. Some of the tales may, once upon a time, have been true, but they are true no more. Gone are the ideas of straitjackets and restraining sheets. We would rather have an attendant stand by each man than use archaic methods. You are here to get well, Grey. I accept no other conclusion, do you understand me?'

'Yes, sir,' I say. I do not tell him what I know, that there is nothing wrong with me. My predicament is due to a misunder-standing, one I will have to work to rectify. Tears of relief, as well as of a natural foreboding, moisten my eyes.

'You're a clever boy, Sandy, too clever, perhaps. I've read the file, and I can read between the lines as well, you can trust me. Already I have had your parents here, insisting on seeing you' – I look up alarmed but he raises his hand to stop whatever I am about to say – 'and, knowing, as I do, what is best for you, I sent them away.'

I close my eyes in relief. A runnel of tension that I hadn't known was there leaves my body.

'You won't have to see them if you don't want to, not as long as I'm here.' I sense his body heat and smell Absorbine Jr muscle liniment as he leans closer across the desk. 'Do you want to see them?'

I open my eyes. 'No, sir,' I say. 'Thank you, sir.'

He gazes into his palms, where calluses round the base of

each finger, and I wonder if he can see the future, then he raises his eyes and begins to outline my treatment.

'Do you understand what I've just said?' he asks when he's finished.

'I think so, sir,' I say. 'There are two points of view. One is that I have a biological fault; the other, to which you're more inclined, is that a mental breakdown, such as mine, is the result of external factors, and these can be addressed through a variety of means. Psychoanalysis, group psychotherapy, narcosynthesis.'

'What I've told you, Grey, is that I'm giving you a chance, rather an unusual one, but you're young, you appear to have had some education and you've taken pains to educate yourself, and there are extenuating circumstances in your history. Recent research has shown that in cases like yours, equally good, if not better, results can be obtained by the methods I've outlined than by the use of the standard treatments.'

'Yes, sir.'

'Not that there'll be any mollycoddling.'

'No, sir.'

'If these don't produce results, of course, we'll look to other means.'

'I understand, sir. I'll work hard, I'll do my best.'

'Good.' He smiles at me. 'You will work six days out of seven, just like the other men. You'll contribute to your upkeep and, as much as you can, to the general war effort. Have you had farm experience?'

I shake my head.

'Then you'll start in the fields, or with the smaller animals, and if you prove yourself capable you can work up to the dairy or stables.' He reaches across the desk and shakes my hand. 'It will all become clear enough.'

He presses a button next to the telephone on his desk. A second later the door swings open and an attendant stands at the ready. I get to my feet.

'We'll have to find something to keep that brain of yours busy. You might think about what that could be. We'll get you settled in the West Wing first.' He nods to the attendant to lead me away. 'Keep your chin up, Grey.'

'Oh, yes,' he says, glancing up from the file which he'd been about to close. 'There is the matter of the attack on your father. We'll have to attend to that.'

The attendant who takes me to my room is Ronald Signet, a neat, clean-shaven, middle-sized man dressed in a blue uniform jacket and with a shirt and tie worn under a grey sweater. As we walk down corridors, pausing as Signet unlocks and relocks doors, he tells me a little of the history of the structure in which I am to live. Originally a jail and a prison farm, it housed prisoners of war and offenders against the Naval Discipline Act during the Great War. There was a hiatus when it became a game and pheasant farm (thus the feathers in Dr Frank's office) and then it reopened as a mental home. Its design is after Windsor Castle, with cut-stone window frames, and various details and castellated features. The corners are decorated with turrets, which along with the crenellated parapet – as I saw when I arrived – add to the general military effect, since such features were originally designed with martial and defensive purposes in mind. He says, as we climb the stairs to my floor, 'So you see, Sandy, you've something in common with King George and Queen Elizabeth.'

'What's that, sir?'

'You live in a palace.' He opens the door, which is not kept locked, to the room that is to be mine. I see four small beds lined up, with reasonable space between them, against a wall. Signet ambles to the bed at the far end, next to a window. Soft spring light filters through the bars on to my suitcase standing on the floor, already there ahead of me.

'This is where you'll sleep,' he says, then he turns to look out the window, the keys at his waist clinking on the bars.

I pick up a printed sheet that gives the daily schedule. Rise 5.40 a.m., Drill and so on, all the way to Lights Out 10.30 p.m. I suppose I must have sighed aloud, for Signet glances over at me. 'Come have a look, Sandy,' he says.

I stand beside him and examine a view of green fields. I watch two lambs stagger behind a ewe as she grazes. The farmer's dog next door is shut away behind a high wire fence: it barks at the helpless sheep family but cannot get to them. Is this not how it should be – that the weak be protected from the strong?

Signet tells me, after he has checked off the contents of my suitcase on a list and I have signed for them, that when the main asylum building was being built, a robin and her eggs were discovered in one of the supporting pillars. Building was suspended until the robin's eggs hatched and the birds were old enough to fly. A stone carving of the robin and her nest was made to mark the incident, and the carving could be found in the very spot between two columns to this day. I say to him, 'When I have grounds privileges I'd like to see that for myself!'

When he has left, I take off my shoes and lie down on my bed for a rest. The other men, my roommates, are at work. I won't meet them until later. I consider my position: I have clean sheets and clean clothes, a shelf for my books, a lamp to read by at night. On Thursdays there are concerts, on Fridays, films; I can say yea or nay to visitors . . . Who could ask for more?

Before beginning work in the rabbitry, I am to spend as much time as I like in the library. Dr Frank wants me to keep my mind occupied until we commence the first stages of my treatment. 'But what exactly do you want from me?' I ask him as we talk the next day.

'What do I want? The truth, Grey.' He writes the word in capital letters in his notebook, then turns it round so I can read it: TRUTH.

'I want facts, not speculations, Sandy. Speculations are

what get you into trouble, eh? You'll tell me what you know – not guess, but know – to be the truth. Investigate, examine, think!' He gathers up his papers and leaves, locking the library door behind him.

While I wait to be let out, I peruse the library shelves. They contain popular novels, dictionaries in various languages – Russian, Polish, Chinese, Japanese, French – and texts of many kinds: elementary physics and mathematics, history, botany, animal husbandry. I find, tucked at the end of one shelf, a scrapbook with a picture of my new home glued to the front cover. Inside are clippings and photographs, all to do with the history of the institution from the time when it was a jail. Some of the first inmates, apparently, had been transferred from other jails; then there were the naval prisoners, mostly from British armed merchantmen, including the famous *Kent*.

I look up at the sound of a key in the lock. Attendant Cooper has come for me. I say to him, 'Why would they take sailors fresh from a naval victory like the Falkland Islands and put them in jail?'

'What's that?' Cooper comes to peer over my shoulder. He points at, then reads, the line that says, 'Charged with breach of the Naval Discipline Act.'

'Yes, but this was 1917 when *Kent* sank the *Nürnberg*! They were heroes! What could "breach of the Naval Discipline Act" mean?'

'A handsome boy like you should know,' he says. He grins and slips a finger back and forth in his fist.

I look at him. 'What do you mean?'

'Buggery, you fool,' he says. 'Don't play the innocent with me.' For some reason he is angry. I wonder about this, as I know that Dr Frank has asked the attendants to answer my questions politely. Ron Signet has told me that the director is writing a book and I am to be a case history in it. He wants to show that his form of treatment is superior to insulin shock and Metrazol. Insulin, in particular, is an expensive therapy. He'll save money *and* get results. I asked Ron to tell me about these other treatments, but he refused.

I flip through the rest of the scrapbook pages – there aren't very many – only lists of names and dates of sentencing, along with the cuttings. A newspaper headline catches my eye: 'Man Once Hanged in Colquitz Yard.' I am just about to read the article when Attendant Cooper reaches over my shoulder and takes the scrapbook away. His hands are roped with veins that run strongly into his forearms.

I follow him to the cafeteria. When we arrive, Attendant Signet is there, drinking coffee. He sets his cup down on the counter then picks it up again. Everyone else is at work on the farm or laying the new steam pipes. Behind him on other counters are the dirty food containers from the hot table, and next to these are mounds of soiled white crockery at the sinks. 'Best get your sleeves rolled up, Sandy,' he says.

Attendant Cooper pours himself a coffee and adds cream to it. He spoons in sugar, stirs it, tastes it, frowns and puts in more sugar. I roll up my sleeves. 'Hey, Sandy,' he says, watching me begin to fill the sinks with hot water, 'did Ron here tell you his robin story?' He snorts as he sips his coffee, then walks over to Signet leaning on his elbow at the counter; he pushes at his arm.

'Don't, Pete,' Ron Signet says. 'You'll make me spill.' He drinks up and puts the cup down for good.

'Did you, hey, Ron, I bet you did. You do that with all the new guys.'

I try to catch Ron Signet's eye but he avoids my gaze. 'Is that true, Ron, was it just a story?' I ask. I drop dishes into the steaming water and add a measure of soap.

'Well . . .' Ron says.

Attendant Cooper explains that the story isn't true. It has nothing to do with us. The incident took place elsewhere, when they were building the cathedral downtown.

'Why would you tell me a lie, Ron?' I ask. He explains that

there are general truths and particular truths. His story is a general truth; he'd hoped, by telling it, to make me feel at home.

'But what would you have done when I asked to see the carving?' I say.

Ron Signet shrugs.

Attendant Cooper laughs. The buttons on the white shirt he wears under his jacket strain, showing his grey undershirt. 'You stupid bugger!' He says it 'booger'. 'Once they start your treatment you won't remember anything, including what Signet here tells you. He could say whatever he wanted and you'd never know the difference.' He finishes his coffee, throws the cup into the sink as he passes, then bangs out through the swing gate and crosses the cafeteria floor, the keys at his belt striking against the baton tied there.

'Is that true, Ron?' I say. 'That's not what Dr Frank has led me to believe.' I trust Dr Frank, but I've had glimpses, on the way to the baths, of the corridor to the East Wing. The floor is tiled black and white, the hallway is lined with cells. I've not met any of the men from there.

Attendant Signet sips at his empty drink. He polishes his glasses on a handkerchief. 'Well, Sandy,' he says.

That night, as I am falling asleep, two pictures come to me. In the first I see my father building a veranda on the back of our house. He tacks wire screening around it to keep out the mosquitoes. I remember that I slept well out there, and I woke up every morning to the singing of birds. I could see the silver gleam of a river when I climbed on to the windowsill.

The second picture is of a little girl who used to play with me. She has blonde curls. Her house was beyond a fence and nearer to the river than ours. To get to our house, she had to pass by the henhouse. My father had built a large pen for the chickens, but the big rooster always managed to fly up and out, jump on her and chase her away; so my father took the bird into our basement and killed it with an axe.

THREE
6 May and following, 1941

It begins to rain before I reach the rabbit hutches. I don't have my hat, but I don't mind the damp. In winter, when I was small, I went with my father, and the grandfather who owned a butcher shop, to watch the ice-cutting on Elk Lake. The men would cut the blocks, load them on to sleighs and pack the blocks in sawdust in the sheds in town. The cold doesn't bother me. I've always liked to be out in all weathers. I feel the cool rain run down my face and rejoice at its cleanliness.

There is, as Dr Frank says, pleasure in work. There's the path from the kitchen door past the newly dug kitchen garden, and then the walk up the grassy rise to the outbuilding where the rabbits and other small animals are housed. My socks are still in the laundry and so I can feel the grass blades as they slap wetly over my ankles above my shoes. Ron Signet is with me; he whistles and jangles his keys. He likes to talk about his family – his wife and daughter. They live nearby in the married quarters. His daughter is four years old and loves horses. We can see her, beyond the fencing, riding a pony in one of the fields.

Most days there are blue skies and small white wafers of clouds scudding over the farm as the spring weather moves through quickly, but today the soft lowering grey cumulus suits my mood.

I have begun to dream frequently, and although very little of these dreams stay with me, their auras remain. In one of these fragments, somebody cut through the wire screening of the veranda I have already mentioned. I told this to Dr Frank. 'Not thinking of leaving us, are you, Sandy?' he said. That was yesterday.

I pick up the rabbitry register from the slot beside the door. I know the names of all the does and bucks; we have just four bucks – one to every ten does, although there are plans to acquire more. I walk quickly round to make certain all the rabbits are well. The hutches stand in two tiers, with wire mesh bottoms that allow the droppings to slip through. The top tier droppings fall on to the sloped galvanised iron roof of the lower tier, then on to the ground. My first morning chore is to sweep beneath the hutches, place the sweepings in a barrow and from there wheel them to the dung heap beside the field compost. I am doing this, rain now falling heavily, my head down to follow the board trail laid across the mud for this purpose, when I hear someone call my name. I look up.

Attendant Cooper waits at the top of a rise ahead of me. He sports a grey fedora and a dark blue overcoat, and I surmise he is on his way out for the day, for some of the staff use the farm gate on their way to the parking lot. I didn't see him earlier, but I suppose he has been on night shift. When I finish dumping, I lower the barrow and walk over to him. Ron Signet expects me back at the rabbitry, so I cannot be long. But Attendant Cooper knows this.

'I've something to show you, Sandy,' Pete Cooper says as I come up to him. He hasn't shaved, and I smell drink on his breath. Myself, I do not drink, and my own whiskers are fine and pale, my skin too sensitive to shave every day, which is just as well, as we are not permitted our own razors. Once, when we sat outside in the grounds, Georgina, who had come to see me, and to give me news of her son in the RAF, leaned close and put her gloved hand on my face; I felt my whiskers catch on the silk. 'Give me a beardy,' she said, placing her cheek against mine, but she was joking and so I didn't.

'Come over here,' Attendant Cooper says.

He leads the way down the little hill past the stables and carpentry shop. He moves quickly ahead of me, not looking back. I turn to see whether we can be seen from the rabbitry, but the slope and a screen of rain shield the hutches from sight. 'I'm in the middle of work,' I say.

'Don't worry, Sandy, you won't be missed,' he says. He walks on until we reach a knot of firs, interspersed with alder. This is the farthest from the main building I have been. When we stop, he says, his breath steaming in puffs of garlic and whiskey, 'You know we read your file?'

I don't know that. In fact, Dr Frank has assured me that our conversations and the writings I have done for him are private.

'I don't believe you,' I say. 'Dr Frank said my file was confidential.'

Cooper faces me; two rivulets stream from the front fold of his hat. 'Then, Sandy, I suppose it's as "confidential" as he can make it, eh?' He winks. One of his eyelids sits lower over the iris than the other anyway, but it is definitely a wink. His pale lashes fringe colourless eyes, and wisps of light-reddish hair show from under his hat. At this moment he appears scrubbed pink and blind like the pigs that hung in my grandfather's butcher shop.

Somewhere, there's a photograph of me standing in front of a row of fresh carcasses, holding my mother's hand. It isn't a happy memory. I hadn't cared for my grandfather and I've always hated to see dead animals.

'You know where we are?' he says. I look around me, but still, all I can see is the green grove of trees. Gold threads of resin stripe the fir bark; the scrolled-up buds of the alder leaves are ready to open. 'We're standing on a grave,' Cooper says. I step back quickly and I look down at the raised ribs of the tree roots where they spread over the ground. There are the usual undulations, the rusty sponge of decayed leaves and pine needles. No stone, no marker of any kind.

'I don't see anything,' I say. 'There's no grave here.'

'People die here all the time, Sandy, what do you think happens to the bodies?'

'You don't place them in unmarked graves,' I say. 'That would be inhuman. Dr Frank wouldn't allow it.'

'Dr Frank? You stupid booger.' He spits at my feet. He rocks forward, almost losing his balance. His face, underneath the sheltering hat, is wet. 'You think you've got it worked out, nice and cushy, and you'll be out in a couple of years when you and Dr Frank are finished talking and the war's over. You're here for life now, boy, and there's nothing you can do about it unless I decide to help you. And you know, and I know, I'm not going to do that. Things for you can only get worse, you bloody shirker.'

'I'm not a shirker!'

He tries to spit again, but the spittle drools down his chin. He wipes the back of a hand across his nose and mouth. 'You wanted a nice safe place to hide while other boys, boys like mine, are overseas giving their lives for your freedom. You ugly little bastard.'

'No! That's not true! I wanted to go!'

'But you're right about one thing, Grey, nobody gets buried here now.' He draws his lower lip up over his top lip, and his chin quivers. Some kind of noise is trapped in his throat. Attendant Cooper kicks a small hole in the humus. He kicks and kicks.

The smell of the spraying wet fir needles, and the turned-over rotting alder leaves, reminds me of the wooded roadside where I'd abandoned my father, hoped to leave him forever. The hole grows deeper. I loosen my clenched fists and look back in the direction of the rabbitry. Nobody is coming to find me. 'I have to get back,' I say.

'No, sir,' Pete Cooper says. He's stopped kicking now. 'We sell the corpses to students who dissect them at the university. It's a funny thing, Grey, what with some of these treatments – you take insulin – people go into a coma and they don't come out of it; or you think they're dead and they're not. They might come out of it, but how would we know? They're already packed into a box and sent off, the next thing's the knife.' He stares straight into my eyes.

'I'm in the West Wing. Nothing like that happens in the West Wing.'

'Not in the West Wing. No, that's right,' Cooper says, 'but you won't be in the West Wing long.'

I turn to go.

'I'm not finished with you, Grey,' he says, gripping my arm. 'I told you I had something to show you.'

I try to find a smile, to stay calm. 'That's right, so you did.'

'People do get their just deserts, sooner or later. You'll get yours, and that cunt who comes to see you will get hers.' He grins as he registers the shock on my face. His words are meant to be knives. He knows how I feel about Georgina: she has been kind to me, even when I was a stranger, and now she is a friend. I have seen him watching her when she comes to visit me, with his blind pig gaze. There is, truly, as my father insists, evil in the world, but it is not confined to unbelievers, and it is not confined to Hitler.

'Under this sod lies the body of Alan Macaulay, hanged by the neck until dead in the exercise yard, when this was a prison. I saw you reading about it in the library. I've read what you wrote afterwards for Dr Frank. How you couldn't sleep that night, and when you did sleep you saw yourself handcuffed to his corpse. You felt like you'd been buried with him. You even wrote that his skin was like hen's skin. Puckered from fear. Like your balls pucker, Sandy.' He blinks his white lashes. 'But you know all that, I don't have to tell you about your twisted mind.'

I look away from him, into the rain. I remember the strawberry birthmark on the inside of my left elbow. I remember I am Sandy Grey.

He takes a step back and laughs. 'Alan Macaulay's ghost haunts the East Wing, Sandy, did you know that? You can hear it at night. It cries and begs for someone to help him. Macaulay committed a crime and deserved his punishment. He begged for mercy, his friends and his family petitioned, but it did him no good. Justice is blind, Grey. Justice gets it right.'

Cooper's fist lashes out and he hits me. I fall, gasping, to the ground and spit out a tooth. Blood and mucus glisten on it in strings. I gaze up through the lank wing of my hair over my forehead. My ear and jaw burn. A spark of curiosity glimmers in Cooper's small, faded eyes. 'You're on my mind now, Grey,' he says. He straightens his hat and the lapels of his coat and goes.

Upon my return to the rabbitry, I lay down a scattering of fresh hay in the hutches, then I set to putting out the feed and water. For now, we use large tin cans tied with wire to the sides of the cages, but I have planned, with the rabbitry overseer, a Jap, to see about constructing a self-feeding system. This would be better for the meat rabbits. The pregnant and nursing does would still have to be hand-fed, but even so we'd have more time to care for the kit conies or any sick animals. When all is done and I've marked off the appropriate boxes in the register, I take one of the younger rabbits and sit with it on my lap and stroke it while Ron smokes a cigarette. He gave me a hard look when I first came back, pushing the empty barrow. 'That's the second time somebody's been careless and stepped on a rake,' he said. 'Now I'll have to write it up.'

It is not that I'm particularly fond of small animals, I only once ever had a pet – a collie dog that my substitute mother had put to sleep when I was ten – but they are living creatures and deserving of our care. I'm well aware that the fate of most of these rabbits is to be used for meat and pelts. Ron shows me how to lift them, so as not to bruise the carcass or damage the hide, by grasping the loose skin over the shoulders with one hand and using the other hand to support the hindquarters. 'I wonder if we could exhibit some of these,' I say. 'Dr Frank thinks showing that we can breed prize stock is good for the reputation of the institution.' I say this, although what I am thinking is that even a grown man – let alone a child or an animal – can suffer from lack of affection. I begin to groom the rabbit from head to tail with a soft bristle brush. The rain has stopped, weak sunlight paints the small table, covered with a burlap sack, that I brought outside to serve as a grooming table. Handling a rabbit is, perhaps, a poor substitute for human contact, but Ron Signet, who has finished his third cigarette, appears to approve.

'You're the spitting image of St Francis, son,' he says.

Today, after supper, they cut off my hair. I had hoped to look like a soldier or airman but, instead, I appear as what I am: a prisoner, an inmate. What is it that makes the difference? I ask the cook, when I am washing dishes. 'They don't bleeding use a bowl on the soldiers, do they,' he says.

FOUR

20 May and following, 1941

Above my bed is a picture of the King and Queen and their family. Although I do not pray for them, they are in my thoughts. I no longer pray at all, since when I do, instead of the face of God (or what I imagine God might be), I see my father's. Perhaps one day I will regain my faith – Dr Frank says we often revert to the principles of our upbringing as we age – although I cannot see it for myself. On the shelf at the head of the bed I keep my notebook and pen and a small shortwave radio that Georgina gave me. At night I listen to broadcasts from around the world, and sometimes my roommates listen also. One of these men, Winchell, likes to interrupt with his stories of fighting in Spain, and of the women he made love to there, but the others aren't too bad.

Bob, who is two years younger than I am, comes from Alberta, and he is visited by his mother who travels by train once every month or so in order to see him. He plays practical jokes, most of them harmless enough, such as turning back the date on the calendar, but aside from offering unwanted advice too often for my liking, he is a pleasant enough fellow.

Karl is the third man, older than the rest of us and with a tendency to be morose. Perhaps it is because he is an enemy alien. Even if he were released, he would not go free but be interned in a camp. I heard him tell Attendant Signet that he had been working as a steam engineer at the Mage Theatre in Vancouver before he was apprehended. I asked Ron Signet why Karl was here and he said I should ask him myself.

Tonight, Bob and Winchell are at the bingo in the cafeteria. I do not go, as I do not know how to play and have no money with which to gamble. Winchell said, as he left, that it was run by Catholic nuns and some of them were good-looking. He liked to imagine how they appeared beneath their habits. This appeared to enrage Karl – I watched the veins of his temples swell where they vanish into the pale outposts of his receding hairline – and I saw him direct a murderous glare at the Spanish Civil War veteran. He restrained himself, though, and got down to the work with which he occupies himself every spare moment, writing in longhand on foolscap paper. I sat and watched him for a minute. He works consistently and doesn't look up. The light glints off the gold rims of his glasses. If I didn't know better, I'd think him Swedish instead of German; he seems, in general, more refined than the average Hun. His nails are clean, he presses his trousers under the mattress, he washes his teeth several times a day and he is always after the attendants to allow him extra baths. Winchell says Karl is a Nazi . . . but I don't know.

'Well, Karl,' I say as I take out my notebook and pen and settle myself at the wooden worktable at the foot of my bed, 'I hope I'm not disturbing you.'

'No,' he says, with his head still down. He dips his pen and resumes his scratches.

We are quiet, then. I sit, staring at the portrait of the royals and try to think how to begin. I want to let Dr Frank know of some of the things that are happening to me, but I need to be believed. I sigh – a bad habit of mine – and Karl looks up.

'Sorry,' I say. He returns to his work. I get up and go to the window, but in the dark there is little to see. The perimeter lights blank out the world. Not even the stars, which have been a joy to me since childhood – they speak of wider concerns than my own – can penetrate that harsh brightness. I tell myself they are up there, that nothing important has changed, and then, I suppose, I sigh again.

Karl puts down his pen with a snap. I hear it roll across the table and on to the floor. I turn with a fresh apology on my lips and he says, 'Well' – he says it, in his accent, *vell* – 'you'd better tell me what's troubling you.'

I attempt to speak, but I can't. Words, I'm beginning to find, are not always available to me when I need them. Emotion is like a tide, and it overwhelms; or perhaps it's more like a suddenly undammed stream sweeping all before it. Dr Frank says I have to not let it build up – but how to do that here and survive?

Karl scrapes back his chair and rises to his feet. He's a tall, muscular man in his forties, with the stooped shoulders of someone who has worked hard for a long time. He clears his throat and steps towards me. 'I wanted' – *vanted*, he says – 'to tell you how sorry I am.' He gestures to the portrait of King George and Queen Elizabeth and their daughters. 'What is going on is terrible.' He shakes his head. 'They have no right to bomb innocent people.'

'Thank you,' I say. I advance and grip his outstretched hand. Only a few nights before, the nightly blitz of London had been particularly heavy. The radio reported that the Queen herself had gone out to inspect the damage.

He points again to the portrait. 'They are very brave.' It is true: the King and Queen have affirmed their intention not to leave the city for a safer domicile, but to stay and show commonality with Londoners.

'You're not a supporter of Hitler?' I ask him. I feel it has to be said. It is better out in the open.

'Me? Pah! No, never. That is why I left Germany. I am a pacifist.'

'A conchie! I'd never have guessed!'

'It is why' – *vhy* – 'I have so much trouble here, with some of them. It has nothing to do with Hitler.' His hands are fists in the pockets of the heavy wool work trousers he wears. We fall silent. Soft hand-sewn leather slippers shoe his feet – I can see him stretch his toes: he always leaves his boots at the door, unlike Winchell who spreads dust and shavings from his work in the carpentry shop, everywhere. Winchell wears an old blue suit with only an undershirt beneath the jacket. I dress in what I have – student's clothes – corduroy trousers, a blue or grey shirt and sweater-vest. I also have a green cardigan, with leather patches at the elbows, that belongs to Georgina's son – she says it pleases her to see it worn – and I am wearing it now. I make myself – with some trouble, after what he's said about his pacifism – meet Karl's eyes.

'*My* trouble,' I tell him, 'is with one of the attendants. He has taken against me. He has threatened me. Even a peaceful man such as yourself will know one must stand up to bullying when it first shows.'

Karl's eyes are blue stones. 'Cooper. It will be him, I think. Yes?'

'Yes.'

'They do not like you to have your own opinions. They are angry if you speak of philosophy. I dislike both Churchill and Hitler. I made the mistake of saying so one day: "You people are barbarians!" I told Cooper.' Karl laughs.

'What did he say?'

'He said nothing! But I was taken off the work party I was on, polishing the gates at Government House, and sent to heavy labour. Now I dig ditches or break stones to build field walls.'

42

He shrugs. 'I do not mind. I am strong and it is good to remain strong.' He smiles at me, removes his spectacles, blows on them, and buffs them with a handkerchief.

'So?' he says. 'And you?'

I tell him about my run-in with Cooper.

'That is bad,' he says. 'You must watch out for him.'

'I have to let Dr Frank know what's going on, so he'll stop it! Attendant Cooper can't be allowed to threaten patients like that!'

Karl peers at me over the top of his spectacles. Standing there near him, I feel small and very young. 'Come and see what I am doing,' he says. I walk with him to his worktable. He hands me several sheets of his writing. 'Read this.'

I begin to read: *Her husband had left her. She did not blame him, because no man wanted a wife that was unable to bear him children. After the doctors had confirmed what for years she did not wish to believe, his answer had been terrible. 'Adopted children are not like one's own . . .'* I glance farther down the page. *With an emptiness of heart and mind she had stepped off the elevator, striding towards the entrance of her apartment.*

'What is it?' I ask him.

'I practise my English,' he says. 'It is a romance. I call it *The Romance of Stanley Park*. Maybe some day it will be published – it is no worse than some of the books I've read – if not, no matter.'

'But why? Why do you write it?'

'It harms no one. It keeps my mind occupied. It stops me thinking about the war and . . .' – he surveys me and smiles gently – 'it stops me thinking about where I am.'

I nod. But still – if he were going to write, why not write something useful, something that could change things? I am going to say just this, but he whispers, so that I have to step near to hear him, 'I have not heard from my family. I do not know what has happened to them. I've sent letters, but there is no reply. Perhaps they do not even send my letters from here, and even if they do . . . Well' – *vell*, as he says – 'you must know the kinds of things that might have happened to them. My mother is a Jewess.'

I return to my own table. Darkness pools on the floor: our two bedside lights are all that keep it at bay. I think about Dr Frank's desire for truth, for facts. I wonder if truth and facts are the same thing. The fact is that Karl is an enemy alien, the truth appears to be that he is a better man than Attendant Cooper. Than most people. The facts are that I have a family near me and want them far away, that Karl's beloved faraway family are, in all likelihood, in mortal danger. What do these things mean?

I have to find facts I can give Dr Frank that will help with my fundamental predicament – the misunderstanding that has landed me here – and also protect me in the interim. I am under no illusion that a direct challenge to Dr Frank's judgement concerning an employee such as Pete Cooper will get me very far: I need to show him truth in a way he can accept so that he will trust me, understand me, help me unquestioningly whenever I reveal my need. There arises unbidden, before my inner vision, an image of the director as the three monkeys: hands over eyes, hands over ears, hands over mouth. The hands must come down. What will do it?

'Karl,' I say, interrupting my roommate who is again hard at work – the stack of completed pages beside him is several inches high – 'what will you do when you finish your book?'

'Well' – *vell* – 'I will start another one, of course.'

'How will you know what to write?'

He gives me a small indulgent smile. 'The idea will come.' He continues writing.

Knowing that my continued questions may not be welcome – clearly it pains the German to be reminded of his circumstances, and relief lies only in the world he has invented for himself – I ask anyway. 'What is Dr Frank interested in? Do you know? The farm, of course, and cases like mine, and being proven right over the opinions of other doctors . . . Ron Signet says he is writing a book.'

'Everyone is writing a book,' Karl says.

'Yes, but there must be something he wants, something I can help him with that would help me!'

'So,' Karl says, pushing his chair back, 'you are an optimist.'

'What else should I be?'

'A realist, Sandy, like me. I do what I must and no more.'

'Yes, you do, you are writing *your* book!'

'Only for myself, not to change the world.'

'I know the world can't be changed, not like that,' I say. 'Thinking it could be was what brought me here.'

'Ah.'

'You'll have heard I struck my father?'

'You were angry with him?'

I take in the yellow light outside the window. The harsh, unreal illumination of my imprisonment. 'Not with him. With someone else. It's a long story.'

'Which Dr Frank is getting you to tell?'

'Yes,' I say.

'And telling it will set you free?'

'Telling it so that he can see the truth, yes.'

'I would be very careful, Sandy,' Karl says. 'Nobody here is your friend.'

'What did you do to get yourself here, Karl?' I ask him.

He smiles. 'I let the birds out of their cages in the park the day war was declared.'

I remember a dream I'd had and which I'd told to Dr Frank. I'm travelling in an open truck with a young woman. We come to some rocks and she shows me a cave. We crawl through it and go back in time – emerging on a plain where early experiments in flight are taking place. I remember that I help design the wings of the experimental craft by watching birds fly.

'Not thinking again of leaving us, are you, Sandy?' Dr Frank had said. He'd told me the dream was a Freudian desire both to return to the womb and to escape. Then he said it could also be, mythologically speaking, a warning about flying too high; that I needed to stay on the ground, rein in my imagination. Remember Icarus.

'Couldn't it mean what it means?' I'd said.

'And what's that?'

I didn't answer, but what I've realised since then is that I could build a similar machine; it isn't much different from the gliders I've flown. I could build it and wait for the right time to try it out. There are certain things I know I can do.

In the meantime Karl has a thought. 'There is one thing that could be useful,' he says. 'When we had our talk, when I first came here, Dr Frank said that he, like me, wanted to make the world a better place, that he was for peace and not war.'

'He is opposed to the war?' I find this unbelievable. Dr Frank has us working hard to support the war, and it is my desire to be a fighter pilot that has gained me his sympathy.

'Not this war, but war in general. He does not like men to die needlessly. It is a waste of resource and talent. It was a philosophical statement.' Karl pauses. 'He expressed a wish for the betterment of mankind. He believes in justice and progress. We talked about related matters, such as capital punishment which he said should only be for murderers of policemen and children. He said that even murderers can be rehabilitated.' He dips his pen in the ink. A blob runs down the nib and on to a fresh sheet of paper. Karl swears in German. He blots the paper then says to me with finality, 'Dr Frank is a practical man. If he does not believe it is right to harm the innocent, show him – don't tell him about it, like this instance with Cooper, but show him that you have been wronged and he will help you. Dr Frank is on the side of justice – as he sees it. Let us call him a humanist.'

'It will be a case study.'

'Yes, that's it.'

'I must present the evidence. Something for his book.'

'Perhaps.'

I think for a minute. Karl has closed his eyes. He might be about to write, *She felt as if she had just come out of a dream*. 'Do you think there's anything in what Pete Cooper says about the ghost of Alan Macaulay haunting the East Wing?' I say.

I catch the glint of Karl's glasses as he lifts his head. 'I do not believe in ghosts,' he says, 'but if there were a place for them, it would be there.'

Today is my twenty-first birthday. I have come of age. The entire world should be open to me. I stifle a sigh. I could be graduating, this month, with a degree from the university; I could not only have shaken the dust of my father's choice for me – Damascus Road College – from my feet, but be embarking on a professional path. I think about all the reading I have done since boyhood, the books that kept the spark of my true identity alive, and I marvel at the thirty-two booklets called *The Treasures of Truth* that make up the entire curriculum of Damascus Road. The phrases 'blind adherence' and 'vain imaginings' and 'threadbare answers' come to my mind, and I realise that these are echoes of arguments with my father. How is it, I ask myself, that I have exchanged one form of bondage for another?

But then, because on this of all days I deserve some happiness, I think about flying, and the golden light of the morning prairie as it unfolds at dawn, and about others I know who must show courage in difficult circumstances – Georgina, for instance, whose family situation is painful, and Karl, who is all alone.

I sleep fitfully. After my conversation with Karl, the other men return talking noisily about their evening. Winchell makes rude comments about the nuns, Bob laughs too loudly. When it is lights out, I hear Bob sobbing into his pillow. My own thoughts whirr. I want to ask Georgina her opinion of what I should do about Attendant Cooper and his threats and how to convey my position to Dr Frank, but I have no way to get in touch with her. I'm not allowed to telephone; I can write, but there is no guarantee – as Karl has indicated – that the letters will be sent, and they would, in any case, be read before they went. I wonder how Georgina is doing. I know she is lonely with her son away in the RAF. Because of this, she has moved from Vancouver to her father's home, but this, as she says, is a mixed blessing. Her husband, a Great War pilot and hero, died ten years earlier. They'd lived in London and had gone to many parties attended by members of high society. Her wedding dress was made of white silk sent by her husband's brother from India. She'd loved her husband, but his family hadn't stood by her, and after her husband died, she and her son had had to return to Canada. There was the lumber baron, her father, in his big house on the inlet, but there were difficulties there – a jealous older sister who had tried to turn the father against her, and the father, himself, bedridden and on the verge of senility. Once, the sister had Georgina taken to a clinic because she drank and visited nightclubs. Georgina calls this 'provincial' – but I can tell that she had been frightened. 'There's no room for bad girls, Sandy,' she'd told me. 'Nor bad boys,' I'd replied. But somewhere inside me I know there's a difference: bad boys are punished; bad girls can be made to disappear.

It was lucky for me that Georgina had been on her way to her father's the night we'd met on the ferry. I would have been a goner if she hadn't intervened. I wonder, not for the first time, from where or from whom she'd been coming, as the inlet crossing is certainly not the route from Vancouver. It isn't my business, but I wish I'd asked her. What if we had met earlier? Could the entire episode with my father have been avoided? Sometimes I think about the workings of Fate, and what it means, and whether within it hides life's purpose.

I have a dream that night that I decide to tell Dr Frank. In the dream I am a woman and meet a small boy. Since he is on his own, I invite him to accompany me on my travels. I am sitting with him and a young girl when he says, 'I want to make a baby with you.' I say to him, 'What you need is a girl.' He nods. I say, 'I will be your mother.' He nods again. Later in the dream I tell him that the pain will go when he finds someone to love him.

I believe this boy is a messenger come to say I should marry Georgina, and that it will be difficult to persuade her, but Dr Frank says it is an oedipal dream, and is about my desire to marry my own mother. Or, mythologically speaking, the boy is an incubus sent to torment and tempt me with sex; that the incubus must be cast out.

'But Dr Frank,' I tell him, 'either way the solution is for the boy to be loved.'

Dr Frank shakes his head. 'I won't waste time arguing, Sandy,' he says.

There will be no more dreams for Dr Frank.

FIVE
2 June and following, 1941

A female nurse I do not recognise stands at a door I have never seen unlocked in my visits to the East Wing. I come here, in a rotation with other workers, to dispose of waste. It is not a pleasant job, and we wear masks and gloves and we do not talk about what we see or smell when a bag bursts open.

It is early morning, early enough that the white-and-green corridors are almost silent and the odours of disinfectant and porridge are at full strength. I gag on the bile that rises from my empty stomach and try not to listen to the rhythmic banging that comes from the direction of the solitary cells. Ron Signet gives me a smile and a farewell jingle of his keys, and the nurse leads me inside.

The room is darkened: heavy green drapes are drawn across the windows, but I believe, from the general orientation, that the window faces south. In which case, beyond it are the dairy barns and the slaughter house; perhaps with a glimpse of the riding ring where Ron Signet's daughter rides Rosie, the

50

sorrel he gave her for her birthday. Most mornings Ron and I stand on the rise behind the rabbit hutches and watch: that is, he watches, and I take the opportunity to do my exercises: five minutes of deep breathing, one hundred push-ups, one hundred sit-ups, one hundred jumping jacks. I have asked for, but so far have not received, my Indian clubs.

'Settle down, Sandy,' Dr Frank says, coming in and shutting the door behind him, 'there's nothing to be afraid of here.' I work hard at controlling my breathing.

The nurse quietly arranges a tray. I see an intravenous syringe, various needles, alcohol swabs and a tourniquet. In the corner, partly hidden by a chair, is an oxygen cylinder.

'Over there, Sandy,' Dr Frank says, pointing to the bed. 'Take a load off.'

I know he smiles, I can hear it in his voice, but the blood pounds so in my head that I cannot see his face. The nurse puts a cool hand on mine and guides me over.

'Shoes off,' she says. She kneels, as I sit, and unties my shoes. She plumps the pillows and encourages me to lie down. She undoes the top buttons of my shirt. 'Warm enough?' she says. 'Want a blanket?' I shake my head and clench my teeth to control my shivering.

Dr Frank pulls up a comfortable armchair, specially made to take his bulk. He nods at the nurse and she pops a pill into my mouth and gives me a drink of water.

'There now. That's to stop you getting too sleepy. We don't want that, do we! You can sleep all you want afterwards.'

'After?' I manage.

'You're a lucky man, Mr Grey. The treatment I'm giving you is the very same I give to the soldiers.'

'It is?'

'Yes indeedy.' Dr Frank leans back, looks around vaguely and the nurse hands him a notebook and pencil. She ties the tourniquet around my arm.

'The drug you're getting is called Sodium Pentothal –

"truth serum" as the press terms it. And that's what we want, eh, Sandy? The truth.'

The nurse is swabbing my arm with alcohol.

'Now, all that will happen is after Nurse establishes the intravenous, you and I will talk. We're going to try to get to the root of your troubles, Sandy. It's in there, you know – the human mind is a wonderful mechanism, it wastes nothing – we just have to dig it out. Now, when I tell you, I want you to begin to count backwards from ten.'

'Ten . . . nine . . . eight . . .' First there's the taste that is no taste I know except that it's pink and sweet and sickening; then there's a fizz, and I'm cold and I hear Dr Frank say, as I surface through a dark green sea and fight for air, 'Tell me where you are, Sandy.'

'In the water. The tide is taking me . . .'

'Yes, yes,' he says impatiently. 'We know all about that. Let's go farther back. Keep counting. Try again.'

Counting is numbers. What are numbers but forms? I'm thinking about triangles, I have a protractor in my hand. I'm in school. 'Five . . . four . . .' There's a gush into my arm, and I've lost all thought but the triangle. The dark bush of a young woman's pelvis. She's standing in front of me, she steps near and I feel the warmth of her breath in my ear. The gush is at the floor of my penis. I know where I am and when it is. In the barn not far from school.

'Where now, Sandy?'

'Three . . . two . . .' I say.

'For God's sake,' Dr Frank says to the nurse. 'He's strong as a horse, open the valve again, but not too far . . .'

'Sandy, can you hear me?'

'Yes.'

'Are you with your father?'

'Yes.'

'Your father loves you. A difficult parent is no excuse for attempted murder.'

'Yes.' I can feel the muscles of my face squeeze and tears come to my eyes. 'All of our family have brown eyes, but his are green,' I say. I bite my lips hard so as not to say more.

'Tell me where you are, Sandy. I want you to go to where you first became angry with your father. You will tell me what happened. Did he harm you in any way?'

'God will judge.'

'Does He say this to you?'

'I speak for myself,' I say.

'You will tell me everything, Sandy. You must distinguish between your friends and enemies. I am your friend.'

'War is terrible and truth is stranger than fiction.' I'm not sure why I say this. But if I turn my head slightly, from where I stand in my parents' kitchen, I can see the horizon. Sunset, I think. It must be warm out, because the window is open. I'm standing on a table. There's another man there – a man with a black bag. A doctor?

'We're not here to play games, Sandy. Where are you exactly? What are you and your father doing?'

'Washing his hands. I can hear my mother's sewing machine.'

'Let's stay with your father,' he says. 'What do you see?'

'A breadboard,' I manage, although the words tear at me. My fist stuffs itself into my mouth.

'A breadboard?' I hear Dr Frank pop a pastille into his mouth. He sucks at it, then his teeth crunch through the candy. Humbugs, most likely. A dish of them sits in his office. 'Is that all?'

'The war did not end with the armistice,' I say.

'Which war is that, Sandy?'

'The Great War, of course.'

'You don't remember that war, Sandy, you're too young.'

'I don't feel too young.'

Dr Frank sighs. 'Tell me something about your family.'

'My father rides a bicycle to work. He was a streetcar

conductor until the strike.'

'What strike is that?'

'My uncle was in the Scottish Regiment and lost his life in France.'

'We don't seem to be getting very far this way, Sandy. Let's start with the facts, just the facts. Your father is a plasterer. Your name is Alexander Grey and you were born in 1920.'

'My mother told me once that she loves her furniture more than her husband.'

Another deep sigh. The director crunches the last of the candy. I hear his stomach rumble, then mine joins his. A duet?

It's a strange place I'm in, like I'm walking along a road with someone. When I look one way, I see my father and mother, the neighbours, the children at school. When I look the other way, it's different. As if it's not my life at all and I've stepped across a gully into a different one.

'Why don't you want to talk to me, Sandy? You know I want to help you. I want you to tell me about the attack on your father. What did you think you were doing when you struck him? Why did you lift the tyre iron? I don't believe you really meant him harm. Did your feelings about him begin with that breadboard?'

'I did not attack my father.'

'There was a witness,' he says testily. 'I've told you I believe there were mitigating circumstances, what were they?'

'I did not attack my father,' I say again, because it's the truth. How can I explain? It's getting hard to breathe. I can feel my lungs compress, as if I've flown too high in an airplane.

'Nothing's going to happen to you, Sandy. Whatever you say here is just between us.' I say nothing, but I have an urge to sing 'Rain Barrel', a song my real mother taught me and we used to sing together when I was fearful. I can hear Dr Frank swear softly under his breath as I begin, and he says to the nurse, 'He's a stubborn SOB. Maybe too bright. Some of them are. It makes the treatment more difficult, not at all what you'd think.'

I start to choke, I stop singing, my lungs are paralysed, a thick cloth blankets my face. It's the stink of ether. 'Help me! He has a knife!'

'Where are you, Sandy! Tell me what's happening!'

But I'm gone. I'm off the table, down the road, out of the house in which I was born and heading towards the visitors who bend over me grinning, wearing my parents' clothing, holding out baskets of poison fruit.

'Get the oxygen,' Dr Frank says. Footsteps speed across the room. I can smell the director's sweat, heat beams from him. He holds my arms down on the bed so I can't move, while the nurse puts something over my face and Dr Frank says, 'Breathe, Sandy, breathe. You're going to be all right.' Because I know he is a good man, I breathe, and I hear him say, 'Next time you will tell me the whole truth.' Then I hear a great sigh, like the noise a balloon makes when it deflates.

I've seen disappointment often enough on people's faces to know it for what it is.

But Dr Frank claps me on the shoulder before he leaves and says, 'I'm sure you did your best. We'll try again. The treatment isn't for everyone. In the meantime, write down everything you remember, whatever comes to you. I want to see it all.'

He's gone before I've even sat up.

I don't like this interruption to my routine. Now the whole morning is gone. There's nothing to do after the session but to wait in the library until Ron Signet or Pete Cooper can take me to lunch. My job is important. Others rely on me. Our production of rabbit meat is part of the war effort. It is the one thing I can do to help in these times, and I like to do it well. I look through the scrapbook again to pass the hour. This time, considering Pete Cooper's comments about the ghost in the East Wing, I read all the clippings about the man, Alan Macaulay, who was hanged outside the walls for murder when the building was a jail. I make a note to myself to ask Dr Frank for Macaulay's files, if he has them. If I know the facts about Macaulay, I will not fear his ghost, I will not make the connections between myself and the fate of the dead man that Pete Cooper wants me to make. Dr Frank always says that truth is an antidote to fear.

I said to him, when we were discussing who I should trust to tell me the truth, 'What about the attendants? Will they tell me lies?' He said, 'Well, Sandy, you know I have personally hired each of them.' Still – everywhere men are in chains, but I am free in my mind and I am not obliged to believe what other people say.

After lunch, when I'm back in my room to change for the rest of the workday, I tell Karl about my morning with Dr Frank. He is resting on his bed after injuring his shoulder lifting rocks. He listens to me then says, 'You must be careful, if Dr Frank loses interest in you, you will' – he says *vill* – 'be on your own.'

'But why would he lose interest? I believe you are right, I could sense it, but what did I do wrong?'

Karl smiles gently, puts down his book, takes off his glasses, blows on the lenses and polishes them with a corner of his shirt. 'The breadboard,' he says.

'What do you mean?'

'Only what I have' – he says *haf* – 'told you before. You must be a success, Sandy. You must show him the causes of your actions in a way that makes sense to him. It must be a logical story so you can be rehabilitated. What (*vhat*) does *breadboard* have to do with that? It sounds like nonsense.' I hang my head. For reasons I don't know, the breadboard is important.

'I don't mean to say that it is nonsense – that is between you and your Maker, where it should remain.' Karl sits beside me and puts an arm around my shoulders. 'Listen to me, Sandy. If you are a big success, Dr Frank is a success too. Things do not go so well (*vell*) for him. So he must defend his treatment, now in particular. His opponents think him unscientific. They want to see results, real cures. Numbers that add up! Society protected from people like us. Not folk tales and fairy stories, like *bread-board*.'

'What isn't going well?' I ask.

Karl's expression darkens. 'One of the soldiers has killed himself. He was the son of an important man. There will be an inquiry.'

'What? Killed himself? Here?'

Karl nods. I think of the handsome men dressed in crisp uniforms I have seen from a distance, led by attendants. I consider my long-standing envy of them.

'But how can that be the fault of Dr Frank? Surely he does his best, surely sometimes this happens, it isn't fair to blame his treatment . . .'

'They think he has exaggerated the importance of his views at the expense of those who were sent here to recover. The families of war heroes want their sons home. They want (*vant*) them to receive different treatment, the latest in science and medicine. They have already managed to have half the facility taken from him.'

'You mean the East Wing?'

'Yes, certainly. You don't think Dr Frank would approve of what is done there?'

I shake my head, even though Dr Frank has indicated to me that that is where I could end up if my treatment with him fails. I had taken it as a threat, but perhaps it was a warning? Certainly, if what Karl says is true, he has compromised himself to keep his job. What is his philosophical position on compromise? 'Who are these men who cause problems for Dr Frank?'

'Pen-pushers,' he says.

For the first time I have doubts about Karl. My feelings, as usual, show on my face.

A wry smile twists his lips. 'Don't worry, my friend. I am not mad. No more mad than the butchers who come once the pen-pushers have prepared the way.'

'What butchers?'

'If I frighten you, I am no better than Pete Cooper,' he says and busies himself with mending.

Karl sews on his own buttons, he turns his shirt cuffs and collars. All his clothing is neat, clean and in good repair. My mending is sent to my mother, but only because I do not know how to do it myself. Everything on Karl's bedside table is carefully aligned. Winchell's area is slovenly, sticky with spilled food; his books, papers, handkerchiefs are all frayed, worried, chewed. Bob is a boy. He drops things without thinking, and tears pictures of pretty girls and cars and motorcycles from magazines and tapes them to the walls.

'You say things I don't understand, Karl,' I say. He bites off the end of the thread. There are no scissors here.

'There are many ways of looking at the world, Sandy. Dr Frank has beliefs about right and wrong. He is a deeply moral man. He thinks we are here because of what has happened to us in the past. He says to himself, "If I can change the past of a man like Sandy Grey with my remedy, he will be well."'

'Well, of course!'

Karl holds up his hand. 'Wait a minute, my friend. The other view is that we are a biology or chemistry problem. What is wrong with us can be cut out with a knife, or altered by drugs. We must be treated in operating theatres and laboratories. Then we are solved into columns. They add us up. We live or we die. These accountants and bureaucrats and butchers. It is exactly what has happened in Germany! But I must not say any more. The walls have ears.'

He notices my frown and explains, 'I'm a foreigner, I speak with an accent. People speak in front of me as if I were an animal, or a servant. I get to know what they really think. You only know what they tell you. But they also listen to what I say: all is reported. One day I will pay for my honesty with you.'

What is there to say to this? If his view is correct, it is probably true. Not only is there a war on in the outside world, there is one here, too, and we are the battlefield.

'You told me before to help Dr Frank, to give him evidence of my innocence. Now you say to tell him a logical story. Which is it?'

'It is both. You provide him with a cause and with a story. So! You will support his belief in goodness and peace and justice. You will recover and return to society a changed man.'

'But Karl,' I say, 'as I've told you, there is nothing wrong with me!'

'That is the wrong answer, but all the better for what you have to do,' he tells me.

I wake up in the night. I know it is three in the morning because the laundry truck has just driven in the gate and I can hear the thud of the sacks being unloaded on to a dolly; and I can tell by where the constellations slot into the sky. Recently, because of fears of attacks by the Japanese, we have observed blackout. The perimeter lights are turned off. On a night like tonight, it is so clear that I am sure that if I could climb to the parapet and look out from there, I could see all the way to Georgina's father's house on the inlet, and then across the inlet to the Malahat ridge on the far side, and to the lake, and to the roadway around it where I began this long last episode with my father. To my change point.

As we'd talked further, Karl had helped me see that my life already is a story and it is made of smaller stories, and that these will, in the end, add up, because all the twists and turns will meet at my death. I need not worry about making things up. My childhood is the story that Dr Frank wants. Karl explained, by using as illustration the structure of the romance he is writing, that there is always a turning point in the story: after this everything that is before drops away and the story embraces the new. This point exists not only within each life overall, as seen from its end, but within each episode within each life. Although these smaller points cannot be as significant as the larger one. But since we do not know which is which, we treat them all the same. So what I must do for Dr Frank is choose an incident in my childhood, and find within it a change point, and present this to Dr Frank, and link it to several other incidents, and place the whole of my childhood into Dr Frank's hands so that he can then design the rest of the story. I am to give him that power.

Karl writes his romances, he says, only because his own story is over. The story he writes is the only power he has left. I dispute this, of course, but the sadness within him makes me wonder.

So I am to make a gift of the childhood portion of my life to Dr Frank and write out the little pieces he asks of me with their embedded turning points, so that he will be able to discover the cause and effect links between them and what this has to do with my father. Voilà! At once, the predicament posed by child-hood will fall away. I will not only be cured, but forgiven.

All this is utterly clear to me as I gaze out the window at the constellations Ursa Major and Draco – Draco lies, of course, over the inlet where the sea creature continues to nurture its young. Which youngster, following the nature of these things, and encountering its own change points, will grow and change and begat. *Ad infinitum.* As is above, so it is below! What a moment of transparency! – the stars set in the heavens, their reflection on the water, the creatures below the surface of the sea, and over to one side, me, Sandy Grey, the observer with what Karl says is a point of view.

My father used to tell me the story of Jesus, but not as a story with events and challenges and decisions that made a pattern, but as if the words themselves were the story. I had to repeat these words until they were memorised. I earned several Sunday-school trophies this way. This is where my father went so wrong! Words, on their own, do not matter: it is the shape they make as they wind their way through the story that counts. Timing within the chain of cause and effect is everything!

To review: a story in words, yes, but in words plus timing and understanding. Take *breadboard*, for instance. When does *breadboard* enter my life? At the age of three or four as I thought? If it is a true change point in a true incident, examining *bread-board* will lead to the other incidents which build upon it. In which case I must ask, what has happened just prior and how had life gone on before? And what place does *breadboard* play in the larger story of my life? For if Karl's theories are correct it will be by this method that I unlock the mystery and find success. For both me and Dr Frank. However much I choose to tell him.

A second word drops beside *breadboard* as I stand contemplating these matters and the stars. It is *footbridge*, and it reveals its mysteries at once. I cross the footbridge to the other side of the creek where I see a little girl about six years old with no clothes on. I take my clothes off and lie on top of her. Then I put on my clothes and follow her to her big white house. In her mother's kitchen we tell what we have done. The mother laughs at us. We go outside again and remove our clothes and then cross back over the bridge. The road winds away from the rented wooden house in Colwood where we lived: pretty farms and fences, tall trees all around. I pick wildflowers for her and we make garlands and put them around our wrists and necks. We know we are married because we have promised to live together forever. When we come to the crossroads we play one-potato, two-potato to decide which way to go. Her hand tops mine and she chooses.

I yawn and go back to bed. As I drop away from my thoughts, holding to an image of my childhood bride, I hear the squeak of rubber-soled shoes passing the door, the jingle of keys, a muffled howl from the East Wing.

SIX

7 June and following, 1941

The question is, which is the best breed of rabbits? Ron Signet and I are standing outside the rabbitry smoking and discussing this matter. He's offered me a cigarette, I've taken a puff and handed it back. Ron stuffs one hand in his pants pocket and rocks casually on his heels. I try it, but I know I look awkward. I catch the eye of the Jap, Kosho, whom Dr Frank has put in charge of the rabbitry. His being the overseer is a sore point with everyone, especially since Japan joined in the Axis pact. Pete Cooper says he doesn't understand why the Americans continue to sell the Japs oil. 'It'll come back to haunt them,' he says.

Working with Kosho doesn't bother me. He keeps so much to himself that I don't see the problem. Right now, he's bringing a hay bale from the storage shed. He's immensely strong. I say, 'Tell us, Kosho, what is your opinion about the best breed of rabbits. Ron here prefers the French Silver. I like the Beveren.'

Kosho smiles and says, 'The white rabbit is best.'

We laugh, because we only breed white rabbits. They're

good meat producers and their skins bring the highest prices. I plan to tell Georgina that a French sable coat is actually a sable-dyed white rabbit. I don't believe this is commonly known. Not that I think that any of her furs would be rabbit!

Ron has told me that Kosho is from New Westminster. He was discharged from the penitentiary (for what crime I did not ask) but sent here immediately afterwards. He is good with the rabbits and with the chickens which he also tends. He is always cheerful, humming and talking to himself in Japanese. The only oddity he exhibits is that he carries a white towel with him everywhere. I asked Ron about this and he said I would have to ask Kosho, which I did. He explained that the towel is so he can hang himself if he has the chance.

'Are you not afraid to die?' I asked him.

'I say my prayers every day. Why should I be afraid?'

The few Japanese have their own hut. A woman, Miss Cochrane, one of Dr Frank's associates, is in charge of it. I've seen her several times walking through the grounds carrying their laundry. None of the other staff will help with these inmates. They cook and clean for themselves. The Chinese, who are also here, do not have the same problem, although they prefer to do their own cooking, and they clean again after the janitors have finished in their outbuilding. This is a sore point with Pete Cooper, who calls it arrogant. They are responsible for the laundry of the entire institution.

In his spare time, Kosho fishes in the pond or in the small creek that runs to it, behind the farm. When he can take the fish alive, he stocks them in the fountain at the front door of the asylum. I've asked him why he does this and he says, 'To bring the birds.'

That may be so, but I've also seen him, when I'm out for my walks with Ron, dusting breadcrumbs into the water. The fish come to his hand. They nibble at his fingers and he talks to them. Pete Cooper says that Japs eat fish raw, they don't even clean them. I cannot bring myself to ask Kosho about this. If it were true, how would I know what to think of it?

Once, when we were on our own in the rabbitry, I had a real talk with Kosho. It was just after my bout with the truth serum, when so uncovered in my soul did I feel that I found heat, cold, light, even normal conversation almost painful. I told him about my leap into the sea from the *Brentwood* and how I discovered the sea serpent. 'Of all the memories I have, Kosho, this is the most beautiful,' I said. He looked thoughtful, and replied that his religion speaks of a kingdom of serpent people under the sea.

I said, 'Are they good people? My religion asserts that serpents are evil. My father says they appear in the end times.'

'Some are good, some bad,' he said. 'People who fall into the sea and live are very lucky. Such people are said to have met Ryu-wo, the guardian of the Shinto faith.'

Since I did not see how that could apply to me – am I not Christian, despite my differences with my parents? – I said, 'What about the bad serpent people? Tell me about them. Could I have met one of these?'

'Their king is terrible. He destroys human villages. He eats innocent children.' I felt from the look in Kosho's eye that he was on the verge of a confidence.

'Can anything stop him?' I asked before he could say more.

Kosho's face closed over. 'Yes, he is stopped,' he said. Kosho made a chopping motion with his hand.

'What stops him?'

Kosho busied himself at the sink, washing the sink and counter surfaces with a weak solution of carbolic. 'He meets the goddess of love and she asks him to stop, and he does. It is a famous story.'

'Not to me,' I said.

I have thought about this conversation in case my first reaction to it was mistaken, but I still can't make my experience fit. The sea serpent I encountered was a mother, and I was clear in my duty to her and her babies. How was she the guardian of any faith? Georgina, in her rescue of me, was my good angel. Without her I would have died. The human encounter, not the animal one – no matter how unusual it was – is what sustains me.

If nothing else, the conversation served to remind me that it is not wise to make hasty judgements. Each mind is furnished on its own terms in its own culture, for its own reasons. Uncover its secret reasons, and you will reveal the pattern behind the taste in furniture. Ha!

Kosho, like Karl, is a good man. This question of who is good and who is not, though, and how to tell which is which, is a troubling one. I asked Dr Frank about it and he said, 'Good question, Sandy, that's just the thing.' He was pleased with me, but I'm still waiting for an answer.

Ron Signet finishes his cigarette. Back inside the rabbitry, Kosho cuts hay into short lengths for the cages. He does this on a wooden table with a hay knife. Ron keeps a keen eye on the knife, and takes it away once Kosho is done. Kosho's access to certain tools is another sore point with Pete Cooper. I am not allowed to touch them yet. I go to the stores and begin mixing feed – oats, wheat and buckwheat – into buckets. Then I add linseed oil cakes, and dampen the mixture before setting it out into the feed troughs. Kosho puts hay in the mangers and I follow along behind him, replacing small blocks of salt in the hutches where necessary. Since it is Saturday, I gather all the water dishes and take them to the sink for a thorough cleaning.

I'm standing there, hosing the dishes. In front of me, on a shelf, are the tins of carbolic acid and cresol we use as disinfectants. I'm just lifting down the carbolic when Pete Cooper enters from the yard and says, 'Okay, girls and boys, hop to it.' Through the open door I see a pickup truck loaded with rabbits in cages. These are the young that have been weaned and quarantined to ensure against the spread of disease. The quarantine period is over. I finish with the dishes, fill them with fresh water and place them in the cages.

Attendant Cooper is walking up and down. 'For Christ's

sake, let's get a move on! Hot time in the old town tonight!' He's
due to go off shift. Winchell has told me that Cooper's wife has
left him for a sailor. If it's true, it might explain his moods. It's
the kind of thing Winchell might hear, since he always has his
ear to the door of the staff room when he's meant to be washing
or polishing floors. Winchell keeps files on us in his head for use,
he says, after the war when the proletariat will rise up and kill
the capitalist pigs. 'Am I on your list?' I once asked him. 'One
of them,' he said. He flashed the smile he knows upsets me:
black stumps of teeth, inflamed gums. 'You're with the milk-
fed virgins.'

Once I've washed and dried my hands, I go to assist Kosho
with the unloading of the cages. Instead of putting the rabbits at
once into their hutches, we leave them as they are on the floor
and wash our hands again. 'What are you nancies doing now?'
Pete Cooper asks. 'I've got to take the cages back.' He points to
Kosho. 'Chop suey, eh? Chop chop!'

'Well, Pete,' Ron Signet says, strolling across to take a look
at the young rabbits that clump together, feathery furred and
blinking, 'they have to sex them first.'

'What's that?'

'They can't put the bucks with the does, Pete, else in a short
time we'd be overrun!'

Ron gives a 'heh heh'. A pink blush stains his cheeks.

'Who's gonna do it?' Cooper says, his eyes sparking with
interest. 'Kosho? Or Sandy?'

'Well,' Ron says.

I've been shown how to do this before, and I don't mind.
You get to hold the rabbit in your arms and cradle it; with the
smaller ones you can cup them in one hand. I've never been
watched before – except by Kosho. Kosho stuffs the white towel
in his pocket, crouches and opens the first cage. 'Girl,' he says
and hands me the doe. I put her in a hutch. He does this several
times, separating the animals with ease, until Pete says, 'No, no,
Kosho. You already have turn. You give turn to Sandy.' Pete

Cooper's sweaty face. His hair, skin, eyes, everything about him washed in red. I don't think he's been drinking, but there's a smell about him. 'You're a lover, Sandy. You love everything, don't you. Krauts, Japs, anything that moves. Let's see you "love" these bunnies.' He grins, pushes Kosho out of the way, reaches in and lifts out a rabbit.

I close my eyes for a second, then I support the small being in my hand. Its fur is soft and smooth, its heart beats rapidly. When you tip them upside down, they go still, so I tilt the animal and murmur quietly to it. I do not wear a glove. To this point, I have never been scratched.

I push down with two fingers just in front of the anus and the vent protrudes. It isn't always easy, when they're this young, to tell which is which, but there is no small tube and I can see from the veins along the central line the pink bands that indicate a female. Pete Cooper is right about me, I am a lover. I love this creature, its trust, its innocence.

'Oh, Sandy,' Pete Cooper says, 'how does it feel? Is it good for you?'

I stroke it between the eyes before I hand it over to Kosho.

'Cute little fryer,' Pete Cooper says. I can tell he's angry, but Ron is there and Pete just pushes by and drives away in the truck.

We finish the job in no time. Tomorrow we'll go through the breeding stock and cull the old bucks and the does that have served their period of usefulness. This part isn't pleasant. Before we do it, Kosho prays. Every now and then we let one go. We don't keep records – we don't have to – since it's all in Kosho's head.

By the time we're ready to leave it's getting late and we've had to turn on the lights. At the last minute, and to my surprise, Pete Cooper turns up again. There is no truck, so he must have walked from the barn.

'I thought you were off home?' Ron Signet says. Ron's been reading a book. He's recently taken up Esperanto. He says that after the war there'll be a big call for it and he wants to be ready.

He marks the page with a turned-down corner and tucks it in his tunic pocket.

'I was,' Pete says, 'but Barker's fallen ill so I'm staying on.'

'Well, it's overtime.'

'Yeah, but . . .' says Pete.

'Big plans tonight?' says Ron.

Cooper winks. 'Heap big!'

I'm not good at hiding what I feel: this has worked against me all my life, first, of course with my parents, and now here. Karl says I have (*haf*) to get over it; Georgina says that I must learn to dissemble; that if I were in the military, I *would* or wash out. Her son dissembles all the time in his letters. He doesn't tell her what's really going on, and for that she's grateful. He won't tell the truth to anyone, except, perhaps, to the new girl-friend he's found in England. This is the way he'll survive the war. I turn my back so that Attendant Cooper won't see my face, and follow Kosho out with the attendants behind us, still chatting.

We all – except for Kosho who has returned to his quarters – enter the cafeteria by the kitchen door. I hang up my work apron and take off my gumboots in the utility room, stepping over heaps of unsorted laundry, then I wash my hands and sit down for a late supper.

There's only me eating. Stew and boiled potatoes and boiled greens. Tapioca pudding for afters. Cold coffee. Instead of the usual long tables in rows, there are card tables in cosy arrangements – ashtrays set out, dishes of peanuts on each – oriented towards the stage at the far end. Soon the others from the West Wing will file in for movie night.

As I push aside the grey tapioca globules (must ask Kosho about fish eggs – does he eat them?) Ron Signet goes through the door to the left of the stage and mounts the platform. There he takes a long hook and pulls down the movie screen. Most of the films are educational, from the Forestry Branch or about safety. We don't mind what they are as it is our main chance to see normal people. Women with make-up, men driving cars.

'What's on tonight, Ron?' I call out.

Ron leaps from the stage and wanders to the back where the film projector hunches, alien-like with its two reels for head and shoulders. He picks up a film can and reads the label. '"Fire in Your Hospital." Sorry, Sandy.' He begins to thread the film.

When I have time, when I'm not busy with my work or trying to understand my position and how I might better it, I like to think about the people with whom I'm confined. Even before Karl comes in, tall, stooped, his spectacles greasy, looking lost, a paper in his hand, and speaks to Pete Cooper, I'm thinking about this difficult attendant. What is it that makes him so angry? The things he says, does he believe them? Or are they just what he says to make his mark? Like dogs do. Pissing into the corners of our minds because he can. Or like the people who came to live in my house when I was small, those who took over from my real parents, who tried to make me believe they were my real parents – did they see it as part of a job, some form of service or improvement? Could they be so deluded they're guilt-less? Judge not that ye be not judged, Sandy.

I cannot say more about the false people, not yet, not before preparing the way first with Dr Frank, but I would ask you to consider: would a mother who loved her children tell them each evening as they settled to sleep that they'd go to hell to burn in everlasting fire if they died in the night? Would she, when she was angry at some misdeed – a broken dish, for instance, or a handful of carrots pulled from the garden – would she shout at them in tongues, engendering terrible fear? I know that glosso-lalia is meant to be God's voice using the instrument of human speech – so how did it come to be used as a lash with which to hurt small children? These are questions which I still consider worth posing.

Karl keeps his head down as he hands a message to Atten-dant Cooper.

'What's this?' Cooper says. 'What hole did you crawl out

of? Who sent you?'

'Dr Frank asked me to bring this to you. He is in his office waiting (*vaiting*).'

'*Vaiting*?' Cooper says. 'What the fuck is that?'

At that moment the doors open and the others shuffle in. These are men in chains, even though there is nothing binding their feet. They scuff their slippers as if they are hobbled; the starved cheeks, the loss of muscle. Don't forget your exercises, Sandy.

The sound of the running film is like distant gunfire, the fire raging through the hospital corridors (men carrying water buckets, women soaking blankets and laying them over windows) is repeated a hundred times a night in the bombed cities of London, Belfast, Liverpool and on the Clyde. A haze of smoke from the men's cigarettes is caught in the cone of the projector light. I'm there, absorbing directions (always know your exits) when there's a soft sigh, the scent of Chanel, and a cool hand on my arm.

'Georgina!'

'Shhh!' she says. 'I had to pull rank to get in here, but I had to come.'

'Why, what's happened?' I look quickly round, but most of the men are still concentrating on the screen.

'I was just too bloody lonely, Sandy. There's nothing going on out there! A girl needs some time off for good behaviour.'

'But how did you get in here?'

'I told your friend Dr Frank my father was thinking of making a donation. I wanted to be sure you were well treated on Saturday nights.'

'He went for that?'

She rubs her thumb and forefinger together. 'Money talks.' Now that she's whispering into my ear, I can smell the gin.

'I don't believe it, George.'

'Well, maybe it wasn't Dr Frank . . .' She gazes around hazily.

'You've been drinking,' I say.

'Not you, too, Sandy! I thought you'd be glad to see me.' She pouts. There's a smear of lipstick in one corner of her mouth. I lick my finger and rub it off. 'I am glad. But I worry about you.'

Shuffle, shuffle of feet. We're being observed. Somebody – maybe Bob – says, 'Hubba hubba!'

'Worry less, play more,' she says. She lights up a cigarette, takes a few puffs. 'Not that there's much scope here.' She stubs out the cigarette in the ashtray.

'This isn't very responsible, Georgina!'

'Quiet,' says a man nearby. He keeps pulling at his ear with his fingers. When Georgina sticks out her tongue at him, he wiggles his ears and goes up-down with his eyebrows.

'You'll have to go if you make a disturbance,' Ron Signet says. He's a brooding shadow; he looms.

'Did you let her in, Ron?'

'Don't be such an old maid, I'm here to have fun,' she says. 'This place needs brightening up!' Ron doesn't return her smile, so she subsides. One leg crossed over the other, she swings her foot, shoe partly off. 'Oh, pooh. This is no good. Come on, Sandy, let's get out of here!' She tugs at my arm.

'Georgina, I can't.' The film continues to unspool, giving more urgent directions, showing evacuations of patients, application of bandages.

'You could if you wanted,' she says. 'If you really wanted.' Her eyes have a glaze.

Her smell is sharp and ripe. She puts a hand in my lap.

'Georgina, please!'

Ron is there again. 'Miss, I don't know what you were told, but you'll have to go.'

'It's okay, it's okay, I'm writing a cheque.' She opens her bag, takes out a chequebook, flips it open and scrawls a figure. 'Is that enough?' She waves the torn-off cheque and it's caught in the film light, a hand puppet. Now everyone knows that she's here. Some of the men laugh.

The spool ends. Ron turns on a light so he can see to change it. There's a different feeling in the room, and I'm afraid for her.

'You'll have to go, George,' I say.

'Spoilsport!'

Then Karl is standing there too. I introduce them and he takes her hand and kisses it. There's a stir. I stand up. 'Karl is writing a book, Georgina. He's a serious novelist.'

'Are you?' she says to him. 'Then I'll send you a writing book that belongs to my son.'

Attendant Cooper motions Karl to accompany him and they both go out.

Even Georgina knows now that she has to go. Ron is on the phone, calling for backup. When four attendants come through the doors, Georgina hands the cheque to Ron. 'Give this to Dr Frank, with my compliments. Excellent entertainment. Superb care. I'll report back to my father.' She gives us a wave – 'Ta-ta!'

Then she's gone. Like the visitation of a spirit, I only half believe that she's been. But then I start to laugh, and can't stop, and laugh and laugh until the tears spill.

Ron sends me to my room although the second reel of the movie is still running. 'A little time on your own, Sandy, that's what you need,' he says.

'Take a cold shower, Sandy!' Winchell sings out.

It's odd, this ability to walk unescorted through the corridors, to pass empty rooms, climb deserted stairways. Being alone, able to walk freely, one might think one were at liberty; although the barred windows, the locked doorways, the double steel door between West and East Wings and the combination of doors, gates, cabinets – like decompression chambers between inside and outside that I can't see but know are there – tell a different story.

I'm thinking about the form of my day: how it began as usual, with work, and then the nature of my work, the contact with the rabbits, the purity of their breath and being that not even an angry man like Pete Cooper can contaminate; how life manages to exist and co-exist on its own terms; and then the surprise of Georgina's visit – like a twist in a tale at midpoint. If Karl is right, the twist should lead to something – and I can't help but think anyway that everything that Georgina does has a consequence.

My room is dark. Winchell and Bob are still downstairs watching the film, and Karl had not returned after leaving with Attendant Cooper: perhaps he's gone to bed early? A soft moan drifts from the direction of his bed and I hope I haven't interrupted him. Although it makes me feel uncomfortable, I can understand the need to take solace however one can, in the dark, where one can imagine it must be the loved one's hands and warmth on your body and not your own. I stand still, so as not to embarrass him. Another moan, then a soft squished sound, like a sponge being squeezed. I hold my breath. There's a smell I know.

'Fucking Kraut, that should fix you.' Pete Cooper lurches out from behind Karl's bed. I smell faeces and urine and sweat. And blood.

I back away, but I'm too late: Cooper has seen me. I try to run, but I slip in a wet patch on the floor. 'It's you, you little faggot, you're next.' Cooper's heavy breathing: I've curled up on my knees, hands protecting my neck.

The light comes on. 'What the hell!' It's Winchell and Bob and behind them is Ron Signet. On the floor, not three feet from me, is Karl's splintered face, his eyes rolled back in his head.

'Jesus, Pete, what happened?' Ron says. 'Bob, Winchell, downstairs, now, call First Aid.' They go without hesitation. They don't have to look to know it's bad.

Ron steps over me and peers down at Karl. I unclasp my hands and sit up. Pete Cooper's shoes and boots are spattered with blood. 'I said, what happened, Cooper?' Ron doesn't try to touch the injured man. He's gone white. He's not thinking about me.

'I came in to check the room and the patient became aggressive. He grabbed and held me,' Cooper says. 'Being alone, I had to become rough, and in the following scuffle the patient received a knock that caused the discoloration of his face.' It's textbook stuff, this.

'Is that so, Pete?' Ron Signet says.

'Are you calling me a liar, Ron? The German rushed me, and to protect myself I flung my arms up and pushed him, he must have fallen against the radiator.'

'Christ, Pete, his face looks like a melon.'

'Any marks on his body will have been caused by his hitting the radiator.'

'Jesus,' Ron says and finally kneels beside Karl. Karl is breathing loudly, there's a whistle from his throat. 'What's that?' he asks. He puts his hand to Karl's face and turns it slightly. There's a hole in Karl's skull and a bulge of glistening gelatinous tissue. Ron scrabbles backwards on his knees, hauls himself up and runs to the door to vomit.

Pete Cooper sits on Karl's bed. 'What did you do that for, Pete?' I ask him. I'm cool, I'm reptilian, I have cold blood. But it's his eyes that blink, lidless.

'An eye for an eye,' he says softly, just under the sound of Ron's retching. 'My son's ship was bombed by fucking Germans, he's missing.'

'I didn't know he was in the navy,' I say, cool as a cucumber.

'Merchant marine,' Cooper says with a proud lift to his chin. '*Europa* went down near Liverpool. I just learned.'

'Then he'll be all right, Pete, they'll rescue him. It happens all the time.'

Attendant Cooper closes his eyes and yawns: his mouth wide, a maw of brown and broken teeth, and the face of a small red devil on his tongue. I hear running footsteps; others are coming, and I have seen that, just as I suspected, Pete Cooper isn't human.

SEVEN
18 June and following, 1941

When I awaken, Karl's bed, kitty-corner from mine, has been stripped. The black-and-white ticking of the mattress and pillow are folded together at one end. Bare bed springs, the scoured bedside table, the empty hooks and shelves inside the cupboard, proclaim his absence. Disinfectant fumes sting my eyes. Someone has done his best to erase him. My stomach, taut with hunger, turns over, but then I find, when I examine the writing table pushed against the wall with Karl's chair upturned on top of it, that Karl has scratched the silhouette of a dove into the wood. I touch the evidence of my friend's existence with my fingers. The dove's wings are spread, and in its beak, it carries a leaf.

I pull on some clothes and step into the hallway, and there's Ron Signet stuffing a string mop into a pail. He gives it a twist in the wringer before looking up. 'Back with us, Sandy?' he says.

I nod and run my tongue over my teeth, feeling fur, tasting vomit, discovering something as I do. 'I was sick.'

'Could have been something you ate.' Ron dumps the water bucket into a utility sink. 'Or it's this flu going round. Half the staff is off with it.'

'But not you?' It's not usually his job to clean. I suppose it's an instance of all available shoulders to the wheel.

'You know me, Sandy. I never quit.' He sponges down the sink, straightens, rubs a hand over his jaw and I see that he's unshaven and tired.

'Where are the others? My roommates? This place is dead.'

He looks wary: there's a slight tension around the eyes, and his shoulders stiffen. 'Now, you haven't forgotten, have you, Sandy? We went over this.'

'I know Karl is gone. I'm asking about Winchell and Bob.'

'They were moved out when you were ill. Once we swab the room down properly, now that you're up, they'll return. We've had men sleeping in the cafeteria. They've been falling like flies, I tell you. What a business!'

'A fine mess you've gotten into?' He'll like me to say this: we're both fans of Laurel and Hardy.

'That's it!'

He still looks cautious: I can tell by his stance, the legs wide apart, the stiff neck. 'Ron?' I say. 'Is there a problem?'

'You don't remember?'

I shake my head. Although I do.

'You must have been coming down with the fever. You were delirious. I can't say that you were easy to handle, Sandy.'

'I didn't hurt anyone, Ron, please don't say that I did?'

'No, no,' he says. He relaxes a little. We're back to being pals. He sighs. 'I know you didn't mean it, lad. It's just the way you took on. We had to tie you down. I was afraid you'd hurt yourself!'

'Took on? Because of what happened to Karl?'

'I know you don't much care for Attendant Cooper. He's a rough diamond, but his intentions are good . . . You'll be glad to hear they found his son.'

'That is good news,' I say. 'It's just that Karl was my friend. I had no idea that Karl could be . . .'

'Such a dangerous man,' he finishes for me. 'Of course you didn't know. He should never have been in the West Wing to begin with. I blame, well, others. Why on earth Dr Frank mixed a Kraut in with the rest . . . Why, to someone like Winchell, it's a red flag to a bull.' He shakes his head in disbelief.

But Winchell, our Spanish Civil War veteran, had nothing to do with it. Nor did Dr Frank, who Ron Signet also wants me to blame. I can see what will happen if this thinking continues – Pete Cooper will go scot-free – so I say, 'You know, Ron, I feel so much better in myself these days. The work I've done with Dr Frank is so important. I've had a chance to examine what happened to me, and now it all makes sense! The last of it has burned away with the fever.'

He frowns. 'You're bound to feel better with Karl gone. You're not the only one he caused problems.'

'Will I see him again?'

Attendant Signet returns the mop to the bucket and puts them away in the cleaning cupboard. He bends to the water fountain to drink.

'Ron?'

Ron swallows. Fever spots chancre his cheeks. He splashes water over his burning cheeks and forehead. 'Well, Sandy,' he says at last after patting his face dry with a handkerchief, 'I certainly hope not.'

Ron Signet is a good man, or as good as he can be in the situation. Although most of Karl's belongings were destroyed or sent to the lockers to await distribution to his family – if they ever turn up looking for them – Ron has saved Karl's writing materials for me. There are several reams of paper, a handful of pens with changeable nibs, four bottles of good ink, used and fresh blotting paper. Ron helps me tuck the supplies away behind my sweaters. 'Out of sight, out of mind,' he says. 'No need to put anyone's back up.'

When Ron has left me to rest, I investigate the leavings thoroughly, but there is no sign of Karl's manuscript. *The Romance of Stanley Park* is no more: Karl will never be a published author. I consider this a tragedy only as long as it takes me to realise that it won't matter to Karl: he won't know of it, or much of anything – Pete Cooper made sure I understood that – and his family will have had no idea of its existence. I'm the only person alive to bear witness to Karl's potential.

I close all doors and windows on the subject of Karl. The East Wing is like that. Once in, never out.

(But to whom will I go for counsel now? Who will be my sword and my buckler?)

Still, an afternoon in all its glory awaits me. I'm a free man in my mind and I intend to behave like one.

My cup of bouillon and soaked bread is brought to me by Bob, who slides the tray along the floor from the doorway, so as not to come too close to me. Ron Signet has ordered a coffee with extra cream for the tray, although he 'wasn't supposed to', but Old Doc Hitchens, still slogging through the worst cases in the cafeteria, let him 'because he's about to send Ron home, though Ron don't know it'. Bob's eyes sparkle: he's the first to carry the news. Then he does something unexpected. He draws out from the large pocket of his student cardigan (leather patches at the elbows, a yellow varsity insignia on the breast) a brown-paper-wrapped package. 'For you,' he says, and tosses it so that it skates over the tiles towards me. 'Well, it's for you now – it was sent to Karl.'

'It's been opened,' I say. It's not a question. A flutter of anxiety runs through me when I see Georgina's name and address in the left-hand corner. I outwait Bob, who wants to see what's in it, by continuing on with my wash and brush-up. When he's truly gone, I slip off the string. *The Storehouse of Thought and Expression: A Course in Creative Writing*, published in 1932. The frontispiece shows the 'Hand of God' by Rodin. A large thumb restrains the struggling limbs of several miniature figures as they writhe (it is an active sculpture) out of the lump of rough bronze. The name of the book's owner, Brentwood Jones-Murray, Georgina's son, is written in a neat round hand very different from his mother's.

The note for Karl says: 'I hope the book will help you in your endeavours. Please return it after the war, when my son is home, or before that, if you can, to my house in person.'

There's something different about this Georgina. I can read, between the lines, within the terse politeness, the fears of an anxious matron. The war, her son, the house, her person. What will happen? she's thinking as she writes to Karl. What will happen to all of us?

Karl. Already. It has happened.

I stand at the window and watch the curl of smoke from the incinerator that could be Karl's life work, or it could be chicken parts and rabbit foetuses and the bags we carry from the East Wing, burning. Thin white clouds, the kind you could tear into tissue shreds with the wings of an airplane, scud across the face of the sun. I look downward. The life of the soldiers in the garden, the workers at the quarry, the husbanding of all the animals, large and small, in our care continues. The world is as it was and ever will be. All in order. I'm ready.

I seat myself at Karl's writing table and pick up a pen. Karl said that the idea would appear when it was ready. I wait. But it doesn't. Not yet. I get up and stretch my legs. I leaf through Georgina's book. I read: 'In the mind ideas may grow or rot. Mental health requires that we submit them frequently to a re-examination.' Well, yes. 'You have a theme and plenty of ideas. Some of you may be going to describe an apple, to show what a wonderful thing it is in itself. There is no predicting what is about to flow down your pens.' The apple must be specific. I should consider that the apple has form.

I close my eyes in rumination. I recall Ron Signet's story about the robin building its nest in the supports and thereby halting construction. That was specific (although not specifically true, as it turned out), that nesting robin . . . and the nest, itself, surely, refers not just to form but to ultimate form: it is a container that contains a container (the egg) that accommodates all the potential of the chicken. But it's no good. The idea turns in on itself. I feel the pull of its vortex and think about the war news, the piling up of the dead beneath rubble in London and in the German cities. I remember how I want to cover my ears when Winchell speaks of the shooting of priests in Spain – the tender voice in which he describes their blood-stained soutanes . . .

Is this what Karl had to contend with? This roar in the ears when you open the doors of the storehouse of thought and expression? I turn to the beginning of Georgina's book, the place to which her son, Brentwood, would have turned without hesitation: this young man who knows right from wrong by instinct, who is an officer in the Royal Air Force, who has already met Churchill and battled German Messerschmidt 109s, as Georgina has told me – yes, he would have begun at page one.

'Our minds are full of ideas as the heavens are full of stars. They are all related in some strange way. We see an apple and think tree.' Quickly I reseat myself and write down *stars*. I don't have long to wait.

> *'Write, therefore, what you have seen, what is now,*
> *and what will take place later.'* (Rev. 1:19)

Prologue

I do not claim to be infallible. I might have made some mistakes in my life story due to witnesses using other people's names to cause the court to make false decisions and believe lies. In spite of this I have endeavoured to keep to the truth. I pray that God will reveal the true meaning and guide you in your decision what to do and not to do.

I, Alan Macaulay, have returned from the dead to plead my innocence. You may say why intrude into the world of the living? I have returned simply to tell my story, so that it will be known in its reality – its turning points and revelations, its ultimate conclusions. For the sake of truth and justice.

Part I: From Whence I Have Come and What I Have Seen

I begin with the dog on the beach in my home village of Cramond in Scotland. I begin at the age of twenty-four, a short time before I left for Canada. I do not begin with childhood. That era is closed to me who am now, on this beach, a man in my prime. I begin here on the wet shingle, under a heavy grey sky, as I gazed across the Firth of Forth to Fife, in the year 1903, on a wet and windy day in early summer that changed my life – although the dog was not mentioned by my mother in the letter in which she begged the prime minister for my life – because the dog and my feelings for it, the state of mind I was in, was identical to that of the moment in which I was said to have formed the intention to kill.

The River Almond, the mouth of which was within my sight, once crowded with transport vessels bringing coal and lime and bar-iron and taking out iron and steel from the ironworks, was an empty sweep of water. The only traffic upon it was the regular crossing of the ferry boat. Within six hours I would ask Andy Mathews to row me across to the west bank, and from there I would walk to Hunter's Crag.

It was eleven o'clock in the morning. The women were watching the tide, some with their skirts kilted up. They carried sacks in which to put the cockles, mussels and limpets with which they fed their families. If I had gone home, I would have found my mother and grandfather in the cottage, she at work with the weaving, and he all too ready with tales of

MARILYN BOWERING

work in the nailery and the sawmill at Dowie's Mill.
Since I had left school, I'd worked for John Weller
making furniture.

Six months ago I'd been squaring a corner of a
cabinet door when my chisel slipped and cut deeply
between my thumb and forefinger. The hand and arm
had become much swollen and I'd had to stop work
for a considerable time, my mother's remedies
notwithstanding. I'd returned to work but found my
hand and arm unsteady and I made mistakes and was
let go.

Every morning I collected kelp from the mounds
that washed ashore. This was women's work, but there
is no shame in work of any kind that is driven by
necessity. When I could find them, I gathered oysters,
although the beds had been largely overfished and
destroyed. I gave the money to my mother for my
keep. I drank little. I did not carouse.

The dog, Dandy, a terrier, ran ahead of me and
darted, suddenly, away from the shore and into the
brush surrounding the ruins of Cramond Tower. I
heard it barking, and thinking that it had cornered a
rat or ferret, followed cautiously. I struck aside the ivy
that had got such a hold of the stones, and when I
rounded the corner, where the stairtower stood
exposed, I found there a young woman, about my own
age, sitting with a sketchbook on her lap.

'Away, Dandy,' I said to the mutt, and to her –
'I'm sorry about the dog.'

She smiled. 'I wasn't afraid.' What did she look
like? She wore a long brown cloth walking skirt over
boots. Her jacket was buttoned over a shirtwaist.
She'd taken off her hat and her hair had loosened
from its knot.

'Can I be of any assistance?' I said.

'I've just finished,' she said, and gathered up her
things.

'May I?' I held my hand out for the open sketchbook and, with a blush, she complied.

From where she sat she had a keyhole view of the strand. She'd shaded cliffs of sky and sea, and a miniature man with his dog, the man with his arms lifted like a bird, as if about to fly, utterly joyous. I made no comment, although it was obvious the man was me. I returned the sketchbook to her. Just then a voice cried, 'Barbara!' and a man appeared. The woman rose. I said goodbye and returned with Dandy to the beach.

Wide open sand and mud flats as the tide retreated. No reason to be anywhere with the kelp already delivered to the buyer, the oysters to the fishwife who would sell them in Edinburgh. I took the raised walkway across the sands to Cramond Island. Deserted today, although on Sundays it was always busy with picnickers from the town. The dog ran away into the trees. I climbed over the rocks to a cleft I knew where I could lie down out of the wind. Noon. The sky broke open its fruit and the pit of the sun shone fiercely. I took off my shirt and my trousers.

I was a young, healthy man. My shoulders and arms were muscled from my trade, my thighs strong from long walks. I had the blue eyes of the men in my family, my hair was dark and streaked light in strips by salt. I'd taken several of the village girls to the kirkyard where we'd lain down among the tombstones. I'd taken one on the long walk to Queensferry and back through the woods of Dalmeny. In my mind, against my closed eyelids, I saw the woman from the tower. My hands unbuttoned her jacket, my fingers felt the sting of her nipples.

I opened my eyes at the sound of a splash and sat up. A seal swivelled its cannonball head, a smooth turn on the waters. I got to my feet for a better look.

'Oh!' I heard from behind me. I turned around. The woman was on the rocks above me. Just cresting the height behind her was her companion. My hand went protectively to my erection.

'Filth!' the man shouted. 'Disgusting!' The woman

did not move. He reached her and pulled her away but not before I heard her say, 'Oh, dear God, your poor arm.' I could not help myself; I came.

It is said that God made us in his own image, and that he made us male and female for a purpose. I had done no wrong, and I did not believe the woman took any offence. Why should she? It was she who startled me and I was where I belonged. Whereas she and the man with her would be met by a horse and cart and would return to Edinburgh. She'd live in the New Town, in a house with high ceilings and where the fire surround had been made by men like me in furniture shops like John Weller's and would cost a fortune – far more than I could make in three months. I knew my place. It was fine.

But what she saw when she looked at me was not a man, but an object of sympathy. I examined my arm and hand: they flopped uselessly, swollen, red, mis-shapen, of no more use to me than a seal's flipper. The future was an open book and my role in it was pitiable.

I returned home with the dog. I took the laudanum from my mother's cupboard. I did not speak to her or my grandfather, but I shut the dog in my bedroom. I walked into the village and from the apothecary purchased more laudanum. When I met my friend, George Falconer, I told him what I was going to do. He said, 'Come now, Alan. What you need is a good dinner, come back with me to my house.' I refused and paid Andy Mathews to row me across the river. I took one last look behind me at the children on the sand. They ran in bare feet, the girls wore hats with streaming ribbons. The mothers and fathers held the hands of the little ones. They were each, in the sight of God and man, perfect.

You will know, of course, that I was rescued. How else would I find myself about to be hanged? I insist I have done no wrong, except to myself, and perhaps, through worry, to my family. I wish I had died that day at Hunter's Crag. If I'd been left alone I would have. It was the right time, the right place, the right reason. George Falconer went to the police and they found me and brought me to the doctor. He pumped out my stomach and took me home. George and my mother kept me awake all night, forcing me to walk back and forth through the rooms of the cottage until it was felt I was safe.

I was not safe. I had made a decision from which none could dissuade me. But what I need to say, so that the whole will be clear to your judgement, was that if I'd had a gun I would have turned it on myself and made an end to it that way. Do you see?

EIGHT

1 July, Dominion Day, and following, 1941

It is not usual for Dr Frank to work holidays, so I'm surprised when I'm taken from my chores in the rabbitry to see him. Miss Cochrane, Dr Frank's assistant with the Orientals, comes with me. Many of the regular staff are absent – off for a day of picnics with their families, I suppose. We meet in his office: it's the first time I've been there since the day I arrived and I experience a flare of hope that I'm about to be released. These things do happen. Anything is possible. I sit in a chair in front of the desk, beads of sweat skating down my forehead. Miss Cochrane takes a chair near the window slightly behind Dr Frank, and flips to a clean page in her secretarial pad.

How precious the view of the garden from that office window, and the glimpse of the fountain stocked with Kosho's fish: myriad rainbows star from the spray, and the long open drive winds between trees to the outside world. When I'm allowed to walk in the garden accompanied by Ron Signet, it's different: the steps, the front door, the swinging gait of those who breeze in and out belong to a different universe from the one I inhabit, and I know it. The same sun, the same stars, but *la condition humaine* is incomparable.

I'm on the cusp of emotion while I wait for him to speak, my desire to leave as hard and bright as a blaze of light from a star thought long dead. He gives me a nod and a glance over the top of his spectacles, then returns to his reading. My pages. My story of Alan Macaulay.

What I notice while I attend: he's lost weight; the shoulders of his navy suit jacket look like epaulettes. Dr Frank's hand does not snake out to the bowl of humbugs. There's dust on the bookshelf where certain tomes have been removed. Which ones? Jung, I believe. Vanished trophies, too. What's left? Medical books. Dead flowers in a vase.

He puts down the papers, loosens his collar and starts right in.

'I see you've been working hard at your writing, Sandy, and Ron Signet tells me you're a paragon of efficiency in the rabbitry. You're making progress.'

Did I say a flare of hope? More like a conflagration. I swab sweat from my eyes. One of the papers on the desk could be a pardon.

'I should also mention how useful is your friendship with Mrs Jones-Murray. Her father, Mr Dunblane Sr, has made a generous donation; next thing you know, we'll be building a swimming pool and tennis courts for the inmates! Ha ha!' Yellow rings pouch beneath his eyes and his fingers are ink-stained. Why is he working so hard?

'I had some difficulty, I must tell you, in getting Mr Dunblane to drop certain conditions relevant to you, inserted in the agreement, doubtless, because of your woman friend's soft heart; but we can't have the welfare of our patients in the hands of civilians and sentimentalists, can we?'

Hope dies. My hands tremble. I clench my fists to still them.

'I said, can we, Sandy?' he says. The eyes in the dirty sunken sockets are neither hard nor friendly. They engage mine briefly and pass on. He has other, more important, matters on his mind than me. He skims the room abstractedly, counting up what's left?

'Are we at war, then, sir?'

'Pardon me? What kind of a question is that?' Life stirs within the stained waistcoat, the dull eyes revive. 'Of course we're at war, you know perfectly well . . .'

'Not that, sir. You mentioned "civilians". I just wondered what you meant. Is this a military institution now? Are you no longer in command?' I've gone too far. He doesn't like sarcasm and I've struck close to the bone. (This could swing for me or against me.)

He draws a slow breath through flared nostrils. 'Which brings me to why I asked you here today.'

'Yes, sir, I was wondering about that. I've been nervous. You'll have to excuse me if I thought, at first – now I understand that I was wrong – that you'd asked me here to impart good tidings. Your office is where I entered the institution: I'd assumed that those about to leave were summoned here as well. I've thought about nothing else since Miss Cochrane came for me.'

He digests this. 'Not a very realistic hope, Sandy, was it? There'd have to be a court pardon first.' He's not unkind by nature. He understands. 'I should have allowed for that. I owe you an apology.'

He pulls himself to his feet. He's added braces to hold up his trousers. He takes my story pages in his hand, walks round the desk to where I sit and places them gently on the desk in front of me. 'What's this about, Sandy? Why aren't you writing about yourself, as I asked you to? I don't understand its relevance. We're here to work for the truth, Sandy, not to entertain ourselves. Why, if we want entertainment, we play golf, or see a film, or go dancing. Am I not right?'

What can I say to this that would be truthful? 'I enjoy movie night, sir.'

'Then you do see this can't continue.' He's back in his chair, nodding pleasantly. I'm a good boy again if I hear and obey. The clock inside him that divides his day into periods of importance has sped up. I've maybe a minute to make my case before he's on to something else.

'I beg your pardon, Dr Frank, but could I please explain?' He temples his fingers below his chin to hide impatience.

'You explained to me that knowing where I am is important. You encouraged me to look into the history of this great building – a not inconsiderable architectural landmark – and I have enjoyed the research. While doing so I came across the account of Alan Macaulay's hanging.'

'Yes, I know. A sad event, to be sure, but the only one of its kind.' Fingertips prick the folds of his jowls. Eyes around the room, looking – for what?

'Yes, sir, but one that must withstand the searchlight of truth if it is not to be wasted.'

'Meaning?'

'Either Macaulay was guilty, as charged, or he was innocent, in which case a grave injustice has been done.'

'You're too clever a boy to be unaware, Sandy, that this is a thinly disguised means of talking about yourself! I've asked you to be direct, yet you insist on fiction!'

'If I may say so, I *am* doing what you ask to the best of my ability; perhaps my abilities will change and develop, but in the meantime this research may help to right a terrible wrong, and bring peace to a shamed family.'

'Fiction, Sandy, it's a piece of fiction.'

'Based on fact.'

I notice as he lays upon me his most heavy, speculative gaze how feminine are his eyelashes: they are thick, black, feathered. Georgina once gave me a butterfly kiss from her eyelashes on the palm of my hand. I told her I didn't like it, but I did. That touch sent prickles through me. 'It was long ago, Sandy. Let sleeping dogs lie.'

'You won't help me further, sir? I'm to return the files? Give up?'

A belch rumbles through him. He lifts a handkerchief to his mouth. Several more suppressed burps. 'I didn't say that, Sandy.' His fingers rustle through folders and he pulls out more paper. These are scraps blotted with ink and food stains. Torn-off corners and long strips. Nothing so grand as my efforts with Alan Macaulay.

'These other pieces you've given me' – he waves a fistful of my dreams and memories – 'these are more what I want, but we're still not there, are we?'

'Sir?'

'Do you remember the poem about the blind men of Hindustan who argued among themselves over what an elephant was like? Each felt a different part of the animal and was convinced that the small area he explored must be the shape of the whole beast. Most of us make as great an error as those blind men in our interpretation of others. These oddments you've given me, Sandy, are my evidence of what you wish to suppress, but what lies between them? Where is the elephant? You understand – Miss Cochrane will back me up here' – he acknowledges her racing pencil just behind him – 'that we may find one facet of a personality and try to judge the whole from that and if we do so we may then make a grave error – one that can't be repaired.'

The scratching of Miss Cochrane's pencil on the steno pad ceases. The two of us wait for more words from on high, but Dr Frank has shrunk into silence. His eyes close, the loose skin of his face drops, his shoulders sag. I remember the suicide of the soldier, the son of an important man. A grave error indeed.

'But that's it, sir,' I say. 'One must see the amazing unique-ness of each individual. Even twins may appear alike, but they differ in their experiences and ideas. We can't make assumptions other than to believe in the fundamental honesty of others. Alan Macaulay insisted he was innocent, his mother and various townspeople testified as to his character. We know that a man was killed, but have we seen into the heart of the man accused of his murder? Do we comprehend his intent, have we considered accident?'

'Into the heart, you say? You want to go there?'

'Yes, sir, I do.'

'You believe you can uncover his secrets?'

'Allowing him to talk, even as a character, gives him the opportunity to express his ideas, and for us to revamp ours.'

'And relieves your emotions, doesn't it, Sandy?'

An image of the young woman Alan Macaulay meets when he's sunbathing naked appears to me, as clearly as if it had been painted on the window glass behind Miss Cochrane. I blink and she fades but not before I've grown hard.

'I won't deny it, sir,' I say. 'But is an emotional safety valve harmful, given the circumstances?'

'Circumstances?' A gaze like a stone shot from a sling.

'I'm not free to do what I want, sir. Not even what I need.'

We hold each other's eyes. His have the glitter of coals on their way to becoming diamonds: heat and pressure over aeons. Mine are, as they say, the windows to my soul.

'There's value in relating a story, it gives some sequence to events, clarifies the problem. Wouldn't you say so, sir?'

He drops his gaze and moves on to words. My own words, written down. Repeated by Dr Frank. He tells me that even today words retain much of their magical power. By words one of us can give to another the greatest happiness or bring about utter despair. By words the teacher imparts his knowledge to the student. Words call forth emotions and are universally the means by which we influence our fellow creatures.

I do not say what I know, that words are not the basis of my problem.

'We'll take one or two of these words of yours, Sandy, shall we?' he says. 'Let's see what we can find.

'Miss Cochrane, would you cancel my other appointments?'

Once more I'm in the East Wing ground-floor room, lying on the bed. A nurse has been summoned. She's not in uniform. She wears a summer blouse and skirt. Her nose sports the beginning of a sunburn. She looks cross. Grains of beach sand cling to the tender hairs of her forearms. Has she left her lover behind on a blanket? Were her husband and children eating fried chicken from the basket she'd so carefully prepared early in the morning? Don't do this for me, I'd like to say to her, but with Dr Frank waiting I only roll up my shirt sleeve so that she can tie the rubber tubing tightly above my elbow. When all is ready, she loosens the tourniquet, opens the valve and the Sodium Pentothal begins to drip into my system.

'We'll stay away from numbers this time, Sandy. That's where we went wrong last time.'

No guidance then? No ladder of figures to hold on to? Just a fall into my own creation?

'Relax, Sandy. Allow yourself to drift. You're on the ocean, fully supported and warm. Nothing can harm you. You allow the current to carry you to a special land. Are you feeling comfortable? What does the word *bridal* mean to you, Sandy?'

I've fallen gently, as if from one of those rooms where you leave your body, float to the ceiling and can pass effortlessly through walls. The word *bridal* takes me safely past all dangers, although I'm aware of them, like tigers prowling dark woods, far below me. Where I settle, light as a feather, is sunshine. A stream rustles between grassy banks. I remove my shoes and socks and step into the water, carrying one of my shoes with me. I scoop up water in it and pour it over the head of the small blonde girl who waits for me. She laughs, tears of creek water on her eyelashes. 'Now I'll have to take my clothes off and dry them!' she says.

I take her hand and we wade to shore, wincing from the pinch of stones, minnows darting from the mud that squishes between our toes. She shakes her fingers dry then reaches behind her neck for her blouse button. Between the two of us, we manage and then she's standing there in her shorts and undershirt. She lays the blouse over a bush, then fumbles with her waistband.

'You can't take your clothes off unless we're married!'

'Oh!' She stops. Blue eyes like the camas flowers at our feet. I crouch and pick some, thrust a bouquet into her hand. 'Well,' she says, 'have you got a ring?'

Many things would do – we could plait grasses, tie a string – but in my heart I know this has to be permanent. I take off my shirt although it is not wet. Sunlight and wind, a chill scrape of air over my chest. I fetch my shoes. Several brass rings hold together the straps of my sandals. I pull at the leather until one breaks free.

'We have to have some words,' she says. She puts the damp blouse on top of her head for a veil; she gives me one of the blue flowers to hold.

I pull her down to kneel beside me. 'Forever and ever, I do,' I say and put the ring on her finger. She stretches out her neck, lips puckered up, and I kiss her, clean and sweet as a lick of ice. It could brace you for life.

'Now I can take all my clothes off,' she says. She pulls down the shorts, shrugs out of the undershirt and panties. Watching me. 'You too.'

We gather grasses for a bed, running back and forth to keep warm, then when it's time, lie down in our nest. Side by side, at first, then I know what I have to do. Lie on top of her, feel the warmth of her. 'You have to touch my boobies,' she says. So we sit up and I do.

'Now I'll touch you.'

Back and forth, everything is permitted because we're wed.

'What's the girl's name, Sandy?' Dr Frank's voice makes her step backwards, away from me.

'Heather?' I reach for her but she runs away laughing.

'Forever,' I say, hearing myself out loud this time, sounding like I'm drunk. Pathetic. 'It's forever. She can't go.'

Dr Frank again, voice booming in a wasteland as I'm plucked away, flung into a grey room. 'You went and told her mother that you were married.'

'Yes.'

'Then you left with her, took your clothes off once more, reached a crossroads.'

'So I've written.'

Two ways to go, one into a gully and back up to the road, the other across the school grounds. We go into the gully because we can't think further than that and we have to find a place to live. It's clear that where we stay must be our secret. Two big girls push their bikes down the path and drop them in a bush. Laugh when they see us naked. One of them takes me with her, and the two big boys who've lagged behind them catch up and they've got Heather. 'I just want to look,' I hear one say. The big girl with me – Dorothy – that's her name – I've seen her before – makes me lie on top of her, but I don't want to do anything. I run towards Heather, and he has her legs spread as she stands and he is poking between them with a stick. She wails, lost, and then her father's voice calls across the field, 'Heather, Heather!' The boy lets her go, pushes me in the face and they're gone.

'I've got to find her!' Tugging at the restraints, out of my mind with worry.

'You're at home now, Sandy. What's happening there?'

Terrible sobs because they won't let me see her. I've been sent to bed without supper. Her parents' voices, raised voices in the living room. Mother comes into my room wearing an old ugly dress, the sleeves rolled up above her elbows, her hands red from dipping them in hot water. 'I don't want to touch him, you do it,' she says.

I'm bundled into the bathroom, my father in his shirt sleeves, steam rising from a tub filled with hot water from the kettle. I scream when he lifts me in – it's too hot!

'You'll burn in hell, Sandy, far worse than this!' That's what I hear, and my mother's gush of syllables as the eyes roll back in her head and she shouts in tongues, rhythmical as the strap. Lashes of gibberish that frighten me to death. I scream and scream but my father has firm hold of me; he takes the stiff wash brush to my skin and scrapes until there's blood. 'I'll teach you to be clean!' he says. I put my hands over my penis, but he takes my hands away and there, too, peeling back the foreskin, soap and brush get to work.

'He had no right to do that, Sandy. You were an innocent child. You did nothing wrong. What happened was natural, most children experiment in that way.' The nurse smoothes a cool cloth over my face. 'It doesn't matter,' I say. She cleanses my hands. Hums a tune, maybe thinking this hasn't taken long, there's still time for her picnic. All the straps are undone. I sit up. I'm getting used to the feeling afterwards: I'm a baby bird, damp from the egg, and I step from the shell.

'What do you mean, it doesn't matter? Why ever not?'

'They weren't my real parents. It really doesn't matter what they did to me.'

'You're not being philosophical with me again, are you, Sandy?' Dr Frank says. 'You haven't been reading up on Freud?'

I shake my head.

'Because if you have, I'll have your guts for garters. No getting into bed with your mother next time, either, or I won't believe a word of it.'

A smile trembles across my lips. He lays a hand on my shoulder: I can hear the rumble of poor digestion from his stomach. 'You do know, Sandy, that Freud changed his mind about all that.'

'All what, sir?'

'Children and sex. It's all nonsense. His patients made it up.' I start to protest and he raises a hand to silence me. 'Not that I don't believe you, in essence. The part about your parents, now that makes sense.'

'Not my parents, sir.'

A baleful look, and he's gone.

I've been given the afternoon off from the rabbitry – although I'd prefer to go there – to 'collect myself' and 'think things over', which is what Dr Frank has suggested I do. When I arrive in my room I find the new man, Tom, going through my things. 'Hey, stop that!' I say. He's pulled out my underwear and sweaters from their drawers. My shoes are scattered over the floor.

He doesn't reply – so far he's said very little to anyone – and walks past me, out the door, carrying one of Karl's pens.

'Hey!' I rush after him and grab his arm. 'Give me that!' He plunges on, ignoring me. At the end of the corridor Pete Cooper stands smiling. 'Attendant Cooper, that man's been pawing my belongings and now he's got my pen!'

'Is that so?' Cooper says.

'Yes! Can you stop him, please?'

Tom doesn't take notice of either of us. 'You there, hold on,' Cooper says.

Tom opens the fire door at the end of the corridor and descends the stairs. He's still got Karl's pen, so I run after him. 'Bring that back, thief!' Tears smart my eyes.

'Been having a session, Sandy, feeling a little sensitive?' If it weren't Cooper who says this, I'd take it for sympathy. I find myself bawling: baby's tears gushing. Just then Bob arrives at the bottom of the stairwell and takes in the scene. Tom is about to brush by him too, but Bob snaps to attention and salutes. 'Sir!'

Tom cracks a salute back and the pen falls to the ground. Bob says, 'Carry on!' and Tom does. Pete Cooper watches in amazement. Bob calls up in a cheery voice, 'He'll be fine now. You just have to give him a direct order.' He glances at me. Both he and I know that Tom pays no attention to Cooper, orders or not. I happen to think it's the way Bob does it: he's playing a role that Tom recognises. At some point in his life, Tom's encountered the military, though why Bob should know this escapes me.

'How'd you figure that out, Bob?' I ask him.

'Observation.' Bob taps his forehead to show how smart he is. 'Saw him watch the soldiers. Figured it was something like that.' I follow Attendant Cooper down the stairs.

'Like what?' Pete Cooper says. Pete's hands are trembling. I know the signs and so I begin to edge away.

'Tom, over there . . .' We watch as Tom reaches a locked door, pauses, makes a brisk reversal and heads towards us. 'You got to keep it simple for him.'

'Is that a fact?' Pete Cooper says.

'Got anything for me?' Bob says. Pete Cooper generally saves magazines from the staff room for Bob who clips out pictures from them. Now that I think of it, I've seen Pete go out of his way a number of times to help out Bob, but this time Pete isn't listening to the younger man.

'Keep it simple, eh?' Pete says.

Tom trudges forward, empty-faced. At the point where he dropped the pen, he crouches and begins searching on hands and knees like a blind man.

'Stop it,' Pete says. 'You, come here.'

Tom ignores him. Pete shoots a venomous glance at me as Bob slips the pen from his hand into mine. 'I'll keep it simple, all right,' Pete says. He opens a cleaning cupboard and takes out a broom and starts poking the end at Tom's side as he crawls, still searching. 'Up on your feet, get up.' Pete mimes a poke with the broom at Tom's rear end.

Bob drops his hand from my shoulder and plants his shoes in Tom's path. 'Reveille, soldier, everyone up.' Tom springs to his feet. Bob salutes him and says, 'Return to quarters.'

I don't see the blow coming. It's there, a crack on the side of his head, then another and another. Tom immobile, cuts in his scalp, eyes swelling. Cooper swings like an automaton. Automatons the both of them.

It takes me oddly, my knees weaken and I'm blubbering. 'Ma ma ma.' No revelations, nothing new, it's that sliced-open feeling, that's all. Tom's buffeting by Pete Cooper finishes the job on my underpinnings that Dr Frank's truth serum began. 'Ma ma ma,' I wail.

A distant door clicks open. Attendant Cooper replaces the broom in the closet. Bob has his arms around me, his hands on my hair, quieting. 'There, there.'

Tom has carried on up the stairs to 'quarters' and, perhaps, to continue his rummage of my belongings.

'BMW, Harley Davidson, Indian, BSA,' Bob murmurs in my ear, words that must have meaning for him, words that at another time I would understand.

He's younger than me, I remember. Only a boy. Mothering me. I take a breath for self-control and open my eyes to meet a ray of hatred beamed my way by Pete Cooper before he follows after Tom to clean up.

NINE

11 July and following, 1941

I sit down to write, but I find I can't begin. Everything Attendant Cooper has ever done to bother me is what comes to mind. More and more of the world is at war, but with Karl's pen in my hand, I write down Cooper's sins:

1. beating Karl near half to death
2. attack on Tom
3. threats against my person
4. numerous insults to just about everyone.

It doesn't sound like much when it's put in black-and-white. Taking Georgina's advice that when you're mentally stuck, you should go in the other direction, I start a list of all the nice things Cooper has done for young Bob:

1. brings him magazines
2. gives him the easiest jobs
3. expresses himself in a kindly fashion towards him.

That's even worse for how little it conveys, but as I stare at the lists I see the problem, and find the page in *The Storehouse of Thought and Expression* to confirm it. 'A writer shows that he observes well when he succeeds in giving vivid pictures.' What's vivid in my lists? Why, nothing! Vivid would be Karl's face, the skin waxy yellow on one side, the other streaked with red, the creases around his rolling eyes forming crepe paper. Marbles on crepe paper. No, try again. The hatred I feel for Pete Cooper is like a vine in flower; in each blossom is the tiny grape that will expand into a globe that ripens under the sun. The grape's sweetness or sourness will be revealed in its taste; its value in the wine. That's vivid, but perhaps it's too metaphorical? I'm getting nowhere in this fashion, but I know what I have to do. The fruit comes of the planted seed, so I must sow the seed, attempt, through words, to convey the flavour of what it is like to live under this man's tyrannical rule.

Report of the attack by Attendant Peter Cooper on new patient Tom

At about three in the afternoon, not long after a session of 'truth serum' with Dr Frank, while I was going about my business in the West Wing, the above-named patient was struck with a broom handle over the head, shoulders and backside by Attendant Cooper.

The patient, although confused, had done nothing to deserve this beating; indeed, he had said nothing at all to Attendant Cooper. I observed cuts like vivid roses on the pale whiteness of his skin. [I cross out the "roses" part of the previous sentence.] Since the beating, Tom has had difficulty with his hearing. The attack was also witnessed by patient Bob Smithson.

Yours very truly,
Alexander Grey

I read this over and put it in my pocket to consider again later. I should get Bob to sign it. The testimony of two of us would count for more. But who to give it to when I'm ready? Ron Signet? Georgina? Is there a way to smuggle it into the general mail? I go back to thinking about Bob. The trouble with him is that he is handsome and knows it, and his joking around makes it so you can't always rely on him to take important matters seriously. Would he, for instance, tell Pete Cooper about the letter? Even as a joke? Remarks made to me by Georgina, when she met Bob, come back: 'He looks like the cat that ate the cream,' and 'That one knows which side his bread is buttered on.'

Indeed, sometimes Bob has 'that lean and hungry look'.

I asked Bob, like I ask everyone, what he had done to get himself here. He said he was 'just having fun'. I said, 'What kind of fun?' He said, 'You know, everything.' I said I didn't know. I asked him what he did for a living. 'Worked two weeks in a drugstore,' he said, 'learned the business in two weeks.'

'Oh,' I said.

'Then I went on a farm for three months, but it didn't pay much.'

'No,' I said.

'I could be a doctor, if I wanted, or a professor.'

'I suppose . . .'

'Or a minister. I'd take the religion of the Shriners Order.'

'The Shriners?'

'You know, like Omar Khayyám.'

'Khayyám the poet?'

Bob laughed. 'Yup,' he said, 'that religion, same as the Hindus and Egyptians.'

Bob surprises me, sometimes, by his references, although when I've quizzed him as to the books he's read, he goggles his eyes and plays dumb.

Sometimes Bob gets up in the middle of the night and strolls around. He doesn't seem to do anything but look through magazines and fetch himself drinks of water. I asked him, once, what he thought about in his night rambles. He answered, 'Yesterday.'

So you see how difficult it is to pin him down.

I recall, as I sit here, waiting for inspiration to strike, that Winchell told me that Bob had once eloped – gone into the airing court and climbed the fence. How he managed, I do not know, for the fence is high and topped with barbed wire. What struck me most about Winchell's tale was that he said that Pete Cooper had brought Bob back, and that although Bob was smiling, Pete Cooper was in tears. Strange. And difficult for me to imagine Bob wanting anything so badly he'd take a risk for it.

I put pen to paper to try to imagine the scene: the attempt to escape comes after a visit from Bob's mother. He's refused to see her. He runs to the fence and, with superhuman strength and total disregard for pain, scales it. He's over, and scarpering across the field; sheep baa away from him, he reaches a road, cars, people, then what? Pete Cooper in a staff car or the farm truck picks him up from the side of the road and brings him back? It hardly seems worth the effort.

I'm puzzling over these matters when Winchell enters. Winchell's looks are brutish. He has a low forehead, thick black hair that curls over his brow, long ears, heavily muscled arms, short legs and a stocky trunk. But I've been thinking over another page of *The Storehouse* where it says that 'we look at human beings with our emotions and our prejudices instead of with our eyes. We have an incurable desire to 'size a man up' which means judge his soul by the shape of his chin.'

Inferences like these, the text informs me, are often wrong, and that the ability to see what a man looks like without making a lot of wild speculations as to what he really is within, is a gift worth developing. I agree. So I am making an effort. I look at Winchell impersonally, just as I would look at an apple.

Winchell crashes on to his bed, stuffs a pillow behind his head and says, 'Still at it, Sandy?' – which, for him, is a friendly opening.

I say, 'Winchell, you were in Spain. You've had military training and seen active service. You've a great deal of experience of life that I haven't.'

Winchell's black eyes stare at me. 'What do you want, Grey? You know I think you're an idiot.'

'It's like this. I've written a letter about Attendant Cooper and I plan to send it to Dr Frank.'

'Jesus, Sandy, I don't want to hear this.' He throws himself round so his feet land thud on the floor, his back to me.

'What he did to Karl was terrible,' I continue, praying that I'm doing the right thing by speaking to him, 'and what happened to Tom was cruel. I'm afraid worse things will occur if Pete Cooper isn't stopped.'

'You're a fucking idiot,' Winchell says. He stands and slides his feet into the bohemian sandals he affects. The trousers of his suit are worn shiny blue. I notice his shoulders twitch, and I recall that Karl told me that a weapon made from a spoon had been taken from Winchell not long before my arrival.

'The thing is, Winchell, there are matters here that are occluded to me. Bob's role, in particular. I'd like to understand why Attendant Cooper is kind to Bob.'

He faces me, eyebrows jerking. 'Occluded! That's the stupid kind of thing you'd say.' He bends over, eyes fixed on me, adjusts a strap on his sandal, then removes an object from his pant cuff. 'See this?'

'Yes.'

'Know what it is?'

'No.'

'It's a chair bolt, know what I did with it?'

I shake my head.

'Sharpened it on a stone. Know why?'

'No.' Perhaps I've miscalculated, but it doesn't appear to be quite the time to backtrack. No retreat, Sandy Grey.

'So that I wouldn't end up like Bob. Understand now?'

Another headshake.

'Jesus H. Christ, you're a case,' he says. He looks thoughtful. 'You raised in a nunnery?'

'I'm not Catholic, I'm not anything, really, although my parents . . .'

'Oh, fuck!' Winchell rests his behind on the bottom end of the bedstead. 'You poor sap.'

'I don't want to be a sap, Winchell, I want to know, I believe I need to know, the characters and situations in which I find myself if I'm to have any chance of . . .'

'Chance! You think you've got a chance!' He blows out his cheeks, then pops one of them with the slap of a hand. 'You know why I'm here, Grey?'

'No.'

'Brought up in a Catholic orphanage, spent two years in the Spanish Civil War and when I came back there was fuck-all. Nothing, nobody cared. Know why I went to jail?'

'No.'

'Begging. No money, no family, no work except a few weeks harvesting now and then. We thought it would change, you know.'

'Change?'

'I went to jail in Winnipeg in connection with the strikes.'

'But why did they send you here, Winchell?'

'I told the truth, Sandy.' He leans forward to wag a finger at me. 'You must never ever tell the truth, or they'll get you.'

'Dr Frank says I should always tell the truth.'

'Dr Frank? That bulbous ox-moron! He wouldn't know the truth about this place if it sat up and slapped him in the kisser.'

'The truth?'

'This is a shit-hole, Sandy. If we get out of this alive, I'll eat my shirt. Dr Frank's got his head tucked so far inside his ass he can't see for whistling.'

I want to tell Winchell that he's used a mixed metaphor, but I stop myself.

'What are you grinning at?' he says. 'What's there to laugh at here?'

'Help me out, Winchell, tell me what you know.'

'The police were chasing me all over the country, trying to get me to kill Communists, because I knew them all. I tried to get friends to help me, but the cops watched all the mail.'

'Everyone's mail?'

'No, you fool, just those of us who fought in Spain together.' Winchell pauses. 'You see everything in Spain. They go at it like dogs,' he says. He explains to me about Bob and his unnatural impulses and how that's provoked Cooper's unnatural impulses which he hates himself for, and then why Pete Cooper hates me. It's complicated. Attendant Cooper had a wife and she left him, and Cooper's looking for compensation every which way, whether he knows it or not, and I don't bite. I'm not that way inclined, and I'm not sophisticated like Winchell so I didn't know I needed a weapon to put an end to the whole question in an uncomplicated fashion. So for Pete Cooper it's personal. 'It's the Catholic Church,' Winchell says, and I note that he's talking to me like a human being for the first time. 'They begin as small boys wearing skirts in church, then there's no stopping them. I tell you, I've seen it all.'

I have my doubts, but I don't voice them. An attendant I don't know wheels Tom in and props him in a chair. Tom's been given veronal, which will hold him for at least a few hours. He's happiest in a chair turned to the corner, so Winchell and I, as one, get up to shift him round.

Then Pete Cooper turns up with a stack of new magazines for Bob, and a bar of chocolate, which he puts back in his pocket when he sees that Bob's not here.

When Bob comes in, he's licking chocolate from his fingers, so I decide not to show him the letter after all.

Bob's gone back to being annoying. He knows I like hot water for a shave, so he creeps out of bed early and turns on the hot tap in the bathroom. By the time I get in the barber's lineup, the hot water's gone – not that it bothers anyone else. They've hides of leather for skin and beards that chop off easily, even with cold water and no strop, but I have sensitive skin and it's inflamed with razor burn. I can't bear to look in the mirror, and almost hope that Georgina won't come to visit. However much I long to see her.

Kosho, on the other hand, hardly grows a beard at all! Lucky.

But this evening, as I rub my hand over my sore and roughened face as I sit at the window, Alan Macaulay's back.

Part II: Leaving Home

Men like to make new beginnings, even when they say they've given up. Ask the dying – one day they'd like you to smother them with a pillow, the next day they're planning holidays.

It doesn't mean they've changed their minds. They just want both things. I heard of an old woman moved out of her house by her family, who went through her belongings and rubbished them – except for the one or two 'good pieces' – a gold locket from her husband, a sideboard handed down. They took the boards from her house and used them to start a new one for themselves. She pled for the mercy of a quick end, then she sent her daughter-in-law out to buy new curtains.

If it's consistency you want you've come to the wrong place for it. It's not our strong point.

I was not sorry that I attempted to take my own life.

I was ashamed that my friends knew of it and I hadn't succeeded.

I went back to the seashore with the dog, Dandy, but I did no work.

We all come to places in our lives where we have to take stock, and this was mine. What were my assets? One good arm, a pair of strong legs and shoulders, a handsome face (so I'd been told), a fifth share in my grandfather's house when he passed on (the others were to go to my mother, her sister and my two cousins). My physical capital, unless I found a means of employment, would rapidly diminish: poor food and cold would lead to sickness in winter and without money there would be nothing to give the doctor. I was a burden on my mother and when my grandfather looked at me he saw only failure.

Dandy and I followed the beach to the tower where we both poked through the nettles at the base in search of anything useful. I retrieved a sharp piece of glass from under Dandy's paw and put it in my pocket. I thought of the young woman I had seen sketching there and her response to me on Cramond Island and I spat on the step where she had sat. Dandy dropped a snail's shell at my foot and I took the glass shard and probed inside at its softness until I saw what I was doing, and wept.

While I was still recovering from the effects of the laudanum, the minister, Reverend Duncan, came down from the manse to sit with me. I had often been to his house because he had known our family for many years. He'd invited me in the first time, when he'd caught me, a boy of six, climbing the kirkyard wall after the manse apples. He hadn't punished me. His wife gave me a meat pie. So I knew him to be a good man, and interested in my education. Several times, when I was older, he allowed me to touch the old pulpit Bible preserved in the church, and spoke to me about the former abuses of the cutty stool where offences against the Sabbath and sexual impropriety were punished before the Kirk Session. 'It's a wicked thing, Alan, to humiliate souls, the Church's job is to rebuke and forgive,' he'd said.

But when I opened my eyes to find my own room in daylight, instead of the Lord Jesus Christ sitting in judgement, Reverend Duncan leaned forward in his chair and he said, 'If you'd succeeded in what you'd tried, young Alan, I'd have had to bury you outside the churchyard. Think of your mother!'

I thought of her, but all I could think was that once her cares were over, her hands, busy at the weaving, enslaved to the weaving, could finally rest. I said as much.

'Come unto me all ye that are heavy laden and I will give ye rest,' he said. I closed my eyes.

'You'll be feeling ashamed of yourself now,' he said. 'Your mind is hurt, it's a long walk back from death.' I began to pay attention, for what he said rang true. 'I want you to remember one thing, Alan, as you come to terms with yourself, for make no mistake about it, this is a turning point in your life. You'll take the high road to heaven from now on, or the low road to hell. You've been given a second chance so make the best of it.'

At the words heaven and hell my ears closed. His voice was the rumble of cart wheels or the spill of foaming water over the weir. Then I heard him say, clear as a bell, 'Don't mistake one for the other.'

'What's that?'

'What I've been telling you, lad. Shame can only come from God. No man or woman has the right to inflict it. Remorse is different. That's where you take steps to correct your habits, put them in line with God's will for your life.'

'What can I do?' I asked him, fearing that all he would say was 'repent' – which I'd already determined I'd never do – but what he said astonished me. He said, 'Have you thought about immigrating to the Colonies?'

Dandy and I left the tower of unfortunate memories and returned to the beach. A pony cart with a man driving a young child in it – holidaymakers – lurched towards us over the stones, so Dandy and I retreated all the way to the river mouth. Several women and men waited there for the ferry boat, the

women wearing caps with buttons sewn along the
brims, the men in the dress of the Territorial Army. I
darted up a lane between the cottages to the main
road and continued on past the inn, scattered a flock
of turkeys in the street, and passed through the gate
into the kirkyard. There, I steered away from the kirk
itself to lie amongst the headstones in a far corner.
Here it was that I'd been with Peggy Moffat. I wasn't
ashamed then, and I wasn't now, of what I'd done with
her. Nor did I feel any remorse. Peggy was a good girl,
and I'd have married her if things hadn't changed.
But what use is a man with an ugly worthless arm to a
healthy young woman? The young woman on the
island had done me a favour by showing me the true
case. Peggy's brothers were my friends. I understood
the situation. One door closes and another opens.

That's how it was that I decided I would go.

Many of the tombstones showed symbols of death,
as you'd expect – skulls, crossbones and hourglasses.
But they also showed the Green Man. I spent a few
more minutes examining these images of catlike faces
or humans with protruding tongues and greenery
burgeoning from cheeks, forehead, nose or mouth. I
touched my own face, seeming to find there my own
germinating sprouts of green as I considered my
new direction.

No life without death. No death without hope. No
hope without a belief in the resurrection.

After I had swallowed the laudanum and as I'd
lain on the rocks at Eagle's Crag, my body cooling, I
had found myself in a new land. Not hell as I'd feared
or heaven as I'd never believed, but at the gangway of
a great ship. I knew that once I boarded, I'd not get
back to land. Not that I minded: I had already said my
goodbyes. Then George Falconer hauled me back.

No one would stop me this time.

I went home and parcelled up my belongings.
The tools of my trade I gave to William Watson, who
had often talked of leaving the mines. I left two gold

buttons with Gordon Moffat to give to Peggy as a keepsake. Both William and Gordon walked with me a way. They promised to tell my mother what I had done and that I would write her when I had a situation. At Cramond Brig we said farewell and I continued to the ships at Queensferry.

Men were wanted for the farms and lumber camps in Canada. I signed up. I drank the last of my money in the pub. I slept rough that night and woke early on the shore with burns on my chest that I could not account for.

'Ye were the Devil hisself last night,' a stranger, also sleeping rough, said to me as I splashed seawater over myself. He joined me at the water's edge. 'Ye said live coals wouldnae singe ye.' He shook his head. 'But there's none can dae that, ye daftie. It's no human.'

TEN

25 July and following, 1941

A ll day, as I go about my work in the rabbitry, I consider what I know of Alan Macaulay. He *should* make an excellent immigrant. Those who have little to lose make the best of what they find. Our country was built by such men and women. Hardship, where it does not destroy, teaches endurance and stubbornness. Alan Macaulay may be a rough diamond, but given the right opportunity, he could make a success of it. I don't see failure ahead for him as he readies himself to cross the ocean, although, of course, I know that things do go wrong. Sometimes that happens. An accident intervenes. Fate has already touched him in the matter of his arm – which, incidentally, begins to heal once he reaches the better food and living conditions of the New World.

How do I know?

From the file folders Dr Frank keeps for me in the library. In them are the kernels of fact around which I construct Alan's story. The rest comes to me, as Karl told me it would, when I wait, in the evenings, pen in hand at the writing table in my room.

You'd think, at first glance, that the statements and letters in the files would make dry reading, but not at all. There's inherent drama in the addressees: the arresting constable, the barrister, the sheriff, the Undersecretary of State, the Governor General and Council. All the underpinning apparatus of the state. This chain-of-being is reflected, on Alan Macaulay's side, by his mother and brother and his friends, people of high standing in the village including the minister, and the local barrister who disputes the fairness of Alan's trial in detail. These are the warp and weft of *that* system. The barrister makes a mistake, I believe, with the patronising tone in which he impugns the legal expertise of colonial officials: it did Alan no good. There is also Alan himself, with his explanations and pleas, his innocence before God.

His restored arm.

Alan's story illustrates no tragedy in a wider sense – there's no epic fall: he's just a man who set out to alter his economic circumstances and ended up hanged. I told Dr Frank this when he checked one day on my progress in the library. He's still concerned I might be wasting my time.

'Is there a lesson for you in this, Sandy Grey?' he asked.

'Man is clay, he is plant, he is animal, he is intelligence, he is machine, he is an angel.' I read the words from Georgina's son's writing text, open at my elbow. I do not read, but I am thinking about, what the text has to say about change points: how Alan came to one, how I may be at one.

'You'll have to translate.' He was impatient with me. His foot – encased in an unpolished shoe – went *tap*.

'It depends which of these aspects we're talking about. As clay, Alan and I are as we were made by God and our parents. As plants we respond to our native environment. Treated well, we grow healthy and tall. Treated poorly, we wither. As animals, we learn to satisfy our basic needs and to cooperate with others.

As intelligent beings we develop higher aspirations; we look to education and to our potential to change ourselves and the world we live in. We have idealistic aspirations. As machines, on the other hand, we are at the mercy of the physical, social and political systems in which we find ourselves. You remember that both Alan and I experience incarceration.' He was listening to me, but his mouth was tight. Nevertheless, I went on. 'As angels we receive direct guidance from above. We may also be of assistance to others or the means of enacting God's will. God, that is, however you conceive of him.'

'You know I don't like display, Sandy, even if it is of education.'

'My education was the library, sir. Andrew Carnegie saved my life when I was a boy.'

'He's got a lot to answer for; I'll say that for him.'

'Are you against philanthropy and the supply of a public library system?'

'I'm against prevarication, Grey, that's what I'm against!'

'Let me be as plain as I can,' I said to him. 'Alan Macaulay's problem is that he's unable to prove his innocence. I'm doing that for him.'

'Better late than never, Sandy?'

'Yes, sir. If by that you mean it is never too late for the truth.' Georgina's son's book – *The Storehouse of Thought and Expression* – had now fallen open to the frontispiece – a photograph of Rodin's sculpture of human figures struggling in the hand of God. I point to it. 'The lesson for me, Dr Frank, is one of faith in ultimate justice.'

'I see.' He rocked forward and backwards on the balls of his feet. 'Do you see yourself as having been dealt an injustice? It's everyone's fault but yours? Is that what's behind all this? Dressed-up self-pity?' He waved an ink-stained hand over the manuscript pages. 'Haven't we been through this before?'

I gathered the papers together in a neat pile. I took a deep breath. 'Do you remember Karl, Dr Frank?'

'Karl? What kind of a question is that? He's one of my patients.'

'In the East Wing, sir.'

'I know where he is. Yes, in the East Wing, Sandy, which is not the end of the world.'

I let that pass. Dr Frank looked away. He was thinner than ever. I'd seen officials carrying briefcases arrive and depart, and with each one it appeared to me that he diminished. Once a car carrying a general drew up and parked near the fountain. The general entered the building without a word to anyone; he glanced neither to left or right; but the driver got out, smoked a cigarette and watched Kosho's fish swim in circles.

'Well, Karl is to me a man trapped by accident. He never meant to stay in this country. He was kept here, away from his family, by the war. He's a stranger in a strange land where his actions are easily misinterpreted. He's a foreigner. That means he doesn't understand the customs. All he did was to let birds loose from their cages. That may be eccentric, but it's hardly criminal.'

Dr Frank's eyes were cold. 'You're talking nonsense.'

'What is he here for, then? Please tell me.'

'You know I can't discuss other inmates. But you were there when he attacked Attendant Cooper. You saw his capabilities. Whatever else you are, Sandy, you're not stupid.'

I held his gaze. I let the silence lengthen. I tried to let everything I knew about Pete Cooper show in my eyes. If I'd had the letter ready, with me, I'd have handed it over. I think it would have made a difference.

'Consider this then, sir,' I said when I could see he was getting restless. 'Mistakes can happen. I believe they occurred in Karl's case and I know from my careful reading of Alan Macaulay's files that they happened in his. If you admit the principle – that mistakes are possible – doesn't that argue for a fresh look at the evidence?'

He leaned forward and placed his hands on the table, so

114

that his face was close to mine. His breath smelled of coffee and there was a whiff of smoke on his clothing. 'I don't want to go through this with you again, Sandy. Now you tell me exactly what this has to do with you.' He said it as an ultimatum, and I responded as such.

'I shouldn't be here. There's been a misunderstanding. I'm innocent of all the charges against me.'

I feel, inside me, as I help Kosho select rabbits to kill, some rodent-sized knowledge skitter into a corner of my mind. When I try to look at it, it's not there. When I turn my attention from it, by thinking about the Luftwaffe attacking Moscow, and the Japanese occupation of Indochina, it peeps out, but I can't catch its eye. The recollection of the conversation with Dr Frank and mention of Karl has stirred it from its sleep. I am imagining my room as it was when I entered and discovered blood-spattered Pete Cooper, and Karl lying on the floor behind the bed.

I get no further, though, as we have now to get on with the killing and dressing. Kosho catches one cony by the hind feet and lets the head drop, then he gives a quick twist to dislocate the neck. I check to make sure it's dead and then hang the carcass by the right hind leg on a nail inserted between the tendons and the bone. We proceed in this fashion until all are done.

Ron Signet comes in to supervise the next stage. This afternoon, Dr Frank accompanies him. Ron unlocks the cupboard and hands over the knives. He trusts me now. We remove the heads and front feet and let the carcasses bleed into a trough. I gather the parts into a sack and take them outside, saving one rabbit's foot for Bob, who has asked me to. This goes, wrapped in a torn corner of sacking, into my apron pocket. Back inside, Kosho begins at one end of the row and I start at the other. We slice off the tail and sever the left hind foot at the first joint, cut the fur around the right hind leg at the hock, slit the fur on the inside of the leg to the root of the tail, and pull the pelt down both hind legs to the tail. We then cut the fat away from the skin before pulling the pelt down over the carcass and off, being careful to remove all the fat from the hide so it will dry evenly.

Dr Frank watches the operation with interest and asks questions as we work. After all the coats have been removed I prepare the carcasses. I carve around the anal opening and follow on down the abdomen to the neck. The rest is removing entrails, stomach and lungs, washing the cavity, then hanging the meat to cool.

I wash my hands and look over my work. Someone else will come in to remove the meat to the cooler. The flesh we can't use ourselves will be sold. Kosho is already stretching the hides before they can harden, making sure that all the legs are on the same side. He smoothes out all the folds and wrinkles and ensures that no parts touch and stick to each other.

'Boys, that's a day's work well done,' Dr Frank says. He claps us both on the back and grins. The quality of the meat and skins we produce has attracted notice in the outside world. There's a write-up in the newspaper. Dr Frank shows it to us and pins the clipping to the wall. 'Mentally Ill Inmates Assist with War Work,' it says. We finish clearing up and Kosho returns the cleaned knives to Ron Signet. He and Dr Frank stand by the door for a moment, chatting. When Ron goes to put the knives in the lock-up I see my chance, reach into my shirt pocket to pull out the letter. 'Dr Frank?' I say. He turns towards me, but Ron Signet is back already.

'It's nothing, sir. I was just wondering when our next truth session is?'

'Good, glad to see you keen to get on with it. I'll let you know.'

'What's that you have there?' Ron asks me as soon as Dr Frank has left. I can't see any point in pretending, since all Ron has to do is ask me to show my hands. I say, 'Ron, I'm taking a risk, but you know and I know that Pete Cooper must be stopped before something terrible happens.' I hold out the letter and put my fingers to my lips for 'shush' so there is no mistaking my meaning. He blinks what I read as agreement, and takes it.

It's only later, after lights out, that I recollect my prior feeling of unease. I had been revisiting, in my mind, the scene of Karl's beating. It comes to me then: although Ron Signet clearly understood what Pete Cooper had done, he didn't report it. How, when Dr Frank reads my letter, will he explain his behaviour? How will he justify his lies about Karl?

In daylight, when my thoughts are brighter, I decide that I can trust Ron Signet. He's a decent man with a family. He's always shown me kindness. He may have been waiting for the right opportunity, himself, to raise the subject of Pete Cooper. It can't be easy to blow the whistle on a colleague, so perhaps I've done him a service.

I decide to continue with my writing while I wait to see what happens. Since the weather is good, there is an early evening baseball game in the airing court to which both Bob and Winchell have gone. This week, brackets were fastened to the tops of the airing court fence posts and four extra strands of barbed wire were stretched on them. Most of the work was done by the patients in the afternoons. I saw Bob standing at the foot of a ladder, but he was forbidden to climb it.

Tom likes to spend the evenings at crafts, although he hasn't progressed far with his rug-making. He pulls out the loops almost as soon as he's finished drawing them through the backing. I've sketched a new pattern of a ship for him to follow. He seems to like it, and I ordered him to complete the funnel and to report to me with it later tonight.

All in all, I have perfect peace and quiet.

The Storehouse of Thought and Expression suggests that when one is troubled – as I admit I am these days – and having difficulty with a set writing task, one should write whatever comes to mind, first imagining that one is in a different place.

I get to work on Karl's paper with Karl's pen and ink at

Karl's table and I imagine myself in the New World where Alan Macaulay lands.

Part III: More Events of My Sad Life

When I arrived at the docks at Montreal I was taken straight to the train with a group of men who had signed up at the same time as me in Scotland. We travelled for several days with little information as to where we were going. West, certainly, but how far west and to do exactly what type of labouring?

We slept in rough berths at night; in the daytime we played cards and examined the scenery and watched other men leave the train at various godforsaken stops. The rocklands of Ontario unnerved me: I felt such an ache of loneliness in them. Mining country, men said as we travelled the empty northland, and I thought of the coal-mining friends I had left behind and wondered, not for the first time since setting sail, if I'd made a mistake in leaving home.

The Prairies, when we reached them, were more alive, with some good agricultural land and a number of farms along the track. After Regina there were sweeps of yellow grassland and a number of alkaline lakes swarming with waterfowl. Wild antelope fled in great herds as the train approached, and I began to take an interest. My companions, much like me, had kept to themselves, but now we seemed to wake up, as if the ties that bound us to our homeland had stretched so far they had to snap, freeing us for what might lie ahead. There was no more rereading last letters or mooning over photographs amongst my travelling companions.

We crossed the river at Medicine Hat and climbed to a new plateau with only water tanks and windmill pumps to look at it. Near the line were hummocks made by gophers: one of the company entertained himself, and us, by taking potshots at them, until I told him to stop. 'Life is precious,' I told him. 'Don't take it unless you must.'

One morning, very early, we awoke to find ourselves running up a steep incline with the Bow River alongside. Ahead were the Rockies. I will not describe that part of the journey in detail – it was too much like a dream, for much of the time I felt I was on a strange planet – suffice it to say I was entranced, it was as if I'd entered a fantasy left over from the imaginary realms of childhood. In these mountains I had glimpses of the better man I could be. A walker and climber, a guide, perhaps as had been my fore-bears in Scotland. I almost left the train at Banff, but was persuaded by my fellows to continue on as I'd agreed in my contract. Honesty, they say, is the best policy and a man's word is his bond. But he should also, I can say with hindsight, listen to his deepest instincts.

In any case, amongst the peaks and ravines and glaciers of the mountains, my spirits lifted, and still we climbed until we were more than five thousand feet above sea level. For a moment we were like gods with the world at our feet, then we began our fall through a series of tunnels, picking up speed as we burst from between canyon walls into another mountain range in British Columbia.

There were more mountain passes and a long run between snowsheds and at length an extended curved trestle bridge over the Columbia River. I stayed awake the night we passed through the Fraser Canyon under a full moon and marvelled at this wild ravine and the furious river below boiling through the shadows and the light cast from the train. I thought of my grandfather's tales of wolves in Scotland and how the last had been killed a hundred and fifty years earlier, and as if I'd conjured it, a lone wolf loped out of the forest, glided over some rocks near the river and disappeared again into the trees.

My grandfather said that an ancestor of ours at Wick had saved the city from invaders when a besieging foe was about to take the city. He'd slept out on a crag after an argument with his father. He was still sleeping when a wolf, alarmed by the advance of the hordes, had howled in terror, waking him. True or not, I had loved that story as a child. Why had it come back to me now?

From Vancouver City we boarded a steamer and crossed a sound peppered with forested islands. From our port at Victoria on Vancouver Island we were loaded into carts and driven on a rough track northwards.

It was dark when we arrived at the camp.

In the morning I stepped out from under the canvas and found myself at the shore of a large lake. Quietness lapped outwards into the dawn. The lake rocked gently in a bowl of treed hills. 'Hey, you!' a voice cried from the cook tent. The figure held several buckets in his hands. I ran over and took them. 'Go out a little ways before you fill them,' he said.

I took out a little rowing boat from the dock and headed into tissues of mist. When I stopped, the land had disappeared from sight. I dropped the buckets into the water and scooped them full. When I came out of the mist I was far down the lake. A doe with her fawns drank at the shoreline. I could have been lost there forever – in the long run I would have been better off – and not minded. In the Highlands they say that a trip in a boat over the water and through the mist is the path to eternal life. If I'd heard singing, I dare say I might have kept on, but as it was, the cook rang the triangle for breakfast and I paddled in that direction.

Was I happy to be where I'd landed? Happy, yes, and more fully alive than I'd felt since before my arm was hurt. The arm I now rowed with, with no pain.

'Glad to see you've made yourself useful,' the foreman said when I staggered into the cook tent with

the water buckets. The others were already at breakfast. One of them muttered something and the rest of
the crew laughed. This was the Irishman, Kennedy.
You know how it is when you make a friend. There's
some affinity, unspoken communication that goes
back and forth. It's the same when you make an
enemy – which was the case with him.

I finish this part of the writing and return to myself. The
work has gone relatively well and I still have time left. With the
longer hours of daylight, the others come in late from their
games and pastimes.

The camp where Alan has arrived is a stone's throw from
the hall at Shawnigan Lake where my father held revival meetings. I know the area well. The coincidence of settings is a bonus.
Not only does it mean that the hanged man and I have a link
beyond our incarceration in this building, but we've seen the
same landscape. *The Storehouse* advises that the insertion of an
object, person or place real to the writer will make the tale more
lifelike. More than that, the coincidence means that when Alan
reaches his crisis, I can see what he sees. 'Write what you know,
or what you think you know or what you can convince others
that you know,' Georgina's son's writing text says. But this is a
paradox, since it also advises how useful it is to write in order to
get away from where we are. 'Dream forward and prophesy,' it
says. 'We cannot be satisfied until we begin dreaming ourselves
out of our skins.' How marvellous that with Alan Macaulay I
can do both!

The text also advises that I recall an experience that has
helped me to feel my relation to the universe beyond mankind:
that is, the world of rocks, plants, animals and stars. I find I'm
biting the end of Karl's pen. How shall I continue? I'll start with
what I know for certain.

It's spring vacation. I'm on a plank bench in the old
wooden barn of a tabernacle on my father's lakefront property.
Earlier in the day I'd climbed on ladders with the men to tack

tarpaper over leaks in the roofing. Sunlight drifts through cracks between wallboards and falls on the upturned faces of the people, and on my father's face as he leans towards them from behind the pulpit. I can hear, through the open doorways at the back, the sough of wind in the tall Douglas fir trees outside. The scents of resin and wet earth from last night's rain, and sun on deep layers of moss, and the murmur of water at the mud and sand lake shoreline – these are more real to me than my father and his preaching. What does he say? Only what he's said a thousand times before – *Repent, the end times are nigh.* I sigh and look down at my feet in their new wingtips. Shoes I am pleased with, shoes that speak of my interest in style and not just practicality. Shoes that let the world and my father know I've a mind of my own. However. They are dirty and half drifted over with sawdust from the floor. I glance to the side. The skirt of the woman next to me has ridden up to show her knees imprinted with tiny sawdust rectangles. She's only just got up from kneeling. Under her breath she keeps saying, 'Praise the Lord.' I can think of many reasons to praise the creator of all being, starting with the handsome trees and finishing, perhaps, with the beauty of the tree-frog I'd regarded that morning. It was a tiny thing with toe-pads that helped it clamber and vault or sit still clasped to branch or shrubbery. It glittered, copper and green, semi-precious. Praise the Lord!

I think ahead to after the service when I will tell my father and my mother who shares the platform with him, her feet pumping the pedals of the small organ, her fingers steady on the chords, that I have long since left Damascus Road College, that I do not believe as they do, that I will not be ruled by them; that the only *calling* I have is to be a university student and a pilot. I'm here to deliver this news as a courtesy. I do not belong with them – I haven't for yonks.

To me, at this moment, my future is self-evident and simple. I do not think of opposition to it – how could there be? Who has rights over the sovereignty of my body other than me?

Only a few nights ago, before leaving for 'home', I'd slept with Maureen, the wife of my former 'Science in the Bible' teacher. When we'd finished, I'd looked at the tiny wrinkles at the corners of her eyes and kissed them. She said I'd made her happy for the first time in years. But when I returned from the bathroom, she'd had time to reconsider. She had telephoned her husband and asked him to come home; she begged his forgiveness.

How sorry I felt for her! Sweet blonde-haired Maureen who'd only just finished begging me to penetrate her, her tongue flicking the roof of my mouth, her finger deep in my ass; the lovely woman who'd adored the holiness of my body had vanished. In her place sat a haggard remnant, a mother of sorrows, a gross forgery. Even the room smelled different. The scent of her had soured. When I sat beside her, she drew the worn chenille bedspread up to her chin. I kissed her one more time, licked her tears dry and told her she was a good girl.

'How could I, how could I!' she'd sobbed. Sadly, accepting this sadness for the truth it revealed, I understood that once more, in the fullness of time, in the blink of an eye, there'd been a substitution.

My father finishes the revival meeting call-to-Jesus and half a dozen come forward. I believe I've seen some of them here before. He walks among them, lays his plaster-etched hands on their heads; some quiver under his hands, and some fall to their knees – axed by the Almighty's power, he says; but it has nothing to do with me or my life because it has nothing to do with being human. Maureen – for a time – was human, and what I'd felt with her was all I require of a 'heavenly' origin.

It is time to go. I slip from the pew. My feet stand in sunlight at the door. My nose lifts at the fresh air. I hear the bracing call of birds. My father's voice rings out from behind me: *Repent, whore of Babylon, yea I say unto you, Repent!* I glance back – foolish as Lot's wife: his fingers point at me, and I run.

Part III: More Events of My Sad Life – Continued

It took a few weeks to get used to procedures in this situation so different from home. For one thing, no matter how far up the hills you'd climb, chasing after the log scalers or out cutting wood, you'd not see anything but trees. I'd never imagined anything like these giants hundreds of years old and so wide around at the base it could take six men to encircle them. The dominant trees varied according to geography. Where it was wet, to the west, you'd have hemlock. The top of these trees (when they were small enough that you could see them) bent in a gentle question mark; mature trees could be three hundred feet tall. On a windswept bluff you'd find Sitka spruce, stiff and unyielding as buildings in the fiercest of gales. These trees, too, were immense. Although there were many red cedar, we did not take them, finding that they died down from the tops and were virtually useless once felled. We were happy to leave them to the Indians who used them for their canoes and other purposes. Nearer the east coast were the yew, and the magnificent Douglas fir, also, like the hemlock, a giant. Wherever there'd been fire or logging, alder sprang up, almost, so it seemed, overnight.

Once on a single hillside I counted six types of trees. The knowledge I had of wood from my years of working with John Weller making furniture made me a valuable employee. I was often called upon for advice. The foreman appeared to like me and once I talked to the bosses about the possible uses to which the wood we weren't yet harvesting could be put.

I saw a future before me. I saw myself with my own company. I made sketches of the furniture I would build. I wrote to Peggy Moffat and asked that she wait for me.

Although in many places the thick undergrowth made walking in the forest difficult, there were many good trails. In places where the forest hadn't been too badly disturbed and the fallen logs had been left to rot, I picked mushrooms and brought them back to the camp to cook. I wrote to my mother and enclosed varieties of fungi that I couldn't identify and asked her to inquire about them through the Reverend Duncan to the Royal Botanic Garden in Edinburgh. I envisioned a relationship with the botanists – I could make a contribution to science through my observations and collections of the many unfamiliar plants I saw.

My new friend, Frank, one of the timber cruisers, showed me where to look for elderberries and huckleberries and I began to acquire a woodsman's knowledge of wild foods. As the days went by, I discovered trails that led eastwards through towering rhododendron bushes, and came out on headlands of Garry oak and arbutus. One Sunday Frank and I packed a lunch and walked all the way to the eastern shore. Frank brought his gun for fear of bear and cougar, but we only saw deer and forest birds such as grouse and woodpecker. I had my first look at the sea. We walked along a beach threaded through with eroded sandstone in strange formations, some of which appeared like flattened mushrooms, others making shallow bowls in which the water collected and warmed. In some areas volcanic conglomerate was scattered among the other beach stones and shells, and all along the banks ran the variegated marks of glaciation. I envisioned my prospects as a geologist.

The landscape was, to me, a book; the forest and sea and sky the education I had never thought to acquire. From where we stood and where we walked we could see how the glaciers had scooped out hollows in between islands which then rose like the humps on the back of the giant sea serpent said, by the Indians, to live in these waters.

Such a creature, as I'd heard from my aunties at home, inhabited our Scottish lochs.

I was in an ecstasy of sorts. The world was spread out before me for my delectation. All things were possible.

I wrote again to Peggy Moffat, and she replied.

Near the end of the summer, I was taken from my forest work to assist the labourers completing a road along the east coast of the island. The work, considered by the government to be urgent, was temporary. In the fall I was to return to my former situation. The lumber bosses had spoken to me about my possible advancement after I'd given them a preliminary catalogue of tree species in the area. I'd also planned, with Frank, to open a furniture shop in the town of Duncan during the wet winter months when there was likely to be little work in the forest.

The road-crew camp of ten men was sited near a river mouth. My tent mate was a man I knew slightly from the several times I'd gone with Frank to the nearest hotel for a drink. Frank himself had headed north to a job cruising timber that he expected to last only a couple of months. He'd left his rifle and a few other belongings with me to look after for him. The only other man I knew was Kennedy, but since he was one of the spreaders, we saw little of each other. Mostly I was on my own. I had no particular friends among the crew, but we all got along well enough. I fell into a routine. All day I loaded gravel into horse-drawn carts that were driven along to where the spreaders did their work. My hands blistered and peeled from the shovel, and then the skin turned hard as horn. In the evenings I swam at the river mouth, invigorated by the cold water. After supper, I'd walk the beach and watch the mist roll in and blur the facing shoreline. I might have been standing on the strand at my own Cramond, staring into the fog that shrouded the Firth of Forth and the Fife coast.

I'd never handled a firearm before, so Frank had told me to practise with his gun until I'd saved enough to buy one of my own. I needed to learn so I could hunt with him in the autumn. Once or twice, after my swim, I thought about taking some shots at the seals that surfaced to see what I was up to, but I couldn't bring myself to pull the trigger. They were doing no harm. It was me who'd intruded on them. Several times I set up tin cans for target practice, but I felt awkward with the gun, I didn't take to it, and hoped I could make myself useful to Frank in other ways.

It was there, on the beach, that I found the stray. She was shorthaired, short-eared and brindled – a mutt if I'd ever seen one – and her tail curled under her belly. She wore no collar or rope around her neck and followed me into the camp. I'd already determined to call her Nellie. MacKenzie, the foreman, was glad enough to have her around to chase off the cougars that occasionally came near, but he warned me that if the bitch caused any trouble, he'd have to shoot her. I took care to keep her always with me.

So things went until I returned later than usual one evening to find Kennedy just leaving my tent. I thought, at first, that he'd been in there talking to Joe, my tent mate, but the tent was empty and I could tell by the look of things that Kennedy had read my letters.

Although I was pleased with the prospects in my new life, I missed the people I'd left behind – my mother and grandfather, my friends, even the Reverend Duncan with his sermons. Of real talk there was little in the camp, unless you counted Kennedy's Fenian rants. He liked to throw his weight around, as the Irish do, especially when he'd taken a drink. I couldn't bear to think he'd touched my letters from Peggy.

'Kennedy,' I said, going up to where he sat by the fire laughing with the other men, 'you were in my tent just now.'

'Is that so, Macaulay? I must have made a mistake. These tents look all the same in the dark.' He winked at the others. 'Just like women, eh? Ain't it hard to tell them apart? You know, Peggy's one of my favourite names. It's a whore's name, ain't it?'

I jumped at him. He was on the far side of the fire and had his knife out by the time I reached him. His knife slashed my arm and I rolled through the flames, burning my hand badly.

Before I could find my feet, MacKenzie, the foreman, was there and the watching men had pulled me and Kennedy apart.

'What's this about? I'll have no fighting here,' MacKenzie said. He looked disgustedly at the two of us.

'He started it,' Kennedy said. 'He jumped me.'

'Is that true, Macaulay?'

'He's been reading my letters.'

'You're here to work. There'll be no more of this, you hear me?' He caught sight of my scorched and bleeding arm. 'Let me see.' I showed him. 'Give me the knife, Kennedy,' he said, and he held his hand out to the Irishman. I hoped Kennedy would refuse, for then MacKenzie would have cause to dismiss him.

'Ah, never mind, boss,' Kennedy said, 'we were having a bit of fun, that's all. The Scotchman here doesn't know when his leg's being pulled.'

'The knife?' MacKenzie said. Kennedy rolled his eyes but handed over the weapon. 'I'll keep this from now on,' MacKenzie said, and left us.

In the morning, I found Nellie sick outside my tent. From the mess nearby I could see she'd been fed meat with glass in it. I said nothing about it, as she didn't appear to have taken enough to do her harm and aside from a scratched throat and mouth she was fine. I kept her even closer to my side from that point on.

Because of the damage to my arm, MacKenzie

put me on general duties around the camp. I carried water and cut firewood, and assisted the cook in various ways. I kept the camp clean. I fully expected to return to the gravel pit, but my arm because of the previous damage to it was slow to heal. One day when I was down on the beach, I heard a commotion and ran back to camp. A cougar had sprung from a tree on to the back of the teamster who was watering the horses at lunchtime. MacKenzie, who was nearby, grabbed his gun and shot it, saving the man's life, but the man was badly injured.

Men started to mutter about 'bad luck.' Mac-Kenzie appointed Kennedy as the new teamster and sent everyone back to work.

Another week went by. Watching Kennedy whip the horses to make them go faster, and neglecting their grooming and feeding, bothered me, but I figured that MacKenzie would see what was happening soon enough, and I let it be. Nellie had learned to stay out of Kennedy's way and I no longer feared for her. There'd been no repetition of the incident in the tent.

I received a letter from the Royal Botanic Garden in Edinburgh inviting me to submit my specimens. Frank sent word that he'd heard of a place we could rent for a small sum in town to begin our furniture work. A carpenter whose wife had died and who'd decided to return home was willing to sell his tools for almost nothing. Peggy wrote that she'd booked her passage. Her mother had finished her wedding dress. I determined to work extra time so I could start to save for our house.

I admit I was tired. I agree that my arm hurt and I was fed up with camp work. I do not admit that I said anything to MacKenzie like people said I did. I hadn't realised that MacKenzie was under pressure regarding the road and that my lack of fitness for heavy work had caused a problem. So it was a surprise to me when he came into my tent before breakfast and said I could have my time. Nellie had followed him in and he bent down to pat her.

'What's that?' I said, struggling out of my bedroll. I couldn't understand.

'We can't keep you on, Alan, not with an arm like that.' I stood up. I was still in my underwear. The wretched arm was swollen and red and scarred. Hot shame flooded through me. I had to stop myself from hiding the arm behind my back.

'You can't mean it! You can't do this to me!'

MacKenzie gripped me by the shoulder. 'I can't afford charity cases, Alan. We'll take you back once that arm is better.'

He left the tent and I shouted after him, 'I'll see you in hell, first, you bastard!'

When I joined the others for breakfast, no one spoke to me. They kept their eyes on their plates. I finished eating, then I stood up and said to Mac-Kenzie, 'You'd better keep an eye on those horses before Kennedy kills them,' then I picked up Frank's rifle and took the dog and went to the beach.

Kennedy drove the others to the gravel pit, picked up and delivered several loads of gravel and then returned to camp. The spreaders were working close to the camp that day, as that part of the road was nearly finished.

I went up and packed my gear. Kennedy walked through the tents singing a Fenian song to which he'd changed the words. No one else was there at the time but the cook, and he was too far away to hear.

> God be praised that I met her
> Be life long or short
> I shall never forget her
> We may have great men
> but will never have better
> to f— Fenian men
> than bold Peggy Moffat.

130

I gritted my teeth. I finished my packing and went back to the beach for Nellie and the gun that I'd left behind. From the top of the bank I saw Kennedy making his way, carrying Frank's gun, along the beach. He pointed it out to sea at what I thought were several seals in the water, then he turned and pointed it back at me. Nellie growled and ran at him, but he kicked out at her with his foot and she backed off.

I slid straight down the slope. He sang on, then sighted along the barrel and pulled the trigger. That was the first shot. I kept running. I could see now that what I'd thought were seals were the humps of some large creature in the water. I caught a glimpse of a long slender head, then the creature rolled over and sank.

I wrestled the gun from Kennedy. I could smell the drink on him. He didn't put up much of a fight. He sank on to the stones laughing. I stood over him, breathing hard. Nellie came to my heel. 'Good dog,' I said. Blood coloured the sea. I felt I was at a turning. That the next thing that happened to me would change my life, for better or worse. I cursed Liam Kennedy. A wave of darkness washed over me and I wished for the first time since I'd come to this country that I'd killed myself that day in Cramond as I'd meant to. From behind me I heard a shout. It was MacKenzie. I swung round, the gun in my arms, my bad hand on the trigger, and the weapon went off. That was the second shot. MacKenzie staggered and fell. I ran up to him, dropped the gun and ran on up to the road, shouting for help. Men came running. 'I've killed him!' I shouted, then I fell to my knees and sobbed. I did not know it at the time, but Kennedy had sneaked back along the river and up to the horses. So when the others arrived, they saw him arrive from that direction.

Every word that Kennedy said in court about me was a lie.

ELEVEN
8 August and following, 1941

Alan Macaulay is innocent! He never meant to shoot
MacKenzie! That he did appalled him! His enemy,
Kennedy, told lies to ensure his conviction! I know this to be the
truth, because I've seen it from the inside! I must pore over the
court records and see what went wrong in the trial and make a
case to present to Dr Frank. After that, we'll take it to the
Governor General and ask for a pardon . . .

I want to get to it at once, but suddenly, I'm busy. It's not
just the continuing work in the rabbitry and my other notes for
Dr Frank that I must catch up on before I do anything else, but
that Dr Frank sits down with us for a cup of coffee in the
evening after dinner in the cafeteria. Tom smiles at him and says
good evening.

'I see progress here, boys,' Dr Frank says to me and Bob
and Tom. (Winchell isn't here. The sharpened bolt he'd shown
me had been discovered. He no longer works in the carpentry
shop where there is opportunity for him to acquire tools. He toils
in the laundry with the Chinese pressing shirts and white

uniforms. He follows their schedule. Winchell is in his element. Some of the Chinese are Communists, and all are united in their opposition to Japan. He has organised a Marx study session – not popular with everyone – in morning tea break and he's made contact with a prominent CCF politician who's promised to raise the plight of the inmate laundry workers in the legislature. All this he whispers to Bob and me – and Tom – at night. There is a great deal going on of which Dr Frank is ignorant.) Dr Frank drinks his coffee and says, 'Attendant Signet tells me that the two of you, Bob and Sandy, are doing good work with Tom here.' We accept the compliment, and Bob explains his theory of Tom's willingness to take direct orders. I tell Dr Frank that as long as Tom is set a straightforward task, such as hooking a defined area of his rug using only one colour, he can do it. What Tom cannot do is take on more than one job – such as hooking loops *and* changing colours. Not only that, I inform him, but Tom has modified my ship design into a trireme. He's added mermaids and rocks. I say to Dr Frank, 'You know, sir, I believe that Tom is portraying an episode from *The Odyssey* in that rug. Perhaps if he were given more artistic outlets . . .? Or if someone could ask what that episode means to him? Someone as well versed in mythology as Tom seems to be?'

'You're not showing off again, are you, Sandy?' Dr Frank says. I must appear shocked – I've said what I said in good faith – because he holds up his hands in apology. 'Just checking, son,' he says. He wipes coffee from his lips with a napkin and sits back looking lost.

I wonder when he's last eaten. His skin is sallow. Yellow folds hang from his jaw, and lap on to his bow tie. Handfuls of skin hang from his upper arms. God knows why he's wearing a short-sleeved shirt – he must know what he looks like! His clothes fit so loosely that he's begun to look like a clown. Should I tell him? Somebody should – appearances will be important to the new Board.

'You two boys keep on top of it,' Dr Frank says. 'I want a

plan for Tom's treatment on my desk by Monday. I want proper notes kept, including weekly reports.'

'From us, sir?' I say and try not to look at Bob. Things are going from bad to worse. The soldiers who occupied their own corner of the cafeteria when I'd first arrived are gone. Fewer of the new inmates pass through Dr Frank's hands at all. The attendants are kept busy preparing men for insulin and electric shock treatments. There is talk of experimental surgery. Now this: Bob and I, who are classified as sick, are being put in charge of Tom, but Attendant Cooper whose job this should be is responsible for assaults on patients; and Dr Frank,   who is supposed to run a tight ship, according to humane principals, has been – to all intents and purposes – overthrown. The entire institution is at risk.

What to make of it?

After Dr Frank leaves, Bob leans over and says to me, 'There's just one thing, Sandy.'

'What's that, Bob?'

'The letter.' He winks.

'What letter is that, Bob?'

Bob glances over his shoulder to see if anyone is near enough to overhear. 'The one about Cooper. The one you wrote to Dr Frank. He read it out in the staff room.'

'With Cooper there?'

Bob nods.

'When was this?'

'Yesterday.'

I consider this. Ron Signet must have held on to it for a period of time before deciding what to do. That he'd ultimately turned it over to Dr Frank and not to Cooper privately or to the Board alone was a good sign.

'There's to be an investigation?'

Bob shakes his head. 'Dr Frank said it didn't matter whether the accusation was true or not at this point, the real issue was Cooper's relationship with the patients. Your letter was a warning sign.'

'What did Cooper say?'

'He asked if, in Dr Frank's opinion, you were paranoid.'

'What did Dr Frank say?'

'He said no, but that given the complexity of your case he'd keep an open mind.'

'Shit, Bob, Cooper will kill me!'

'Not so,' Bob says. He puts his hand over my hand and squeezes it. 'Dr Frank's asking us to help out Tom is his way of showing he believes in us. Cooper won't dare to try anything.'

'Us?'

Bob's eyes blink his hurt.

'I'm sorry, Bob,' I say. 'I wasn't sure you'd want to be involved in this. To tell the truth, I wasn't sure about your loyalties.'

He blinks again. 'I have feelings, Sandy, just like you.' He turns his head away.

'Bob, I am sorry. It's just that, well, things can't be easy for you.'

'You have no idea, Sandy,' he says.

'I've been wondering, Bob' – I touch his shoulder so he'll look at me – 'how you know all this?'

Bob raises an eyebrow then tips his head in Cooper's direction. Cooper lounges against the front of the stage watching us. 'From the horse's mouth, of course.' He scrapes back his chair and stands up. 'If you need anything, just let me know.'

What could I need? I wonder as I watch Cooper follow Bob out of the hall. Magazines, candy, extra pocket money? Would something in this scene explain why Bob has stopped playing practical jokes? I realise that I no longer conceive of him as a boy.

I think for the first time in a while about Karl. What would he have done in these circumstances? 'Bird cages,' I say.

'Good evening?' Tom says.

'Just thinking aloud, Tom, don't mind me.'

Karl's action had been a metaphor for freedom. At the

outbreak of war, when many freedoms were being curtailed and men were about to be sent to their deaths on the battlefield, he had released all the birds in Stanley Park. The point was that living things were meant to be at liberty, not held in contravention of their natures. Not rounded up by the Nazis, not confined in camps, not conscripted into armies. The irony, for me, was that I *wanted* to join the military in order to *show* my freedom. I desired to contribute to the overall independence of humankind. Life followed a natural order, not only species to species but individual to individual. Respect it, and all went well; overturn it, and you risked chaos. What could I do to show that kind of respect?

Bob returns late to the room. Tom is already asleep. 'Sandy!' he says.

I sit up. 'What is it?'

'Shush!'

He comes close to whisper. 'I took a letter from Cooper's pocket. It lists three more complaints against him. Ron Signet signed it.'

'What does it say?'

'A post-lobotomy patient in the East Wing struck Cooper and Cooper beat him with a chair until they had to take the man to the hospital, where he nearly bled to death. Then one of the soldiers – that should do for him, Sandy! – started to argue with Cooper and Cooper struck him with his fist and broke his jaw.' Bob falls quiet. He moves away and I hear him preparing for bed.

'Don't you like Cooper, Bob?'

'Fuck you!' Bob says.

I think about this. 'Bob? What's the third case?' I say.

I hear Bob sigh. He fluffs his pillows. He sighs again. 'Signet claims to have caught me and Cooper at it in the garden, one Sunday.'

'At it?'

'It's against the law, Sandy.' Bob laughs. It's the first laugh

I've heard from him in some time. 'My mother thinks I'm sick, she thinks they'll cure me here.' His head, a black oblong in the darkness, turns in my direction. There's no laughter left in his voice when he says, 'I'm getting worried, Sandy. I'm afraid of what Cooper will do to me if Signet's complaints go ahead. He could go to jail, just like I did, if they think the claim is valid. I need your help. I have to get out of here.'

Opening bird cages? Perhaps this is it? 'If you go,' I say, 'you can't ever come back. No one must know how you did it.'

'They won't.'

'You came back before. Winchell told me.'

'That was different.'

'Why is it different now?'

'I've a friend on the outside. He'll help me.'

There are many questions I want to ask, such as who is this friend and how is Bob so sure of him, but I decide to proceed on trust. If I can't, what's the use anyway?

Before we can take our completed treatment plan to Dr Frank, Tom appears before the Board, which recommends him for surgery. When we say goodbye to him, Tom makes me a present of his completed rug. Bob gives him a hug. Cooper, who stands watching, says, 'The best laid plans of mice and men, eh, girls?' It's the first time for days he's spoken to either of us. Ron Signet who has also come to say goodbye whispers, 'I'm sorry.'

Why is he sorry? Is it because he could have done something?

Bob and I stand together and watch as Cooper leads Tom along the corridor, down the stairs and through the door at the far end into the East Wing.

Bob and I have set up a routine. In the evenings, when we've finished work – me in the rabbitry, Bob in the garden – we play chess or take ten or twelve turns around the airing court. Since Winchell is no longer available to play baseball, Bob has given up sports. If anyone asks, we say we've seen all the movies. If anyone listens, they hear Bob chat to me about his interest in design and the course he'd like to take after his release – I'm pleased to learn that there is a purpose to the cuttings he takes from magazines. We find commonalities in our families. He refuses, now, to see his mother when she comes to visit because of what he's learned about her role in his incarceration, and I refuse to see both my so-called parents because – well, you can see it the same way. Cooper – who is on probation – watches us closely, but he can't be there all the time. Bob is really a kind soul, all gentleness now that he's dropped the annoying practical tricks. They were, he says, a way to attract attention. His greatest fear had been that he'd disappear in here, that no one would know he'd ever been. It's a problem I recognise. Now that we're friends, there's no need for him to show off.

My initial aim was to send Bob out the same way I'd been planning for myself with Karl, but the more I think about it, the more I'm sure it's not a good idea. Karl and I had devised our scheme for ourselves: it plays to our strengths, but it can be safely done only once. Karl and I could have gone together, but Bob is no Karl, and I can't leave yet. I owe it to the memory of Alan Macaulay to finish his story and prove him innocent. I've made a commitment to Dr Frank. I still hope for a pardon once I'm finished Dr Frank's treatment.

I present the revamped plan to Bob during our walks around the airing court. I build on what Bob has told me about himself: his boyhood in Alberta riding horses, jumping from barn roofs, swinging on ropes, vaulting fences; his athleticism in high school (before all his foolishness): Bob was a hurdler and pole-vaulter! As well, Bob, as a gardener, knows the layout of the property almost as well as I do, although he cannot go so far afield as can I with my wheelbarrows of refuse from the rabbitry. He must stick to the formal gardens.

Naturally there are no trees left standing close to the outer wall, but the ground rises not far from the wall and that gives a slight advantage. Kosho and I often go as far as the stand of trees where Alan Macaulay's grave lies – ostensibly to disperse rubbish – but on the occasions when Ron Signet allows us to go by ourselves (he's a lazy bugger, is Ron), to say our prayers. These trees are within a hundred feet of that rise of ground. Since our conversation about the sea serpent, Kosho and I find we can pray in common.

I present the plan to Kosho. He says nothing, but he holds the white towel he carries to his face a moment, then nods. The next day he presents me with the first length of bamboo he's filched from the stand of bamboo near the pond.

Bob and I stage an argument in the airing court. From then on we scarcely speak to each other in public, and Bob returns to playing sports. He runs around the court instead of walking with me; he sets up hurdles with Dr Frank's permission, and jumps them. Dr Frank says to him, 'A healthy mind in a healthy body, eh, Bob?' Privately, I teach Bob what I've learned from my Indian club exercises. Bob is strong, but not yet as strong as I am.

Kosho and I take the bamboo lengths, one by one, and hide them near Alan Macaulay's grave. When we are on our own, we begin the process of lashing them together. When the pole is complete, I let Bob know. Bob says, not for the first time, 'You're taking a big risk, Sandy.'

I know, and Kosho knows, but there is no other way. It's all up to Bob.

At the end of August, Dr Frank holds his annual garden party. The night before, Bob asks Ron Signet if he can work late to ensure that the flower beds are at their best. Ron agrees, watches him for a while, then returns to his Esperanto and coffee in the cafeteria. The long, pale, moonless summer evening continues.

Kosho is seen at the fountain feeding the fish, then making his rounds near the rabbitry and pond. It is not Kosho, of course: Kosho hides within the hutch. Bob has donned his clothes. A Bob hunched and made to appear smaller, wearing Kosho's hat on his head and Kosho's white towel around his neck.

We come and go, all of us, as if in a dance.

The night darkens. I return to the rabbitry to make certain all is well. Because it's me, because of everything, Ron comes with me. Kosho – the real Kosho – is there, too. Many of the does are pregnant and we're keeping a close eye on them. We do not open their hutches unless we must; we keep quiet in their vicinity. This night we see that a number of the does have begun to make their nests and we add plenty of soft hay for the purpose. Several of the does have already kindled. We continue to leave them undisturbed so that the anxious mothers will not turn on their young and eat them. Young rabbits are born blind and do not leave the nest until their eyes are open after they're about sixteen days old. Until then we are watchers, Kosho and I.

We watch, this night. When Ron goes back to the main building for another coffee break, Kosho and I take wheel-barrows of dirty straw to the compost. Kosho returns to the hutch, but I continue on, at a run, to Alan Macaulay's gravesite. From there, peering out between the trees, I can see the long snake of the bamboo pole fallen in the grass near the wall. Bob is gone. I only wish I could have been there to see him – that leap of faith in his old training, the hard kick to propel himself over the wall – Bob's rise, climax and denouement, with his friend – all being well – waiting in a car on the far side.

I crawl to the pole and tow it back, then cut the lashings with one of Winchell's sharpened bolts – he'd told me where he'd hidden his tools when he was moved to the laundry. Within minutes it's done, and I'm giving a final sweep and clean to the rabbitry when Ron returns. 'Where's Kosho?' he says.

'Gone to bed.'

Even I am amazed at how lax the supervision is: where's Dr Frank? Putting last-minute touches on reception details? It feels like the calm before the storm. If the Board had any idea . . . which it will, tomorrow, when Bob's absence is discovered.

Ron peeps in at some of the nests. He knows better than to stick in his fingers or make a noise. He comes over to me and whispers, 'Cute little things, aren't they. Isn't life amazing?' I agree. Ron locks up behind us and we walk to the kitchen door.

'Hey, Sandy,' Cooper says, when Ron and I sit down to drink hot chocolate. 'This came for you today.' He hands me a letter. It's from Georgina, who since the episode on cinema night has stayed away. I don't want to open it in front of them. Cooper has a smirk on his face. It's the first time he's spoken to me since he was put on probation. Ron won't catch my eye.

'Open it, Sandy,' Cooper says. 'We all want to hear what your girlfriend has to say.' He winks at Ron Signet.

There's nothing for it. If I don't open the letter, he will take it away. The note is brief.

> My beloved Sandy,
>
> I'm in hell with worry. A letter came today from Brentwood. He was on reconnaissance – he couldn't say where – but it's somewhere in France – when they were attacked by fighters. They dived, right down on deck with the rear gunners answering. The fighters sheered away. While Brent's plane was still down there – 'going like hell between houses and trees' – three Messerschmidt 109s attacked them. They got one – it fell into the forest in flames – and some French fighters got another. One got away. But one of Brent's gunners was shot and later died. Sandy, he wrote, 'It was our first real engagement and the only sensation I can remember was thinking, "Can this be real? Some other bloke is actually shooting at me – there must be a war on!" It was just about the strangest feeling I've ever had.' I have a very bad feeling about this, Sandy.
>
> If there is a god, pray to him for me.
>
> George

Cooper cranes his neck over my shoulder at the letter. He knows what's in it. 'Now, ain't that too bad?' he says.

TWELVE
30 August and following, 1941

Gone! His bed empty! The gardening tools put away neatly! Not a sign of him! My father would say 'in the twinkling of an eye' to describe how Bob has vanished. He'd speak about the Rapture, when all the saved in Christ will be whisked to heaven, leaving the damned behind. The damned – that's us; the saved – that's Bob! Free on the other side of the wall! Only Kosho and I know how it was done. The heavier bamboo sections of the pole have been burned in the incinerator with the other rubbish.

I don't know who sounded the alarm. To avoid suspicion I had mentioned to Ron that Bob wasn't back yet when I went to bed, but Ron only said, 'That boy does like to work hard!' and returned to his magazine.

Lazy, our Ron.

Cooper checked the beds at 2 a.m. Shortly afterwards, we were all awake: footsteps ran down the hall, alarms rang throughout the building, sirens screamed in the streets outside. Cooper rousted us – I took a quick look out the window and saw teams of men with dogs roving the grounds – and led us all into the cafeteria where we were locked in for the rest of the night.

Breakfast is late. No one comes to tell us what's going on. For lack of anything better to do, I begin to organise food for the reception: unfreeze the canapés, mix the fruit punch – some of the others join in. Soon we've made sandwiches and arranged neat trays of cutlery and set out cups and saucers. We prepare coffee urns and hot water for tea.

It's lunchtime before anybody checks on us: they're speechless. We're still in our pyjamas but the cafeteria is spotless, the tables are placed in rows, and we've done our best to decorate with the supplies that we have. Some of the men have constructed paper roses from serviettes, twisted wire for stems, and linked them into garlands.

At 3 p.m. the guests begin to arrive. We are sent to our rooms to wash and shave. Those who specialise in crafts will man demonstration tables. The rest of us will be at our work, as usual. But there is nothing usual about today. Police patrol the grounds and the attendants are armed. What do they think the runaway Bob will do – come back and shoot them? I catch sight of Dr Frank, dressed in a suit that fits him, leading a party of visitors towards a circle of lawn chairs. For some reason I glance up at the top windows in the East Wing: from one of these hangs a red flag.

What a cacophony of images! How will Dr Frank explain them? Do the guests know that a dangerous lunatic (sic!) is at large? Gentle Bob meek and mild! They eye me as I pass by on my way to the rabbitry: I wish I had dragging chains to show them. I am, we all are, a disappointment. I think about drooling for effect but decide that it is bad long-term policy. Truthfully, most of them look more *interested* in what's going on around them – police and police dogs, inmates carrying tea trays – than frightened, even the Board members, who are identifiable by the name tags they wear, and who one would expect to be most disturbed.

The red flag is withdrawn from the East Wing window. A phalanx of doctors and nurses – none of whom I've seen before – come out of the East Wing doors to shake hands with various personages. All is as well as it could be.

I'm in the rabbitry on my own. Kosho has been tucked away out of sight. When the ladies in their tea hats and the gentlemen with their cigarettes come to tour, they don't want to find a Jap in charge, even if it's just of rabbit droppings and hay bales. Despite Japan's recurring assurances of its peaceful intent, many in the general populace have doubts. It's only weeks since Japan occupied French Indochina and Roosevelt seized all Japanese assets and placed an embargo on oil supplies. Pete Cooper is pleased about that, but doesn't think Roosevelt went far enough. As for Canada – well, we've done nothing, as always, except talk talk talk. So Pete Cooper reports.

As if I've conjured him up, Pete appears. He taps a whip against his leg. 'Think you're pretty smart, eh, Sandy? Think nobody knows it was you. You're dead, pal.'

I smile over his shoulder at the group of ladies entering the hut. 'Shush,' I say to them, and point at the signs I made with Kosho: 'Baby Rabbits Sleeping! Mothers Need Their Rest!' The ladies laugh. One whispers, 'My, isn't it clean!' They tiptoe past the hutches; they poke their noses into everything. They ignore Pete Cooper who is fuming.

I lead the party into the room where we deal with the pelts. I shut the door behind me. They cluster near. 'The best way to keep skins from spoiling,' I say, tying hides together at the top end to demonstrate, 'is to make small bundles and hang them from a beam.' I hang them. 'We don't keep them long. We sort and grade them' – I take down a different bundle and begin the process of separating it into piles – 'and then we offer them to market. Most of our skins are "firsts".'

A woman wearing a blue felt hat with a peacock feather attached to it puts up her hand. 'Will these be made into furs?'

'Some will.' I flip several pelts over and invite her to stroke them. 'The thicker and denser the underfur on a skin, the more valuable it is.'

A Board member (he's wearing a name tag), followed by Pete Cooper, shoulders open the door. 'It's no way to run an institution, Attendant Cooper. These are dangerous men.' Pete Cooper's face is bright red.

'Can you keep the noise down, gentlemen,' I say, pointing to the still-open door. 'We don't want to upset the babies.'

The tour groups are gone. I'm tidying. Each time I pass by the door to the outside, I see patrolmen and dogs. Kosho has tied the slighter bamboo lengths into a crude rake: the dogs have found it and sniffed it up and down, but no one can figure out what it means. I'm at the sink with my back to the door when I smell the scent of cigarettes and Chanel. And gin. Georgina. Before I can turn she's right behind me, 'Will you look at what I've found in the dark.'

Her arms come round my waist. She leans her head against my back, her chin sharp between my shoulder blades. 'Sorry I'm late, Sandy. I had some business to attend to.' I try to turn round but she won't let me. 'I had to see a man about a dog.' She laughs and the laugh changes to a snort. She's drunk.

'Georgina!' I pull her hands away.

'Now, don't you lecture me, Sandy. I've had enough for one day.' She stumbles back a step. She's a picture in an old-fashioned tea dress with slim sleeves that fall in vees over her hands. The neck is cut deep and fringed with lace, the skirt is long. A moth-eaten muskrat wrap winds round her shoulders: its eyes glare.

'You're too hot in that stole,' I say strongly. It looks ridiculous. 'What are you doing here? Everyone else has gone.'

'*Et tu*, Brute?' she says. Another step back and there's enough light to see that one of her eyes has been blackened.

'Oh, George . . .' I lift my hand to her face. She moves her head so that her cheek slides under my fingers. 'Who did this to you?'

'I can't stay there any longer, Sandy, I hate the old bugger and my sister.'

'Your father?'

'He says terrible things about me. He says it will be my fault if anything happens to Brent. He doesn't mean it, I'm sure, and he's old . . . but . . .'

'Nothing will happen,' I say, but a cold reptilian hand has pinched me. My spine, and brain stem. Knowing.

'Why is your father so cruel to you, Georgina?'

'Ah, now, that's the thing. I'm his favourite, Sandy, can't you tell? Don't you always hurt the one you love?' She leans against the wall and starts to slide.

'No, George, stand up!'

'I can't!' She's laughing again, great whoops of it.

'You've got to be quiet!'

'Who cares? Who the fuck cares?' she cries. Whoop, whoop.

'Georgina, you'll upset the rabbits!'

'Fuck the rabbits!' she cries. I hear footsteps.

'It's mothers and babies, George, please! You'll upset them!'

'Oh! Mothers and babies!' She puts her finger to her lips and tries to stand up straight.

'All right then, shhh. I know all about mothers and babies.' She winks. 'Brent's my baby.'

The thought seems to sober her: her blue eyes swim with tears.

'It's a hell of a way to run a battleship,' I hear. A Board member in full naval uniform enters followed by Ron Signet.

'Sandy, here, is one of our most trusted inmates, Admiral . . .' Ron begins.

'Madame,' says the admiral, taking in Georgina and the situation at a glance, 'we've met before. Would you do me the honour?' He offers his arm. Georgina snaps to and places her hand in the crook. She's not from a military family for nothing.

'We'll be off?' She blinks hard, tries to concentrate.

'Where to, Madame? I'm at your service.'

Ron Signet doesn't bother to escort me back to the building. In fact, I don't see any of the attendants. Something is very wrong. I've been convicted by the courts of attempted murder of my father, but I'm allowed to roam freely. Only a day ago, one of the inmates eloped and now everyone from the West Wing is permitted to wander? It makes no sense. I notice men who aren't normally allowed outside at all stumbling through the trees, their faces lit by the glow of paper garden-party lanterns, their hands hanging loosely at their sides, or their hands wringing in anxiety. They're worried: where should they go when they're let off leash with no preparation? The guests have dispersed, of course, but the police are still here, not sure why they're patrolling or what the rules are.

There are no rules.

It's misrule, late summer madness. This is not how Dr Frank runs things. What's happened to him? Could it be that they, his opposition, want something to go wrong – something even worse than harmless Bob gone missing? Have they unlocked the locks and countermanded all Dr Frank's orders? Is 'Director Throws Party While Madmen Wreak Havoc' the head-line they want? Throw in an 'Escaped Inmate Terrifies Neigh-bourhood' or 'Innocent Women Menaced by Lunatic' and you have multiple reasons for Dr Frank's banishment. Sent into exile, just like Napoleon, who was the best general the French ever had. Able was I ere I saw Elba.

Georgina! I think, suddenly. Is she all right? But even as the thought crosses my mind, I see her stumble down the driveway still with the admiral. He's a gentleman. His hand remains firmly under her elbow. He laughs with her at whatever she says. He'll see her home safely, whichever side he's on.

I enter the building and walk myself up to my room and put myself to bed.

The world is electrified. Humm. I wait for the clock to strike midnight, and for the noise outside to settle down. My skin feels itchy. There's no Bob or Tom or Winchell in the room. I get out of bed and look out the window. Shadowy figures slip through the grounds. Flashlights flicker. I remember the red flag at the window. What could the flag have meant other than a Communist uprising (where's Winchell when I need him?). Could it have been a message from Karl? Is he keeping an eye on things? Does he think we're in danger? Red flag for danger? Does he approve of our freeing Bob? I hold tightly to the windowsill. I'm on edge. Things are slipping from me. I need facts, just the facts. I need Dr Frank.

In the morning, while I drink coffee in the cafeteria, I consider the events of yesterday and try to sort them. I recognise that I'm under extreme pressure – who wouldn't be, what with Alan Macaulay's case and Pete Cooper's antipathy and Georgina's instability? She told me once how her sister had had her picked up and confined to a clinic, claiming she was addicted to dope and an unfit mother; how the sister then tried to take Brentwood for herself. All out of jealousy and narrow-mindedness. Only Brentwood's pleadings and her own evident sanity, and the money her husband had left her and that she was able to access through a friendly lawyer, had resulted in her release. 'Good girls don't smoke, Sandy, good girls don't stay out late or drink.' Georgina knows she walks a fine line: lions and tigers wait for her. She'd gone on, 'Smart girls don't live in the backwoods, Sandy, but what am I to do? This is my home!'

Well, this is my home, and my entire destiny is in the hands of others, none of whom will listen to me.

The heaps of cups and plates still to wash, the limp garlands strung above the stage testify to the actuality of yesterday's reception and party. Bob – thank God – remains absent. I decide to go over everything.

I know that the rabbitry is real and that the tour groups

visited. I remember giving the demonstrations. Pete Cooper and his animosity towards me is certainly verifiable. Others have commented on it. What about Georgina? Did she arrive drunk last night or not? Yes. She put her arms around me. She left with the admiral, a Board member.

Georgina has me particularly worried. Going back to live in her father's house was a bad idea. But what is one to do when one is lonely and afraid?

Well, Sandy, I say to myself, if all these things are genuine – troubling, but definitely substantive – what are you so concerned about? Nobody's path runs smoothly.

How I feel. I'm not settled. The strings that hold the world I'm in have loosened. Why?

It's early afternoon and I'm with Dr Frank in the truth serum room. To tell the truth, I don't feel I need the drug, but I submit to the nurse's ministrations. While she prepares my arm Dr Frank says, 'I'm pleased that you asked to see me, Sandy, I've been waiting for this.'

'You have?'

'Yes, I have. You'll remember that last time we reached an impasse.'

'An impasse? We did?'

'I thought so.' He waits for me to speak, but I'm not sure what he wants so I remain silent.

'You'll be worried about Bob.'

'Bob?' I say.

Dr Frank frowns. 'Don't be irritating, Sandy.'

'Bob's missing,' I say.

'I know Bob is missing,' Dr Frank says. He throws a sharp glance at the nurse to see if she's ready. She nods. He holds up his hand indicating that she should wait a minute. 'Bob is your roommate. The fact that he's gone is bound to be upsetting. You don't want to be upset. You're ready to change.'

'I don't like it when things change,' I say.

'Ah. Now we're getting somewhere. You don't like it when things change.'

'No. Unless the change is for the better.'

Dr Frank sighs. I know him well enough by now to understand that he thinks I'm speaking platitudes and being evasive, but I'm not. 'Dr Frank,' I say. 'May I be honest?'

'I wish you would be.'

'I want to get to the bottom of this. I want to get out of here.'

'Like Bob?'

'No, not like Bob, sir. I want to walk out the front door a free man.'

Dr Frank signals the nurse and this time once the drug enters my system I'm on a raft that drifts backwards on a river. The river isn't unpleasant, even in reverse. I can dip my hand in it and pull out objects – books I've read, even toys I played with as a child. These items are real, in their way, as stimulants to my imagination. I drop them back in the water. I want facts.

'Now, Sandy,' Dr Frank says, 'do you remember what you said to me last time about your parents?'

'They're not my real parents.'

'Exactly. I want you to tell me how you know this.'

I'm outside in the street where I lived as a child. The little girl to whom I'm married is with me. Heather. She says, 'Let's go and find my father.' I tell all this to Dr Frank.

'Why does she want you to help her find her father?'

'We need his blessing.'

'I see. Then what happens?'

'We look for him up and down the street. We walk to his shoe store, but he's not there. He's not at her house for lunch. We go back to the shops and look in them all. We even check inside the beer parlour, but someone shouts at us to get out.'

'You don't find him?'

'No.'

'Then what?'

'I say to her, "Let's go and find my father."'

'Why do you do that?'

'The same reason. We want his blessing. We love each other.'

'I see. So you search for him, too?'

'Yes. But we can't find him either.' I feel myself getting agitated. I try to keep a lid on it, but my heart is hammering. 'We look everywhere he should be – he's not at home, not at my gran's, not at work.'

'How do you know he's not at work? I thought he was a plasterer, he could be anywhere, couldn't he?'

'No! He's plastering in the apartment building on the corner. He's been working there for weeks. He comes home every day for lunch and has a nap with mother.'

'So you don't find him.'

'No.'

'Then what do you do?'

'Heather and I make a nest.'

'You . . . ?'

'We build a nest, like birds do, only it's bigger and it's on the ground. We've decided to live there together.'

'Didn't your parents ask the two of you not to play together? Didn't they punish you?'

'Yes. But our parents aren't anywhere. We can't find them and I know what's happened to them.'

'What's happened, Sandy?'

'It's the Rapture.'

'The . . . ?'

'Our parents are gone because they've gone to heaven.'

'They've died?'

'No, no, they've been taken into heaven before Jesus' return. It's in the Bible, my father told me. It's called the Rapture.'

'I see.' There's a pause while he thinks and writes. Even on my river and in my nest with Heather, I hear his pen scratching.

'Has everyone gone? Is there no one left?'

'Bad people are left.'

'That includes you and your little friend?'

'Yes.'

'What do you do after you build your nest?'

'We go to my house.'

'Why do you do that?'

'The nest isn't warm enough and we need to live some-where. Our family house has food and beds in it. We'll be all right if we stay there.'

'Then what, Sandy?'

'We do what mother and father do at lunchtime.'

'That is?'

'I told you. We have a nap.'

'Where do you take your nap, Sandy? I need to hear all of this.'

'In my parents' bed.'

'You and Heather go to bed in your parents' room?'

'It's nice,' I say. 'We take our clothes off, hold on to each other and we fall asleep.'

I start to zoom back. I've gone as far as I care to. I say to Dr Frank in my grown-up voice, 'That's all there is, folks.'

A surge of truth serum jolts through my veins.

'That's not all, Sandy. Tell me the rest of it.'

I don't want to tell. I do want to tell. I want it to be over.

The next thing I know is that Heather and I are yanked out of bed. Heather screams, and I scream. A woman who looks a little like my mother, except that I can see as she shouts into my face that she has a moustache, throws me into a closet. I don't know what happens to Heather. A long time after – a very long time – so long that I pee my pants – the closet door opens.

'You can come out now, Sandy.' At first I think it's my father who waits there. It smells like him. He's chewing Sen-Sen. But it isn't my father because he picks me up roughly. He carries me into the kitchen and stands me on the breadboard. He picks up the bread knife. 'Ho, ho!' he says.

Another man – I recognise him as the doctor – yes – he would have been left behind – I've heard my parents talk about his drinking, says, 'Don't tease him, Alfred.'

I look at the man holding the knife. My father's name is Fred, not Alfred. The woman with a moustache says, 'Let's get on with it.'

The doctor says, 'Put him on the kitchen table and hold his arms and legs still.'

The woman and man who are pretending to be my parents do this. I try to kick but they grip me tightly. The doctor puts a rag over my face and I can't breathe. I can hear and see, though, because I rise up out of my body and look down at it, still as ice, on the table.

The doctor takes a pair of scissors, pulls on the foreskin of my penis and snips it off. He uses a scalpel to do some additional cutting. I can't see much because of the blood. I scream but the boy on the table doesn't make a sound. The pain makes me faint and sick. I plunge back into my body.

When I come to, the doctor is tying off the stitches. He places a gauze wrap around my genitals. 'You should have had this done when he was an infant,' the doctor says.

'I told him,' the woman says. She watches the doctor finish up his work with an expression of satisfaction on her face. She's a cruel, wicked woman. 'I hope this will put an end to the nonsense,' the woman says.

'It will,' the man who pretends to be my father says. He hasn't been able to watch the operation – he has a weak stomach – but now that the doctor is done, he takes a look at my bandaged privates, my white face and the bundles of bloody rags on the table. 'It will do that for some time to come.'

'Well, well,' Dr Frank says, when I've fully returned to the present. 'Do you understand what we've uncovered?'

'I understand.'

'Tell me, Sandy, in your own words.'

'I was circumcised in a crude way when I was six or seven.'

'Why were you circumcised?'

'To stop me and Heather from our sexual explorations. They didn't understand that we loved each other.'

'Your parents hated and feared their own sexuality. They took it out on you. You did nothing wrong, Sandy. You have cause – a child's cause – for hating them. A memory like that, suddenly surfacing under stress, could certainly explain the apparently unprovoked attack on your father.'

'He's not my father,' I say.

'At the time, as a child, you believed in – what was it – the Rapture? You thought that people who hurt you couldn't be your parents. Real parents wouldn't treat a child like that. Therefore your real parents had been taken up into heaven and these substitutes left behind to do their worst.'

'They were dressed up to look like my real parents, but they weren't.'

'You attacked your father when the memory of his part in the punitive circumcision reappeared. We'll have to find out why it did, what exactly provoked it.'

'If you say so, Dr Frank.'

'What do you mean?'

'I don't think it matters.' My eyes feel heavy. I'd like to sleep.

'Why doesn't it matter? Without that knowledge, you can never be free!'

'Because he's still not my father.' How many times do I have to say it?

'Are you telling me that you still believe they aren't your real parents?'

'Yes.'

We go over it and over it: it's he who doesn't want to let it go. He points out that what I'd told him was my childhood means of dealing with intolerable pain. That is true. But it doesn't explain everything. How can I convey the certainty of my knowledge that the people I loved and knew as my parents disappeared when I was small, and never returned? It isn't, as Dr Frank thinks, a notion I made up. It's a simple fact. Nothing in my experience since that day has contradicted it.

My one hope is that this 'exchange' serves some important purpose; also of note, as I've observed, is that occasionally the process is reversed. Not only are the good exchanged for the bad, but an evil person may be changed into good: take Franklin Delano Roosevelt, for instance, a pacifist (no slur intended against Karl), but who has agreed to Lend-Lease and wants the Americans to help us in the war. These are not the qualities of the same person.

'Do you believe in God, Dr Frank?' I finally say.

'Yes, I'd say I'm a God-fearing man, Sandy. Why?'

'How do you know there is a God?'

'I just know, in the same way that thousands have known before me, century after century.'

'You're saying that a commonly held belief is equivalent to truth. In the Soviet Union, millions do not believe in God, therefore, according to your own criteria, Dr Frank, there is no God. Is truth, then, a matter of dogma or politics or fashion?'

He looks disconcerted. His thinned features harden. Before he can say anything more, I interrupt. 'I'm disappointed in you. You're a doctor, a scientist, you should respect the truth. You shouldn't buy into all that mumbo-jumbo.'

'It's my mumbo-jumbo, Sandy, and if I choose to believe it, that's up to me.'

'That's exactly my point, sir, don't you see?'

'Don't forget who's in charge here, Sandy, will you?'

The subject of belief is a large one. I skim through several chapters of *The Storehouse of Thought and Expression* to see if it offers advice on this subject, but it doesn't. I wish Karl were here to talk to. *The Storehouse* is concerned with the nuts and bolts of the writing craft, not with the meaning of life. That subject is the writer's private concern.

What I do know is that what is real to me is different to that which is real to Dr Frank. It is possible that neither of us is in touch with absolute reality since belief lies behind the perceptions of both of us. It could be that a consideration of time past is the only means to bring us both to our senses. Is that not, in fact, the basis of Dr Frank's treatment of his patients? To go backwards in time with them until truth becomes apparent? Why, then, does he not apply these principles to himself?

I also know that a sense of time can be influenced by emotion. People say 'after the flood' or 'before I was married' to indicate a significant experience. Time speeds up or slows down, depending. My time with the sea serpent, for instance, is a long, slow unspooling in my mind, although it may have lasted only a few minutes. I can also say, 'before my parents disappeared' or 'after I met Georgina' to indicate massive change within my life – not only *change*, but a revolution of belief as to the nature of reality.

Does this help with Alan Macaulay, whose story I have yet to finish? Although his version of events is, I believe, the truth, his version was not accepted. An account of events presented by people who disliked him prevailed. Beliefs – in this case, the commonly held belief that Alan Macaulay was guilty – don't alter truth: they run parallel to it. Sometimes a belief and the truth coincide, but not always. These are big ideas.

I look out the window. Once again, although it is night and all inmates should be locked indoors, numbers of them roam the grounds. Once again, a red flag hangs from an East Wing window. Sirens sound and searchlights spring up from the town. They crisscross the sky looking for I know not what (not Bob: Bob's not up there). Are we under attack? Are German or Japanese planes set to bomb us? No one comes to say. We've been abandoned.

If we have indeed been left on our own, it may be time to put our plan, mine and Karl's, into action. I raise the sash and loosen the bars over the window, then lift them out and put them into a pillowcase. It is not the first time I've done this. Karl had the window prepared even before I came along, and we've gone through many dry runs. Karl is big on preparation.

I swing myself out, then feel with my fingers for the gaps in the brick Karl showed me. Before I begin to climb, and while I still have the sill for purchase, I close the window and set the bars back in their holes. The work is treacherous and I'm sweating from the effort and – to be frank – from fear. I can't jump from here – it's too high up: if I fall, I die – but even if I could I'd never escape the property. Not to worry, though: Karl has thought of everything.

It is a truism that people on the ground rarely look up. In this instance, with the building dark and only flashlights illuminating the path of the police patrolling through the trees, and the searchlights sectioning the sky, I have little fear of discovery from below. Nevertheless, I've taken care to wear dark clothing. I stuff the pillowcase under my shirt so it can't be seen. Now I'm at the stepped bricks at the corner and within minutes I've spidered myself up them and over the castellation and on to the roof. From there, it's a jump and scramble to the top of the turret and on to its small roof. I crouch up there and feel with my fingers for the opening, raise the hatch, and edge down the ladder into the room that Karl found.

There are no openings inside the body of the turret, other than in the ceiling, so it is reasonably safe to light the hooded candle we have left there. Karl stole matches from Ron Signet, and Kosho made the candle for me from beeswax. The attendants' rounds and our work and meals are normally on such a strict schedule that finding time to work here posed no problem; and with the two of us, one could always keep lookout in the room below while the other laboured above. The distance from floor to ceiling is over twenty feet – thus the need for the ladder which had been left by the original builders. We've speculated, but have come to no conclusion as to the room's original purpose.

I've not been here at all since Karl was taken away.

Since I know this is the last time, I take care, as I place the finishing touches, to destroy all evidence of what we've been up to. Even though there is little further they can do to Karl, still I do not want to leave a trail that leads back to him. Every scrap of leftover material, I put inside the pillowcase.

So very little remains to be done: Karl's drawings are simple but professional – after all, he is an engineer, even if he'd been reduced to working in a steam plant before his incarceration, and I have had glider training at the flying club, where it was taken for granted, not only by me, that I would go on to be an air force pilot. I was praised for my abilities: it was said I had aptitude!

Let bygones be bygones, Sandy. Onward!

We've constructed a simple monoplane – a single-wing shape with a hole in the middle. There's not much we could do for controls, but they won't be necessary if the machine is light enough to fly. It only has to carry me from the roof and above the trees and over the wall. We're sure it can do it: we've made the frame from balsa wood stripped from crates, and with sections of Kosho's bamboo. We've glued and stitched canvas mail and laundry bags over the skeleton and then painted the whole with a doping paste made from boiled millet. We fabricated the harness from lengths of electrical wire that Karl took from the worksites to which he had access. The harness is basic: strictly speaking, I'll be hanging by my armpits, but it will provide some security.

The golden rule, as Karl said, is never to fly higher than you care to fall.

Rules, we both said, are made to be broken.

I'm proud of our glider. The wing stands upright against the wall, one tip near the opening. It is light enough that I should be able to haul it up through the hatch by myself, although in our original plan, one of us would have assisted the other. If there is sufficient wind, and if I pick up enough speed during my run across the roof, I should be able to maintain sufficient height to clear the trees. There's been no opportunity for a test flight, unfortunately, but I know how to control the dimensions of flight – roll-tipping, pitch and yaw – by adjusting the position of my body. It would help to have a tail and rudder – but, well, you can't have everything!

I climb the ladder, haul up the stuffed pillowcase with a length of rope, finish fastening myself and the case into the harness, then ease the wing up and out. When I'm clipped on, and it, and I, are on the biggest section of the roof, I set up a windsock made from a tube of sacking. The wind is light and gusting. When it's as dark as it's going to be, and the searchlights play at the far end of the city and the flashlights of the ground patrols are at a distance, I place my head through the hole in the wing, and tie the remaining straps.

One two three and I run, the wind catching the wing's edges; I reach the lip and jump.

The principles of flight are simple: air flows over the top of a curved, fixed wing, creates lift and opposes the pull of gravity. At first I drop, gain some speed, then I'm supported and carried away from the building and across the gardens beyond the rabbitry. I can see the other outbuildings, dim and quiet, where the larger farm animals are kept and I pass over the Chinese and Japanese quarters with the distinctive smoke of cooking fires rising from each. I adjust my body so that I turn towards the woods and the wall beyond, keeping the wing as level as I can. The strain on my arms is terrific.

Not far to go, Sandy.

When I'd flown in a glider before, I'd been towed by an airplane in a steep climb over the prairie, hot air rising from the ploughed fields to make columns of air for support. Once in one,

I'd spiral up and up until I reached the top and then level out and head where I wanted to go, looking for more cloud-capped thermals: it was a dance of air, the most delicate of relationships. Nothing like this. I sense the stall the instant before it happens – I'm too slow, and too low, the left wing dips and I'm pitched forward and down into the trees. It is over in seconds.

The Wright brothers failed many times before they succeeded, I think . . . I'm not badly hurt, I can try again . . . but – I hear shouts behind me – the Wright brothers didn't have to deal with pursuit. Quickly I break what's left of the wing into pieces and bury them in leaf mould. The pillowcase and harness are another matter – too difficult to hide – so I keep these with me, and move as rapidly as I can on my bruised limbs towards the rabbitry. There I can catch my breath, clean up, appear to be doing something useful if I'm discovered. I wipe my wet nose with my sleeve several times before I realise it's pouring blood.

'Now, now, Sandy, what's this?' It's Pete Cooper's voice from right in front of me. He's materialised out of nothing. I've had just enough time to secrete the pillowcase and harness in the straw bales. I squint in the sudden bright light next to the hutches. I hear running footsteps, the sound of heavy breathing – there's a crowd behind me now, silent, at the door, and in the new light I can see what they see: the walls and floor of the rabbitry are splashed with red; smashed and broken cages lie strewn over the floor, and everywhere I look are pieces torn from the bodies of dead rabbits. I squat and put my head between my knees.

'Feeling squeamish, Sandy?' Pete Cooper stands over me. 'Dear, oh dear.' He points to the splashes of blood on my face, arms and shirt. 'Had an accident, have we, Sandy?' He grabs me by the shirtfront and hauls me to my feet. 'You stupid little pervert!' He shoves me hard against the wall.

I feel, as well as hear, Dr Frank push his shrinking body through the onlookers. 'What's going on, here?' Then, 'Ah . . .' as the shock hits.

'What's "going on" is perfectly clear,' Pete Cooper says. 'Sandy here has been playing with knives.' He indicates the bloody carcasses, my clothing and the knife – which I notice for the first time – with which I prepare the hides, and that is lying on the floor.

Dr Frank looks at me with grief and astonishment. 'Has it come to this, Sandy?' His shoulders slump. It's a mortal blow to the both of us. He turns to leave.

'No!' I say. 'I didn't! I just came to check on things and found this!'

'There's the small matter of the blood on your clothing,' Pete Cooper says, looking smug.

'I fell! It's dark out.'

'Tsk, tsk. Shouldn't you be in bed?'

Dr Frank seizes on this and turns to Ron Signet who has been keeping out of the way in the shadows. 'Ron, you did the bed check, was Sandy there?'

Sadly, reluctantly, Ron shakes his head.

'No one's in bed tonight – everyone's out, you know that, it's not just me! Where's Kosho, he can tell you I'd never do anything like this, I couldn't!'

'Couldn't?' says Pete Cooper. He takes my work apron – which I'd last left at the kitchen door – from a hook on the wall. 'Some people just can't resist a souvenir,' he says, and takes from the pocket the rabbit's foot I'd placed there earlier. He'd seen me do it, too. Now I know, as if there were any doubt, who's responsible.

'Where's Kosho?' I say again. 'He'll tell you about that, too.'

Ron Signet gives a discreet cough. 'Dr Frank?' he says. 'I can't find Kosho, either.'

'Can't find . . . ?' Dr Frank takes a step back. There's no doubt now, it's out of his hands. 'Well go and look, damn you!' He pushes his way out through the onlookers and they close behind him as if he'd never been.

I hardly notice when the police escort comes. A photographer records the 'evidence'. I'm handcuffed and shackled. Before I'm led away, Pete Cooper manages to say to me, 'About Kosho, now, I know you were friends. He popped in, Sandy, just before you did and left in a hurry. You know what I think? I think he's found a use for that white towel.' He winks.

You know when things have gone too far: you can't keep up, it's an overload. Too many details and events in a flood the brain can't process. There's no story here, just a great fall. Will anyone pick up the pieces? I should refuse to believe Pete Cooper, but I can't. I can imagine what Kosho would do if he saw this room. All this slaughter for nothing.

'Get the Chinks to clean up,' Cooper calls out to Ron Signet, who is still lounging, uncertain as to his position. 'Hop to it, Ron.' Ron goes. Pete goes. My escort and I make our way over the lawns Bob was so proud of to the front door. Why the front door? What's happening? More police cars idle at the entrance.

'Take the goddamn shackles off!' Dr Frank shouts when he sees me hobbling up the steps. A policeman complies and leaves me in Dr Frank's hands. He shouts further directions for the roundup of all inmates. He's asserting some control!

'My, my, Sandy,' he says to me. 'You'd better come in and sit down while we have a chance.' He leads me through the lobby and into his office. He motions me to sit and he remains standing. 'You understand how serious this is?'

I nod.

'You have an explanation?'

I nod again. 'I would never . . . I didn't . . .'

'It looks bad, Sandy. There's little I can do for you at this point. You'll be taken for examination by other psychiatrists, you understand? There'll be changes in your treatment.'

'Changes?' His gaze tells me that this, indeed, is a change point after which things will never be the same. To my great sorrow, I also understand it is a change in belief: Dr Frank's belief in me.

He stares out the window at the cars, the police, at the bands of inmates gathered into neat knots by attendants. We're still in blackout other than for the flashlights. The blaze of the rabbitry lamps is behind us. 'It's madness, eh, Sandy? Who knows the depths of the human heart?'

'I swear, sir, I really didn't . . .'

'What were you doing out there, Sandy? Tell me the truth.'

'Flying, sir.'

He sighs. 'There's more bad news, Sandy, I'm sorry to tell you, but you'd best have it all now.' He picks up a piece of paper from the desk. 'Would you like me to read this to you?'

'Just tell me, sir.' I brush at the blood drying on my hands. It flakes on to the carpet.

'It's from your friend, Mrs Jones-Murray.'

'Georgina?'

Dr Frank keeps his eyes on the paper. 'It's about her son, Brentwood. He's missing and believed to have lost his life as a result of air operations over France.'

'No, that was his gunner. He was shot and killed; Georgina wrote to me about it.'

Dr Frank hands me the letter and I read the details that have been sent to Georgina by one of her son's friends. The weather was good – one of these clear September nights with a bright moon – and at about 22:00 hours there was an enemy intercept. Brent turned and made visual contact and closed with a JU-88 and attacked from level and dead astern. One of the other fighter pilots saw flashes in the enemy aircraft fuselage, and then it returned fire from the rear. Brent attacked twice more, the JU rapidly slowed, and Brent's aircraft overshot, narrowly missing a collision. The observer then saw a red glow in the cockpit; Brent's plane started vibrating then went into a steep dive. There was a patch on the water where it hit the sea.

'Yes, I suppose that's clear,' I say.

'Sandy?' Dr Frank's eyes are wide and brown, they brim with tears. 'Is that all you can say?'

'Just one more thing, Dr Frank.' I get to my feet. 'Why didn't Alan Macaulay run for it when he could? There was time after he accidentally shot MacKenzie – about four hours – before the police came. No one would have stopped him. He must have known, with Kennedy there to lie about what happened, that he didn't have a chance. He could have escaped to the woods, changed his name and appearance . . . Yet he stayed and waited for justice.' I shake my head. 'But you know, and I know, Dr Frank, there is no justice.'

It takes me three long steps to reach the window. I punch my hand through the glass and grab a piece of glass.

'What are you going to do with that, Sandy?' Dr Frank says calmly. His hand reaches under the desk for a button. Never mind. They'll be too late.

'If a member offends you, cut it off,' I say. 'I'm going to finish the job.' I open my trousers, close my eyes and cut.

THIRTEEN

31 December and following, 1941

I turn on my side and see a guard carrying a tray and a newspaper stop in front of my cell. Keys jangle from his belt. 'How're you doing today, Sandy?' he says. 'Think you can eat something?'

He's friendly enough. He unlocks the door and swings it wide. 'Still feeling woozy?' He sets the tray down at the foot of the bed. I try to sit up but only get so far before the room tilts and I fall back. The guard catches me and holds me upright until I can get my legs over the side and look down at my bare feet on the floor. I'm wearing pyjamas.

'What time is it?'

'Time for you to wake up.' He stuffs a pillow behind my hips to keep me straight. He places the tray in my lap. On it is a serving of turkey, mashed potatoes and Brussels sprouts. 'Dr Love will be here any time.'

'Dr Love?'

The guard checks over his shoulder then bends down, his face close to mine. 'Between you and me,' he murmurs as he uncovers another plate to reveal two cookies, an apple and a piece of cake, 'you're a lucky man.'

'Why am I lucky?'

'Yes, why are you, Sandy?' a new voice says. A tall man with a long bearded face stands at my threshold. 'That will be fine, Don,' he says to the guard. 'Leave the door as it is, I won't be long.'

He turns to me and holds out his hand. 'I'm Dr Love. We've met before, but you may not remember.' My hand is sweaty, my whole body reeks with perspiration. I wipe my hand on the sheet. 'Don't mind that,' he says, watching me, 'it's just the drugs wearing off.'

We shake hands. 'You don't remember me at all, do you, Sandy?'

I shake my head. He pulls a stethoscope out of a pocket and leans forward, and as he does, I recognise his scent of Bay Rum.

'There's something familiar . . .' I say, but he holds up his hand so that he can continue to listen to my chest without interruption. He checks my heart and lungs, then takes out a penlight and looks into my ears, my throat and lastly into my eyes. I have to struggle to keep them open. The lids feel weighted. 'Everything tickety-boo?'

'Just fine, Sandy, just fine.' He sits beside me, crosses one leg over the other and swings a brown oxford-clad foot. He seems entirely at his ease. 'Don't mind me, eat your dinner before it gets cold.' He's waiting for something, what is it?

I'm raising a forkful of turkey to my lips, worried that I'll spill in front of him, when the image of a figure dressed in red silk shirt and cape, and tall black boots, and with whiskers drawn on to its cheeks springs into mind. 'I remember something! It's Puss in Boots!' It is so vivid and sudden and stupid that I'm shocked. Not only that, but how grey my world is by contrast: grey walls and flooring, grey blankets and sheets, the grey pyjamas I wear. Even the overcooked food on the plate partakes of shades of grey. Grey, that's my name, I think. I'm Sandy Grey.

'Very good, Sandy,' Dr Love says. He grins. 'That was the pantomime three weeks ago, ten days or so before we put you under. Considering the state you were in, that anything stuck is tremendous. With any luck, the rest should come back to you relatively quickly. You've made the bridge.'

'I'm a lucky man!'

Another smile. I find the courage to look at him more closely. He's dressed too warmly for indoors. He has the usual doctor's stethoscope, yes, but he wears no white coat. Instead, he's sporting a sweater vest beneath a heavy tweed jacket. His trousers are wool, walking weight, the clothes of a gentleman. Instead of a tray of instruments (what tray? how do I know he should have a tray?), he has carried in with him, and placed on the floor, a black doctor's bag. 'Do you work here?' I ask him.

'Your friends, Mrs Jones-Murray and her father, Mr Dunblane, sent me. We agreed with your other doctors that I should sedate you for a period of time to see if we could bring you back.'

'Sedate me? Bring me back?'

'You've been away, in a manner of speaking. Not yourself; not permitted to be yourself. Mostly, in my opinion, because of the treatment you've received. Not that I've said that, not even to you. Do you understand?'

'You don't want to be seen to criticise.'

'Exactly.'

'It won't do me any good.'

'There's my boy.' He pats my knee in a friendly manner. 'From here on in, Sandy, it's mostly up to you. Your friends and I have done what we could. As I said, you will begin to remember now and the memories may be difficult at first. You must prepare yourself. They will become less painful with time.' He gives me his gentle smile. 'Sleep is a marvellous cure, too little used.'

'How long have I been asleep?'

'Ten days. We've managed to keep you fed, more or less, during this time, but you must be hungry. You should eat to get back your strength.' He gets up to go.

'I'm a Rip Van Winkle.'

'Or Cinderella.' He holds my gaze. 'Now, I have to go.'

'Don't leave. I don't remember. I don't understand . . .'

'I'm afraid I must.' He's out of the cell now and closing the door behind him. The guard pops up from his post nearby and locks it. 'You have a visitor waiting, Sandy,' Dr Love says. 'I'm sure she'll do her best to answer your questions.'

He's gone, with rapid footsteps, then sharp heels click my way over the black-and-white tiles, and she's here, Georgina, looking thinner, and a little stooped. From what I can see of her hair, beneath the hat, I believe it's been dyed! The blonde strands are dark! She raises her veil. Her eyes are set deeply into a white face. She peers at me through the bars, 'Geez, Sandy, you look like hell. For Christ's sake, you've gone white!'

I put my hand to my hair. I can't see the colour – I had no idea – but I can feel short, stubby, unfamiliar bristles on my scalp. My head has been shaved. Why?

'Georgina! What are you doing here?'

'Getting you out of trouble, as usual.' In the aisle in front of the cells are groupings of tables and chairs. Georgina draws a chair close to the cell door, sits, then leans forward, and reaches a gloved hand between the bars. I stumble to my feet and grab hold.

'Oh, George,' I say, reading the lines of grief on her face, and remembering why they are there, 'I'm so sorry.'

'I thought I'd die, but of course I didn't,' she says, talking quietly. There are others in the cells nearby, scarcely breathing, listening. I've only just become aware of them. We're like fish in a tank, on display. 'I'd just heard about Brent, and then you – I couldn't believe it, none of it, I didn't believe it, but there was nothing I could do.'

'I'm so sorry, Georgina,' I say again. Tears spill from her eyes and run unchecked into her collar.

'I was saving his letters – he would have made a beautiful writer, Sandy – his descriptions of England and the way he made me feel, even that I could fly a plane myself, and so marvellous. I was going to put the letters into a book so he'd have them later. He was all I had.'

I squeeze her hand. 'You've still got me, Georgina. I'll help you make a book. It will be a greater success than *War Birds*. He won't be forgotten.'

'I know I was drinking, but who wouldn't have, what with the worry? Oh, God.'

She's going to break down completely; her face scrunches up; but then she gets hold of herself. She dabs her face one-handedly with a hankie, blows her nose and sniffs. Fumbles the hankie back into a pocket. 'But I didn't come to talk about me. We have to get you fixed up first, don't we?' She smiles bravely.

'Yes,' I say. Then there's a silence, for I'm sure there are things I should say, but what are they? 'Dr Love says I've been asleep,' I try, for it's one of the few facts I've got. I'm getting tired, so I lean against the bars.

She nods vigorously. 'He thought it might work in your case. He indicated to me, when I saw him just now, that it has! He's been such a help. Without him, I'd still be locked up too.'

'You, George? What happened?'

'I was shanghaied – kidnapped! – Sandy. My sister talked our father into it, said I wasn't responsible, I'd drink through his money; she had him sign papers. Well, he's a senile old coot, he can't be blamed, but it's the second bloody time! What do they think I'm made of, wood? You'd think, in the circumstances . . .' She takes several deep, sustaining breaths. 'They took me to a clinic and left me there. It was only through the help of the admiral that I got out. He couldn't find me – well, I'd disappeared, hadn't I? – so he investigated, God bless him! You remember him, don't you? He discovered where I was and contacted Dr Love. And then, voilà!'

Voilà? It's a horrifying tale: it's one thing for me to be locked up, but Georgina! She's a woman, and she's not as strong as she thinks. 'You're a lucky woman, Georgina,' I say.

'Yeah, I guess.'

'Why would your sister do such a thing?'

'You know what she told me the night the telegram came about Brent? That she was glad, that I'd always been spoiled and now I might get what I deserved. She said terrible things about the love I had for my son. She thinks I'm a monster, and I'm not! How would she know? – she's had no one to think about except herself!'

'Oh, George!'

'She was jealous of my husband, too. She thinks it's all about money. You don't know how lucky you were to be born poor.'

'I'm a lucky man.'

'I was drunk for a week afterwards and I'm still glad of it. I couldn't have borne it otherwise.'

'I don't blame you, George. Of course you couldn't.' But I'm thinking, am I lucky, really lucky, in ways I haven't before understood? Has my ignorance of the rest of the world and how it lives led me to misconstrue my own case? Are terrible families and terrible parents normal?

'I can't drink a goddamn thing any more. Dr Love says I shouldn't.'

I look around for some clothes. I feel naked in my pyjamas with Georgina here. I don't see any, so I make do with a blanket from the bed. I sit on the floor so, if we like, we can hold hands again.

'I've missed you, Sandy.'

'What can I do to help?'

Once more she tears up. The tip of her nose is red, as are her ears where they show between the too-dark strands of her hair. 'Just be well, be my friend.'

'What kind of a friend would you like me to be?'

For an answer, she reaches a hand through the bars to touch me.

We talk for a few more minutes about her family problems: the vicious sister, the increasingly incapable father who is used to, as a lumber baron, wielding unlimited power. We discuss where she should live and decide – now that she has Dr Love and the admiral on her side – that it's best if she remains at home, with her father, 'to keep an eye on things'. Her sister, who is married and lives in Victoria, won't repeat her attack on George, we think, not now that she'll face real opposition. In fact, Georgina is going to visit a lawyer with a view to prosecuting her.

'Can you do that?'

'Sue her? Goddamn right I can. At least scare the pants off her! But we must talk about you before I go. You've had a bad time of it, Sandy.'

I bob my head in agreement, but then I say, for there is no point in not being honest about the fact that my memory is like Swiss cheese, full of holes, 'Why am I here? What happened to me?'

She nods as if she's half expected to hear something like this – briefed, perhaps, by Dr Love – and she tells me what occurred in the rabbitry and how I was blamed for it. I close my eyes and I see Pete Cooper's face and behind him the smashed rabbit hutches and rabbit blood. My gut clenches with sadness for the poor blameless creatures, but not with guilt.

'It wasn't me, Georgina, I didn't do it!'

'I know, Sandy. Everyone knows that now.'

'What about Attendant Cooper? He said . . .'

'Pete Cooper!' she says, and laughs. 'His lies caught up with him. While I was locked up, somebody sent an anonymous letter to Dr Frank, explaining that you were innocent. You were set up. The letter writer suggested that we count the corpses and the number of rabbits' feet and that if we did, we'd find one extra foot. Dr Frank, who understood what that could mean, got on it right away. There was indeed one too many, and then Ron Signet said he remembered seeing you tuck just such a rabbit's foot into your pocket after you and Kosho had spent a day dressing rabbits.'

'Kosho!' Pete Cooper's terrible words about Kosho's suicide return with a rush.

'Yup, even the Jap stood up for you. Can you imagine? Although, especially after all that's happened, without Signet's corroboration, he wouldn't have been believed.'

'Kosho's alive!'

'Of course!'

I tell her what Cooper had said, then ask the next question that troubles me. 'You said he wouldn't have been believed, on his own, because of something that's happened . . .'

'The Japs bombed Pearl Harbor and the Americans are in the war. They'll have to round up all the Japs now or we'll be sitting ducks.'

I try to digest this news, but what she's said doesn't make sense. 'But why? What Japs?'

'All the Japs. We're not safe. The coastal fishing fleet is full of them. The admiral says . . .'

'George,' I interrupt, now I see what this means, 'can you look after Kosho?'

'Oh, Sandy,' she says. She won't meet my eyes.

'He saved my life.'

'He and a few others,' she says tartly. Her foot, on the floor, starts tapping.

'I know, George, Dr Love told me that it was you and your father who sent him to help me. That must have cost money; and in the midst of your troubles . . .'

'Well, the old goat will sign anything these days if I get him by himself.' She clasps her gloved hands round her knees. Both feet still. She sees me watching her and tugs her blue wool skirt down farther. I can tell by the stitching at the hem that it's been shortened and by the fact that the stitches show, that she must have done it herself. She stands up. She's not wearing stockings. I stand up, too.

'I'll do what I can, Sandy, of course I will.' She steps close to the bars and we're nose to nose.

'It won't be long,' she whispers.

'No.' Her perfume of cigarettes and Chanel. 'I can't bring him back for you, George. I wish I could. I'd do anything . . .'

'I know you would, Sandy.' She sniffs deeply and digs in her pocket for the damp handkerchief. Wipes her eyes, blows her nose.

'What happens now, Georgina?'

'For you? Well, we have to wait until you've fully recovered, then you'll be examined by a Board and then, well, we'll see.'

'But if I'm innocent, what do I have to recover from?'

She looks at me sadly. Those blue eyes – 'You tried to harm yourself, Sandy, don't you remember?' Her lids flutter. Her body is a crucible of pain. 'I'll see you soon.' Then she's gone, and I scarcely know what to think, but it doesn't matter much because already, as I turn towards the bed, it's like walking through water. It's up to my knees, my hips, my neck. Over my head.

It's night when I next awake. I lie on the cot – for that's what it is, not a real bed, there's no proper mattress, only a sheet of canvas and a blanket – and try to ignore the stench from the toilet next to me. The guard paces the corridor. It's embarrassing to have to pee where anyone can watch, but at length I get up and try to time it so I have at least a minute or two before he comes by again. I finish and lie down and listen to the sound of other men, awake or sleeping, coughing, sighing, crying out.

I know, now that I've read the newspaper Don left for me, that it's New Year's Eve. For all I know, it could be after midnight and we've already begun 1942. I wonder what the new year will bring, and I feel terribly frightened. Not so much by what I recall, but by all the chasms in my thoughts. Sometimes a thought will begin, it trips along, and then it's just swallowed up. Some of these thoughts are important. They have to do with who I am. What I can remember, though, and what I hold on to, is that consciousness is a light and that the light exists even when I can't see it. It's up to me to find it, I have to find my way.

I try to follow the thread of this idea to its conclusion, but I can't. Instead I see a face – it's Karl! My former roommate and mentor who was taken from me! But it's not Karl as I knew him. This is a different man: this one speaks to me in winks and nods and baby words: *Da-da. Ma-ma. Wa-ter.* What does this mean? I've been here for weeks and months, nearly three months. I've been rescued, more or less, I'll be all right; but what about Karl, what's happened to him? What have they done? What is it that I've forgotten?

I can't help it – I turn on my stomach, jam my face into the pillow and sob.

In the morning, when Don comes in with bread and tea, I ask him: 'Don, I don't suppose you know my story?'

'Some of it, Sandy.' He bustles about, strips the bed, hands me a blue suit of clothing not unlike the pyjamas I've been wearing.

'I was accused of something I didn't do.'

'Oh, yes,' he says, carting the bundle of laundry to the door which he's left, casually, open.

'Well, did they find out who did do it?' I'm expecting, I'm hoping, that he'll say, 'Pete Cooper.'

'It was another one of the inmates – Winchell – he confessed.'

'Not Winchell!'

'Apparently promises were made, assurances given.'

'Who promised, what did they say?'

'I'm not at liberty to discuss that, Sandy.' Don purses his lips and the tap of gossip is shut off. He busies and bustles some more.

It is all too much. It is one thing to be betrayed by an enemy, quite another to be betrayed by a friend. But then I remember Winchell's face as he spoke of the rape and murder of nuns by the Republicans in Spain. The glee in it. My heart hardens against him. Yes, he is capable of it, yes.

'Are you coming?'

It's only then that I realise I'm expected to follow. By the clothes I've been given I know I'm not being set free, but there is certainly going to be a change. I feel happier at the prospect, and stumble along after Don, still buttoning my shirt. All I have for shoes are paper slippers, so my progress is more of a shuffle than a walk. As I slough down the hall, I feel the others in the cells watching, envying me, but I don't look at them. I can't. I won't.

'What's happened to Winchell?' I ask Don when we stop at a steel door. He takes the keys from his belt to open it.

'You can probably ask him yourself in five minutes.' I follow after him again. We descend stairs and then climb another set, go through doors and stop. Don pulls back a slot in a forti-fied door and peers through an opening. He gives a signal and the door is opened from the inside by another guard. This man is fat and slatternly, his shirt untucked and with grease stains on it. He grins at me.

'Abandon hope!' he says cheerfully. I turn to say goodbye to Don but he's on the other side of the locked door and I'm in a room of madmen.

I look quickly around for Winchell, but as far as I can tell, he's not there. I am relieved. What could I say to him? He'll know how he's wronged me. And now that I've remembered Karl, I recall that life is a story and it is full of turning points. Something happens and you're shunted off in a new direction. There is no bad or good, there is only how well the story is told.

In *The Storehouse of Thought and Expression* – I'll ask

Georgina if she can get the book to me – I've read that whatever our circumstance, we have a choice as to whether to take the narrow, the broad, the short, the long or the deep view. The narrow view sees only one face of the cube. All inferences about the cube must be tentative. As I think this, I see the pages of the book in my mind, and find I can turn them at will. This is surprising – is it the 'other side' of my loss of memory?

In any case (the slovenly guard has returned to the papers on his desk near the door), as I make my way to a chair stationed against the wall, I tell myself that I must be careful not to make up my mind or take decisions, before examining the broad view. I must consider not only myself and my business, but the whole community and even the entire human race.

I look up. The unkempt attendant stands in front of me. 'Sorry to keep you waiting, Sandy, but I had to get our order finished.' He waves a sheaf of papers. 'You wouldn't believe how many needles and catheters we go through. And the wrist supports! Tsk, tsk!'

I don't say anything. I don't know what to say.

'Cat got your tongue, Sandy?' He peers at me closely. 'Word is you don't remember anything, that so?'

I've an opportunity, I remind myself, to collect material for my story – however it is going to turn out. To be on my best behaviour. To act human.

'So, special instructions for you, eh, Grey?' says the attendant. His breath stinks, his teeth are dirty. I don't turn my head away.

'Are there?'

'Oh yes!' He cackles.

'What are they?'

'Wouldn't you like to know!' I've given up on him, on obtaining help of any nature from him. I've already turned my thoughts in a different direction but then he says, 'We've a watching brief. See how you do.'

'You're watching for . . . ?'

'Signs!' he says and makes a quick and not unfriendly throat-cutting motion, and laughs heartily. He's a fountain of jollity, he is. He's a moron; but I've remembered what Georgina told me about my harming myself. Is this to what he refers? That I'm a suicide risk? Or they're not certain about me but are willing to give me a chance since my self-destructive behaviour was provoked by lies?

I could do with a broader view, but I only know what I know. Which isn't much. The short view highlights the aspect of a specific view: its disadvantage is that it says nothing about yesterday or tomorrow; its advantage is that it takes the emotional temperature of 'now'. 'To become despondent over a zero or too highly elated over a perfect mark are both bad results of the short view.' That is in *The Storehouse of Thought and Expression*, and I believe it to be true.

So. 'Well . . .' I say, taking the Ron Signet approach to tricky conversations.

'Well, well! Let's get you settled, shall we? We'll start by introducing you to your colleagues. On your feet, Sandy. We want you to feel at home.'

What a funny man! Settled, but on my feet. In an insane asylum but at home. I can't help but think he's been here too long himself!

He takes my arm. 'One of the finest rooms in the whole building,' he says. 'We've the most air, the most light!'

I look around. Now that my blinkers of fear are off, I see a large rectangular room painted green. Windows there are, indeed, but these are very high up and small in walls that must be fifteen feet high. In one corner, on a platform reached by steps, sits a second guard or attendant.

The scruffy overseer, noticing the direction of my gaze, says, 'Oh, don't mind him! He won't bother us.'

'What is your name?'

'What's that?'

'What should I call you?'

'Oh! Everybody calls me John.' He blinks his eyes coyly.

'Should I know you?' I say. 'Have I been here before?'

'Oh, no!' he says, and titters. 'This is your first time.'

By now we've reached the north end – judging by the slant of the morning light. Here are two rows of men, six in each, sitting as if in a bus station, slumped over and waiting, each with a wide cloth band around his waist to hold him to his chair. 'We won't get much out of these ones,' John says. 'They're still waking up.'

'Waking up?'

'They were up early' – he giggles – 'but then went back to sleep. I have to keep an eye on them. If there's any trouble, I'll give them glucose. Sometimes they stop breathing.'

I nod. But there isn't anything I particularly want to hear about insulin therapy. Pete Cooper used to frighten me with his accounts of it: those who scream in terror before reaching complete oblivion; those who never wake up. 'When will I be able to talk to them?'

'After lunch,' John says. 'Then we'll see.'

Now I hear what's been bothering me. The room's stillness. So many men, shadow figures against the wall, all quiet. The free limbs of several of the insulin patients jerk. 'They're all much better,' John says, 'some of them were such grumblers! You wouldn't believe! They kept such irregular hours!' He lowers his voice to a whisper. 'The awakening is quite dramatic – and they don't remember any of it! Then they doze away like babies . . .' He leads me away.

'Over here we have our Russians.' We're standing near a knot of crouching men who gaze straight ahead. I'm sure they're looking at something – what could it be? A lost landscape? Snow? The towers of St Petersburg? 'No one can understand them, but it seems they want to go home. Of course, they've no idea of the conditions there these days!'

'Why are they here?'

'Bank robbery!' John lowers his voice. 'That one' – he

points to a muscular, clean-shaven man in his thirties – 'asked to have his head cut off! Can you imagine! He said it would be more merciful than his sentence here!' John's merry laugh rings out. In the silence immediately following I hear the Russian say, quite clearly, in English, 'My wife!'

'But now, Sandy, at last here we are.' He's been dragging me with him. I'm aware of the awareness of our progress through the room – it's a ripple in a big pond; the big fish are waking up. I can see them – the big fish – at the south end and I know that my guide has been saving them until last. They lift their heavy heads – they're like bulls more than fish – and their red eyes are turned on me.

But first, John stops at a 'room-grouping': a sofa and armchairs, a coffee table. A cluster of hunched-over men. On the table is a small tea urn and cups. 'Elevenses, boys?' he says to the gathering. 'I've brought you a friend.' He bends over the urn and opens the spigot. A reddish liquid dribbles into a cup. 'There you are, Sandy, drink up!'

There's a knock at the door – 'Oh, no, not again, just when I'm in the middle of . . .'

John dashes off and I'm left standing holding the luke-warm cup. What goes on within this silence? Sleeping? Suffering? I raise the cup to my lips.

'Don't drink it, Sandy, it's laced with saltpetre!'

One of the hunchbacks has moved – it's Karl! Not Karl quite as I used to know him, but neither is he the terrible figure of my dream.

'Jesus, Karl, you're all right!' The head is shaved revealing scars from his Pete Cooper-smashed skull; the hair on it is white instead of blond, his skin is the colour of old curtains, and the muscles of his eyes twitch, but it's him! Him!

'Be quiet, Sandy,' he says, but I've already noted the re-turning footsteps.

'Found a friend?' John says. 'I'd forgotten you already know some of the men. Karl, is it?' He moves close to Karl and

I'm aware of a prickle on the back of my neck. A quick glance round confirms that the guard above is watching us closely.

'I've ordered something special for you, Karl. Take a look.' John holds out one of the pages he's continued carrying. I look, although Karl doesn't. On the paper is a diagram of a black box. 'Can't be bothered? Too tired? Sandy will help you out, won't you?' He makes me read aloud: '*Electro Convulsant Therapy Unit featuring Glissando control: many psychiatrists feel that the prevention of even a single fracture makes the B-24 a good investment.*' John tucks it back in the pile.

'Karl's strong as an ox, isn't he! That German physique! It doesn't matter how much electricity you run through it! He's been so well-behaved, haven't you, Karl.' John reaches down, cups Karl's chin and gives it a little tweak. He addresses me: 'Most of them remember nothing, but our Karl – why he's a regular encyclopaedia – just listen to him.' He swivels his attention back to Karl: 'Karl, why don't you tell us all about – what was it the other day – opera? Ha ha!'

Now I've got it. I've deciphered Karl's cue. I must be quiet and low-key, draw John's attention as little as possible. He delights in cruelty. But as long as I behave, as long as I don't do anything . . . take the long view, which is to give myself enough time to see what things lead to . . . I can shape my course and make it mean something as a whole.

'Shall we move on?' John says.

We cross a small patch of sunlight on the linoleum floor. As I look up, a tiny paper airplane wings into view. It floats above me, then slowly, gently, settles to the floor. 'They're like children!' John says and steps on it. His crepe-soled shoe leaves a print, but I know, I know! I see myself with the wings that Karl and I built, soaring in the dark, cool air carrying me – and I remember that I flew – briefly, it's true; but I did fly. I did.

'What was done to me, John? What was my treatment?'

'Why, Sandy, what makes you think I know?' He bats his eyes at me. There's a gleam of malevolence.

'You're in charge, John. I'm sure you know everything.'

'Not everything, Sandy, no, not that.' He's flattered – good. He puffs out his cheeks and blows – *puh*. 'You were given a little of this, a little of that – you were very upset, dear boy.' He glances over his shoulder at the far end of the hall where the big fish-bulls wait. There's a glint in the bank of red eyes, and the sudden stink of faeces.

'Oh, my, not again. I thought we were finished with that.' I track his glance and discover one of the men down there in the deep shadows smearing shit on to the wall. His hands move as if he is writing. 'Come, Sandy,' John says and we go to him. John claps his hands and clears a path through the others who move slowly out of our way.

Now that I'm near, I see they're fat, most of them. Not bulls but cows.

The man in the corner takes his hands from the wall as John approaches. 'Why do you do this, Philip, why?'

'I have money,' the man says. 'What I do is my business.' He notices me. 'Thank you!' he says.

'Why do you thank me?'

'Thank you.' He tidies his clothing. 'Thank you.'

'The pail, Sandy, in the cupboard over there, go and get it.'

I go and return with cleaning supplies and begin to wash the wall. 'Thank you, thank you, thank you,' Philip continues.

'You're welcome,' I say. John is occupied at the intercom near the door.

'I was not born, I was put together at the age of two by the Natural Power,' Philip tells me. 'I was sewn together.'

'Yes.'

'I see Hitler,' Philip says. I follow the direction of his gaze. It's on John who is coming back to us, smiling, chatting with some of the men on his way.

'Yes.'

'Why is everyone so fat?' I ask Philip as I finish with the cloth and disinfectant. Nothing has been done about Philip's clothes, also heavily smeared with shit.

Philip lifts his fingers and makes a motion with them as if with scissors.

'Quite right,' John says from behind us. 'You had a close call yourself, Sandy. Snip, snip.' He too makes the scissors sign. 'All of them, every one' – he gestures to the lump of men, from whom I feel waves of antipathy – 'snip, snip, snip!'

'What's wrong with them, John?'

'Murderers, rapists, nancy boys.'

'Yes, but what's wrong!'

'It's not a punishment, Sandy, oh, no! It's for their own good!'

'What did they do to them?'

'Cut their balls off.'

It's more than this, but I'm afraid to ask. 'I want to see Dr Love.'

'Oh, I don't think Dr Love wants to be bothered just now.'

I gaze upwards. The guard on the platform watches over me. 'I want to see Dr Love!' I shout. And then, after a few minutes and rather to my surprise – I do.

'You're on trial here, Sandy,' he says to me. He's come bustling, energy shooting from him, into the room. 'You're fortunate I was in the building and got the call. I'm not usually.'

'I know, sir, and I'm grateful, I am, truly.'

'You have to show signs of normal socialisation if you're to have any hope . . .'

I swallow all I might say and thank God for the watching attendant who'd called in my request over John's objections.

'Please try to understand, Dr Love. I feel absolutely fine, but I'm remembering things and I have no context for them.'

'Ah,' he says.

'If you could let me see my treatment sheet, then I'd know.'

'Know what, Sandy?'

'What was real, what I'm imagining.'

'Are you imagining?'

'I don't believe so.'

'What do you remember?'

'Hot water. Cold water. Out of a hose. It pushed me back and forth in a room. I couldn't breathe.'

'Hydrotherapy,' he says.

'I'm an Egyptian mummy. I can't move. The cloth I'm wrapped in is wet. I'm sorry, sir, it makes no sense.'

'You were wrapped in wet sheets. You went into shock.'

'I'm in a room full of men in suits. No – there was a woman, too.'

'The Board.'

'The Board?'

His foot taps with impatience to be gone. 'Nothing came of it, it doesn't matter.'

'It matters to me. What I know I can put behind me. What I don't . . .'

'It was the Lobotomy Board. Fortunately for you, because of the intervention of Mrs Jones-Murray, Dr Frank, and me, we put an end to it.'

Lobotomy. Brain surgery. After which things are never the same again. The other shoe drops and I realise what I saw in the red-eyed men and what scared me. Nothing but the animal brain at work, nothing human. 'You spoke up for me?'

'As I said.'

'Who spoke against me, Dr Love?'

There is silence. He's considering how much to tell me. He says, 'Your parents. They want you home. They believe if you have a lobotomy, they can manage you.'

I find myself, in my mind, with my arms around the sea serpent I found so long ago. Her reptilian skin is cool and soothing, like the hand of a mother on the brow of a fevered child. She was a mother; she was giving birth.

Dr Love sighs. A deep sigh. 'There's a school of thought that says it's better to forget. Many of our treatments are based on it.'

'Not Dr Frank's.'

He gives me a sharp glance. 'No, not his.'

I want to ask, but am afraid to, what has happened to the West Wing director? Is he back in power? Is his regime safe? The fact that he was able to help stop the Lobotomy Board from harming me argues that he is not completely out of favour. I hope it's more than that, that he's in the ascendant. It's my turn to sigh.

'Look, Sandy. I'll see what I can do. It's a matter of time. Until then, just try to behave . . .'

'Normally?'

He smiles. 'Exactly.

The narrow view, the broad view, the short view, the deep view. Which is it to be if I'm to survive? I reject the narrow and the broad as being too dangerous. Only the deep view looks at the pattern that lies behind the obvious and has the potential to open any situation to its past and future.

If I examine everything that has happened to me, as far as I can remember it, I see that it is I, Sandy Grey, at this moment in time, who links what has happened to what may come. In such a way, I am the pattern. But of what especial quality does the pattern consist?

In a story, the main character finds a solution to his problems through his response to obstacles and delays and danger and struggle and waiting. Interruptions and distractions and indecision are also elements that impede his progress. This is the state of things in the middle section. Unbeknownst to him, tension is building; he heads towards a climax. His own especial quality will determine the outcome. I ask myself again, what is mine?

The answer, which I see at once, is nothing new, but it strikes me afresh. The quality of my pattern, the truth behind the details, the essence of my life, is my innocence. Both Dr Frank and Dr Love have told me as much and it is the aspect of myself that I believe Georgina values. In a world gone to ruin, where so many have given up, I, Sandy Grey, from the time I was an infant, am and continue to be innocent of all accusations against me. Slowly but surely others are coming to know this. The false accusations of Pete Cooper were not able to stand against it. Its strength directs the efforts of my friends: firstly, Karl, who gave me the tool of writing, with which I am able to work for my own *and* Alan Macaulay's salvation – the pen, truly, is mightier than the sword; secondly, Georgina, who has demonstrated unbending faithfulness and loyalty; thirdly, Dr Frank, who despite his own difficulties has fought for me against the prejudices of his profession; fourthly, Bob, who accepted my help and thus became free and along with poor Tom – an emblem of innocence also – gave me the opportunity to demonstrate my better human qualities; fifthly, Ron Signet and Kosho, supporters who have surely surprised themselves with what they have risked for me; and sixthly, Dr Love – so aptly named – who has pulled the burning brand of my breakdown out of the fire.

They are the engine of my life and direct the plot within its overall pattern towards an inevitable triumph. There is no other way to look at it! QED!

The Storehouse of Thought and Expression says, 'If each human being is a nerve centre in the body of human kind, which are the more important centres? Those that respond only when they are touched directly, or those that respond no matter where the great body is touched?'

My friends are the important centres! They respond to the nuances of the great body of mankind, just as I, as a member of a fellow species on earth, responded to the plight of the sea serpent in her hour of need.

I'm pleased with my thinking. It has reaffirmed what I knew from the beginning (and now can remember). As Sandy Grey goes, so goes the universe. Not that I'm puffed up with pride – it isn't that, it's not a matter of my own importance, but of equality, fraternity, liberty. The pillars of civilisation. At this moment in history, in this place, I'm a weathervane. Watch me, watch the world.

In the afternoon John takes me to see Winchell. He is in a room on his own. John does not tell me so, but I believe he has been ordered by Dr Love to arrange the meeting. Perhaps it is a test of my equilibrium? Winchell sits on a cot coughing blood into a handkerchief.

'Fuck you, Sandy,' he says.

'I'll just leave you two lovebirds,' John says.

'Fuck you, too,' Winchell says.

John closes the door and we're alone, although I'm sure that he, or someone like him, is listening.

'I've got TB, you bastard,' Winchell says. 'They've had the Spanish Civil War Veterans Association to see me. Half of us have got it. But what the fuck can they do?'

'If you're ill, they'll have to let you out.'

'You're a kidder, Sandy. That's what I like about you.' He gazes at the blood spots on the linen, red on white. 'You know I wouldn't have done it if I thought there was another way, Sandy. Cooper fucking lied to me. He said you'd written a letter about me, about the laundry strike; you'd exposed us.'

'I didn't do that.'

'Yeah, I know that now, but somebody must have. You know what they did to those poor bastards? Put them on a slow boat to China. Can you imagine that, these days? If the Japs didn't sink them, they'll have been shot on landing. There's no safe haven for crazies, Sandy. He said I was next, they'd ship me back to Spain – and guess what, we didn't win that one. One look at me and I'd join thousands in the *barrancos*.'

'The what?'

'Fucking ditches.' He raises the cloth to his mouth and spits. 'But if I did this one thing, told a little white lie about you, he'd get me out. Said the CCF would look after me. He knew a man, a socialist member of the legislature, who's always here, poking his nose in, said he'd speak to him . . .'

'You believed him?'

'I'd heard of this guy he talked about, he got the heat turned on and lights for the cells.'

'I'm truly grateful.'

Winchell finally meets my eyes. 'Yeah, I believed him. I'm an asshole.'

'I understand. It's all right.'

'You know I never had a real job? Just harvesting, and then the war. You know the only thing I ever read?'

'Karl Marx?'

'You're a kidder all right. You ever read him?' I shake my head. 'Don't bother. Stick to the comics like I do.'

He thwacks himself on the chest and spits up again. When he's done he says, 'Why'd they bring you to see me?'

'They're going to let me go.'

'They won't do that, Sandy. Oh, no, no no. Once in, never out. Like they said of the Bishop and the nun . . .'

'I've been promised.'

'Yeah. Talk to me about promises.'

'I'm innocent as charged. They'll have to let me go.'

'You poor sap,' he says. This time there's a flood of blood. The handkerchief is soaked.

'I don't want to be a poor sap.'

'I know, you told me once,' he says, when he can speak. 'It doesn't make any difference.'

We sit quietly in his room. There's a kind of hum in the walls. I point it out and he nods.

'They do that to you?' he asks.

'What?'

He goes, '*Bzzztt bzzztt*. You know, that machine.'

'I don't know.'

He shakes his head sadly. 'Who'd have thought it, that it would come to this. We didn't know when we had it good.'

'What will happen to you?' I ask him.

'Me? I'm going before the Board.'

'The Board?'

'You know.

'The Lobotomy Board? Why you?'

'About that brain surgery – they say you don't feel anything afterwards. Maybe that'd be better, eh? What do you think?'

'I don't know.'

'Christ's balls, Sandy, you do know. You've seen them. They're fucking Frankenstein's monsters. Maybe I'll be one of them.' He stands, sticks his hands in his mouth and pulls back his lips, bulges his eyes, walks stiffly about the room.

'No, Winchell. They won't do it. There's nothing wrong with you.'

'I organised the laundrymen. I'm a Communist. They'll never forgive me. You have no fucking idea.' He starts to laugh. 'You should have seen it, Sandy, we barricaded the doors with laundry tubs, we threatened them with hot water.'

'Did you raise the red flag? Was it your flag hanging out the window?'

'Eh? Somebody did that? Well, I'll be . . .' He is pleased, almost happy. 'There's hope for us yet, Sandy.' A thought crosses his mind. I can see it arrive and linger in the way he shifts his eyes away from mine. The thought – whatever it is – makes him uncomfortable.

'You already said you're sorry, I forgive you. You can say whatever you want.'

'Fuck it, Sandy. I was wondering . . . they said you tried to hurt yourself.'

'So I understand.'

'Well, did you, you know . . .'

'Did I what?'

'Do it, cut your prick off?'

It's nighttime and I'm in a room by myself. I have no proper sheets and not even a blanket this time, only a canvas cover and no window to look out of. Compared to how I started off in the West Wing, it's a major comedown, but compared to the possibilities in the East Wing, it's not bad. At least it is quiet and I can think. In this privacy I can do what I want, which is to examine myself as carefully as possible. There are scars low on my belly, and the marks of stitches on my penis. I don't remember doing it: I remember right up until that point, then nothing.

Does that mean I'm insane after all?

The Bible says, if thy hand offends thee, cut it off. I don't believe the Bible. It's just that it's been sown – planted – in my mind by my parents. I reap what they sowed.

So. Ha ha! So, then. This indeed requires the deep view (the narrow one's a bitch), the one that sees pattern and its relation.

As I think it through, I am able to summon the events: Bob's escape. The lack of reply to my letter about Pete Cooper. My truth-serum session with Dr Frank. The breakdown of order in the institution. My flight from the top of the battlements. My crash. The massacre of the innocents in the rabbitry. Pete Cooper's lie about Kosho. The telegram announcing the death of Georgina's son, Brentwood.

What I did might have been crazy – self-inflicted harm is that, of course, since it is an act contrary to the individual's normal self-interest – but it was logical. What other out did I have?

But why, Sandy Grey, if you're to be honest you must ask yourself, did it take the form of attempted self-emasculation?

Because what was done to me by others I do to myself. Simple, isn't it? There, in a nutshell, is the answer to the problems of the world. Christ said, Do unto others as you would *have them* do unto you. It may be subtle, but it's an important difference.

In a story, once the pattern becomes evident, there's a reversal that marks revelation for the protagonist: the events of the story are seen, suddenly, from a new perspective; they are turned inside out, or there is the arrival of a new character who brings the required revelation; that is, the story interrogates itself. It puts an end to the clutter and tyranny of words and emotion with their endless clatter clatter clatter and reaches for fundamental oneness, beauty, resolution of conflict in perfect chords. This is my reversal.

What exists within my terrible attempt to castrate myself? What lies within the bonds of cause and effect that link my father and me? What is Sandy Grey's answer to his self-hatred?

The answer is love.

It has been a busy day and I'm tired, but I'm not so fatigued that I cannot will myself back in time to a bed in which I lay with the little girl who loved me, and whom I loved, and to whom I pledged my heart and soul in all its innocence. A promise that I've kept. For I have never lost the innocence or the love: they were stored within me, seeds to ensure my survival against all odds, which now that I have found them again, I will nurture.

How? By finding her.

FOURTEEN
1 April and following, 1942

I t's nighttime in the East Wing. I'm back in the cells, this time on the top tier. No one tells me why I've been moved. From up here, the sum of individual existence in the bottom two tiers makes a hum, as if I lived on top of bees. Deep at night, when I lie awake, the hum breaks into episodes of coughs and cries, and I think of a jungle more than a hive. Or of caged animals. I try to pick out from this who I am. The metaphor matters in my search for unity and harmony among my ideas and thoughts. I must keep order in my mental chambers. Bees, I think. Honey and pattern and sweetness.

In the daytime, in the Great Hall where no one dares to talk because those who protest their treatment disappear (I've not seen hide nor hair of Winchell since our meeting; what has happened to him? how did it go with the Board?) . . . in the daytime, I draw the cloak of silence around me and do my best to forget. I'm done with remembering, as here, in these circumstances, it is an evil and not a blessing.

I make myself as useful as I can to John. I wash walls and floors; I carry lunch trays.

When I can, I whisper words of hope and encouragement to Karl. But each time he returns from a session of electrotherapy, there is less of him. He's a candle guttering out. What could save him now? Even a German victory might not be enough, for the Nazis, as he has told me, have no tolerance for the imperfect. One look at us and they'd put us up against a wall and shoot us.

In the daytime – I'm a dead man if John catches me – I collect the names, addresses and stories of the Russians. When I get out I will contact their families and tell them what has happened. The same goes for Karl's family. After the war I will visit Germany and tell them about Karl's writing, and *The Romance of Stanley Park*. I'll take them a copy – it will be my own work, but it will contain an essence of Karl, because Karl is my teacher and mentor. While I and *The Romance of Stanley Park* exist, so does he.

In the daytime, I do what I can: I look to the future.

Georgina visits me when she can free herself from her obligations to her father. She tells me that Singapore and Rangoon have fallen and there are fears of a Japanese invasion here, on the coast. She says that all the Canadian Japs have been moved inland.

'Why?'

'In case they are spies.'

'Any of us could be spies.'

She puffs out her cheeks and gives a small, dismissive blow. 'Not me, not you, not the admiral, Sandy!'

'What about Kosho? What's happened to him?'

'I said I'd look after him.'

'Where is he?'

For answer, she recites the poem 'The Lake Isle of Innisfree' by W. B. Yeats. I join her for the final two verses. I'm puzzled, but all she'll say is, 'The walls have ears, Sandy.'

I resolve to think about the poem later on. For now I put my fingers to my lips, 'Mum's the word, Georgina.'

When the air-raid siren sounds, Georgina leaves. We, in the cells, don't go anywhere. They say that only a direct hit would affect us. They say. They say. Like all the alerts so far, it is a false alarm.

In the daytime, when I am in the Great Hall and I'm thinking about the future and not the past, I pass on what Georgina has told me. To Karl I say that the Germans have called off their assault on Moscow: soon they will be able to return home. To the Russians I say their army is fighting back, regaining lost territory. They are brave, and although in difficulties at the moment, we are bound to come to their aid by opening a western front. In the silence that I then draw around myself, I try not to think about how I might have been able to help win the war by bombing Germans or taking part in patrols that search for submarines, or even by scanning the skies for enemy airplanes. When doors close, Sandy, I tell myself – the cell door, the Great Hall door, the door of the truth serum room, door after door – another door opens. I am looking for that door.

But at nighttime like this, the small world I have contracts further into the sighs of the others, and the voices of the dead and those worse off than dead. It narrows into a tunnel to the past. In the tunnel I find poor Tom. Karl whispered to me, weeks ago, when he could still talk, that Tom was gone. 'Gone?' I'd whispered back. Karl pressed his index fingers to his temples, by which I knew they'd done the brain thing to him. John has told me how it's done. They drill holes in either side of the head, insert a tube to make a path for the knife, introduce the knife and swing its blade in arcs. 'It goes through just like soft butter,' John said. I close the door on Tom.

Next in the tunnel I find Misha. After arriving in New York from Russia, he travelled to Prince Rupert to work on the railroad. One night he was drinking heavily and with several others of his countrymen robbed a bank of a thousand dollars. He was shot in the back, arrested and sentenced. While in jail, in his natural despair, he tried to cut his throat. He has been here ever since. Misha says that sometimes his bed is burning. Why not? Is he not in hell? He is married with three children. He has never attended school.

But, but, but! The tunnel itself has a door, and so I shut it firmly, and try, as I do every night, to clear my mind of all but sanity, health, sociability, cheerfulness and tolerance. Dr Love has told me that soon, within days, I will go before the Board. That I am not guilty of the crime that brought me here to the East Wing matters somewhat, but only to the extent the Board allows. What counts is the here and now. Sandy Grey, his state of mind.

I do my exercises: sit-ups, squat jumps, push-ups, jumping jacks until I'm sweating. After this, I splash my face and torso with cold water from the metal bowl of water I'm allowed. Although I have no soap I'm clean enough, my circulation sings, my skin stings pleasantly.

Then I choose with what I will occupy my thoughts when I lie down to sleep. I have made it my resolve to be emotionally integrated, never to think a painful thought without balancing it with one that brings pleasure.Georgina says she sees a positive change in me. I have a better outlook. Dr Love says the same thing.

I lie on my cot in my cell and listen to the guard walk up and down. *The Storehouse of Thought and Expression*, which Georgina has retrieved for me, recommends relaxation as a means to gaining self-control. Mastery of the ego is essential in life as in writing. Such mastery requires integration of mental, emotional and physical health, adjusting to others, acquiring ideas and expressing them. I tense each muscle and let it go. 'When do the best ideas come?' *The Storehouse* asks.

In the twilight between waking and sleeping, in the truce between conflict. Plant and animal life are locked in the pitiless struggle for survival, but there are gardens, there is cake as well as bread.

I sink into spaciousness, the bounds of my body loosen, my mind is free. I recall the lines of the poem 'The Lake Isle of Innisfree': *I will arise and go now, and go to Innisfree, / And a small cabin build there, of clay and wattles made*. As I do, a vision of the marsh and pond area behind the institution comes to me. I imagine Kosho cutting bamboo canes and packing them with mud from the pond bottom and constructing a hut; but of course that won't do. He'd be caught. But where else could he be, *in the bee-loud glade* and with *lake water lapping with low sounds by the shore*? – for surely that's what Georgina meant? My vision expands until it is as wide as when I flew from the top of the roof: there's the rabbitry and other outbuildings and the farms spreading through bog and ridge and wood, networked by creeks and flooded flatland. At the edge of the expanse, the inlet shimmers and the ferry, *Brentwood*, cuts across its living back to the far side.

What else is there? Georgina's father's house, with its rear to limestone quarries, and out of sight and nearly out of mind, the labourers' cottages, long disused. Is that where she's hidden Kosho? It's not a perfect fit with the poem, and there remains the question of how he was spirited away . . .

I let the questions float off, and I'm in an airplane that dives and spins and climbs and soars to the heavens. Up there, in the unclouded sky, I remind myself of what is most important of all, what I hold in my breast like a nugget of gold – the truth of my love for Heather.

In this state of unity and harmony I sleep, and am restored.

'Sandy!'

I jerk awake, my heart pounding. I get to my feet and stumble to the bars of my cell just as the guard passes. 'Did you call me?'

'Call you? No, Sandy, go back to sleep.' He's a young guard, and new, but he's taken time to get to know me. He moves on.

Once more I settle down and pass through the stages I require to summon rest. It takes longer this time to disregard the snores and snuffles below. I curl myself around the idea of Heather.

'Sandy!'

I'm on my feet and at the bars again. There are no footsteps, but I can see, if I crane my neck towards the light, the young guard sitting quietly at a table, reading a magazine.

'Psst, Ed!'

He looks up, puts down the magazine and tiptoes my way.

'Having trouble sleeping tonight, Sandy?'

'Say, did you call me, Ed?'

He shakes his head. 'Having nightmares? Something bothering you, Sandy? Do you need anything?' He steps closer. 'You hearing things?'

I've put my foot in it and aroused his suspicions. 'No, not at all! It must have been a dream.'

'Well, sweet dreams, then.' He returns to the table, but instead of continuing with the magazine, he makes a note on the night sheet. This is worrying. The notation will go on my chart and will be there in black-and-white when I meet the Board.

I get back in bed and tuck myself in. It wasn't a dream. I've heard my name called, twice now, clear as a bell. Whose voice is it, if not the young guard's? I lie awake for some time, but at length I sleep again.

'Sandy!'

This time I don't move. It comes once more. 'Sandy!'

'I'm here,' I whisper into the darkness. 'Who are you? What do you want?'

There's a pause and in that pause the words I need come to my consciousness, just as they were said by the boy Samuel in the Old Testament when a voice spoke to him in the night. 'Speak, Lord, I am your servant.'

I feel a hesitation and then the voice replies, 'It's me, Alan Macaulay.'

'Macaulay!' A wave of relief washes over me: it's only Alan, and not the Lord!

'You made me a promise.' I sit up and crane my neck but I can't be sure where the voice is coming from. 'It would have been better not to start at all if you weren't going to finish.'

That's it. Not a syllable more in that rich Scots accent. Memories jibble and jabble – there's no more sleep for me. There's Pete Cooper showing me Alan Macaulay's grave; there's his assertion that Macaulay's ghost haunts the East Wing; his threat that I'd come to a similar bad end; there's all the work I'd done with the files to convince Dr Frank of the justice of Alan Macaulay's cause. How had I let it drop? Even worse, I'd left off with Macaulay accused of murder, weeping beside the corpse of the man he'd mistakenly shot. I'd abandoned him at the lowest ebb of his life. No wonder Macaulay has rent the veil to speak to me!

But there were reasons for leaving off, good ones, events beyond my control! Yes . . . but reason doesn't come into it, as I know well.

In the morning, as I'm squired to the hall, I watch for my chance. I'm not on my own any more, I'm not special enough for that: I'm in a long tail of men who are being dropped off at various points – at the treatment rooms where the psychiatrists and their students wait with instrument trays; at the visitors' room where 'loved ones' nervously greet the slack-faced, drool-lipped, fat-bodied or emaciated-to-bone, cardigan-wrongly-buttoned, socks-inside-out souls about to be released to their care (the fate my parents wished for me). I have not, thank God, so far seen anyone I recognise, and – which is not the same thing – I have not been recognised, thank God, by any one of these lost souls.

At the top of a flight of stairs I pretend to stumble and I crouch to fix my paper slippers.

Others pass by. I wait as long as I can – the rearmost attendant isn't far behind – then I see *her* as she passes the bottom of the stairs along the ground-floor hallway as I have seen her so many other mornings – it's the once-sunburned nurse on her way to the truth serum room.

'Nurse, please!' I cry out. 'It's Sandy Grey. I need pencil and paper. Please tell Dr Frank. I have to finish my work on Alan Macaulay!' That's all I get out before I'm scooped up from behind and shoved on my way.

Sometimes a subject means more to me than it means to anyone else, but I'm reasonably certain that the topic of Alan Macaulay is important to Dr Frank. He took a chance with me. He went out on a limb. If the message gets to him, he'll understand. I believe that the nurse has some sympathy for me: she has heard my story as it came from my mouth. How could she have been unmoved by it? She's a woman of feeling, not an automaton: she had grains of sand in her hair and on her clothing.

At 10 a.m., when the orderly wheels the tea urn into the hall and sets it and the cups on the table near the couch and chairs of Karl's grouping, I'm vindicated. The orderly hands me a blunt pencil and a notebook.

'What's this?' John asks sourly, hands on hips, shirt and belly slopping over his belt.

'Doctor's orders,' the orderly says. He winks at me when John's back is turned. No one likes John. I glance up at the observer on the platform: he winks at me too.

I sit on the couch next to Karl. He is dazed and speechless. I hold up the notebook. He bubbles saliva and nods excitedly, making the risk I took to obtain the writing materials worth it.

'What are you writing, Sandy?' John peers over my shoulder.

'Poetry, John. It's for you.' I write a few lines and show him:

> It is not only in the rose
> It is not only in the bird
> Not only in the rainbow
> That always something sings.

'Ooh, Sandy, who'd have guessed?' He preens.

All morning I scribble such nonsense and read the results aloud to John, being careful to use as little paper as I can. After a while he tires of watching me.

Part IV: The Trial

When I first stepped out of the police wagon and viewed the courthouse, I felt relief. It was a monument to British justice in pale dressed stone, two towers, an upper portico, and large arched windows and entrance: it was a building to inspire faith. I'd seen its like in Edinburgh with defendants and lawyers strolling solemnly in and out amongst the pillars of the porch and steps that fronted the high street. My friends and I, on a day trip from our village, had gawked at the men and women, guilty and innocent, going in and out. We'd talked of our glorious Scottish history and the long struggle for fairness before the law (and quarrels with the English) and congratulated ourselves that in our day the battle was over: we were confident of the principle of presumed innocence. I remember deciding that architects think long and hard about such buildings; and citizens think serious thoughts about paying for them; and that this was only right, since the result was that nothing in such a structure could be taken lightly. Now, here, in the New World, where the majority of buildings were higgledy-piggledy wooden ones and staggered brokenly along the muddy, rutted streets, a structure such as this, magisterial in design, and well set back, with room for the planting of a lawn, conveyed an inspiring message.

I knew that, although it looked bad for me at the outset, the killing of MacKenzie was an accident. I believed that my side, once presented to judge and jury, would prevail. How could it not? Did not judges and juries rule on the weight of truthful evidence and not on hearsay or perjured testimony?

I entered the courtroom with my head held high.

As soon as I could, over the next few days, I wrote to my mother and asked her to break the news of my unfortunate arrest and incarceration to Peggy Moffat, but to tell Peggy to continue with preparations for our wedding. I wrote also to Peggy's brother Gordon, and to my friends George Falconer and William Watson and to the minister, the Reverend Duncan: to him it was most difficult to write as I felt, accident or not, that I'd let him down. It is a terrible thing to deprive a man of his life.

I would have written to my old dog, Dandy, if I'd thought I wouldn't look like a fool.

All in all, I marshalled my forces: I called upon the army of my friends and neighbours and family to put in a good word for me with the authorities; I didn't neglect to request their prayers.

I took courage not only from the edifice in which the proceedings went forward, but from the measured pace of the process. The judge, an Irishman named Flanagan, sat at a raised desk in the small courtroom given over to my trial, the jury of twelve men to his right, and twirled his thick black whiskers, and paid close attention to the evidence against me. From the prisoner's box, I kept my eye on my counsel, Batterbury. Although I could not speak directly to him there, he led me to believe, with his nods and winks, that all – eventually – would be well.

I looked forward, patiently, to the presentation of my case.

Night after night I waited in vain for Batterbury to come to my cell and discuss with me our strategy.

My first real inclination that the judge was biased against me came like this: the Crown counsel, Fitzgerald (another Irishman – I mean no offence, but you can guess what I think), asked to have admitted into evidence a pencil sketch, made by the cook, of our camp ground and the nearby beach. Cook, on his own admission, was no artist: he stated that the drawing was meant only to be an approximation. Nevertheless, over the objections of Batterbury, it was taken into evidence.

Then Batterbury neglected to correct several errors of date and time as they were given by witnesses – this despite my urgent signals to him to do so – and these were also entered into evidence. So it was that when Joe, my tent mate, was questioned, he reported on the fight with Kennedy that resulted in the burn to my arm as having taken place shortly before MacKenzie's death. This was followed by the Crown's assertion that I was a man with 'a chip on his shoulder' always 'spoiling for a fight' and that this behaviour had 'rapidly escalated'. Batterbury wiggled his eyebrows, conveying to me that time and date were insignificant, but I knew better: on such small matters can hinge life and death.

'It seems clear,' Judge Flanagan said to my counsel's mild objection at this description of my behaviour, 'that your client had a chip on his shoulder in general. Wasn't there also something about a dog?'

'Yes, your Honour,' Fitzgerald intervened, 'he claimed someone in camp had tried to poison the animal. We'll be leading evidence that the men believed Macaulay to have done this himself.'

Poor Nellie. I hadn't given her a thought since I'd been jailed. I hung my head – an action which the jury may have misconstrued.

The 'evidence', when it came, was from the liar Kennedy.

The other men were asked about my argument with MacKenzie. It sounded poor – I admit – although I hadn't said more than any one of them might have in the same circumstance. I'd called the man a 'bastard'. But I'd been let go because of my arm, and not from a question of character, and MacKenzie had said he'd have me back once the arm was healed. If Batterbury had put me on the stand, I could have said all that. In fact, the weakness in my arm should have been helpful to my cause, for how could I have aimed and intended to hit MacKenzie with such a handicap and at such a distance? Here's where Cook's sketch map proved fatal. As Fitzgerald put it: 'The distance from myself to your Honour, as you can see from this map, is not much less than that from the accused, Macaulay, on the beach to where MacKenzie stood on the road: Alan Macaulay could scarcely have missed.' His tone implied that even a fool with a gun could have done it.

Nobody said, because they weren't asked, that I'd spoken to MacKenzie about Kennedy's treatment of the horses, nor that it was Kennedy's invasion of my tent and property that had led to our fight; nor that it was Kennedy who had attempted to kill my dog. I had no chip on my shoulder, but I did have an enemy.

I explained all this to Batterbury in the few minutes he eventually gave me in the corridor.

When it was our turn and Frank testified as to my character, Batterbury only asked him what kind of a man I was. Frank said, 'A good one.' Frank was shy and he didn't like speaking in public, he needed to be pushed. But Batterbury didn't ask him how hard I worked, or how I saved my money, or about my work for the Royal Botanic or about the plans we'd made to start a business together. He only asked Frank what was the reason behind his loaning me his gun. Frank replied, 'He asked for it,' and Batterbury said, 'Why did he ask?' and Frank replied, 'To be a better shot.' It was left like that! I could hardly believe it! I knew Frank wanted to say more, to explain that I scarcely knew one end of a gun from the other, and that we had plans to go hunting, but Batterbury simply turned away and sat down. Why? It was after lunch – was he

drunk? Or was he a lazy bugger more concerned with
mending fences with the judge than looking out for
me?

I sent a note through the sheriff: 'Ask about my
competence with the weapon.' Batterbury got to his
feet to ask the judge's permission to do so, but Frank
had already stepped down and Fitzgerald interrupted
Batterbury's request to say it was well known that
Frank and I were friends and he didn't think that the
testimony of such a biased witness on such an important matter should be admitted.

I cried aloud, 'Ask the cook then!'

Fitzgerald rolled his eyes, fitted a pince-nez to
look at me, and opined that although he imagined
Cook to be a dab hand at pork and bannock, he
hardly expected him to be an expert in weaponry.
Indeed, he doubted the man 'could tell a cracked egg
from a crack shot'. Everyone in court, even the judge,
laughed.

So it went.

When it came to the actual killing not only the
cook's map told against me. There was the matter of
the two shots.

'My client claims he never fired the first shot,'
Batterbury said, and hooked his thumbs in his watch
pockets. Crown counsel snorted out, 'Claims!' and
was not reprimanded by the judge.

I could have told them about Kennedy being
there, I could have explained how he had time to run
away, once I'd taken the gun from him after the first
shot, and was then able to appear on the scene from
the far side of the camp where the others saw him.
Batterbury could have questioned the witnesses as
to Kennedy's whereabouts – which were utterly un-
accounted for – during the crucial moments. But
Kennedy, who'd lied through his teeth about me at
every turn, didn't have to account for himself at all. I
cried out to Batterbury the moment I realised that he

wasn't going to put me on the stand to refute the false-hoods: 'Ask him! Ask the bloody Fenian devil why he's lying!'

The judge's face blackened. Batterbury frowned. 'I apologise for the outburst, Your Honour,' he said.

'Gentlemen of the jury,' Judge Flanagan said, 'the accused is indicted for having committed murder.'

So began the last act of the charade in which I had placed my hopes. As he went on to lay out the definitions of murder and homicide and culpable and not culpable homicide, I cast my eyes over the spectators. Some of them I knew: they were my friends from the camp, or those I knew by sight, from town or the hotel where I sometimes drank. With a few, including Frank, I had discussed my future plans for business and marriage. Others were perfect strangers, a number of young women amongst them. Did they have nothing better to do? Why were they there if not to have a near view of my sufferings? Despite myself, I found myself searching for Peggy Moffat's red hair.

'Culpable homicide is murder, first, if the offender means to cause the death of the person killed; second, if the offender means to cause to the person killed any bodily injury and is reckless whether death ensues or not. If this case is one of murder, it is because the accused either meant to cause the death of MacKenzie or it is because the accused meant to cause to MacKenzie some bodily injury which he, the accused, knew was likely to cause death, and that he, the accused, was then reckless whether death ensued or not.'

It didn't take a genius to hear the presumption within the judge's words. What if, I wanted to shout, there was no intention at all? What if a man – MacKenzie – had simply been in the wrong place at the wrong time, had come running at the sound of Kennedy's shot at the sea creature, been in the line of fire as I pivoted to look at him and my useless hand had slipped?

'This case is very simple,' the judge said. 'There is no doubt that MacKenzie is dead; there is no doubt he is dead as the result of a bullet wound; and there is no doubt that the bullet was fired from a gun in the hands of the man in the box. He says so himself. That, gentlemen, is, *prima facie*, murder. It is necessary, of course, that a man should intend to kill another in order that he be found guilty of murder, but the only way that we can judge of the intentions of a man is by what he says or what he does. Therefore, if you believe that this man fired that gun at such a distance from MacKenzie that any man would have known that the reasonable consequences of so doing would be the killing of MacKenzie or the doing of grievous bodily harm to MacKenzie, the accused being reckless whether he killed him or not, then gentlemen, that is murder.'

I looked over at Cook who sat amongst the spectators grim-faced. He did not meet my eyes. There were half a dozen of them who could have raised the issue of the distance from the beach to where MacKenzie had fallen, but would they? Why would they, indeed, if they believed, due to Kennedy's perjury and Batterbury's inability to ask the right questions, that I had shot a man on purpose? They had liked MacKenzie, I had liked him: he was a good man.

I looked away from them and examined the wood panelling, the polished tables, the unyielding face of the Irish judge.

'So far as I can gather from the evidence,' he said, 'this was either murder or an accident, and if it were an accident the man ought to be acquitted. If the gun did accidentally go off without any intention whatever of killing MacKenzie, unless you find the accused was so reckless in handling the gun that he did not act like a reasonable man, and unnecessarily exposed people around him to danger, then you should acquit him. If you think he did not intend to kill MacKenzie but was handling that gun in a grossly negligent manner, and it accidentally went off, and killed the deceased, then in that view you could bring in a verdict of manslaughter.

'Now, what is the evidence? It is not incumbent on the Crown to prove motive. If that were so most of us could be killed, and there would be no after-result for the person who killed us, as motive is a very difficult thing to prove. There is, however, the question of the two shots, which strongly suggests intention. One shot could be accidental but that two are so strains credibility. What the Crown has to prove is that the dead man was killed by the person in this box, and also prove, in addition to that, that the accused man intended to kill the dead man, and the Crown proved that by bringing evidence before you what the man said and did, and as I say, you judge what a man intends to do by what he does and by what he says and the law says in addition to that, every man must be presumed to intend the reasonable consequences of his act.'

I turned my gaze on Kennedy, who sat at the back of the courtroom with his arms folded over his chest. A faint hope had sprung within me that now, with so much at stake, he would stand up and tell the truth. 'It was my fault, Your Honour: I fired the first shot, I was drunk. Macaulay wrested the gun away, MacKenzie shouted, Macaulay turned and the gun accidentally went off.' Was that too much to ask? Whatever happened to me, he would have to live with it. He was a Catholic, and Catholics believed in hell. Would he risk eternal damnation because of an unfounded dislike? Liam Kennedy raised his eyes to mine, and smirked.

'You were told what occurred in camp, the prior quarrel with another worker, the accusations concerning the dog, the threats to MacKenzie shortly before the killing with demonstration of ill feeling towards the dead man. You were told about the accused's possession of the gun and his own admitted use of it. You were told that the first man to come along after the killing spoke to the accused and asked him what happened. 'I've killed MacKenzie,' the accused said. He admits to this still.

'You have, therefore, gentlemen, if you believe the evidence of these men who have testified, indications as to Macaulay's motive. In addition to that you have the actions of the man himself. You have what happened. Not long after he threatened MacKenzie and the others had gone away to work, two shots were heard and that is what caused the death of MacKenzie.'

I lifted my face to the judge, willing him to look at me: mine was the face of innocence, how could he not see! Others had read my face before him: my mother who had nurtured me, who knew the depths of despair to which I had sunk and from which I had raised myself; the Reverend Duncan, who had seen in me not a sad man with a bad arm, but a person with abilities that could be put to good use in the New World; and Peggy Moffat, who had loved me. Did not that investiture of love count in the balance?

'The suggestion of the defence is it was an accident. The Crown has brought home to the accused the killing, and has brought such a quantity of evidence pointing to a motive. There is the onus on the defence to clear up in your minds the case which the Crown has made out against the accused. If it fails in doing that, then the Crown has fulfilled its duty.

'You are at perfect liberty to disregard anything I said about the facts. You must take the law from me.'

Quod erat demonstrandum. It was over. The fact that I was innocent had had no bearing on this trial. Innocence was not in question. The preservation of a single point of view was: that men, particularly Irishmen, who had lived in the community much longer than I had, did not lie under oath.

Frank murmured to me as I was taken out, 'Don't

worry, Alan, I'll take good care of Nellie.'

It took the jury less than an hour to return a verdict of Guilty of Murder. The judge pronounced sentence. I was to be kept in close confinement until I should be taken to the place of execution and there hanged by my neck until dead may God have mercy on my soul.

You will already be considering the irony of my position: that I, a man who had once tried hard to take his own life, should now be determined to fight for it: but so it was. I had been on the verge of making something of myself, of having a wife and family and making a contribution – one that might be remembered (either through my botanical work or through my business) – to society. I had come up the hard way, through poverty and shame and ill luck, to the brink of success, only to be brought down by the ill will of a single man – Kennedy – who probably couldn't have said, if you'd asked him, why he hated me.

The police cart waited in the dark and the pouring rain. I was manhandled from the courthouse, handcuffed and shackled; my limbs trembled and I had to be helped up into it. Batterbury stumbled after me, and grabbed my arm: 'I'm of the opinion,' he huffed, 'that the judge charged very strongly against you.'

We drove away, water splashed up from the horses' hooves, the road wound in a ribbon of pale gravel along the side of the mountain. Down below, the waters of the inlet surged and fell: in the distance were the few and scattered lights of houses. I thought of my own country with its several great cities and the empty hills and glens between them. I might have been driving into the north of it. I might have left behind, and had waiting for me, in Cramond, my mother and my friends and the Reverend Duncan and Peggy Moffat, all of whom might have been thinking

kindly of me. I might have been travelling into the
unknown some other time and in some other way. As
it was, there was no one on earth who cared for me at
that moment and who knew of my terrible fate.

At length, after hours of this rough and cold
travel, we arrived at the new jail in Victoria. We came
here, Sandy Grey, in the early morning hours as dawn
flowered over the woods and fields and lit the turrets
of the castellated redbrick prison.

I put down my pencil. It is late: dimming light slants
through the high windows of the hall giving barely enough illumination for me to read over what I've written. There's the
tinkle of cups beside me as the orderly gathers up the day's
accumulation of china and debris. John remains seated, sullenly,
at the table by the door, waiting for the escort to come and
relieve him of his charges.

'All done?' The orderly holds out his hand and I place into
it – with a prayer for its safekeeping and delivery – the notebook
and pencil. My personal hopes go with it, along with my dream
for Alan Macaulay's peace of mind.

'Justice,' Karl says to me, 'has to be seen to be done.' I blink
in surprise. Karl couldn't have spoken. He is slumped over, tied
with bandages to his chair. With his head shaven so as to make it
easier to attach electrodes to the skull, the striped uniform and
emaciated frame, he looks like a victim of Stalin or of the Nazis.

(I append the poem mentioned above for your enjoyment.)

The Lake Isle of Innisfree

I will arise and go now, and go to Innisfree,
And a small cabin build there, of clay and wattles made;
Nine bean rows will I have there, a hive for the honey bee,
And live alone in the bee-loud glade.
And I shall have some peace there, for peace comes
    dropping slow,

Dropping from the veils of the morning to where the
    cricket sings;
There midnight's all a glimmer, and noon a purple glow,
And evening full of the linnet's wings.

I will arise and go now, for always night and day
I hear lake water lapping with low sounds by the shore;
While I stand on the roadway, or on the pavements grey,
I hear it in the deep heart's core.

W. B. Yeats (1865–1939)

FIFTEEN
8 May and following, 1942

'Do you know why you're here, Sandy?'
I absorb the words of the man in the dark suit, but I'm thinking, *I'm in the West Wing!* It's a room new to me, on the second floor, with a view of spring green fields and of the corral where Ron Signet's little daughter liked to practise her riding. A corner of the rabbitry's tin roof reflects a ringing morning sunlight.

Dr Love, seated in the corner, clears his throat and I pull my gaze back to the real world. I point to the window. 'Yes, sir, sorry, sir, it's just been so long since I looked outside.' As one, the four bodies behind the long wooden table (they sit with their backs to the light) turn to examine the view. They swivel back, each equally grim-faced. Clearly, it's not spring for them!

'Would you answer the question please, Sandy,' the woman says. She wears a navy suit that's a little too tight for her. Her several chins disappear into the cream ruffles at the neck of a rayon blouse. She keeps steady eye contact. She's the spitting image of my old piano teacher.

'I'm here to see about my release, ma'am.' There's a squeak from Dr Love's chair. I make a quick emendation. 'That is, my release from the East Wing to the West Wing.'

'Why were you taken to the East Wing, Sandy?' My interlocutor, this time, is a thin gentleman in a pinstriped suit, balding and with wire-rimmed glasses. He looks, to my eye, a little scruffier than he should. A sea-spray of dandruff on the shoulders. A used handkerchief poking from his breast pocket. *He* won't hold my eyes. He stares down at the papers in front of him.

'I was accused of a crime I didn't commit.' He glances up with glittering ice eyes and I fear I may have misjudged. I regret the missed 'sir'. His nostrils flare with arrogance, his thin lips purse. He'll be the lawyer.

'What would that "crime" have been?' he says.

'The rabbits in the rabbitry were slaughtered. Sir. I was suspected of having done it.'

'You were suspected, why . . ?' He thinks he's pinned me; he leans back, ready for a litany of excuses. How many times must he have heard the jailhouse plea of innocence? But I remember the lessons I've learned from *The Storehouse*. When the narrative matters, stick to the facts. Don't elaborate.

'I have no idea, sir.'

'Do you know who did commit this act?'

'Only what I'm told, sir.'

'And, that would be . . .?'

'I was informed, by Mrs Jones-Murray, that it was another inmate.'

'Who is this lady?'

'Mrs Jones-Murray is a friend of mine. I believe it was she, along with Dr Frank, who launched the investigation . . . '

'Yes,' says a high voice from the end of the table – it's the man I'd been thinking of as 'the senator' – 'that's been taken care of. Can we move on?'

He shifts his heavy rump and adjusts his broad shoulders.

His noble large head, with its thick wings of white hair, is giving me its full attention. I attempt eye contact, then have to grip my stomach muscles to quench a laugh when he looks at me. The senator is wall-eyed!

There's a noise from the door behind me and someone slips in. No, two people, by the sound of the footsteps and the twin scrapes of chairs. I throw a glance their way as they take their places along the east wall. I have to steel myself not to react. It's Dr Frank and Pete Cooper. Dr Love coughs a warning.

'Sandy, I see you've taken on our *cause célèbre*.' The senator turns the pages of my Alan Macaulay notebook and riffles through the manuscript left behind when I was moved from the West Wing. There's a murmur along the table and they're all turning pages. I notice they're supplied with a typescript and carbons. A pang goes through me at the waste of the typist's labour: I would have liked first to have made my edits.

'Yes, sir. The case of Alan Macaulay. I decided to write it up.'

'Tell us about it, Sandy.' He leans back and eases his braces.

I give him a brief, succinct rundown. I emphasise that the project has kept my mind exercised and helped me to develop my writing skills. I finish with, 'Dr Frank was kind enough to allow me to examine some of the files.'

'There's more than files here,' the lawyer says, as if he's caught me in a lie. The ruffled throat woman looks interested.

'I'm a writer, sir. I am learning to write.'

'Then we're dealing with fiction?'

'Not when it comes to the actual facts. I made up none of them; I simply tried to fill in the missing coloration and to give a sense of what kind of person Alan Macaulay was.'

'You've done all this while you've been in the East Wing?' the woman says. A stupid question, since she should know the answer from what she's read, if she's read it.

'No, ma'am. Most of it was completed earlier. I've only written the last section here – that is, there.' She raises her eyebrows; turns left–right to the others, then leans back, as if to say, 'See!' Although I'm not sure what a 'see!' would indicate.

'Be more exact, if you please, Grey,' the lawyer says.

'Most recently, while I've been kept in the East Wing, I wrote about the trial and conviction of Alan Macaulay.'

'But you had no access to the files! How can you claim what you've written to be factual?'

The hearing is at a turning point and everyone knows it. Is Sandy Grey a lunatic liar or does he tell the truth? The four interrogators lean forward. Dr Love recrosses his legs. I smell tweed and soap and lace and lavender. I can feel the burning smirk on Pete Cooper's face and sense the sweat beading on the loose skin of Dr Frank's forehead.

'I didn't say I had access to the files. I said the material was factual. I had read the files before, in the West Wing. I remembered what was in them.' I can't say, mustn't, mustn't say, that I've had contact with Alan Macaulay directly.

'Is that so?' It's the first man, our chairman as I've been thinking of him, imprisoned in his expensive and poorly tailored suiting. 'How could you remember such detail? I've read the pages, they follow a series of arguments, they quote judge – what was it?' – he shuffles his carbons – 'Judge Flanagan verbatim.'

I say a quick prayer to Karl, and to golden Heather, and to Georgina and the admiral, and to the memory of Tom. Even to the merciless God of my parents. 'I have a photographic memory. Sir.'

'Really?' The lawyer is sceptical. He adjusts the wire-rimmed spectacles and makes a show of searching through my file. 'I see nothing here to indicate a photographic memory.'

'It hasn't come up, sir.'

'Hasn't come up?' He's just too polite to snort. Instead, he takes a handkerchief from his pocket and gives his bony nose a blow.

'Well, then,' the senator says, 'let's have a demonstration!'

They fall silent. There's a tug of wills going on. Are they going to make me show and tell or throw me out as a fantasist? The lawyer draws a breath. I have to act. I dart forward and take a page from the space in front of the woman. It's an index of names, birth dates, incidents and medical opinions with the heading, Eugenics Board. She must be a member of that, too. 'Give me a moment and I'll recite this back to you.'

I read. Swallows fling themselves past the windows. Skylarks begin to nest.

'All right.' I hand the paper back, and recite. I'm a phonograph, a camera, a parrot, a freak.

'That's enough, Sandy,' the lawyer says. 'I don't think any further purpose is served by having you . . . '

'The man's done what he said he could do!' the woman says. 'Honestly, Donald, let's give him that!'

'This isn't a circus, Mira.'

'Then don't you treat it as one!' They glare at each other: her bulging eyes to his gold rims. The chairman and senator sigh, and adjust clothing and pens.

I can't stop my trembling. I'm a blade of grass and they're the wind, or the reapers come.

To reason well and be sympathetic, so instructs *The Storehouse of Thought and Expression*, and I remember that it is all up to me. I have one chance, and one chance only, to send my story in a new direction.

'I'd like to tell you more about Alan Macaulay,' I say.

The chairman, to my surprise, folds his hands on the table and says, 'What would you like to tell us?'

I imagine myself dressed in a good suit with a watch-chain across the vest and a stiff collar circling my neck. My hands, in my pockets, hold back coat-tails. I stand with legs apart and slightly bent, my hair is neatly combed. I rock slightly on my well-polished shoes (begone paper slippers!). I'm wearing spectacles from years of reading and thinking and studying and arguing in front of juries. I begin.

'You have in front of you all that I can tell about how Alan Macaulay was sent to jail, but you have not heard about his attempts to have his conviction overturned.'

There's a general bustle of papers as they confirm what I've just said.

The lawyer says, 'You believe there are grounds on which this Alan Macaulay should have been pardoned?'

'Yes, sir. I do.'

'You're saying there was a grave miscarriage of justice?' It's not hard to behold the sneer that lurks within that argument-honed face. He wants me to overstate the case so that I show myself a fool, and he doesn't want to be met on equal terms on his own territory.

'I am saying, sir, that there were grounds, in my opinion, for remission. If you care to examine the dates involved' – more general shuffle of papers – 'you'll note that Macaulay was sentenced, jailed and executed all within three months. These days that would be considered . . .'

'Barbarous!' the woman says. With her flushed cheeks she appears much younger.

'Barbarous,' I agree. 'It goes without saying that we cannot turn back the clock . . .'

'I'll go along with that,' the lawyer murmurs under his breath. I stop, turn politely to him in case there is more. He gives me a sour go-ahead nod. 'As I was saying, there is no means of changing what happened, but it is still important, I believe, to clear Alan Macaulay's name, for the sake of his family.'

'You know them?' the senator says in a high, incredulous tone.

'An execution for murder leaves its stain on a family. It is not so very long ago as these things go, less than thirty years. Macaulay's mother may still be living. Almost certainly some of his brothers and friends are. Those who weren't killed in the last Great War, that is.'

Solemnity descends on us, and I have them in my palm, I

think – this Board used to forcing its will on whomever it likes. Although I'm already over my allotted time, no one glances at his watch. The vast army of the war dead march through our minds.

I lay it out for them: the petitions and letters and testimonials from Scotland; the request from the minister of justice to re-examine evidence; the slipshod nature of replies to this request; the further petitions signed by hundreds of citizens in Scotland and Canada begging that Alan not be hanged; the letter from the Scottish solicitor that so clearly put somebody's back up; the incontrovertible evidence of the dates – the rushed procedures – that shows that a determination was reached by the Governor General in Council before all the evidence was in; and the *pièce de résistance* – the urgent telegram from the well-known Presbyterian minister David Knox to his dear friend the Solicitor General, Arthur Meighen, pleading, 'There are extenuating circumstances!' All of it ignored in order that a man be cut down in his prime.

When I finish, there's quiet.

The chairman clears his throat. 'Yes, it does seem odd that nothing was done at the time.'

'May I take it then that the Board will take this matter under advisement?'

'Which matter?' the stickler lawyer says.

'To have the conviction quashed and Macaulay pardoned.'

'That's not why we're here,' Pete Cooper pipes up from the sidelines. And the spell is broken. Now they feel awkward at having listened to me, a purported madman, and of having had their hearts and minds changed. I hold my breath.

'I'm sure the Board doesn't want to waste any more of its time listening to this nonsense,' Cooper says. I smile to myself – he's gone too far. They'll remember his involvement with the rabbitry question. They turn, once more a unit, look down their noses, and prepare to put him in his place.

'We'll make up our own minds,' the woman says.

'This isn't a public gallery,' the chairman says.

'You're not on our speaker's list,' the lawyer says.

The senator contents himself with a 'harrumph.'

The woman addresses me. 'Mr Grey. You've been very persuasive. You've given us much to think about today. Our immediate question, though, is what to do with *you*!' Her smile softens any rebuke. 'It's my opinion, and I'll have to consult with my colleagues, that looking into the case of Alan Macaulay might do some good. If a wrong has been done, then let's right it. Where's the harm in it? The publicity might be advantageous. I congratulate you on thinking about someone other than yourself. But we must return to the matter now before us.

'Dr Frank?'

Dr Frank scrapes to his feet.

'Dr Frank,' she continues, 'you were Sandy Grey's primary physician when he came to us. What is your opinion now?'

'I'm still of the belief that this young man can be helped. We were on the road to completion of the investigation of the basis of his neurosis when there was the occurrence of this unfortunate incident.'

'Yes,' the chairman says. 'Let's not forget what brought him here in the first place: the unprovoked attack on his father.'

'Apparently unprovoked,' Dr Frank says mildly.

'You took a risk with this patient,' the lawyer says.

'A considered risk. My trust hasn't been misplaced.'

'He's obsessive and he . . .'

'He's completed a comprehensive case study, made himself useful, exactly as I'd asked him to. He demonstrates considerable intellectual and emotional acumen.'

'In your opinion,' the lawyer says.

'Well, I am the doctor,' Dr Frank says.

Now Dr Love's on his feet. He's noticed what the others haven't: I'm about done in. I won't be able to hold myself together much longer. 'Are we finished? I have another appointment,' he says. There's a general epidemic of watch-checking as

Dr Love gathers up his doctor's bag, overcoat, gloves, hat.

'Yes, I suppose so.' Our chairman gives a dismissal wave. 'You may go.'

'But you should watch that impulsive behaviour,' the lawyer, the blackguard, eager for the last word, says to me.

Dr Love has my elbow and the door shuts behind us. 'Steady, steady now, Sandy, just a little longer. You've done well.'

I'm back in my top-tier cell, resting on my cot. I've had lunch – chicken noodle soup and a bun and coffee – which has helped to settle me. I'm thinking over what Dr Love said on the way back: that I'd stood up to them and I'd demonstrated my reasoning abilities, my socialisation, my ability to withstand pressure. 'You've done what many of them couldn't,' he told me. 'They'd crumble, most of them, under such a mental assault. You don't belong here, it's evident.'

'Here?'

'In the East Wing, Sandy.' He touched my arm. 'We'll take one step at a time, shall we?'

'Dr Love?'

'Yes, Sandy?'

'Could I have paper and pencil again? I'd like to do some writing.'

One step. One step at a time. A voice isn't a voice until it is fully expressed, so instructs *The Storehouse*. Any notion can be divided into smaller parts or be shown to be part of a bigger one. This applies to both the concrete and abstract. It's only natural that Alan Macaulay wants one more crack at the subject of his life and death.

Och aye. Och aye. Och aye. It's like a tap dripping, this mournful Scottish voice. It's been at me full force ever since I met with the Board. Alan Macaulay wants me to fill in the blanks, to flesh out the bare bones that I presented to the Board on his behalf. *Not fair. Not fair*, the voice wails. I try to stop my ears against it. I grit my teeth and begin the hard work of

organising my thoughts. It's a relief when the young guard
delivers a notebook and pencil with my supper.

Part V: My Sad Life

I had never expected to find myself in such a
situation. In the dank, cold jail cell, which was the
last home I would know, I understood, as never
before, my choices. In the short time left to me, I
could attend to the needs of my soul, or I could fight.
There wasn't time enough for both.

I spent a day during which I revisited, in my
mind, and said goodbye to, all I held near and dear
in life. Goodbye to Peggy Moffat, love, marriage and
children. Farewell to a thriving furniture business in
the New World with my new friend, Frank. So long to
the prospects of an historical mention in the cata-
logues of botanical discoveries. Godspeed to old
friends who knew and trusted me without question.
Even if my hopes were to be realised and I were to be
pardoned, my life would never be the same. I'd be
launched – one way or the other – either into the
cosmos (or as the Reverend Duncan would have it, to
heaven or hell) or into another form of reinvention.
Cut off, through shame from my family . . . and tied to
my own loose ends.

With a clean slate, I dusted off my hands and set
to work.

Within three weeks, sworn affidavits witnessed
by the provost and two magistrates, solicited by
telegram, had arrived from my mother and brothers,
from three of my friends and from the family doctor. I
do not mean to be critical, but I believe they – each of
them – took the wrong tack, choosing to emphasise
that I had tried to kill myself with laudanum and that
afterwards I'd been a different man. My mother
referred to my 'frequent curious turns of mind';
William Watson to my being subsequently 'restless,

depressed in mind and in a dazed condition'; George Falconer wrote of my 'rambling and incoherent manner'.

What no one took the trouble to point out was that this had been an aberration! One that could, with little difficulty, be explained by my ruined arm and hand and the loss of my employment and self-respect as a man!

I wept when I read these documents – not out of anger, but from knowledge of the wasted effort that lay behind them: the meetings in the village hall, in the manse, or in the church itself where all agreed as to a strategy to follow and to which all directed their minds. Wrong! Wrong! If I'd been there, I would have asked them to ask *themselves* if any of *them* had ever considered suicide when they'd been young: for it's a truth I've often observed that the boundless enthusiasms of youth are perfectly matched by youth's boundless despair. It's only as we age and our dreams diminish that we understand life's intrinsic preciousness . . .

The minister of justice inquired as to whether or not I'd been examined as to my sanity, although it was evident that this would go nowhere. My conduct from the time of my arrest onward had shown explicitly that not only was I sane but I was willing to take responsibility, so far as it was mine, for the accident.

I wrote to the minister. I pointed out the errors in my trial, the failures of my counsel in calling evidence, the various erroneous statements admitted into the record and so on. I wrote, too, about Kennedy and his role in the affair and I asked for a pardon not only for my own sake but for my poor mother's.

My letter and the other affidavits from Scotland were placed before His Royal Highness the Governor General in Council.

Over two hundred and fifty men who had known me from Shawnigan, and the road gang work, and from the hotels and shops in the area sent a petition. I was moved by the kindness of those who had taken up pen in my cause. But here, again, what was meant to help, hindered. The petition stated they believed that I had 'committed the deed while temporarily insane'! The basis of the petition, thus, was not the fundamental miscarriage of justice, but my state of mind!

The Reverend Duncan wrote of my mother's heartbreak and of the fine Christian conduct of the rest of my family: this was no doubt helpfully meant (as was everything else), but – pardon a murderer on the basis of his family's church attendance! Duncan was too unworldly a man to do me much good.

It was then November. I was brought out every few days for exercise in the courtyard. I'd been kept apart from my fellow prisoners, but they knew who I was. One managed to show me where they would soon construct the gallows. When he did this, fear creased my bowels and I soiled myself. I had not thought of my execution as being near at hand.

I was led back inside and given a bucket of water to clean myself. It was Guy Fawkes' Night: I remembered how, as a boy, I'd collected rubbish for the bonfire; how we'd built the fire at the end of the village street; how when it was lit, it coloured the whitewashed walls of the houses, and threw an oily bright stain over the park and sea; and how its smoke and stink and fire obscured the church. We'd danced like pagans around it. On one of those nights, as a young man, I'd taken my first girl.

I spent that night in my cell enshrouded in the black weight of my sins. I suffered until I saw that no god could be so cruel as to punish the creature he'd created in this way. *Ergo cogito sum.* I think and *therefore I make* what I am. By morning, I was a non-believer.

My mother wrote: 'It will break my heart if the death penalty is carried out. As it is, I am beside myself with grief.'

I could read between the lines. She'd already been bereaved, she was only quibbling about time.

It was at this late date that Batterbury finally put in a word for me. As well as joining the chorus as to my 'peculiarity' and emphasising that I had once attempted suicide, he mentioned that 'the judge charged very strongly against the prisoner'. Hurrah! I thought when I read this. I read on. But he did not dispute the judge's charge or point out why and in what way the charge may have been mishandled. To my mind, Batterbury's letter exuded fear of upsetting the apple cart, although he may have wanted to do the right thing.

I imagined Batterbury, sleepless, picturing the letter's consequences. Of which there were none.

I lay awake anticipating the sequence of events that would take me to my death. What time of day would it come? How much warning would I be given? Would I feel the cold (it was set for January)? This mattered to me: I did not want to tremble in front of the witnesses. I did not want anyone to report that Alan Macaulay had died afraid. I began to plan my last words.

In late November a petition containing the names of over fifteen hundred citizens – nearly the entire adult male population of the borough – was sent to the government. Although the issue of my so-called insanity was now dropped, this petition appealed on the grounds of my family's 'respectability'! As if such niceties would have any bearing! Oh, the naivety of my stay-at-home countrymen.

I read the names and addresses on each page – I knew each one – and the signatories were not exclusively male. I looked for the name of Peggy Moffat, and I found it. The woman I'd hoped to marry had joined with the others to beg for my life. I felt my heart collapse with shame.

We had reached December. The days were short and the nights were long. When I went outside, and I paused to break the ice on a puddle of water with the toe of my boot, the other men came to me and slipped candy and chocolate into my pockets, as if I were a child in need of treats. War news dribbled in from the guards. Off the Falkland Islands, a British squadron under command of Rear Admiral Sturdee sank three German cruisers which had destroyed the *Good Hope* and *Monmouth* on 1 November. The escape from this battle of *Dresden* was on everyone's lips. All over the world, men were dying and suddenly the rumour went round that we would all be released to fight. Why keep healthy young men in jail when there was need for them elsewhere? If I was to die, why not in a trench? It made sense! My expectations recovered.

I was not informed that a letter had already gone out from the sheriff's office asking as to when to send for the executioner from Toronto.

So little time!

Night letters and telegrams clicked back and forth over the wires. The various provincial police officers involved in my case were asked to send 'all particulars possible . . . which might have a bearing on the case . . .' One replied that I drank, another that he 'could not add anything to the existing information'.

A letter arrived from the Scottish solicitor to whom my mother and family had turned in their desperation, castigating Canadian officials for their mishandling and carelessness in my case:

If the statements of Alan Macaulay are true, or if there is even a particle of truth in them, the matter should be fully investigated as no man can be condemned without a fair trial. I have to request therefore that you give very careful and serious consideration to the matter and order a retrial of the prisoner for the alleged crime.

Failing this, I trust you will exercise your prerogative, commute the sentence of death and substitute a term of imprisonment. I shall be glad to receive satisfactory intelligence from you for submission to the prisoner's mother and brothers who are anxiously awaiting the same.

Did he not perceive the insult? Nothing could have been better designed, with its dismissal of Canadian justice, and its assumption of superiority of judgement, to raise the hackles of the minister of justice. To turn stubbornness into intransigence. A final telegram was sent on my behalf in late December from the Presbyterian minister who had come to visit me in prison. As a personal friend of the Solicitor General, his plea was on the basis of common decency, that I appeared to him 'not to be a criminal'. Not even that cry, human to human, was enough.

On the last day of December letters and telegrams went out from His Royal Highness the Governor General that, in my case, the law was to be allowed to take its course.

I awoke, that first day of a new year, to hear the carpenters in the yard hard at work on the scaffold. I prayed, in my fear, to the God in whom I no longer believed. I waited for a last-minute commutation of my sentence.

(I, Sandy Grey, come up for air. How far must I, as writer and recorder for Alan Macaulay, go? He's finished, isn't he? Must I follow him even unto death? I search the pages of *The Storehouse of Thought and Expression* for guidance and find nothing but such truisms as 'Men are not moved by the prospect of remote rewards' and 'Children prefer stories which end happily.' More Scottish *grrroans*, with rolled *r*'s from Alan Macaulay.)

The evening before the day of my death, the jailer brought me a large package. It was wrapped in oiled paper, tied with string and the knots sealed with wax. I recognised the knots as my mother's work. I undid the wrapping, careful not to break the string, but to wind it into a small ball and place it in my pocket; neither did I tear the paper, but folded it into a neat square and placed it inside the Bible I'd been given as my only reading material.

The package contained an overcoat. I shook it out. It was made of the heaviest cloth and lined with sheep's wool. The close and careful stitches were in my mother's hand. How many hours had it taken her to make it? I put it on, and my body, for the first time in months, for the first time since the accidental death of MacKenzie, was warm. I huddled in my coat and leaned my back against the wall: I did not sleep. No one came to visit, not even Frank, although he'd sent a letter to say how sorry he was about how things had turned out. I'd raised the note to my nose and thought I'd caught a faint whiff there of the dog, Nellie, still in Frank's care.

What had my life come down to? Many coloured memories, an affectionate recollection of a dog, and a warm coat.

I felt in the pockets, but they were empty.

To say I wept all night would be wrong: I spent most of my time imagining the wheel of the stars across the sky as I had seen it from the deck of a ship. I felt, for a time, that I'd found a place amongst them: something to aim for.

At seven o'clock in the morning, the jailer brought tea and porridge with cream. The cells all around lay quiet. Not a mouse squeaked. When I was taken out, just before eight o'clock, I saw that a black flag flew from the flagpole. Seven men, in good dark suits, but none with so fine an overcoat as mine, stood ranged at the foot of the gallows. The hangman bound

a belt over my arms behind my back and led me up
the steps. At the top, he instructed me to kneel on the
trap.

I had no thoughts at all, Sandy Grey, none at all.
The neat and intricate spiralling that bound me to my
body had already unravelled. I felt nothing when the
rope was placed around my neck and adjusted to fit,
but the texture of the rope. Texture! Fine fibres of
hemp, hand-picked by sailors; a texture reminiscent
of grass on the *machair* where it falls smoothly to the
sea; my skin prickled alive by wind and salt.

The hangman's blows on the bolt to release it
were a thunderclap. Only then did I try to cry out,
only then did I think, 'But there have been no last
words!'

'And so to silence,' says Alan Macaulay, utterly visible to
me now in the dim light of my cell, with his hands tucked inside
the sleeves of his overcoat. 'Now I'm done. You get me that
pardon and I'll leave you alone.'

'That wasn't our bargain.'

'What say?'

'Our bargain was for me to tell your story. I have no power
over the rest.'

He rubs his hand over his chin. 'That's so. But I'm not
happy about it, Sandy Grey.'

'I've done what I can.'

'Aye.'

'I'll ask.'

There's a deep sigh from the shadows that now occupy the
place where he sat. 'As for the hanging,' I say, 'the witnesses
reported that you never moved after the drop, they considered
your death a success.'

I tuck my cold feet back under my blanket, turn my back to
the bars and follow the dark.

SIXTEEN
24 May 1942

Each morning when I wake up, I feel like a baby – secure and content in my innocence. The Board has let me go. Not for good, of course, and they took some time to think about it, but I'm out of the East Wing at last. It's been a long haul, a hard road. But it's over. I sleep on an iron cot with a thin mattress, but no matter. I have a pillow and a warm blanket and I sleep well and dreamlessly. Most importantly, no one bothers me, not even Alan Macaulay! At night, in my room, one of four on the top floor of the newly acquired farmhouse, I tune my ear towards the main building – just in case – but he isn't there. No ghost. Nothing but the hum of the power line that now links the former dairy farm to the main building. On my first morning outside, after I'd been shown round the changes, I managed to slip away (I'm a trustee these days and have grounds privileges!) to the wooded hillock where Pete Cooper had told me Alan Macaulay was buried. There's nothing there, either, except for the firs and alders, a little taller than when I first saw them. Some animal has snuffled through the roots, but all sense of

Alan's presence is gone – wherever his bones may lie. May he rest in peace.

It took two weeks for the Board to make up its mind and for Dr Love to spring me, but spring me he did. Paul (the new guard), who was on top-tier cell rotation, brought me a suit of work clothes: heavy wool trousers, a flannel shirt and twill jacket (an attractive moss colour) and a sturdy pair of boots. 'What's this?' I said.

'You like outdoor work, don't you, Sandy?' Paul placed the items on the bed.

'I'm going back to the rabbitry?'

'Not the rabbitry, no. Haven't you heard?'

I'd heard that Burma had been lost, Australia attacked and the Americans had surrendered the Philippines, but nothing about the rabbitry or what was going to happen to me. I shook my head.

'Dr Frank's gone and bought the farm at the southwest corner.'

'The Speller farm?'

'That's it.'

'I'll be going there?'

'So they say.' Paul retreated to the other side of the bars.

'What about the rabbitry?'

He shrugged his shoulders. 'You'll have to ask Dr Frank.'

So I did, in the interview that followed, once I was dressed and ready to go.

'It's not in your best interests to return there,' he told me. 'We've decided to place you in as normal an environment as possible. Anyway, we're closing the rabbitry for the time being.'

I pondered that. I had loved the work, been proud of my abilities in small animal husbandry, had learned, I felt, to distance myself sufficiently that I was not overly sentimentally attached to the creatures (although my hands recalled the sensation of silky fur under my palms). My thoughts plunged on, however, to the scene in the rabbitry as I'd last viewed it.

'I can understand that,' I said.

'Good boy.' Dr Frank clapped me on the back. 'You'll have more freedom than you're used to, Sandy, I know you'll repay my trust in you.'

'Indeed, I will.'

We looked at each other, he and I, measuring. We'd both been through a lot. He'd recovered some of his health but not his weight. I'd gone to the edge of what I could endure.

'Sir?'

'Yes, Sandy?'

'What's next for us?'

He sighed, stood up with his back to me and peered out through the slats in the new venetian blinds in his office. 'We'll take up where we left off. We'll complete your treatment.'

'I know that, sir. I was wondering . . . your health?'

'Ah.' He faced me. 'Diabetes, Sandy. I've had to make adjustments.' He pointed at a tray on the sideboard. It contained a large bottle of dark blue liquid, a test tube, a metal measuring cup, a small Primus stove, a set of scales, a number of vials, and a box labelled FRAGILE: GLASS SYRINGES. A colour chart, ranging from blue through shades of orange, was tacked to the shelf above it. He gave me then a smile of utmost sweetness. 'A little discipline and all my problems are solved. I wish it were that simple for everyone.'

'I'm sorry, sir.'

'Nothing to be sorry about, Sandy.' He gazed at his desk and gave it a solid knock with his knuckles. 'I'll have to get a new one.'

When Dr Frank sat in the space that had been cut for his former bulk, he seemed childlike. A little lost. 'I'll be sorry to see the old desk go, sir,' I said. 'It served you well.' What I was really sorry about was the diminishment of his world. You could find it in the too-clean shelves and desk surface. The trophies and certificates had vanished. It was hardly like his office at all.

Once, he'd been larger than life; now he was an adjunct, an accessory. What was he doing here?

'You should know that I'm director on a temporary basis while the new director is needed elsewhere. For health reasons I'll be leaving as soon as possible, but we've a severe labour shortage because of the current crisis and I'll stay as long as I'm needed.'

I must have raised my eyebrows, for he went on to elaborate, 'We expect an attack by the Japs any day. Just about everyone has been called up to deal with the emergency.'

'I didn't know it was urgent.'

'No reason you should. You've had other things on your mind. It's a problem for the farm, though, Sandy. I'll be asking you, once you're settled in, to assist with all the farm projects.'

'I'll be glad to do it, sir.'

'You'll also run Deceased Property. We've moved that from the main building to the former Chinese quarters.' I recalled Winchell's comment about the Chinese being sent 'on a slow boat' to China. Had they had a choice as to whether to go or stay? Was it purely a function of their medical state?

'A lot of changes, sir.'

'You'll note, as well, once you're outdoors, the installation of anti-aircraft guns and searchlights on the roof.'

My consternation must have shown on my face – what about my turret room? How could I return to it now? I'd hoped to have another crack at building a glider. He mistook my expression for concern for my personal safety.

'You'll be safer, by far, living in the farmhouse where we've put you, than here, Sandy – and I doubt we're the Japs' first target, anyway.'

'We're on the flight path to the airport.'

He frowned, long creases gathering in the loose skin of his face. 'And what would you like me to do about it?' This was a testy Dr Frank, another change!

'I meant it as a statement of fact, sir. You'll recall my interest in aircraft.'

He made no response. His attention had shifted to that medical tray.

'I know you're busy, sir. I don't want to keep you, but can you let Mrs Jones-Murray know where I am?'

'Of course.'

'May I write to her?'

'You may have all the writing materials you require, Sandy. We'll consider it part of your treatment, just as before.'

'Yes, sir, thank you, sir, I realise I may write, but will the letters be private?'

He gave me a long steady look. 'You know the rules as well as I do, Sandy. If you're asking me will your letters be sent – yes, they will. If the question is, will they be censored, the answer should be obvious. All mail is censored, these days. Because of the war.'

Dr Frank prevaricating. Dr Frank not being straight.

I'm not entirely out of touch with those in the main building. Once the farm is ready and the other trustees and the overseer are installed, we'll cook for ourselves in our own kitchen. But for the moment, I sleep on my own in the farm-house and take my breakfast and dinner in the cafeteria. I make a lunch to carry with me. I'm pretty much on my own, in fact, while the barn and outbuildings are being renovated. My duties consist of sprucing up the farmhouse living quarters with a scrub brush and paint brush in the mornings, and in the after-noons, sorting through boxes of 'deceased property'.

Today, a particularly quiet day because it's both a Sunday and Queen Victoria's birthday, I take time for two sets of exer-cises. I face the sun through my open window, thank God for it and the clean, invigorating air, then set to using Indian clubs I've devised from old table legs I found in the basement. After break-fast, I sweep out my room and make my bed. Then I return to the basement and haul up a door and trestles to make a writing surface. I hand-sand the door until it's smooth, wipe it clean, place a kitchen chair in front of it, lay out my writing paper and pens and *The Storehouse of Thought and Expression* and sit down. I tack a postcard on to the windowsill. It came while I was in the East Wing; Dr Frank kept it for me. The message says only, 'Wish you were here!' The card is unsigned. The front features a soldier on a Harley-Davidson motorcycle. The caption is 'Save Gas, Oil and Rubber.' The rider peers over his shoulder at the viewer from under a peaked cap, and he bears a remarkable resemblance to Bob! My heart lifts, and at the same time I become aware of the sound of a motorcycle engine – it's not the first time I've heard this – as someone rides by on the road beyond the perimeter walls. The noise fades.

My window faces northwest from the eastern border of the farm. From there I can see the slope of the land towards Kosho's pond. What's beyond it, I don't know, but bearing in mind the clues given to me by Georgina in 'The Lake Isle of Innisfree', I know I must begin my search for Kosho there.

I return my thoughts to the project at hand. I make a number of beginnings, but none of them sticks. 'Beware,' cautions *The Storehouse of Thought and Expression*, 'of believing you'll get something for nothing.' Well, I'm not afraid of hard work. 'Have your main thought clearly in mind, express it as plainly as you can, emphasising it by repeating it in various ways, and be sure that it is logically developed.' There's the rub. My main thought isn't at all developed! If I'm to write *The Romance of Stanley Park* as it should be written – that is, as a partnership between me and Karl – I'll have to find whatever Karl and I have in common; and whatever that is, it certainly isn't logic! Indeed, I don't believe – despite what *The Storehouse* says in these chapters – that reason is the source of literature. All I know, all I *feel*, argues against it. Is Shakespeare reasonable? Are Lady Macbeth and Hamlet? Or, to bring the matter home, was it *reasonable* for Karl to set free the birds in the Stanley Park aviary?

It wasn't an act of madness; it had an inherent, sophisticated logic to it, but was it both rational and prudent? Likewise, was it *reasonable* for me to sacrifice my freedom for the sake of a primitive sea creature? Has it been a *reasonable* act for me to spend so much of my time on the case of Alan Macaulay? None of these acts was reasonable, but they were not without cause or purpose or justification.

Philip Sidney wrote, '"Fool," said my Muse to me, "look in thy heart and write." Guidance comes not from the mind and what "should be" but from the heart and "what is".' But what's in my heart is unfinished; and what's in Karl's is now dark – occluded (that word that so upset Winchell) – and likely to remain so forever.

I turn the page and *The Storehouse* leaps from Reason to Art. 'Art is a way of looking at Nature. But you must remember that your own mind is a part of nature. Your chief task is, thus, to discover yourself – let us say, by a walk on a May morning.' So here it is, the answer I need on this bright May morning as I turn my full attention from Alan Macaulay to Sandy Grey.

I put down my pen and run downstairs and outside. The sky is a seascape of blue and white – clouds roll and break on the far hills. Swallows fly and flip in arcs of silver. Sheep move and stop across the green and yellow grass, a workman in blue overalls crosses from the barn to the dairy. I've been in there: there's a milking machine and steriliser and cooler, separator and tubs. The barn has now been 'beefed up' with Beatty stalls and stanchions. There are hay storage and feed bins and a steel bull pen. The earth in the fields, where turned, shows rich and brown, all cleared and fenced and ready for a first crop of potatoes. From some such scene came the great pastoral symphonies; from the play of light on water, on grasses and spring flowers came the poems of the master artist (Yeats) himself. What infinitely complex rhythms, what atoms dancing, what waves and pulses of the great tides of life as they form and reform in innumerable patterns are here. 'What is it in Nature that has an intensely personal significance for you?' *The Storehouse* asks.

I walk, 'between the stars and the fishes' – that is, this morning, through the brilliant landscape of daylight, each step uncovering a pleasure: the long unmown grasses abuzz with insects, the skylark nests, the overgrown path, moister as it falls towards pond-bottom; and lilies and pink shooting stars, and camas. A hummingbird slips its minute long beak between the lips of an orchid. If I were not overlooked by the anti-aircraft battery on the roof (who knows who is up there?) I would fall to my knees and worship.

Wouldn't I?

It's darker down here. The reeds close in, and I find Kosho's stand of bamboo from which we constructed Bob's vaulting pole. I move near. Duck and swan footprints splay through the shore mud. I push through, rushes and reeds sharp against my skin. I can see where the bamboo was cut, the puckering of the split, but there's nothing else that speaks of Kosho. I thrust my way out of the thicket, slog through the shallows of yellow and green skunk cabbage to a sudden surge of upland. Behind me the asylum looks like a castle in a tale; ahead is thick wood; before me is a wall topped by barbed wire and glass, and strung above with electric wire. Not even Bob could have leapt clear here.

I gawp – a thin trail . . . a deer trail? – follows along the bottom of the wall and then just vanishes. I'm about to investigate when I hear, 'What in tarnation are you up to!' and it's Ron Signet, red in the face and sweating, looking madder than I've ever seen him as he emerges from the swamp below me. 'What the bloody hell, Sandy! You've got half the institution watching your antics. Where do you think you're going?'

I fix my position in my mind – the nearest trees, the face of the stone wall, the hint of a trail that appears to disappear under the wall – then batter my way back through the brambles at an angle. Ron shadows my progress, stumbling along below; he's swearing a blue streak. I jump down the last of the slope and land beside him. He wears a portable two-way field radio strapped to his chest. A set of headphones clings to his neck. 'Just a sec,' he says, 'I'm going to call you in.'

He puts on the headphones, turns a handle, twists dials and finally speaks into the mouthpiece.' Got him,' he says. 'Exercise stand down.' There's a blast of sound from the other end. 'That's what I bloody well said!' More squawks, then, 'Over and out.'

He tucks the parts back in the box, adjusts the straps and glares at me. 'Well, I've covered for you this time.' He stalks off.

'But Ron, I don't understand! I was just out for a walk . . .'

'Walk my eye!' He's stopped, lost his way in the reeds. I come up beside him.

'Really! I wanted some exercise, I . . . '

'Save it for someone who doesn't know you,' he says. 'You're just lucky it was me, out here. Haven't you any idea what's going on? There's a war, Sandy. We're on high alert. There are soldiers with field glasses manning those guns you see up there' – he points to the canvas-covered battery on the castle's roof – 'we're watching for saboteurs . . . and you decide to go for a stroll in the bushes!'

'I wasn't in the bushes.'

'All the way to the wall.' He eyes me up and down. 'I may not be the brightest penny in the lot, Sandy, and I know you've had some bad breaks, but God help you if you make a run for it now.'

'I wasn't!'

'You could get shot, Sandy! Nobody's playing at soldiers any more. It's the real thing! What were you doing, son' – he kicks at the bulrushes – 'looking for Moses?'

'In a way. There's a poem, 'The Lake Isle of Innisfree', by W. B. Yeats. I was walking and thinking about it and I saw this and I thought . . . '

'Just stow it, Sandy.' He takes a deep breath. The sky has paled; it's colder. 'We'd better get back for lunch. I don't want to see you out here again.'

'I've packed my lunch. It's at the farmhouse.'

'You'll eat with us today and you'll work in Deceased Property this afternoon.'

We start walking. Ron tests the radio a few more times. We pass the rabbitry, a boarded-up and slouching sad reminder of our former lives. I stop him there. 'Ron, what are you going to say about me?'

He smoothes the damp hair from his forehead. It has thinned and greyed. I should ask him about his daughter and the rest of his family. He's a person, with feelings, like me. His life can't have been easy, whatever his failings. 'I'll say you were working with me today. It was a misunderstanding, that's all.'

'Will they go for it?'

'Once, maybe. Not more than that, so you'd better watch it.'

After lunch (heavy with potatoes and cabbage) in the cafeteria, I ask Ron's permission to stroll through the gardens before going to work. 'Ten minutes, Sandy,' he says. I nod agreement and hit the paved paths. You can see, at once, in the lawns and flower beds that line them, the lack of Bob's thoughtful designs. Whereas Bob worked to a concept, the new gardeners, whoever they are, plant to a system: a clump of hydrangea here, a set of spring bulbs there, shrubs in regular stepped order, shortest to tallest. There's no flow, no heart to it. Bob's colourful insertion of vegetables among the flowers in order to maximise the efficacy of good soil and fertiliser, and without sacrificing beauty, has been abandoned. Instead great patches of herbaceous border have been stripped and turned over to kale and turnips – neither of which is doing well. Both turnip tops and kale shoots are yellow and mouldy. 'There's no need for ugliness,' Bob used to say, whether of gardens or of his beloved motorcycles; 'to achieve it takes hard work.' It's true. Beauty takes effort, but not nearly as much.

Pete Cooper appears from the farm borders (what was he doing there?), crosses the lawn, skirts the fountain, and takes the steps two at a time, heading for Dr Frank's office: I've not seen him since my meeting with the Board. A scant minute later he emerges at a run, rounds a corner of the institution and beats it in a beeline for the attendants' housing. Dr Frank steps out and down the stairs after him, but he pauses at the bottom, looks around without seeing me beneath the cypresses, seems to think better of something, and retreats.

These are puzzles, but they are not my puzzles.

Ron Signet materialises from the main entrance a few moments later, and also looks around. He sees me, however, and waves me away.

Deceased Property is housed, not as formerly in the lower regions of the main building, but in the disused Chinese quarters. Once this outbuilding was forbidden territory, and those who lived there and who worked the fields or in the laundry were scarcely glimpsed by the rest of us. We know why the Japanese have gone: they're a security threat, and have all been relocated inland. I know, because Winchell told me, that most of the Chinese were sent back to China, and some of them, those few who stayed, are now working on the Alaska Highway. I don't, however, know how they felt about it. Only Winchell spent any time with them and might be able to say.

The wooden building consists of a large open room outfitted with tables and a cook stove, and four smaller rooms lined with bunk beds. The windows are small and dirty and there is no electricity, so I light a lantern and candles by which to work. Three large boxes wait on one of the long tables for me to sort through them. Materials that clearly are to go to families of the dead have already been removed, so that what remains are articles that are unwanted or those that belong to men who have no next of kin. It's a sad business, in its way, but I feel that I'm doing a service as I place useful items in a box to go to the poor, and the rest in the garbage. A third category – the 'questionable'

– is where I place anything I'm unsure of: perhaps a book that could be of interest to an inmate, or a pocket watch, somehow overlooked, and too valuable to give away. The work requires discretion and trust: it is up to me to treat these remnants of a life with respect. Naturally, it comes to mind, as I make my distributions, to wonder what became of the belongings of Alan Macaulay – was he buried in the coat his mother made for him? Was he sent cold and naked to the grave? Had he no pen or watch-chain or comb? Were these items returned to his family? But I do my best to push such thoughts away. Some day, in some way, someone will do me a similar service, and I like to think that my care and calmness in this task now will be rewarded then.

Each box contains a sheet of paper that lists the name of the deceased and the box contents. Where little property is involved, the box may contain the belongings of several men.

There's Stephen Batt, who has left behind him a cufflink, a collar stud, a tie pin and a gold tooth. I place these items in a tackle box where I store jewellery to go to the Salvation Army.

With him is Gilbert Cruickshank who owned an alarm clock, a writing tablet, prayer book, pocket diary, steel mirror, razor, stick pin, a ring, a chequebook, a tobacco pouch filled with stale tobacco, a chemistry book and a book of poems. I add the ring and stick pin to the tackle box, place the razor and steel mirror in the poor box, and set aside the alarm clock in the questionable pile. I toss the chequebook and tobacco pouch into the garbage. I've left the books to one side. After some thought, I add the pocket diary and its jottings to the trash and the prayer book to the poor collection. The book of poems (by Emily Dickinson) and the chemistry book I place in 'questionable' with the intention of asking Dr Frank to place them in the library. The book of poems was a gift to Gilbert Cruickshank from his sister. I tear out the frontispiece that says so.

I work in a similar manner for some hours. Ron Signet comes to check on me several times, and the last time he brings me a cup of coffee. He watches as I make my decisions and says nothing until he's ready to go, then it's 'Hard work, eh, Sandy?' and gives me a pat on the shoulder.

The dirt-filtered light dims, the candles burn down. With one more box to go, and a heavy spirit – (that book of poems! the piano-tuning tools! and the rosaries, and more books than I could have ever imagined!) – I retreat to one of the other rooms. The candle I carry casts a pale glow on bare boards and plank beds. I lie down on a bed near the door. I'm tired. One of the last items I placed in the garbage was a writing pad of notes on constitutional law. The handwriting was neat, the arguments solid. What good was it? I hadn't closely examined any photographs or letters – these were automatic garbage – but somehow their images had stuck. Mothers, sisters, brothers, parents and sweethearts; locks of hair between pages. Words. Words. Words.

I close my eyes and sleep – not for long – I can tell by the candle it has only been minutes, but when I open them, my face inches from the wall, I view Chinese characters cut into the wood beside me. They are faintly done and visible only at this angle and in this uncertain light. I can't read them, of course, but they appear to me to be names. I get up and lift the candle: now that I know how and where to look, it's the same everywhere. The walls are alive with writing.

I flee back to the large room and open the door. Late sunlight slants from the direction of Kosho's pond – I think I catch a glimpse of water. I shrug away the cobwebs and colly-wobbles and return to my labours.

Box three: I lift the flaps with care. What else have I missed? What else is all around me that I haven't noticed? For one thing, a thumbnail sketch of the hammer and sickle on each flap underside. I examine them closely. Yes, so it is, the Soviet insignia in drawings in pencil.

The property of the late Leonard Clatt is in a valise containing a monumental catalogue and monument designs, and a bunch of keys and tax bills. I dispose of these as garbage.

Next down are the effects of Boris Godunov. I pause. I believe I know all the Russians but I'm not familiar with this man. Who is he? I pause again. The name belongs to a character in a Pushkin drama that has been made into an opera by Mussorgsky. Does this mean something? I move aside the packing materials and find an old billfold and glasses. Below this are items wrapped closely in paper and old clothes: two pocket knives, a set of awls, a pair of shears, a telescope and a case holding calipers and compass, and another case housing nine metal files. These are forbidden materials! My hands shaking, and with a quick glance at the door, I remove the last layer of packing and unwrap the heavy cloth bundle that remains. Two revolvers lie there gleaming. They're .45s. We used these for practice at the university cadet training. I was never good with them. I lift them out and place them beside the other objects on the floor. Then I put with them a box of ammunition that contains, when I count, seventy-four rounds. What a hoard!

I have two choices: keep them or give them up. If I give them up, the sender is bound to be discovered and I, myself, will fall under suspicion. Given the hammer and sickle drawings the sender may well be Winchell. Who else could it be? Who else would dare! But how had he placed them there? How would he know I'd be the one to find them? Indeed, how had he escaped the Lobotomy Board? Was he planning an insurrection? What should I do?

I think through the problem and quickly come to the conclusion that what I need is more time.

After dinner I play a brief game of chess with Ron Signet – it's movie night, and Ron has other duties. Ron, a little grim around the mouth, finally lets slip that Pete Cooper's son has been killed in an Atlantic convoy. He has no more details, but Pete, of course, is devastated and has been given time off work.

'I'm sorry to hear that, Ron,' I say. I am. 'The sins of the fathers should not be visited upon their children.'

Ron gives me a bleak look. 'Nor upon their friends,' he

says. He coughs. 'I didn't mean that, Sandy. I didn't know the boy, but that's what he was, a boy. I'm sorry for him, and all the others.' Somebody wheels in the projector and Ron gets to his feet. 'Well . . .' he says and slopes off to set up the reels.

I recall how that afternoon Pete Cooper had run as if the Devil were after him. As if he could outrun time and catch up with the son who had left him behind. I think, for once, about my own family, from whom I am estranged. Would they grieve if anything happened to me, or would they be relieved?

Back in my room, a large half-moon rising above the trees, I sit at my desk and look out the window. My feet rest upon the box that I've turned into a footstool and that contains Winchell's weaponry. That the weapons do belong to Winchell I'm now sure. I'd questioned Ron about where the boxes I worked with in Deceased Property came from. 'Why, from the mortuary, Sandy,' he'd said, his fingers hovering over his knight. 'I pick them up and bring them over. Your old friend Winchell works there.' He changes his mind and hovers over a bishop.

'How is Winchell, Ron?'

'Oh,' he says, the fingers back-pedalling to finger a pawn, 'as well as can be expected.'

'How well would that be?'

'You're still friends? Really? After what happened?' Ron advances the pawn and reluctantly lets it go.

'We had a talk. It's all right. He was sick . . .'

'He must be feeling better.'

'Yes, he must be if they've given him a job. What is his job, Ron?'

Ron begins to look as if he's thinking too closely about what I'm saying so I take his pawn.

'Shit, Sandy, whad'ya do that for?'

If Ron talks to Winchell like he talks to me, Winchell will know exactly where I am. He'll know, too, naturally, how much looser we are in the West Wing than the East Wing where he is. It's much less likely that a cache of arms would be discovered here than there. But where did the guns and other tools come from? I shuffle the box a few inches forward to make my feet more comfortable. I've padded it with straw and added stones in case anyone is interested enough to peer between the slats. Unless they actually open it up, that's all they'll see: straw and stones. I let my mind drift without thinking (as *The Storehouse* directs) of any particular direction at all. There's 'Bob' on the motorbike postcard directly in front of me. There's the message on the back, 'Wish you were here!' and the frequent thrum of a Harley engine in the background of our daily lives.

That's it! The guns must be from Bob! Repaying a debt! Exactly how Bob passed them to Winchell I don't know yet, nor how Winchell has got word out to him – unless, somehow, through his Communist colleagues? Maybe even through the red politician he spoke of, who isn't, perhaps, quite as useless as Winchell made out?

It all fits, but is it correct? No matter. For whatever it is, I have the hard evidence.

I try, once again, to make a start on *The Romance of Stanley Park* but I'm too stirred up. Plots, characters, feelings, worries, consequences swirl but won't sort. I give up and go to bed and close my eyes, straining to translate the constantly shifting stream of Chinese writing and coded messages and motorcycles and dead and drowned boys that assail my consciousness. I gasp and sob and stop myself with a corner of the pillow in my mouth, the pillow over my eyes, and a hand, as if it were Heather's, between my thighs.

SEVENTEEN
15 June and following, 1942

All my love of animals has returned over the past few weeks as I've become more involved in preparations for the full start-up of the new farm. I hadn't realised how much I'd missed working with them while I was living in the East Wing. It's not just the scent and feel of animals, breathing their breath, bridging the gap between species, but of being in their presence, having to consider their well-being as much as – even more so than – my own. Of course the rabbitry is no more, and I've still full responsibility for Deceased Property, but now that I've finished the cleaning, painting and general repairs of the farmhouse, and Ron Signet, as temporary overseer, and the three assistant inmates have moved in, I've been given charge of 'projects subsidiary'.

The way we decided was like this: a meeting with Dr Frank, me, Ron Signet and Pete Cooper – who was officially still on bereavement leave, but who'd shown up in Dr Frank's office: we turned over the possibilities.

Although, at first, it looked like my work would be nothing more than managing the distribution of milk and the production of cheese at the dairy, Ron said he thought it a waste of my talents. The three new men could do it: he'd train them. After all, this was to be a modern, mechanised dairy farm. A question of organisation rather than of heavy labour. If, indeed, we were to branch out, then he thought we should use my imagination and expertise.

Dr Frank, thin, jowls sagging, templed his fingers and leaned back in his chair. I saw him glance at the shelf where his trophies used to be. I said, 'It seems to me, sir, that the way has to be forward, but without losing sight of the past.' He nodded. 'You told me once that this institution had a history as a game farm. Might not an aspect of that be reconstituted?'

'Reconstituted?' I could almost hear him go through the sorry list of foods he was allowed on his diabetic diet. 'Reconstituted', I understood, didn't have a happy ring to it. It made one think of dried egg and mock chicken.

'What I mean is that we could take advantage of existing game on the expanded land, and farm it. There's plenty of wild pheasant, for instance.'

'What the fuck for, Sandy? Not many gentlemen out bagging pheasant these days. What the fuck planet are you from?' Pete Cooper guffawed. Ron Signet turned his head aside and coughed. Dr Frank furrowed his brow. I understood that Pete was to be forgiven his coarseness of speech because of his recent tragic loss, but I pressed the advantage his crudeness presented.

'Yes, that's true. Even the leisured classes have been pressed into service. I wasn't thinking of hunting parties, but of morale-building in terms of food.' He glared at me balefully. 'We have pheasant and quail in abundance in the fields and woods: perhaps with some management they could become an important source of nutrition and a welcome change.'

'A food source?' Dr Frank said.

'For variety of diet, sir. Here, at Colquitz, if you like; but also perhaps with a contract with the military? They must be weary of those endless tins of Spam.' This was my attempt at a joke. Everyone knew that one of Dr Frank's favourite dishes was Spam in orange sauce. It used to be made for him, as a treat, by the asylum chef when he could come by the oranges and sugar. Sugar was now out of the question for our acting director.

'Roast quail and stuffed pheasant, sir; we could even have a sideline in feathers for ladies' hats.'

'And fuck you a duck,' said Pete Cooper, who, for sure, was drunk.

'Ducks?' I said. 'Not a bad idea, Attendant Cooper. We've the pond already. I'll see what I can discover about raising duck-lings.'

'There'd be duck eggs, too!' Ron said, with sudden enthu-siasm.

'Possibly fish, as well. I'll have to look into that. I'm not sure what the pond will sustain.'

'Why not fucking squab?' Pete Cooper said. 'Why not fucking mink!' He placed a thick hand on his crotch, and leered generally. Mink, of course, have a reputation for sexual excess: I took another look at Pete Cooper's blurred face and could see in it the small glittering eyes, sharp teeth, even stray long whiskers of his mink friends.

'That's not a bad idea! We'd kill two birds with one stone!' I said.

Dr Frank had begun to look grim. He lifted the earpiece of his telephone, joggled the receiver, reached the kitchen and ordered black coffee to be brought to his office. 'I'm serious, sir,' I said to him. 'Squab. Pigeons. The pigeons we could raise for food *and* communications. Think of the possibilities!'

'Well, Sandy, I dunno . . .' Ron Signet said, and glanced at Dr Frank for a cue. 'We've a lot on our plate as it is. You don't think this might be, well, excessive!'

'Fucking excessive,' Pete Cooper slurred.

'But that's it exactly! We're about the only outfit left that has time and resources to attempt it! We're not going anywhere: we have labour, and natural advantages, and . . .'

'Now, Sandy,' Dr Frank said, 'Attendant Signet is correct: we have to continue to do what we're already doing well: there's the vegetable growing, the cattle production, the . . .'

'It was your decision to take on the Speller farm. Sir.'

'*And*,' Dr Frank said, 'we have our basic defence responsibilities and in case you've forgotten I have an institution of sick men to take care of. Not excluding you.'

Pete swivelled his head my way: his eyes glinted. They telegraphed happily that I'd gone too far.

'The Speller farm was a good decision, a brave one,' I plunged on. '*You* could see the possibilities, sir: it's a courageous man who during times of danger when all others are scrambling for cover, can take the long view, find the advantages . . .'

'Don't bull-feather me, Sandy,' Dr Frank said. But he was interested. He hadn't shut the door.

The office door opened and the once-sunburned nurse who worked with Dr Frank in the narcosynthesis room, the one who'd helped me when I was in the East Wing by passing on my message to Dr Frank, came in carrying the coffee tray. His face softened. He smiled at her, then looked at me. 'I suppose it could be part of your therapy, eh, Sandy?'

'Yes, sir.'

'Write me up something. I'll see what I can do.'

Ron and the new men all sleep in the farmhouse with me, with Ron downstairs and the others in the remaining upstairs bedrooms. We farmhouse inmates live in a kind of no-man's-land: linked to the institution for our room and board, under armed guard, assigned to specific jobs, but free in most other respects to do and say what we want.

I've tried to begin conversations with the new men along the lines of the parallels of our situations with Nazi-occupied countries – you could call us forced labourers or collaborators or some of us (perhaps) resistance fighters, even prisoners of war, in which case we'd have a duty to escape. I suggest these topics but they won't bite. They keep their heads down and mouths shut except for some heavy chewing at mealtimes. Even Ron Signet smiles when I refer to them collectively as 'the bullocks'. I have qualms about the term: they could well *have* been castrated under the sterilisation programme and I wouldn't know; I should show more tolerance. But I have nothing in common with them: they're older than me, more worn around the eyes; they have massively developed upper arms and shoulders and low-slung sloping bellies; they know each other, and communicate in grunts. They do exactly what they're told. Thank God I have Ron to talk to! And Georgina, when she comes by. Which she's started to do again, now that the admiral has been recalled to duty. I suppose I'm her second choice as a confidant, but if so, I don't mind. Georgina's happiness comes first.

I mention the squab/homing pigeon plan to her – as I think, upon reflection, that it has the most potential. 'If all goes well, George, and we train them up, we can send messages back and forth, we can write what we want!'

'Short messages, Sandy. Don't they carry them in little tubes on their legs?'

'Yes, but I could get hold of you and you of me in an emergency.'

She frowns. 'What kind of emergency?'

'I don't know, George. We're at war, aren't we?'

'I'd have to have my own set, wouldn't I?'

'Can you do it, George? I don't suppose your father could help build a dovecote?'

'The old man? Are you kidding? He'd nail himself through his palms. God, though, Sandy, I like the idea of slipping past the censors. Half the time I think my phone's tapped and somebody certainly reads my mail. I wouldn't put it past my sister to have hired a private investigator. She's convinced I'll get my father to change his will. She'd like to have me put away – for good!'

'Are you going to?'

'What?'

'Have him rewrite his will?'

Georgina looks shocked. 'Sandy, no! That would make me just like her! There's nothing wrong with his will: it's split fifty-fifty between us. Besides, the admiral would be cross. He doesn't like that sort of thing. He's a truly moral man, Sandy.'

I don't want to get off on the subject of the admiral, her admiration for him, her worry about his new sea duties chasing Japanese submarines. The plans they are discussing for the future. He's too old for her: it isn't right. I remind myself that Georgina deserves to be loved and that I'm not available, at the moment, to be more than a friend, but it doesn't help.

'So, will you do it? Get your own pigeons, build a dove-cote.'

'You bet,' she says. She winks.

'You have to keep it secret.'

'Of course I will, Sandy,' she says. She pats my hand.

I worry about Georgina. Although things are going better for her, it is clear to me that her grief over the death of her son, Brentwood, continues to be corrosive; it has undermined her skin so that you can see right through it to the veins below; it has thinned her bone structure – she looks like she'd fall over in a puff of wind – and it has, I fear, damaged her spirit. Her eyes, when she lets me meet them, still show shock. She no longer bothers much with her dress. She wears trousers instead of fashionable suits, although she can still look smart when she wants to. It hurts me when I think about Georgina and all the trouble in her life. With the admiral absent – much as I dislike the way he's taken over, he does look after her – I'm afraid she'll start drinking again. And then what? Would the sister and the medical men move in? I don't want anything bad to happen to her.

'Someone will have to know what you're doing. You can't build the lofts by yourself.'

'I have a carpenter in mind,' she says. Her dark blue gardenia eyes sparkle. I think of the very first time I saw her, on board the ferry. How beautiful she looked then. For the very first time I realise that the name of the ferry is the same as her son's! Both Brentwood! This only adds another layer of meaning to our meeting. 'It's right up his alley,' she continues. 'Just don't ask me who it is.'

Can it be who I think it is? Kosho in hiding? I know better than to ask.

From what I can tell from my reading, with the right breed and the right feed, pigeons are easy to train. Once they're six weeks old or so, they leave the nest to practise flight. You just show them how to use a trapdoor entrance and start releasing them short distances from the loft. They quickly get the idea and can be taken farther and farther afield until you can exchange them with those to whom you want to send messages.

In the paper I draw up for Dr Frank, I give particulars of all the projects we've considered but suggest that we start with the squab and homing pigeons first. For practical reasons, of course. The pigeons can fly up to forty miles. If the Japs arrive and shut down the phones and telegraph offices, this resource will be invaluable. The military will only thank us.

After his first quick perusal of my paper, Dr Frank says, 'Don't you think our generals have already thought of this, Sandy? Have you checked to see what they're already doing with carrier pigeons?'

His comments remind me of his initial objections to my project concerning Alan Macaulay. In that case, with persistence, he came to see reason.

'If they have, sir, they'll be thinking of communications between bases; they won't have a civilian backup. With the kind of operation you run here, sir, we could be completely unde-tected by the Japanese.'

'Hmmm,' he says. He has his back to me. He fiddles with the objects on the insulin tray.

'We'll start with squab. We can begin selling these within a few months. Once we have our markets we can think about pigeon training. Depending on how that goes, we can then add in the pheasant and ducks.' That's me, Sandy Grey, giving Dr Frank his instructions.

Stage one: build a suitable loft. We won't need much space, but there must be an indoor and outdoor area. The outdoor area must be caged in with wire. Set up roosts inside, with nest boxes, provide nesting materials of hay and straw. Order grains and pellets. Set up records and banding procedures. Order breeding stock. Initiate inquiries as to interest from restaurants and the officers' messes, army, navy and air force. Contact local butchers and game suppliers.

At the same time I lay the groundwork for ducklings and pheasant. There are similarities in the requirements of each – secure sheltered space, adequate light and food and clean water – but it's clear to me that eventually I'll need an assistant. All things are possible, but all things are not possible by oneself. The trouble is, who should I ask for?

I want to request Karl or Winchell but I don't dare. Dr Frank's jurisdiction over the East Wing is limited, and I've lost touch with Dr Love. Where can he be? It won't matter to Dr Frank – not the way it does to me – that securing their release might save their lives. Dr Frank believes they belong there. Karl, even in the state he's in, might be capable of directed labour. He couldn't be worse than the 'bullocks' who do nothing unless they're told. There's nothing wrong with Winchell other than tuberculosis – at least there wasn't when last I saw him, and not now if he's indeed the one sending messages through Deceased Property. But I know better than to open up a subject when I'm not sure of the outcome. Bob, if he were still here, would have been perfect. Bob's another subject not to mention.

'One thing at a time, Sandy,' Dr Frank says when he comes

to check on the loft building progress and I tell him I'm going to need help. 'Don't try to go too fast. Take it easy. Prove this will work. Show what you can do with the squab, and if that's successful, we'll move on. We've plenty of time. The main thing is the new dairy farm.' He looks over his shoulder to where Ron Signet and his boys are waiting to take him through their operation.

'Righty-oh, sir.' For a second I feel downcast – where's the enthusiasm my work deserves? It's abundantly clear it's not high priority for Dr Frank. How I miss Kosho! He would understand the potential and pitch right in. We'd have quick results. Still, it's those who work behind the scenes who often achieve the most. The important thing is that Dr Frank, acting director, has signed the necessary documents. Squab and homing pigeons and then ducklings and pheasant.

'You're a devious man, Sandy,' Georgina says to me when I outline the whole of my plans to her later. She sits in our warm kitchen, her shoes off, her feet up on a chair. There's a hole in the toe of one of her socks – men's socks. Her father's? The admiral's? Or old ones of Brentwood or even her husband? I get up and take a fresh batch of cookies from the oven. Georgina has given me her ration of sugar.

'Don't forget we're at war, George,' I say. 'We have to be cunning to survive.'

As an enterprise, the management of living creatures requires whole-hearted commitment. Once the breeding pairs arrive I've little time for anything else. The boxes in Deceased Property pile up. I worry about it until Ron claps me on the shoulder and says, 'No hurry there, Sandy! Nobody's punching that particular time clock! Ha ha.' He loves being in charge of the dairy. He's king of the cows. I don't begrudge it to him. He would have made a fine farmer.

I have five pairs of mated breeders. These pairs, so I'm told, generally bond for life. I've banded them with the same colour leg bands and given them the same number. When the hatchlings come, they'll be banded and colour-coded too so we can keep track of our results. Each pair has selected a nest and three of the females have already laid their eggs – two white eggs each, about one and a half inches in length. The males and females take turns in sitting. I have two weeks before the first set hatch.

Tonight I'm finished early: all's well in the loft. The door is shut and the wire netting of the enclosure is pegged down and secure. The others are quiet in their rooms in the farmhouse, doing whatever they do after dark. Ron sits in the kitchen downstairs and listens to war news on the radio. I adjust the objects on my desk, set out some fresh paper, check the nibs of my pens, smile at Bob's postcard – and settle my feet on the box containing Winchell's tools and guns.

With the window open I can smell the sweet smells of early summer. The warm, damp weather brings out the richness of the earth, the fertile loam threaded with worms, the hay and vetch crops showing well: on the old part of the farm, they're already harvesting vegetables. In the asylum garden, roses wind through hedges and over trellises: the heady scent of jasmine heats the air. If I didn't know better, I'd say Bob was back on the job! As if summoned, the throb of a Harley engine sounds from the road beyond the wall.

God's in His heaven. All's right with the world.

I turn to my writing and go over the progress I've made so far with Karl's *The Romance of Stanley Park*. Precious little, it seems. What with being so busy, I'm no closer to understanding how to approach the subject, and am certainly far from the source of inspiration that served me so well with Alan Macaulay. With Alan, I suppose, somehow, I was writing what I knew. An injustice had been done: it was up to me to rectify it. The case for Alan Macaulay's pardon is, indeed, Dr Frank informs me, making its way through the bureaucracy: there's cause for hope. Where Karl is concerned, on the other hand, I have no real expectation of a result: only a sense of duty, a desire to reclaim a remnant from the wreckage of Karl's life to present to his parents after the war. Karl's subject matter was a story of a tragic marriage – a state of which I've no experience. The wife in the story could not have children and the husband rejected her. The husband refused to adopt a child. Since he behaved in a cruel and unfeeling manner towards his wife and would have done so, doubtless, to any children in his care, it seems to me this was fortunate. Their failure to have children was a blessing. But this kind of attitude is anathema to romance. Perhaps I'm just not the right person for it?

The trouble also is that I don't know what Karl planned. Were the parents to stay together? What role, if any, did Stanley Park occupy in the story, or was the title merely a device to indicate setting? What elements of Karl's own life were to play a part? Was the story he told me about freeing the birds to be an element? I only have questions now and no means to ask them. Karl's been taken from us, he's deep inside what remains of his thoughts and feelings, whatever elements of his brain he's been able to protect from the barbs and jolts of electricity.

I put my head in my hands. There *must* be an answer!

What else? I try to relax and think.

I lift my head. I reach for *The Storehouse of Thought and Expression* and flip through. 'Story writers should keep in mind that the opening situation should show that trouble may follow. The incident that starts the trouble should be unmistakeably the whistle of the referee, Fate.'

This strikes a chord.

Once more I open the pages at random. A sentence jumps out: 'When all else fails, change your point of view.'

I sit back and close my eyes. I let the advice resound through the caverns of my being. Some door opens on a beginning. Writing on a wall. Chinese characters. A face that belongs to someone. Not myself. I'm away.

What it Takes to be Human

A Tale: Not The Romance of Stanley Park

There's no telling what can set things off. You step out, for instance, from your uncle's shop on a Vancouver street. The weather is brilliant, the sun showers its coins over your hands and arms; when you see a woman, she, too, is sprinkled with gold: of course you follow her. You could have chosen not to: you could have turned your back on the summer's day and remained indoors. You are only eighteen.

The woman is young, like yourself, but she is no one in particular. It's just the hat she wears, its glitter of feathers – a hand's width of blue iridescence sewn on to black velvet. You feel it in your throat like a drink.

You're new at this: you've only just come from China. You could have stayed at home and lived with your mother. She wanted you to: she took you out, the day before you left, for one last walk along the estuary and pointed out the birds – as if you didn't know them, as if this could have any effect on your desire to go. The green valleys and great rivers of your province were not going to be left behind: they had entered into you.

You trail the woman: you're a young Chinese boy training to be a herbalist. The scents of musk and fungi cling to you: but you throw off this persona. You've discovered gold in the mountains or you're the owner of an island producing sugar and coconuts; you're a musician and painter. Your being is the green of trees and full of song. Your gift to the woman whom you will never know is your unlived life.

When you reach the park, you stop. The woman sits down on a bench. She opens her handbag. Time hangs on a slender golden thread. Almost you return to your uncle. Instead you sit down too. You're close to her. You can sense her body, deep in its reeds and bamboo, but you're an innocent. You turn to her with

255

a smile: you want to tell her about yourself, and about another uncle, at home – a silk merchant. You would like to give her a bolt of silk to match the feathers on her hat. You have no words. Your silence slices the air. The woman holds her purse to her stomach. You reach out from your youth with thoughts of the silver beauty of ponds, and what you might see if you looked below the surface, and the woman runs.

She stops and faces you: you want to show her who you are. You open your palms to display their emptiness. Her summer dress lifts in the breeze and brushes your legs.

Every day there are choices, and this is yours: to raise a hand to the smooth skin of her face. To treat her like a friend.

You lie on a wooden bunk in a cramped room. You are facing the wall. Your days are spent washing the clothes of strangers. Your nights are full of sobs. The men around you listen to you weep as if it is water running into a creek. Sooner or later you lift your eyes as you cross between buildings in the morning and see the surrounding trees: their voices whisper poems of abandonment. After a time you listen carefully, and begin to write them down on the walls of your prison.

Now you are on a ship: no one has told you why. You've been gathered with the others into trucks; you've ascended a gangplank and been given a chair and drunk soup and visited a lavatory. Through the portholes you glimpse snow-covered hills. They pass away. Light and darkness pass away. An old man dies. You sit up in your bunk and you're hungry again; through the porthole you count the variations of grey. Questions frame and reframe themselves. One day the bed linen is changed; another day you eat an apple. You spend weeks like this.

You arrive at a port. The ship is unloaded and loaded. Once more you set sail, and travel among islands and past boats: all this is familiar. You could be dreaming, but you're not. You feel old. Your youth waits for you far away in that left-behind park. Your uncle still stands on his threshold, a hand shading his eyes, watching for you. In the park, a man has opened the aviary: the birds fly free. You dream of your return, and of the woman, of course.

Some of the men stop eating; all have boils on their gums. This time the ships in the harbour have guns. Still nothing has been said about where you are going. Then you anchor offshore, and you're told to gather your parcel of underwear. The police, when they come on board, are armed.

There's a knocking. Knock knock! I stumble to the door and open it. Ron Signet stands there. 'Were you asleep?' he says, taking in my dishevelled appearance. My pyjama jacket is mis-buttoned. My flies gape. I hold them together.

'This won't take a minute, Sandy, I need to talk to you.'

'It's all right, Ron. Come in. What is it?' The fragment of an ending that I'd held in mind slips away. Ron Signet from Porlock.

He steps into my room. 'I thought it might be better if you had some warning.'

'Warning, Ron? What about?' I'm annoyed. Another few minutes and I'd have been done. I thought it was going well.

'It's just that . . . it's just that . . .' – he toes the floor in worry – 'I'm sorry things have turned out the way they have.' He stops. I nod at him. Ron plods on, 'The thing is, Sandy, the farm overseer. Not that Dr Frank wanted it this way. There wasn't much choice.' Ron hems and coughs. I sit down, for I begin to sense what's coming. 'You see,' Ron says, 'considering his recent bereavement, it seems the best thing all round. Less demanding. More outdoors. The simple life. Nature . . . I thought you should know. The appointment came through today. Pete Cooper's going to be in charge of the farm.

'I'll be gone in the morning. Back to my old job. I'll still see you, I'll check up on you in Deceased Property.' Ron's smile is strained.

My stomach tightens. 'Pete Cooper? Here? In charge?' Ron backs out of my room.

I shut the door. I sit down at my table. There was more. I know there was more. I can't believe I've lost it, the story cut off. Just like Karl. It's gone. I put pen to paper for one more line: *The water is warm, the sea calm, the current carries you home.*

They say that the second attempt at writing may not be the same as the first, and so I have found it to be. Now that I've had time to reflect, I see that this 'tale' wasn't what I wanted to write at all! There's too much Sandy Grey in it and not enough Karl. Karl – even with his German background in the psychological – would hate it. It describes a grey area, part real and part fantastical. It contains Sandy Grey's thoughts about a character not unlike himself. There is no escape in it, no romance at all! The tone is cool. I'm sorry, Karl, I think. I've let you down. I put out the light and then I lie down and close my eyes. Othello leans over his wife: 'Put out the light, and then put out the light.'

It's not as bad as I'd feared, although I admit I'm keeping notes, just in case there is need for documentation of Pete Cooper's rule. I won't risk losing my hard-won modicum of freedom because of him.

We rise at dawn and breakfast together: each of the farmhouse inmates takes a turn at the cooking. Mostly, Pete Cooper stays out of the way, except to give daily orders.

We meet again at dinner, but generally, because we're all so busy, the dinner's brought over from the main kitchen and we have little to do but eat it. Pete sleeps in Ron's old bedroom. In the evenings he goes out to the pub and one of the other guards checks on us; but since we're all hoping for release, and we have our own rooms, there's no trouble.

The only ruffled feathers now are when Georgina comes to visit since she and Pete don't get on. Why would they? He knows that she knows what I know – which is that he was behind the massacre at the rabbitry.

I give my story to Georgina to read. She looks it over quickly: 'Champion of the underdog, eh, Sandy?' she says. 'It's a little different from your usual, isn't it?'

I put it away. I'm sorry about her response, which seems curt. I suppose my face betrays a sulk.

George lays a hand on my arm. 'Don't misunderstand me, Sandy. It's just fine, but it makes me think.' There are tears in her eyes and I recall that George too has had her freedom taken away more than once and felt helpless.

'How's your father?' I ask her.

'Mad as a hatter. Setting fires in the basement. He thinks we've still got a wood furnace so he puts in paper and kindling and tries to light it. I've told him a hundred times we burn oil now, but he doesn't remember.

'He's still "the lumber baron", though,' she says. 'He follows the company investments and goes over the household accounts. I have to explain every penny.

'Then my sister turns up and I have to do it again.' She shakes her head. 'She sneaks around, poking her nose in.'

'George,' I say, deeply concerned. I can smell the gin by this time. 'You need something to look forward to. You can't spend all your time with your father.'

Deep shadows patrol her eyes. The loss of her son, other losses. 'I'm fine, Sandy.' She smiles the slow smile that makes my stomach flip. '*Really* fine,' she says.

'I'd do anything for you, Georgina,' I say. 'I owe you my life.'

We're sitting at the kitchen table. It's evening. Pete's out and the others are in their rooms. I take her hand. 'You know that things are going pretty well here. I'm working hard . . .'

She removes her hand from mine and squeezes my bicep – 'I've noticed! You're getting in shape, Sandy!'

'Don't joke, Georgina.'

'Why not?'

I start over. 'I'm close to finishing my treatment, Dr Frank says. Once I'm done, they'll have to reconsider my sentence.'

Her eyes are steady headlamps. I blink in their brightness.

'With the war on and all, I think they'll let me out. I'm young, I'm strong, I'm not stupid. More to the point, I haven't done anything wrong.'

'I've never thought you were stupid, Sandy.'

'What about it, then?'

'What about?' Her eyelids flutter as if she knows but doesn't know what I'm trying to say. I swallow hard to clear the way to get the words out.

'Georgina, will you marry me?'

She jumps away – the chair skitters back a good two feet. I guess it's the shock, but she recovers quickly and laughs. She's on her feet. 'Sandy, you're just a boy! And what about Heather? Didn't you say you'd love her forever?'

'There's love and there's love, Georgina, it's not the same!' I get up and grab her hand again. 'I love you, and I know you love me, it's always been that way.' The hand in mine stills, chills. I let it go. I know, from my work with rabbits and pigeons, when a creature is frightened. 'I'm sorry, Georgina, but you have to listen to me. I shouldn't have sprung this on you but I've been thinking about it. We understand each other, you and I. You need me.'

'Need you, Sandy?' There's something in her voice that bites my soul.

'Someone has to look after you, George.'

We hold eyes.

'We have kindness and friendship, Sandy. What else is

there? You know I'm too old for you.'

'You'll never be old.'

She turns away and looks out the window at the main building. If you don't look outside, it could almost be a normal household. The wood-burning kitchen stove warms the evening. Dishes drain in the sink. Somebody's left the milk pitcher on the counter. Georgina sits down at the table again. Her fingers gather crumbs from the surface into a little ball.

'I'm going to marry the admiral,' she says. 'He's asked me and I've said yes.'

'You're not!'

'He's good to me, Sandy. I am going to marry him.'

'*He's* too old for *you*! He's already left you on your own when he knows you can't manage!'

'Is that how you think of me?' She's made half a dozen spheres of crumbs by now. Her head's tucked into her collar. I can see the effort it takes her to look up. 'Listen to me, Sandy. After Beau – my husband – died, there was just Brent and me. It wasn't easy. I lived for that child. Nobody helped me. Not my father, not my sister – they stayed away. Then Brent grew up, and it wasn't enough.'

I can feel, like splashes of icy seawater, all the thoughts Georgina doesn't say. Her life with her son, her drinking and staying out late. The effort it has cost her just to survive. And me. Once a stand-in, maybe, but no more. Just Sandy Grey.

We're still sitting there, our spines ramrod stiff in the kitchen chairs, listening to the electric clock on the wall tick, when Pete Cooper ambles in. He stops short when he sees Georgina, scratches his balls, then shrugs out of his jacket and hangs it on the back of the door. He walks round behind her. He catches my eye, makes an airplane diving motion with his hand, shakes his head, twirls his finger at his temple. Sign language for 'Since the death of her son she's crazy.'

'Fuck you,' I say.

'Pardon, me, Sandy?' Georgina says.

Pete turns pale. My words mean 'Your son's dead too, you bastard.'

Now Pete's face is dark. 'No visitors in here after sunset, Mrs Jones-Murray.'

Yes, it's nighttime and we hadn't noticed. She stands. She holds out her hand. 'Goodbye, Sandy.'

I stay where I am and refuse her hand. I'm aware it looks bad, but I can't help it. She should have said earlier about the admiral. She shouldn't have let me make a fool of myself.

'Oh,' she says, right on the point of going, while Pete Cooper folds his arms to watch us. She flips open her handbag. 'This came for you. I found her, Sandy. I found your Heather.'

She's spoken gently, so gently that I'm able to raise my eyes and meet her look of earth and sex and love and loss. I suddenly see, as I hadn't before, how far Georgina's travelled ahead of me. It's time for me to catch up.

Everything's changed and not changed. I still love Georgina, but I can't stop myself from raising Heather's letter to my lips. It smells of hay and meadowsweet. It smells like Heather, her small triangle of a face lit up from beneath by the buttercup I held in my fingers.

'I'll be seeing you,' Georgina says. 'Don't take any wooden nickels, Sandy.' Click of her heels. Turn of handle in the door.

Upstairs, on my own again, I sit at my table with the letter. Heather lives in Winnipeg. She's been to business college. She works for the Hudson's Bay Company in the fur department. She's married to a pilot in the RCAF. He's already won some medals. She remembers me. She writes, 'Weren't we funny as kids!'

How will I answer her? What will I say about me? She knows where I am but not why. It is kind of her to write. Kind! How hateful.

I pick up my pen.

Dear Heather,

I'm glad to hear from you. There's not much to say from this neck of the woods. Maybe some time you could come and see me and we could talk. I'd like that. Do you remember when we ran away together? It was the happiest time of my life.

Yours, as always,
Sandy Grey

EIGHTEEN
29 August and following, 1942

I keep waiting for Georgina to say she's sorry for not wanting to marry me and for keeping me in the dark about her engagement to the admiral, but she doesn't. We carry on like always, we're kind to each other, but I still think she's making a mistake. Georgina needs someone warm and young to love her! Georgina thinks, for her part, that I take Heather's letters too seriously: Heather is lonely because her husband is away in the war, and she's young and not used to being on her own; once the war is over and Heather's husband returns, that will be the end of it. So Georgina says.

I know that a relationship by mail can't go far. But the fact that Heather writes at all from her prairie city means that she remembers what passed between us. Our bond is deep and permanent. One day she may remember it all, in every detail, and come to the right decision. One day the promise of 'forever' will mean what it means.

I've grown to enjoy composing letters: writing to Heather has taken over, for the time being, my attempt to pen *The*

Romance of Stanley Park. Not that I've given it up entirely, but every work has its time and place – does it not? – and at the moment I'm too busy, anyway, for anything longer than a note.

The Storehouse of Thought and Expression advises that a letter should never overstate or be afraid to declare the truth. I describe my life, truly, as a *via media*. I'm neither in the war nor quite out of it; I'm not completely imprisoned, neither am I free. I am deeply involved in small animal husbandry but would you call me a farmer? I dream of the dead (lost Tom and the other deceased of the East Wing, and Georgina's husband and her son, Brentwood) as if they are living and of the living (Karl, Bob, Winchell, Kosho) as if they are dead. I'm walking a path looking neither to left nor right. The troublesome Alan Macaulay is a distant memory. I navigate between Pete Cooper and Dr Frank, between Georgina and Heather, between all that I know and the great realms of my ignorance. Between – as a pilot would say – heaven and earth.

Waiting for a letter from Heather, now that Georgina is pre-occupied with her wedding plans, gives me something to look forward to.

Ten days ago the Canadian troops in Britain were sent to attack the French coast. When Heather wrote to me about this, she knew that her husband had been in the raid, but not what had happened to him. The newspapers drew a picture of fierce sky battles on the scale of the Battle of Britain, and of landing craft storming the broad grey beaches with troops and tanks. They reported German sources as describing a successful coun-terattack and many prisoners taken. She was angry that while her husband was 'risking his life' others were safe in their beds. I, for example (she did not have to point this out), was raising pigeons and dabbling in writing. I could have answered that I am not incarcerated in an asylum for the criminally insane by choice. I could have drawn her attention to other newspapers which reported that the first units of allied commandos had returned to their British base in gay spirits. That there wasn't anything to worry about. I didn't. I do not trust the newspapers, one way or another. There are bound to be casualties, and none of the accounts will be strictly true. Truth is always a victim of war. In any case, my troubles are my own and not to be mis-understood as anyone else's, even Heather's. I remained silent. I thought of Karl and cultivated the art of patience.

Since then, Heather has telegraphed that her husband, Dave, is safe. She is sorry if anything she might have written has offended me. I do not know everything about my love for Heather, but I do know that not only is love patient, but love endures. Love, such as ours, forged in childhood, is a lifelong contract.

Every day I spend as much time as I can in the fly pen. It's made of one-inch wire mesh to keep out sparrows and rats, and I've extended the wire, and pegged it down a foot into the ground; there's another foot or so bent away at the bottom of the pen for extra insurance. I scrape the gravel and sand clean, rinse off the landing boards, change the bathing pans and refresh the bowl at the base of the drinking fountain which is connected to a constantly running hose. For feed I'm using a corn base with some kafir, peas and red wheat. I also add in vetch and hempseed and mix my own mineral mixture of oyster shell, limestone, charcoal, granite-grit and salt for the hopper. Several times a week I change the nesting material – the pigeons like the commercial oat straw and sage grass the best – and I'm experi-menting with adding in small amounts of our own hay. Best of all, these mornings, while the air is still cool and you can smell the hidden scents of the vegetation of the fields and woods in that hour of the sun's first touch, is that I get to handle the birds. Already most of them will come to me, even without grain to lure them. They are intelligent, gentle birds: when their wings spread and when they take flight, and the sun streams through their pale feathers, they make me think of angels – how I imag-ined they might be, the size of fairies or doves, when I was a child. Heather and I used to say that angels watched over us:

hers sat on her shoulder; mine hovered near an ear, whispering, so I believed, into my dreams. I used to have such dreams! It was the greatest pain to me that the angels didn't help us when we needed them.

I've always made the best of things, and even when relations between me and Georgina are strained, I take care of my birds. The squabs started leaving their nests nearly three weeks ago. Pete Cooper complained that they should have been killed before they were fully feathered, but I explained to Dr Frank that we needed to see the entire first batch through. We had no way of predicting the survival rate. As it turns out, we lost three of the ten through accidents – two were pecked to death by the adult pigeons and one became caught in the larger mesh netting I used at first: I've learned from my mistakes, and they won't happen again. The remaining pigeons, those that mate, we can add to our breeding stock. The next fledglings will have to be killed and dressed, but I'm prepared for that. It is part of the deal I struck with Dr Frank.

Georgina's progress with her flock is proceeding more or less in step with mine, although she is a little behind. This week I showed her how to let the pigeons leave the loft through a small slot, and then try to get back in as she tempts them with grain. We have to be careful with the training as I do not, as yet, have Dr Frank's direct permission for the undertaking. I'm not sure, in fact, that he understands that my stock is homing pigeons at all! He's so taken up with the dairy and the prospect of fresh cream and prize cheeses that he just lets me get on with it. Even better, he keeps Pete Cooper and his helpers on the hop.

Georgina urges me to be careful: since she's become involved with the admiral, she's taken to saying that I should learn to accept things as they are. I don't like this 'wise counsel' of hers: it doesn't suit. It's as if she's trying out a set of views, not hers. Is this the Georgina who rowed out in the dark to save me in the inlet? Is this she who bulldozed her way into the asylum on movie night? Who moved mountains to inveigle Dr Love into my treatment? I understand that life hasn't been kind to George and, at the moment, she's in retreat. I am patient with her, but I reply, always, when she resorts to these platitudes, that we must resist what is and exchange it for something better. How else would humanity have progressed from the caves? I think to myself that her son, Brentwood, would have been appalled at her talk: he died trying to stop Hitler and Mussolini and the Japanese emperor from enslaving us. Would she have had *him* give up? I don't say this, of course: where Brentwood is concerned, and Georgina's grief, it is better to let sleeping dogs lie.

It's just like old times! Dr Frank summons me to his office and from there we walk together to the East Wing and through the pea green and dirty white corridors. I think I'm fine – it's not a problem to be going to treatment because I've done this several times before. I'm sure of it – until he's opening the door ahead of me. It's dark inside, the heavy green curtains are already drawn. I start to sweat, my breathing quickens. 'Now, now, Sandy, it's all right,' Dr Frank says, surprised at my gasping. 'We're all old friends here.' He switches on a lamp beside the bed and I see waiting for me – just as he has indicated – old friends. The nice nurse and – surprise! – Dr Love.

'Dr Love!' I cry, and step forward to shake his hand. 'What are you doing here?'

'Come now, Sandy,' he says, and lays a kindly hand on my shoulder. 'Did you really think I'd forgotten you?'

No. Not forgotten exactly. But I'd imagined I'd dropped from his radar. There are plenty of people in need in the world and not so very many Dr Loves.

'It's so very good to see you!' I'd like to embrace him. Tears gush. He lays a gentling hand on my shoulder. I wipe my face with my sleeve.

'And you,' he says.

The nurse begins the familiar preparations. I note the orderly tray of vials, needles, swabs and tourniquets; the oxygen cylinder tucked behind Dr Frank's chair. Dr Love leads me to the bed, his hand under my elbow.

'You know how this goes, don't you, Sandy?'

'Yes, sir, I do.'

'The drug will help us help you,' he says, as if I hadn't answered. As if it's he and not I who needs assurance. 'We think, Dr Frank and I do, that it's time to finish with this neurosis of yours and be done with it. I've heard good things about how you're doing.'

'Yes, Dr Love. Things are going well. There's the pigeons, and I have plans . . .'

'You're ready to face the world, are you, Sandy?'

'I am. I'm ready.' I sit on the edge of the bed and wipe my hands dry on the sheet.

'Fully ready, Sandy?' Dr Frank pipes up. He moves his notebook from the seat of the chair so he can sit. 'Prepared, now, to face a world that includes your parents? You'd be ready to stand up to them?'

This shocks me, although I try not to show it. I slap on a silly grin. My parents! He hasn't mentioned my seeing them since when I first arrived here and he told me he'd protect me from their visits. Their prying and pushing and wheedling. Their pulling the strings of my feelings. I'd almost grown to think that they didn't exist except when *I* thought of them. I haven't missed them. I have no longing for a mother, no need for a father – I was done with that long ago. Why should these strangers be allowed back in my life? Nothing good can come of it. I'm drenched in sweat, and I recall in harsh flashes of thought what I went through the last time in this room. The recollection of my separation from my beloved Heather. The brutish punishment of a bloody circumcision – engineered by those so-called parents! The fact that this act had shown they couldn't be my true parents at all, whatever Dr Frank thought. My mouth warps under the strain of the grin. I open it to call for my lost mother – she who had held me safely in her lap to read to me, sing to me, give me comfort. And my father – the one who had taken me with him to his work, given me my own set of miniature tools with which to mimic his labours, my hands dipping into and out of buckets of water and sand. I grieve for whatever terrible fate these good people have suffered. My mouth is open, but I'm silent.

'Sandy?' Dr Love says. 'Can we count on you?'

I close my eyes. I hold the sorrow of the child I was in my hands. It's a multi-coloured ball. No, it's a ball and chain. Fetters. Prison. An asylum for the criminally insane.

Tears wash my cheeks in a sudden spill. I want to plead with Dr Love to stop this at once. I can't bear it. I open my eyes.

The nurse, who is once more sunburned, fresh and ripe as approaching harvest, helps me lie back. Her nose, cheeks and forehead are rosy and freckled. She has even toasted the tips of her ears where they peep though her dark hair. Her arms and hands are shiny and pink-skinned against her white uniform. She gives me the pill that means I won't drift off to sleep instead of facing hard reality. She ties the tourniquet around my arm. I watch the glances – bright as sunbeams – that zing back and forth between her and Dr Frank. They're in love! How well Dr Frank looks! He's tanned, too; his skin fits him: he's wearing a new shirt and tie.

Fear for myself, love for him and all he's done for me, contend.

I glance at Dr Love. He hasn't trimmed his beard recently, harsh lines of fatigue show in his face; and his clothes – always of good quality – look slept in. Who is he saving day and night? What life and death matters weigh him down? What, in reality, do I know of either of these men?

The nurse slips the needle into my vein and waits for the signal to open the valve. Sandy! I say to myself. Quick, remember what you've learned! All depends on it!

I've learned that men who suffer may be good or bad.

I've learned that appearances don't tell you everything.

I've learned that love is complicated: sometimes it includes lies and betrayal.

I've learned that in all matters of love, including the love of animals, you have to give before you receive.

I've learned that everyone is human. The Chinese, the Russians, the Germans – everyone.

Except for those who are not. Like Pete Cooper, or Attendant John in the East Wing, and the substitutes who take over the personalities of those who care for us and use their shapes and minds for evil purposes.

What about the substitutes, Sandy? What do you really think of them now? Wasn't that the easy way out, the old way?

The bite of the drug is under my tongue; my eyes drop into the other world that waits for me. I hear Dr Love say as I'm counting backwards . . . ten . . . nine . . . eight . . . under Dr Frank's direction, 'Now, Sandy, Dr Frank has filled me in on your other sessions. In those you went far back in time, into your life as a child. This time, we want you to stay with us, allow yourself to travel back only a little. Can you do that? We've cut the dosage back, it will feel different, you'll be more in control.' I nod. 'Where are you now?'

'With the rabbits,' I say. 'They're so soft to touch.' My fingers make little stroking movements, but it's only the blanket under my fingers.

'A little farther,' Dr Love says. 'Tell us how you came to be here at Colquitz.'

'In a car.'

A chair scrapes nosily. That'll be Dr Frank. 'Of course you came in a car. We want to know why. None of your nonsense now, Sandy.'

'From the boat.'

'You jumped from the ferry, you were rescued,' Dr Love says. 'By your friend, wasn't it?'

Then I'm on the ferry and in the water and . . . Shit! Shit! There's such pressure to tell them all that happened. I'm swim-

271

ming towards the landing lights, then scooped away by the current and then by the great dragon of the deep, she who inhabits the origins of time, without whom I would have died, and then – zoom – I'm on that sandy island shore my hands on the heaving sides of the ancient sea creature and there slips from her underside, new as dawn, wet, raw, copper-eyed, the miracle, the sea serpent's infant, and I'm there at the beginning of all things, and I can't think of it, mustn't allow myself to, in case I let it out . . .

Dr Frank's impatience rescues me. He whispers, *Don't get him started on Jones-Murray!*

Dr Love says, 'Before the ferry.'

'The police brought me . . .'

'Even earlier. You were with your father and mother in the family car; you had driven from Victoria that night, isn't that right? It's the Sunday war is declared. You've told us before. This time tell us exactly what you see.'

I could say Alan Macaulay's ghost has made an unexpected appearance, winking from the corner of the narcosynthesis room at my fluttering eyelids, but I don't. I've sent him on and I don't want him back, even as an ally.

I'm just home from university and a stint in air cadet camp. My parents know nothing about this. They've picked me up from the bus station in Victoria. I smell the familiar odour of hot tyres and stamped metal from the machine shop out back. The sleeves of Mother's too-heavy coat hang to her bitten fingernails. When she looms towards me, arms out, I cough into my handkerchief. 'Hay fever,' I say, and give my nose a blow. My nostrils sting with bus diesel. I'm holding on – as if I could grasp them – to the pictures I have in my mind of what I've just left: green and gold fields, skies burnt rust with sun; the glider that I train on ready and waiting at the flying club airfield. Me, at the controls, flying, in swoops and swings through rushing air. My father avoids my eyes, says, 'You'll come to the mission with us, we can talk on the drive home.'

We get into the Studebaker for the short run to the water-front. The back seat is covered with a canvas tarpaulin. I shift the pile of buckets and trowels. The rest of the car is clean, spruced up for my father's Sunday evening preaching. I lean out the window: dusk and the heavy smog from the gorge mill, and the salt and salmon tang of the wharves, in layers over the quiet: everyone's at home, except for a handful of government workers, summoned by the emergency, cutting through the streets towards the legislative buildings, briefcases important with papers. The street corners bristle with the stark cries of the news hawkers: War! War! War!

My heart hammers with excitement. Now! My life is about to begin now! But I can wait a few days and endure the passage of my parents' obligatory company, and then I'm free.

There's a feeling of deep unease. It's there through the entire service my father conducts in the waterfront mission in Victoria. It's there in the pump-organ squawks my mother wheezes from the organ. In the stink of cheap liquor and smell of damp musty suits that cling to the men who have to listen to this rubbish before they can get a coffee and sandwich. In the hope that flares, like damp matches being struck again and again, in the eyes of the younger men who are thinking perhaps that this war means an end to the waiting, the hopelessness, breadlines and pity. War means jobs and money and everyone pitching in. Doesn't it?

The drive after the mission service is silent and slow. The general tension in the air coalesces around my father and his sourceless anger. Sweat runs down the back of my mother's neck from beneath the thin colourless knot of her bun, and into the collar of her dress: not a flowered summer dress, like girls and women – even farmwives – wear in Saskatchewan, but a dress like a shroud. Purple crepe. Ugly. Her rank sweat. Her sharp unprettiness.

Steady, Sandy, Dr Love says.

The road, once we're away from the town, curves north

through steep blue rock cuts: I open the window to smell the baked forest, the reek of drying streams, exposed alluvia, bird bones and fish bones: the secrets of wood and creek bed revealed by the season; then the leaked and drained odour of mud flats as we climb the dirt road of the Malahat as it rises along the border of the inlet. Up and up until we glimpse the scattered lights across the water where there are farms and the rare houses of the rich; where – though I do not know it yet – Georgina's father lives.

For God's sake, don't let him get started, Dr Frank says.

To pass the time, I make a list of the houses in which we've lived, and say goodbye to each. The first, in Langford, where there were farms and hedges of bramble and roses and where I met my sweet Heather; then, in exile, the move to a two-storey duplex on the fringes of the naval base where my father picked up extra work at the dockyard and from where I walked to school through a daily shower of stones thrown by bullies; and yet, even there, in my childish suffering, I discovered a secret path to the sea and the bracing sight of ships riding high on a glitter of waves, and kept close to myself the knowledge that in the wide world in which I felt so alone, I wasn't, for somewhere there was Heather: and what can separate us from love?

For a while, after a failed attempt to start his own church and a fall into debt, my father took a job as a watchman on industrial land: we lived in a nearby apartment over a grocery store. From my room, at the back, I could see the high, black fuel storage towers that belonged to the oil companies and knew that my father climbed their ladders and walkways every day, naked to fate, and I hoped . . .

Hoped for what, Sandy?

Hoped for an end, that's all, to the steady slippage of my parents' prospects and God's 'testing time'.

Throughout the moves (now I'm bored with the counting) there were annual summer trips up and down the island to rural settlements, villages with a mill or a mine and a union hall where my father would preach, my mother pass the collection plate, and I would stand on the platform with a grin pasted on my face, and play hymns on the accordion. Later on came the building of the Bible camp beside the lake and the hours I spent on the plank benches of the tabernacle I'd helped to construct, stirring my toes in sawdust. Sometimes, at the camp, I slept outdoors, under the stars. I could place my sleeping bag where I liked and spend the night in contemplation of the heavens – not Heaven – but the deeper mysteries of the planets and constellations. It was on that land that my parents now lived in a winterised cottage.

Wherever we'd lived, there was the constant embarrassment of wearing old clothes to school and having bad skin from a monotonous diet and being taken, door to door, to 'witness' for the Lord, despite the fact I didn't believe a word of it.

So, you're a snob now, Sandy, are you? Dr Frank says. *Ashamed of your family and of being poor? You managed to get yourself to college! Something must have worked for you!*

And so goodbye, once and for all, to a life that cycled between the stations of my parents' lives. A triangle, these days, of the Victoria Lighthouse Mission and the premises of villagers and farmers where my father does his plastering work, and the lakeside camp and cottage.

My mother, in the front seat, gargles a wet cough as we turn from the main road on to the lake road. We chutter along, the tyres crunch on gravel, the headlights cast weak piss spots on a grim slice of white road. She hums under her breath, her fingers rustle a packet of mints as she passes them to my father. The air grows heavy round his loud sucking, he smells more than ever of earth and fox; the heat and anger of him balloon.

The cough must have been a signal, for he begins to speak. His voice twitches quickly into the cadences of the pulpit as he embroiders the theme of my failings. Primarily, there's the waste of my education, paid for out of his savings and from the collection plate of his congregations – *and by me! I've worked for it, gone harvesting, laboured on the roads, won scholarships.* He's learned I've left Damascus Road College and all prospects of entering the ministry, for the company of atheists at the university! Words, phrases, whole sentences and paragraphs spew from the cabinet of mimicry that suffices for his mind. 'You're a sinner and a liar, wallowing in whoredom and fornication.' I pay no attention. Through the window, I catch a glimpse of a pale doe and its speckled fawns at the roadside waiting for us to pass.

'Don't think I don't know what you've been up to. You've broken your mother's heart. You're a disgrace, a son of Satan . . .' I examine these words clinically. A son of Satan, am I? Is this an admission, finally, as to *his origins*?

The car smells of horse: it's the sum total of the body odours of these two creatures. The nerve! To call themselves my parents!

'What the hell are you talking about?' I say.

The silence is crushing; but I lean across the heaped plastering buckets and open the far window so that dust clouds – more pure than my father's poison – rush into this prison. My mother coughs out something about 'you've no idea of the work to keep things clean' and we reach the east–west fork in the road. We scrape along the eastern shoreline for ten minutes or so and I think it's over – whatever this is that he's up to – but he steers the car to the shoulder and stops. 'Don't think you're going to get away with it,' he says.

'I'm a grown man. You have no say in my life.'

'You'll have no more help from me. It was a mistake to let you leave home.'

'I'm not going back there anyway.'

'You bet you're not. You'll stay home and help your mother, and pray for repentance.'

'I'm enlisting in the air force.'

'You'll stay home and do what you're told.'

'No.'

He gets out. I wait in the back until he yanks open the door and pulls me out after him. I don't resist – why should I? The polished chrome that bands the cylinder of the hood shines in the spackle of moonlight that falls through the trees. The gleam of whitewall tyres anchors the car to the night. I can see in the yellow spill of the headlights that his Sunday collar and cuffs are smeared with dirt.

'I'm not staying home,' I say to him. He stands in front of me, thick and solid and puffed up with his views. 'I'm joining up tomorrow. There's a recruiting office in Duncan.'

'You'll walk, then.'

'I'll walk.'

He's angry and swings his arms in my direction to let me know it, but I duck my head to avoid the blow, and he doesn't touch me. Then I walk away. There's nothing he can do to me any more, nothing.

I light a cigarette. I hear my mother's gasp and glance over my shoulder to see her out of the car and standing beside him – my father, so called – with his bull's body, ape's shoulders, and simian arms still swaying. He gives a snort. I return to my smoke, and hear, as I inhale, the air part just to the side of my head. I drop and roll, and spring to my feet: the tyre iron is on the ground beside me. I pick it up.

Did you get that nurse, Dr Love? Is it self-defence?

The mother – so called – is crying fat grease trails of tears. I throw the burning cigarette to the earth and grind it under my foot. The father and I lock eyes. He gives his great laugh. He's facing me, not turned decently away, while he unbuttons his flies, pushes the vent of his underwear aside, and pulls out his winkle, stands there, legs planted apart, cradling himself in his hand, and sends an arc of urine that spats the dust at my feet.

He finishes, grins, keeps still so I can see in the cream headlights of the Studebaker that his fingers hold back the foreskin, then he slides it over the end, gives his member a shake and tucks it back in.

Christ, I hear the sunburned nurse say. There's a *hush* from Dr Frank.

So, that's it, Dr Love says.

It's a classic all right.

So, Dr Love repeats, but to me, *You, Sandy, understand at that moment, exactly what?*

'The son of a bitch who had me circumcised wasn't circumcised himself.' There's a sigh from all three of them: the room deflates.

You attacked him with the tyre iron. Struck him several times over the head. Why?

'He treated me like a dog all the while he pretended to me and to the world that he was my father and loved me.'

Are you sorry about what you did? Dr Love asks. The nurse removes the needle and helps me sit up.

I rub my arm. I'm buzzing with anger. 'No. Only that I didn't succeed.'

The remaining implements of therapy are put away. Punctures swabbed, blood dabbed, cold cloths administered.

Dr Frank, particularly, keeps busy, he won't meet my eyes.

'What happens now?' I ask as I watch him snap his notebook shut with an elastic band. 'Will my case go in your book?'

'There'll be another Board,' Dr Love answers. Dr Frank slips from the room.

'What will you recommend?'

'I can only speak for myself, Sandy, not for Dr Frank and not for the Board. I'll suggest that you acted while in a state of diminished responsibility brought about by a subconscious memory of your traumatic circumcision as a child. I'll recommend that you serve the rest of your time in safe custody.'

'What does that mean?'

'We'll have to wait and see. Don't worry. You did well.'

'Dr Frank doesn't think so. I can tell he's not pleased with me.'

'You're wrong there, son.'

'No, I'm right. He didn't want to hear the truth.'

'Truth?' The good doctor sits beside me on the bed. He gazes into his clasped hands. 'There's a kernel of truth here, Sandy. You may even have told the whole truth, as you know it, but you know what I think?'

'No, sir.'

'I think a drug is an imperfect tool and that no one knows the entire truth of life in your family, not even you.'

'Ah.'

'I also think the world isn't ready for your kind of truth.'

'So you do believe me!'

He rests a hand lightly on my shoulder. 'I believe that you believe what you've said. I know you did your best for us. That's as far as I can go. Not just with you, with anyone.

'The rest is . . .'

'Guesswork?'

He smiles down at me after he stands, his tired face a beacon of light. The nurse has bustled her crisp white uniform out the door, in a hurry, after Dr Frank. 'I was going to say "professional opinion". You're not a danger to anyone, Sandy. Not even to your parents any longer as far as I can tell. You've kept your opinions but you're no longer so certain about them. Am I right?'

I nod. How can one be certain about an opinion that no one else shares? In the end you have to admit doubt. There's no other way to tell a story. There are many possibilities, but for the sake of simplicity you choose among them. I've learned that from Karl.

'There's one more thing I'd like you to do, Sandy,' Dr Love says.

'What is it, doctor?'

He tells me.

There's no one around. Pete Cooper and the boys are making cheese or grooming cows or disinfecting the stables. Ron Signet has popped his head into my room to say he's had instructions I'm to be left alone for several hours. 'You're on scout's honour, Sandy,' he says.

'Can you do me a favour, Ron?'

'What's that, Sandy?'

'Would you mind feeding the pigeons for me? Just fill the troughs from the bag. I'll do the clean-up later.'

'Okey-dokey.'

I've been asked to do some funny things in my time, but this one takes the cake. I clear my writing table of all but paper and pen. I take a quick look at the passage on Descriptive Writing in *The Storehouse of Thought and Expression*. It reminds me that I should first indicate clearly what I see, and to observe very carefully shapes, planes, lines, proportions, colour. And, for the purposes of the exercise, to avoid indicating likes and dislikes. I feel a little funny, but it's Dr Love who has asked me to do this. Once it's done, I'm to bring it to Dr Frank, with a copy for Dr Love. I arrange writing paper and carbons. Just before I go ahead, I take the chair at my desk, turn it round, and slip the back of it beneath the doorknob; in case of interruption I'll have some warning.

I stand at my desk naked from the waist down. If anyone could look in – which I doubt, as the window is too high up – they'd see my head and my shoulders and chest dressed as usual, and the backs of what are now four motorcycle postcards sent by Bob, lined up along the windowsill.

To begin:

The shape of my penis is ordinary, as far as I can tell. It's cylindrical, a dark salmon pink in colour with a little brown mottling here and there. Its size is – well, it grows under my regard – but is nothing different from what I've observed in others. You can see, though, the scar line from the circumcision where there was a jagged open wound on the remaining foreskin and on the glans: it healed with some adhesion, as the wound wasn't well cared for. I'd had to have that dealt with by a doctor when I was thirteen, but he'd assured me that no deeper structures were involved and I was 'right as rain'.

Now to the self-inflicted damage. The attack had been on the penis itself, not on the testicles. I'd hacked with broken glass, but hadn't succeeded in dismembering myself. There is certainly damage: a lump of diagonal scar tissue remains from where the wound was sutured, and disappears into the pool of the scrotum. Dr Frank has said that he thought the attempt 'symbolic' although I could assure him that there'd been nothing symbolic in my mind at the time! Since the injury, I'd had a minor problem of incontinence, but that has resolved itself.

I get dressed. I read over my notes. It isn't poetry or *The Romance of Stanley Park* but it will have to do.

I have the notes all ready when I get the call to bring them with me to Dr Frank's office.

NINETEEN
21 September 1942

It is always difficult to wait, but it has become more so since Dr Frank has forbidden me to write. He says I must use this time, while the Board is making up its mind as to what shall be done with me, to think about my life and about the forthcoming meeting with my parents.

There is certainly much to consider:

Georgina tells me that I need to straighten out my ideas regarding her and Heather. Winchell's messages sent through Deceased Property have me increasingly worried about Karl. They've stopped the electric shock treatments and he's soon to appear before a new Board. In the meantime, Pete Cooper has taken to wearing a white towel draped around his neck, and grinning at me like a maniac – an obvious reference to Kosho and the white towel he wore over his shoulders in case an opportunity for suicide might occur. But why is Cooper doing this at this point? Kosho, as far I know, is safely hidden away at 'Innisfree' by Georgina. Is the towel wearing meant as a threat to me?

I look out the window from where my writing table used to be and view the land that slopes towards Kosho's pond. The long summer and dry Indian summer have turned the fields golden: but I know that only a little farther off, the area surrounding the pond remains green with sphagnum moss and water plants. To keep me busy, Dr Frank has had Ron Signet set me to preparing the pond for the ducklings we will acquire next spring. We'll raise mallards, because this species most rapidly becomes accustomed to captivity and is a persistent breeder. The irony of it, particularly when I lift my head from my work with a shovel, dredging mud or digging the foundation for a rock retaining wall, to watch flocks of ducks migrate south, does not escape me. Overhead are free creatures following their inbuilt natures, while down here I, a prisoner, address my efforts to the future imprisonment of their fellows.

Pinioning ducks is very simple if you snip the wing joint when they are only days old.

The parallel, Sandy? Your wings clipped long ago? No, not *wings*!

The heavy work of digging is making me exceptionally strong.

I cast an eye at my dismantled writing table: the sanded door, somewhat ink-stained, leans against a wall. The trestles are stowed beside the entrance. Dr Frank says I may set the table up again once matters are resolved. Which matters? How resolved? I tried to ask him these things at our last meeting, but his mind was on plans for his honeymoon. He and the sunburned nurse have married. 'No point in waiting, Sandy,' was his comment to me when I offered my congratulations. 'There's a war on.'

The remark has remained with me. Not that I don't know about the war, of course I do. But is there a point in *my* waiting? Is there?

Although I am not permitted to 'write', Dr Frank has allowed pens, ink and paper to remain in my room: I'm on my honour. I did manage to smuggle out, by pigeon, the briefest of notes for Georgina to send to Heather, but even the strongest of George's birds can only carry a snippet, and the sending and receiving require the utmost caution. The watchers on the roof are nearly always at their stations, and even when they aren't, there's still Ron Signet or somebody else patrolling with radio and binoculars. Recently, I've managed to interest Ron in bird-watching. All I have to say is 'Ron, look, a Townsend's Warbler,' and point to the distance for him to swing his glasses that way. This gives me a moment to let fly the pigeon I've tucked into an inner pocket of my jacket – it's better, if it is seen, that it be flying in the wild rather than from the coop so that the going can't be traced to me. So far, all such messages have been safely delivered and no one has taken any notice of the pigeons fluttering back and forth over the woods. In the words of the Yeats poem, 'And evening full of the linnet's wings.' Although there are no linnets in our marsh. But I have, in the coop, ready to go, several more of George's own pigeons. Evening, indeed, is our usual time to 'talk'.

This morning, with Ron Signet in a meeting and Pete Cooper involved with the cows, I've hurried through my work in the loft and pen so that I can make an inventory of the contents of my room. I've wanted to do this for some time, since it is clear that there have been alterations in my quarters beyond the dismantling of the table. Today is my earliest opportunity.

What's impossible to miss is that all four 'Bob' motorcycle postcards are gone from the windowsill. I've looked every-where, in case they were simply knocked aside when the table was shifted, but they aren't here; and my books and papers are arranged differently. It is vital, considering the feeling I'm having that a story pattern is being made by the intersecting lines of development that concern me (Georgina and Heather, Pete Cooper, Winchell and Karl, Kosho, etc.), and that the pattern is about to reveal itself – or as *The Storehouse of Thought and Expression* says, I'm near the point at which 'the writer must be keen enough to recognise what is indicated and skilful enough to carry it out' – that I know exactly where I stand. The story – whether written or of a life – as I've begun to understand, can't be predicted ahead of time: one has to pay attention to the indications, to see what *is*.

I push a trestle against the door to the hallway, fetch the footrest box from beside my chair, and begin the most urgent part of my search by prying loose several of the wooden slats. I remove the top layer of straw and stones and wiggle my fingers through the remaining straw all the way down one side to touch the envelope of letters and addresses entrusted to me by the Russians. Then I extract the wrapped packets of knives, awls, shears, files and Winchell's revolvers and ammunition. I quickly clean and oil the guns and put everything back. All is well. I take a moment to leave the room and wash my hands before continuing.

There's not much else in here besides my clothing and papers. On the top shelf of the cupboard I keep my writings; the more personal of my letters, notes and observations are hidden within the pages of what remains of the reams of Karl's blank paper. I find the stories and letters, but several pages of my observations of Pete Cooper's work are gone. I double-check using my system of a knotted measuring string, but no matter how many times I look through the paper stacks, these items remain missing.

This is worrying. If Cooper has found them, that would explain the white towel. But wasn't Ron with him? Wouldn't Ron know?

I'm thinking this over when I hear the outside door slam. At the same moment a pigeon flutters through the open window and alights on the windowsill. That it is a bird trained to my window and not to the loft is significant. This is no simple social call. George and I have only a few of these 'emergency' pigeons. I quickly remove the capsule from the pigeon's leg, then put the bird and capsule in a sock in my pocket.

Ron stands at the bottom of the stairs gazing up at me, light reflecting off his spectacles. 'You coming down to the pond, now, Sandy?'

'Not just yet, Ron,' I tell him as I skedaddle down the stairs and past. 'I've got a couple of other things to do.' He drifts lazily in my wake as I make my way out the door and towards the fly pen. Quickly, before Ron can catch up, I place the messenger pigeon back in its nest and sprinkle out a little extra feed.

Ron watches as I check the pins in the wire netting and make sure that there are no breaks. Georgina recently found a raccoon prowling near the coop at her father's house. As I do, I coo softly back to the pigeons which bob their heads and watch.

'You'd make someone a good mother, Sandy.'

'Listen, Ron, would you mind if I didn't work at the pond today? I'm a little tired, and I'm behind with some other things.'

'What things?' Ron says. His eyes screw up behind the lenses of his spectacles and he looks like he's trying to see inside my head. 'Everything here looks fine to me.' I know that I'm a problem. Nobody knows quite what to do with me. If I'm not crazy, why am I here? If I'm guilty of a vicious attack on my father, why aren't I behind bars? I'm in limbo, no longer quite one of the loonies, but neither one of 'them', the regular folks. It's a social problem. It makes nice people like Ron worry about how to do their jobs.

'Everything's hunky-dory here, Ron, as you say, but the boxes are piling up in Deceased Property. I realise it's not high priority these days, but, well, I don't like to fall too far behind. People are waiting. It might not mean anything to us, Ron, but a memento of a loved one can make all the difference to the peace of mind of a family. Even if the loved one was a nutter.' I hope that Ron won't remember that the 'mementos' are distributed before the boxes come to me.

Ron is shocked at my terminology. He ducks his head. 'Well. I know, Sandy, I know.' He sighs and lifts his gaze to the distance. Who or what is he thinking of? Ron, one of my most constant companions in my time here, is a mystery to me. I know nothing of his home life beyond the little daughter who used to but no longer rides her pony in the ring beside staff housing. Things change. *Mutatis mundi.*

From the corner of my eye, and through the brush and trees, I catch sight of Pete Cooper and two of his helpers as they emerge from the barn.

'The trouble is, I can't be in two places at once, Sandy.' Ron chews his bottom lip.

'Don't you trust me on my own? You used to, Ron.'

His neck above the buttoned shirt collar reddens. 'It's not that, Sandy.'

I believe I understand the dilemma. When I'm at the pond he can stretch his legs, bird-watch, smoke cigarettes. Fiddle with the radio. Deceased Property, on the other hand, is boring: there's nothing for him to do but look in on me through the window. He can't just sit there and babysit me, can he? How close *has* Dr Frank told him to stick?

'Dr Frank's away, Ron.'

'It's not Dr Frank.'

'What is it, then?' I ask, but Ron just shakes his head. Pete and friends disappear into the trees.

'I'm on patrol this afternoon; I'd only be able to check on you every now and then.'

'What's the problem, Ron, you can tell me.' I'm genuinely puzzled. He shifts back and forth, cleans the toes of his shoes on his trousers, plucks invisible threads from his shirt sleeves.

'Nothing, there's no problem, Sandy, I'd simply prefer it if you came with me to the pond.'

'Whatever you think best, Ron.' I don't look at him. I, too, can examine the distance. 'But it's a terrible thing to lose a loved one, no matter how it happens.' I give a gentle – as-if-disguised – sorrowful sniff. I believe I can count on his humane instincts and his laziness, and I'm right.

'For the families, you say? I thought that everything to go to the families was removed already?' He offers me a stick of

American gum.

Here it is, make or break. 'Supposed to be, Ron,' I answer, taking the gum. 'But you know how it is. Things are missed; no next of kin may be marked down on admission – they're ashamed, see, they don't want their families to know – but I've found the names of family in books, or overlooked letters or twice – I swear it, Ron – on pieces of paper tucked into shoes.'

'These are hard times, hard days . . .' he opines.

I keep quiet.

'Well,' he says, obviously still somewhat troubled by my request, but weakening, 'I can't see it will do any harm. You've worked hard on the pond. We'll have it finished in a few days. You go on over there' – he points in the general direction of Deceased Property – 'and I'll drop by when I can.'

I'm on my way to the old Chinese quarters, cutting across a corner of the main building's lawn, when I spot Dr Love sitting on the fountain wall. He's got his jacket off, his shirt sleeves rolled up. He dips one hand in the water and flicks droplets on to the walk. When I am close to him, he looks up and I'm shocked at how gaunt he's become. His skin is the colour of the pale fountain stone, and with a haze like its green scum. 'Dr Love!' I say. 'What's wrong?'

'Oh, it's you, Sandy.'

'Who else?'

'I was just thinking about you. I've come from a meeting of the Board.'

'About me?'

'Among many.' He dries his hands on his good, but crumpled, grey trousers.

I take another look at him. 'You've shaved off your beard!'

'My wife says I look like the walking dead.'

'You have a wife?'

'I am human, Sandy, whatever you may think.' He stands and I walk along beside him as he heads down the drive. I'm taller than him, now; I've grown; or maybe it's that he's begun to walk with a stoop. The war, and his work, all the people he tries to help – it's been hard on him. I look away. The surrounding trees have been trimmed back, the hedges given a military clip. Oh, for Bob and the care that went into his gardening.

'There's something I need to tell you, Sandy.'

'About the Board, sir?' I've been waiting, my heart in a flutter.

'I know you're anxious about the result. Your case is a difficult one for them. More difficult than some.'

'Why's that, sir?'

'There's some dissension. There are the opinions advanced by Dr Frank in his report: he believes that you're cured, that the narcosynthesis sessions have been a total success.'

'You were there, Dr Love. I'm sure you know what to think, as well.' I twist a button on my shirt. I shove my hands into my pockets so as not to further betray my nervousness.

He stops, and I stop. I am permitted to go no farther towards the wall and gate. The soldiers, who guard us day and night ever since they began using the rooftop as a battery, have their eyes on us. 'Yes, I was there, and on the whole I agree with Dr Frank.'

'On the whole?'

'What happens to young children can affect their perception of reality. It may lead, in later life, to serious mental illness.'

I feel like I've been kicked in the stomach. 'You think I'm ill – in that way?'

'You're a clever lad, Sandy. I don't think this is the right place for you.'

In my pocket, my fingers find, and roll back and forth in its cylinder, the still unread message from Georgina.

'They – the Board – see it as one way or the other: you stay here and receive treatment, or you go to jail and serve your time. Dr Frank, on the other hand, has put forward an alternative.'

A skirling wind picks up leaves from the grass and blows them on to the walk. The maples and alders are shedding their bright leaves, quickly. I look into the trees, and catch sight of two crows: they jump from branch to branch, setting the tree limbs shaking. 'Just tell me, sir.'

'You're to be released, under strict supervision, and beginning with a series of day visits, into the care of your parents. In order to minimise the possibility of' – he pauses, waits until I meet his eyes – 'any unfortunate incidents, you'll be put on a new treatment programme.'

'What kind of programme?' I ask, although I'm still trying to absorb the words 'in the care of your parents'.

'Insulin.' He watches my face closely. What does it show? I have no idea, but it feels frozen as my life divides neatly, as it has done at least twice earlier, into before and after. I will not allow it to happen: I will not live with them and I will not undergo insulin shock. I don't care what the Board has decided, I won't. The crows lift into flight together, and they're away, over the wall, gone. 'It's done routinely when patients go on day trials,' he finishes.

'You agreed to this?' I remember the men I'd seen in the East Wing visitors' room, slack-jawed, slack-minded, waiting for their families to take them out for an airing. I take in his face once more: its hollow shadows, its defeat.

'It's rare that a patient doesn't derive some benefit from the treatment, Sandy.'

'I've been in the East Wing, Dr Love. I've seen what happens.'

'You've seen the failures. In our experience, half make good recoveries and can return to normal lives.'

'Will I have a normal life? With my parents? Like that? With all that you know can you truly say you believe that?'

'Would you rather be in jail, Sandy?'

'Would my father press the issue?'

'If you do not go home with them, he will prosecute to the full extent of the law. It could mean years, many years, of further incarceration.'

One of the crows – if it's the same one – flies back and sits on the wall. *Caw caw,* it cries, *are you coming?*

'Your life is different now, Sandy. There are people – friends – in it who care for you. Mrs Jones-Murray; the young woman, Heather, you write to . . . you're not alone any more.'

'You, Dr Love? Do you include yourself as a friend?'

I wait for him to say he's done his best, to offer excuses, to indicate that I'm just one of many patients in his life. Instead, in full view of the soldiers, he sets down his doctor's bag and puts his arms around me. He sets his forehead against mine – I feel its heat and sweat – and he whispers, 'Never give up, Sandy.' He clasps my hand in his long thin fingers before he goes, leaving behind, in my palm, a wad of money. 'That's the best I can do. God be with you. I couldn't help your friend Karl, either,' he says. 'I guess I'm a bust.' He turns once, and waves, and I know I will never see him again.

The pain of the heart is unlike any other pain. It is fluid, it sloshes back and forth through memories, good and bad, and yet it strengthens because of its sincerity. Because of its purity, it opens the world of alternatives. In this pain I turn my back on the front gate and cross the lawn and then the dry, harvested fields to the empty Chinese quarters.

I have my work cut out for me. I estimate it will be only about another hour before Ron comes to check on me. I wipe away dust and spider webs from one of the waiting cardboard boxes, open it, remove the contents list and spread some of the items on the table – bills, receipts, photographs, a broken watch, a miniature chess set: the lot belongs to G. Tupovich. I set out the categories – for the poor, garbage, and questionable – and do a superficial sort. Then I take out the pen, ink and onion skin paper I have brought with me and quickly write the letter about Pete Cooper I've been composing in my head.

It outlines his fraudulent use of farm supplies and equipment for personal gain; his theft of gas and oil, beef, paint, lumber, cement, poultry, milk and cheese for personal use or to sell on the black market; his forcing the helpers, sometimes at the point of a gun, to work on his personal projects, his pointing his rifle at me when he loads and unloads it in the kitchen. It contains as much as I can remember of what I'd put in the missing notes. I fold the onion skin scrap as small as I can, take the messenger cylinder from my pocket, remove Georgina's note and replace it with my letter.

A deep breath now. I go to the windows and wipe away enough dirt so that I can see there's no one approaching. I open George's note and read it: it says only: *Help. Please!* The brevity of the note underlines all too clearly both her distress and her fear of discovery.

So much in my life has changed since I met Georgina. Some would say it was for the worse, since it marked the point of my loss of freedom; but I believe it has all been for the best. Was I free before? Did I know who I was? What was I before she entered my life but a lost soul, a boy who one way or the other was about to give up? George saved my life and bought me time in which to grow, and if it hasn't been on the terms I'd have selected, well, never mind. I've not been idle: I've done my work and become ever stronger; I've learned to write a decent story, I've helped construct a glider, I've built enough of a case of miscarried justice to launch an appeal on behalf of Alan Macaulay. None of my suffering has been useless. How many on the outside could say as much? Georgina has been my angel. Of course I'll help her, whatever her trouble.

I must hurry. I'm just finishing with G. Tupovich when Ron Signet barges in. He's huffing and puffing but looking pleased with himself as he places another Deceased Property box on one of the tables. He blows dust from the surface, brushes his hands on his blue cotton trousers. 'Geez, Sandy, you should take the time to clean this place up.'

'Who's got time, Ron?' I open the next box. He watches me

sort, and I can see him working himself up to a question. I know the signals: the little cough, a polish of the glasses on his shirt sleeve, a practice or two of a smile.

'Say, Sandy, I saw you talking to Dr Love earlier.'

'Yes?' I put some collar studs and a watchband into the Salvation Army tackle box.

Another throat clear. 'Well' – Ron shuffles his feet – 'did he say anything?'

'Say anything?'

'Well, you know he's resigned.'

Now I look up. 'I didn't know that, Ron. He didn't tell me.'

'Oh . . . I just thought . . .' Suddenly he's got on my nerves.

'You thought what? That he was my friend. Well, you know what, Ron? I once did too. But now I'm not so damned sure.'

I wait for the reprimand about my language, but I don't care; not just that I don't care what Ron thinks, but I've noticed a pencil drawing on the side of the box that Ron has carried in. It's Winchell's hammer and sickle.

Now it comes. 'Sandy! You can do better than that!'

'I'm sorry, Ron.' Three deep breaths: I consider the ways I can deal with him. I pick the shortest. 'It's just that . . . what he told me . . . I never thought he'd agree to send me back to my parents.'

'Aw, Sandy, that's not it, not it at all! That's why he resigned! He wouldn't stand for it or for the Board saying that the German, your friend, has to have his brain done.' Ron makes the scooping motion that is a reference to lobotomy. 'He asked for you to be released to him and for Karl to be sent to a POW camp but they said no.'

What Ron has revealed about Dr Love finally sinks in. 'He asked for me to be released to him? He stood up for Karl?'

'Yes, that's right!' Ron nods furiously. 'He said he'd take care of you himself.' I slump against a table. Have I misjudged Dr Love? His defeat isn't a moral one after all, it's tactical. He's been outmanoeuvred, out-gunned. The poor sap! So what, in that case, is the money for if it's not, as I'd assumed, blood money? What do I need money for? Everything is done for me here, I don't pay for anything.

The answer, when it comes, is startlingly obvious. I need money for when I'm on the outside.

'Look, Ron,' I say, digging in my pocket. I pull out the message cylinder with the Pete Cooper letter squashed into it. 'Would you see this gets to Dr Love?'

'What is it, Sandy?' Ron jiggles the grey cylinder in his hand.

I hold his eyes: he has washed blue eyes – like a sky that can't imagine either snow or hot sun. 'It's best if you don't know.' Ron drops his gaze. 'Can you do that, Ron? Just get it to him? Otherwise . . .' I put out my hand to take it back.

'No, it's all right. I can do that for you, Sandy. I won't even look.'

'It doesn't matter.'

'But I won't!'

'I said it doesn't matter!'

A stiff breeze rattles through the loose boards of the walls, and a swirl of dust scurries across the floor. The Chinese must have been cold here in the winters. Did anybody know? Or care?

'That's it, then. I'll be on my way.' He backs out the door, either to do as I've asked or to betray me. Which will it be this time? 'So long then, Sandy.'

'Yeah. So long, Ron.' I lift my hand, but he has already walked away.

Time is running out. *Now Sandy* – it's as if Dr Frank is speaking right into my ear – *you'd better start with the bird in the hand before you hare off into the bushes.* Georgina's message is urgent, but there's also Winchell's box to open. Georgina or Winchell?

I open Winchell's box.

TWENTY
22 September and following, 1942

To follow knowledge like a sinking star
Beyond the utmost bound of human thought . . .
– *The Storehouse of Thought and Expression*

'I'm a party man,' Winchell writes. 'Ever since Stalin's historic call to action of the Soviet people, this war has been my war. If we don't unify against the fascist armies we face complete Nazi victory and enslavement and the return of the Dark Ages. Such are the fundamental alternatives confronting mankind, Sandy, and such they were in Spain. Not that anyone gave a pig's ass then or will now, but I'm in again.' It's Winchell at his most literate – a sure sign of his desperation.

I wipe my sweating hands on my shirt. It's midnight. There's been much to do since I received the note from 'Boris Godunov' in the Deceased Property box. It said that Dr Love had been to the mortuary with medicine for Winchell's tuberculosis – he does this regularly because he's treating him, keeping him in the land of the living while Winchell sorts the East Wing corpses . . . And it's a good job for the Spanish Civil War veteran – his bloody handkerchiefs are burned along with the clothing of the dead, he eats well enough, and he sleeps alone; on fine days he sits in the sun in the loading bay, waiting for the ambulances or for Bob to pop by. It's just as good as – better than – a sanatorium . . .

The *reason* Dr Love visited Winchell this time, though, was to tell him that Karl is scheduled for lobotomy – 'the brain scoop' is how Winchell, like Ron, puts it. So Winchell wants to do a good deed. Get Karl out *and* go to Russia to fight. No easier said than done! Bob's your uncle! Or, as *The Storehouse* tells us, we simply watch the flower unfold.

My role is simple: watch for the lights to go out. Bob – yes, Bob! – will stash his motorcycle at a distance, arrive quietly on foot, and cut the power lines from the road. The door of the ambulance bay will be left unlocked by the fellow-traveller politician Winchell knows. He'll do this because he's ashamed that the government refused to help bring home the shattered remnant of the Mackenzie-Papineau Battalion from Spain, and because the war hero Winchell is incarcerated here, and because of the pro-fascist attitude of some of Mackenzie King's cabinet, and because the Communist Party supported the conscription plebiscite – in short, for no shortage of reasons. Or, as Winchell says, people who can't do much, do what they can. Guilt is a wonderful thing. It turns mediocre men into heroes; it really does open doors.

Once the lights are out, I'm to creep out and meet Winchell and Karl at the pond. How Winchell will extract Karl from the coils of the East Wing, I have no idea, but if it's not a problem for him, it's not a problem for me. I'm to bring the weapons and as much tinfoil as I can to deflect radio waves. Not that, as far as I know, tinfoil will have any effect, nor am I likely to find any to speak of in the kitchen or on the farm. But who am I, Sandy Grey, to question at a time like this? It's all or nothing. What have I got to lose but torture by insulin and the rest of my life with my parents? Rise up, as Winchell would say, and lose your chains.

When the lights wink out, the helpers are asleep. Their snores rumble through the house. I gather my few belongings and slip out of my room. It's not hard to avoid the creaking stairs – I've had plenty of practice. I ease my way down. Outside, men call quietly back and forth as a patrol begins to search for the source of the electrical outage. There's no anxiety; they're not worried. No Jap planes or submarines have been sighted. We're not on alert. The searchlights sleep. Electric lights twinkle merrily beyond the wall. It's merely darkness; we're in a state of nature here. The gibbous moon slopes its way west – I'll be heading northwest, and can use it as a guide.

I'm standing at the kitchen window, stuffing bread and cheese into the top of the rucksack I'm carrying and watching for the moment when I can slip out the door and behind the flash-light-equipped patrols, when a hand grips the back of my shoulder.

'Can't sleep, Sandy? What's the matter? Guilty conscience?' I spin round, and let the rucksack slide from my hand behind my back. It's Pete Cooper in his briefs and T-shirt. He's a grey shimmering ghost in front of me. Also shimmering, poking out from under his arm, is the long barrel of the rifle. He pushes me away from the window and peers out himself. I note, with some relief, that the white towel is not around his neck.

'That's right, Pete. I've got a lot on my mind.'

'I just bet you have, you little bastard.' He's turned to face me, and moved a step closer. His breath is a witch's brew of tobacco and beer. He sees the flinch of my nostrils and moves even nearer, the foul odour of his person washes over me. In the wisp of moonlight that is our illumination, thin strands of his fringe of hair move independently, as if by thought, or by the current of the deep lost sea in which he swims.

'I've seen what you've written about me. You don't have a chance against me, you little squirt. You're dead, Sandy. You're fucking dead.' He steps away and raises the gun.

'How are you going to explain this, Pete?'

'I caught you trying to escape. You're a known criminal. I'm just doing my job.'

Every now and then we're given the gift of clarity, and I have it now. Just as the essence of night is to hide, the essence of Pete Cooper is to destroy: he's a negative force, it's nothing personal; the hatred that possesses him is transcendental. Perhaps more than anyone in my life, he's responsible for teaching me what I need to know. In this moment of understanding, I see him as perfect of his kind. Perhaps, even, I love him.

'Did you ever think, Pete, that you and I are part of one mind?'

He gapes at me, the rifle barrel wavers then steadies, his finger tightens on the trigger, but in that instant a large rock smashes through the window and strikes him down, and the bullet ploughs harmlessly into the ceiling.

'What's the use of a fucking gun if you don't fucking use it!' Winchell's low brow and long ears poke through the hole in the glass. I pick up the rucksack in which I've stowed the revolvers and everything else I need. Pete is down for the count; blood swells from a long gash in his scalp. 'He got the drop on me, Winchell,' I say.

'Fucking amateurs.' The head withdraws.

When I meet up with him outside, he pulls me into the shadows of some trees. We wait, stifling our breathing, until a soldier has walked briskly by. No one's paid any attention to the disturbance. Perhaps they think it's a signal? Then we're on the move. We skulk through the cut hay fields along dark furrows to pillowy hay stacks; we zig and zag the long way through brush near the perimeter wall, then cut back from the west, across the marsh and to the pond. Kosho's pond, where Karl waits, hunched over, in the bamboo stand. He's too skinny and his shoulders won't straighten even when he tries. When I greet him with a hand on the arm, he lifts his heavy head and I catch the glint of his glasses.

So it is that the threads join.

All the East Wing Russians are dead, but Winchell was able to tell the last of them – Kudikov – that the tide is beginning to turn against the Germans at Stalingrad. He knows this through his Spanish Civil War comrades who get the information straight from the horse's mouth, that is, from the Party that gets it direct from someone who knows someone who knows Stalin. Who knows if the 'source' can be trusted? But are you going to give bad news to a dying man? I have the Russians' letters with me, wrapped in oilskin and tucked in an inside jacket pocket. I bring them out and take Karl's arm with my other hand. Many dancing lights are beginning to converge on the swamp.

'We'd better go,' Winchell says.

'You really headed to Russia, Winchell?'

'You bet, Sandy.'

'Then you'd better take these.' I hand over the letters.

It's a terrible thing to know that a tragedy is unfolding in front of you, and yet be unable to stop it. Personal tragedies are one thing – they're a dime a dozen in a place like this – but it's a whole other level to watch the world break up as you stand by helplessly. This is what's on Winchell's mind and what he talks about endlessly as we tramp the terrain. There's the Spanish campaign he's lived through – the grenade launchers sounding like birds as the Canadians crossed the Ebro in boats and on pontoons; they swam the mules and arrived at the encampment as the fascists were about to say Mass; and then a shell exploded in Winchell's group killing all except him. He crawled away and found a cave where he hid until the barrage lifted, then he went up a hill where he was hit in the arm by a bullet and couldn't lift his rifle. He could do nothing but lie there in the dry red earth. The smell of blood was everywhere; and anyway his Russian rifle had jammed.

'Thanks for the encouragement, Winchell,' I say. I'm puffing and out of breath. Moving Karl is like hauling logs.

'You'd better get the guns out, Sandy,' Winchell says.

We stagger on a little farther and I stop tugging on Karl's arm. We're on a ledge on one of the rocky hillocks that rise out of the marsh to form the ridge near the wall. Dry moss crumbles under our feet as I push Karl down to sit in the deeper shadows of a scraggle of stunted oak. I open the pack and hand the weapons to Winchell.

'Did you kill anyone in Spain?'

'I hope to Christ so, Sandy! What kind of fucking soldier would I be if I didn't!' Then he's on to the subject of Stalingrad – which is where he's planning to go – and we're edging forward again, trying not to pop up like sitting ducks on the skyline. There's the occasional burst of gunfire as some fool in a patrol in the swamp lets off a burst at the waterfowl that start up in panic to get out of his way.

I'm moving Karl up the last of the slope, and I'm thinking about Georgina and whether I can reach her in time to help her with whatever she needs help with. Each breath could be my last. Each second of life beneath the starry sky means I'm born again. Time – this time – is a spider's web of spectacular beauty. Me and Karl and Winchell – we're like raindrops trembling in its threads. We're not caught: this is only an instant of arrest in something more general: rain as it falls from the clouds to earth – like that – and the cycle renewed. I glance at the low half-fist of moon. Where did I, Sandy Grey, begin? Where did I come from? Is it a dream of that home – who knows, maybe the moon? – my true home that I've been chasing all my life? The puzzle and the longing and the lack inside me, is it simply what I'm made of, and nothing to do with my parents? Am I the alien, the substitute, fallen out of the sky of nothingness to which all returns?

Well – as Ron would say, and I wonder if he's one of them out there now, after us, under arms – these are not abnormal

thoughts in the face of death. Your life flashes by: Alan Macaulay's did; everyone's does. There's no stopping it.

Winchell rattles on: the city's been smashed to smithereens;
the Russians have thousands of men with no rifles and those
who do have weapons possess no ammunition and the rein-
forcements have no maps – they don't know the city's blitzed
terrain and the memory of streets is lost to all but archaeologists,
or maybe to a new ice age or to experienced veterans like himself
. . . But even so, Winchell asserts, they'll hold off the Germans
when the tanks approach from two sides and fire at point-blank
range and the Russian Maxims are blown up and they can't see
one another for smoke and dust.

We're at the wall now. There's a *ping* into the stone above
my head and I shove Karl over and fall on top of him. Winchell
squashes in next to us. I look up at the drunken stagger of trees –
but it's only me pitched aside on a tilt, and maybe the roaring of
the hunt. For a moment I think myself into the safety of the
Chinese quarters, and imagine I'm lying quietly on a wooden
bunk, puzzling out the characters scrawled on the wall next to
me. Wall scratchings, messages to the future – which has turned
out, sadly, to be only me, Sandy Grey. The building's made of
stone, and concrete and wood. It will stand forever. Long after
I'm bone fragments, like the makings of my father's plaster.

Winchell's still mumbling: the Germans appear next from
behind their tanks and throw grenades in front of them, and the
Russians catch them and throw them back. They can hear the
enemy soldiers' breath and footsteps but they can't see them in
the smoke; they fire at the sound.

Karl's sweat has soaked through his shirt. He's not said a
word, and his eyes, when I catch their glint as he lies beneath
me, are closed mouths – they say nothing. I lift my head: barbed
wire, broken glass and electric wire defend the top of the wall.
How did we imagine we'd get over it? Is there a handy glider
and a launching platform nearby, or are we to leap over, like

Bob, with vaulting poles? But we have not trained for this moment! Beyond and below where we lie in our little stack against the wall – it's a mountain from this point of view, with its implacable force that seems to reach sky high – I can see that emergency lighting now illuminates the asylum. Newly unmuzzled artillery points from behind the parapet. I recall my flight from the roof: what dreams Karl and I had had – we'd removed window bars, climbed to the roof, found a hidey hole, and in there, like gods, we'd fashioned our creation. I'd followed that one as far as it would go.

A truck screeches into the farmyard. Doors slam, dogs bay: we hear the crackle and shout of more men arming themselves with fury. They'll have found Pete by now. If he's conscious we're condemned; if he's dead, we're dead.

Flames blaze from the farmhouse roof. 'Christ, Winchell, the balloon's really gone up now!'

'You and Karl take off, Sandy!' Winchell's stuffing ammunition by the handful into his pockets. 'You both better get the fuck out of here now!' His fingers jab at the fine scrawl of the deer trail that mirrors, so delicately, the base line of the wall. He's on his knees, he pushes the revolvers into the waistband of his trousers. I coax Karl on to his knees and we begin to crawl. More *pings* smack the wall near us, then Winchell scoots away downhill and northward, returning fire as he runs – he's fast, he leaps and bounds over the rough ground; he flops, as if nothing can get through that tough skin, into a nest of brambles. I glimpse – I swear to God I glimpse – Pete Cooper's face on the other side of one of those marsh guns: he's a chalk inflatable of skin and bandages rising up from the reeds.

By the time we come to the blown-out section of the wall, and Bob holds out his hands to pull us through the hole, Winchell is hunkered down hundreds of feet away on level upland, drenching our pursuers with gunfire.

At the end of time, my father said, there will be two kinds: the lost and the saved. The lost are damned to hell, the saved rejoice in heaven. At the last judgement, the dead will arise: the sheep will be parted from the goats, and those that are saved – the sheep, I suppose – will be those who fed the hungry, gave the thirsty a drink, took in the stranger, clothed the naked, visited the sick . . . We cannot know which we are ahead of time – for what we see now we see through a glass darkly – but *I* know, in the deepest hidden part of myself, that Winchell, who has set us free, is one of the saved.

Bob's lean young body is cocooned in black leather: his white face candles the dark; he's chewing gum like there's no tomorrow. 'Where's the Winch?' he says. I thrust Karl in his direction.

'Back there. He's holding them off.' More tat-tat-tatting shots ring out.

'Jesus Christ!' Bob says. 'What've you gone and done, set off a war?'

He starts up the motorbike, I lever Karl on to the seat behind him and wrap his arms around Bob's waist. 'Hold on tight, Karl!' Karl does, but he also turns his head and leans his cheek against my body a moment. Through my clothing I feel a pulse, a thread of intelligence in his skin. Something, someone in there, is still alive.

Bob revs the engine, I straighten Karl up, leap back and start running in the opposite direction down the far side of the ridge.

When I was a boy, I could run for miles. I'd head out from the house, some angry words or fashioned cruelty at my heels, and I'd outrun those knives. Out across the farm fields, over the cattle bridge where Heather and I once played, along paths, through dirt and grass, across the railway tracks, deep into the network of farm roads where, at night, only rabbits and deer travelled: I'd run right here, sweat washing me clean, on the road that is now under my feet. It curves into a triangle of low-lying fields, then climbs steeply into the hills.

This section of the hills is surprisingly clear of bush. My

feet kick up gravel. I cut away on to another trail, heading north-west. The moon's adrift over the woods, like a small barrage balloon fading into the inlet.

I slow down a little, anxious not to lose the way. After some hesitation, I single out the landmark of poplars at a dark farm-house lower down, and I pick up speed; the cedars and firs spiral around me, the crowns and flames of trees send their energy upward; the lower branches have dropped away under shade. Light and light only can draw them away from the earth to the stars and whatever lies beyond them; as if the darkness needs their green. My heart pounds in pieces, its separate give and take of pulse.

Sandy! This is what you were made for!

The runner runs because he must. The prisoner is obliged to escape. The child loves the mother who gives him birth. I run, shadowed by the swish and swoop of an owl and the hanging froth of tree moss. The earth is dry, the leaves under my feet snap and crinkle. Everything has its cause and its effect, even the shallow pockets of soil that prevent the conifer forest from closing in; and I've found the trail that hems the lake.

I stop and splash cool water over my hands and face. The lake – seen from above, or on the map – makes the shape of a dove, its beak pointed straight to Georgina's. This is as far as I've ever been. When I was a boy, at the end of my run, I'd jump in, rinse the sweat and salt from my body here, then turn back towards home. When I arrived, they'd say nothing, there'd be nothing in their faces.

My fingers trail in the water's silk. When I plunge my arm deeper, a swirl of cold circulates its tendrils over my skin.

A nest of cabins inhabits the north end of the lake. I skirt these and search for the path of which Georgina has told me. She and her sister used to walk here from their house on the inlet when it was too cold to swim in the sea. I've tried to imagine Georgina as a girl, but I can't. She sprang forth, for me, on the *Brentwood*, a fully formed woman. The trail unravels just where she said it would, a finger of moonlight along a rib. Sword fern and maiden fern gently waft the night air as I travel through the lush green of this hidden world. And my mother comes to mind: how it must have been when as an infant, I was held in her arms and breathed in the scent of her milk. When I was as I was before; when she was as she was, before she became resentful and hardened. I no longer believe she was two women, as I'd thought for so long, but just one human being, saddened and broken by life with my father, also only a single, solitary person. It's as if a record of this truth has been pressed deep inside me, its evidence beyond erasure, waiting for the right moment, the right amount of effort and darkness and transport, for it to resound in my memory. Now here it is.

The earth grows softer, piled deep with pine needles and moss; I've covered some distance and all the noise of battle has been left behind. I try not to think about what might have happened to Winchell. In that brief final glimpse of him, I'd seen him pull a red scarf from his pocket and tie it round his bicep . . . I skid down a creek bank and into water. I stand still for a moment, then allow the pull of the current downstream to take me knee-deep into the flow. My feet test the way round boulders and over slippery crystallised igneous rock: I'm following the shaping of glaciers, as all the land, the lakes and the inlet towards which I'm heading have been carved by ice. In the bushes along the banks, small animals such as mice and sala-manders rustle as they negotiate pathways through the twisted stems and glossy leaves of Oregon grape and salal, their progress parallel to mine. My heart thumps with fear and glad-ness because of this and of nothing more than that I, Sandy Grey, am still alive.

I'm doing fine. The single buttock of the moon has dropped from sight. I remember Winchell saying, 'I'm the guy who gets to stand at attention with his hands covering his dick going *Jesus, Mary and Joseph*; the one who climbs from a shit-hole of a childhood to the shit-hole of Spain; from the scented crap-hole of the West Wing to the bloody dung pit of the East – that's why I'm the guy who has to go to Russia to fight.' So I don't believe it, I don't believe they'll get him: he'll never give up.

There's a big bang from behind me, I turn: the whole sky is alight. Searchlights, sirens, the wail of an ambulance, anti-aircraft guns. The whole lot.

I come out at a dirt road. It passes between tangled hedgerows and through orchards and rolling farmlands north-westwards. The night scent of cut fields, of earth and gold, of the rich odour of ripened blackberry and the faint perfume of rose-hips with dried petals attached – these are my food and drink. Behind the hedgerows are the squares and oblongs of farms; the occasional gate marks a farmyard entrance. Sometimes, through these, I glimpse the sheen of high windows in a farmhouse. I move as quickly as I can, my body sings with energy. I know they will think of Georgina, and that I might be headed towards her, and will sooner or later take the route I'm following. How soon depends on information that I don't have: the nature of the explosion and what it does or does not have to do with Winchell; the priorities the soldiers have been given; whether they know that Karl is missing as well; the route Bob took on his motorbike; whether they think I'm dead or alive; the lies that Pete Cooper (if he is able) will tell them.

As I come to the path that returns me to the creek, and which will take me the rest of the way to Georgina's house, I remember there's another possibility: we could be experiencing enemy strikes. After all, we are at war!

There have been, according to Georgina's information from the admiral, several attacks by Japanese submarines on the coast, most recently only a few weeks ago, when a submarine-launched seaplane dropped phosphorus incendiary bombs into the forests of Oregon. Perhaps submarines and seaplanes are bombarding us now? In any case, everyone will be on the lookout for Japs. Could Georgina's *cri de cœur* mean that increased vigilance has put Kosho at 'Innisfree' in danger? Is the admiral really on our side? How much has Georgina told him? I turn the trouble over in my mind, but get nothing from it but a sense of increased pressure in my brain. Don't speculate, Sandy, and for God's sake don't make assumptions, it'll only make things worse.

I run past the last of the farmhouses – this one with a light on, despite the blackout demanded by the explosion – my head down so as to hide my face from any farmwife gazing from her bedroom. Now, here's a narrow bridge over a small ravine, one of the quarry cuts with which the creek path intersects, and I'm across it and the warning voice in my head says, *Sandy, don't get too far ahead of yourself.* But how can I not imagine what the future might hold? How can I not invite myself to live the union of hearts of which I've dreamed?

The path ahead is a keyhole into the dark, the earth beneath my feet is dry and light. There's a whisper of leaves, and hanging moss, and I can hear the susurration of the stream picking up strength as it nears its end. My feet fly, I'm weightless, the sky glows with fire. The path twists and turns and the way winds downward. I have a glimpse over the bushes, of hills across the inlet, those hills from which I once came, then the path drops steeply and I've passed a crisscrossing of broken branches and sticks and leaves, and I sight, to my left, shimmering water, and I've leapt down the bank and landed on the tidal flat where the stream loses itself in the sea.

I watch a line of foam write its way along the eastern shore of the little island, barely visible at the far end of the fjord, where Georgina had taken me to hide so long ago, and where I'd stumbled over the sea serpent as it had brought its baby into the world. I listen to the roar of my breath as it subsides to a hum in my ears, and I wait for the pounding of my heart to keep time with the gentle surge of waves at this juncture of fresh and sea water. If I could start all over again, open the end of the loop in which I'm standing, would I? Return to that small open boat with Georgina at the oars, stagger ashore, keep myself hidden, betray the dragon of the deep in exchange for the three years I've spent in prison? But it's not a real question. There's no going back, there's only what I've done and who I've become, and I think about how Karl taught me that even in a circular story there must be change, and that this Sandy Grey has got to keep going. I crouch in the mud and dip my hands in the water and splash the sweat from my face: the water is cold and it stings my skin, but even as Heraclitus said so long ago, you can't step into the same water twice. The night releases a brief rain shower over my head and shoulders, and my shirt sticks to my rapidly cooling body and I'm shivering. So it's once more into the moss and trees and the path to Georgina's house.

The clearing, when I come to it, is long and wide, and with an air of once having been tended. Overgrown shrubbery edges a wide sweep of pea gravel that faces the rippling inlet and the navy blue, almost black, forested hills on the opposite shore. Behind me, on the slope, is a large dark house. Below me is a little clay-and-stone beach with an upturned skiff resting on it. Something about it catches my eye. I jump down the bank and tug out from beneath it, by a protruding corner, a wet white towel. Even before I've seen more than a fraction, I know it for Kosho's, and I look up immediately, half-expecting to see some-where on the stirring water, my friend swimming to meet the king of the serpent people, Ryu-wo, the guardian of his faith. The waters grow flat under a scud of wind, the surface pocked by rain, but if anything lingers within that face of crumpled silk, it is not apparent to me. I hear footsteps behind me, turn and there's Georgina skidding in a spray of stones down the bank to join me.

'Christ, Sandy, what took you so long!' she says.

It only takes a few minutes for us to make our way across the clearing and into the trees to the hut which George and Kosho have made into a dovecote. Although most of the pigeons are sleeping and quiet, a few wake and coo as we enter the fly pen. I pick up a handful of grain, and several of the birds settle quietly on my arms to peck at it. They are sleek, well fed and unafraid, and I'm struck through with a pang of longing for the simple creatures that I've had to leave behind. Who will look after them? Ron Signet, I hope – and that he knows enough. When the food is gone, I dust my hands on my trousers and follow Georgina through a low doorway into the living quarters. All here too, is neat. A few shirts and undershirts hang on hooks, a pair of boots lined up underneath. The plank floor has been swept clean and there are no unwashed dishes on the counter. The washbasin is empty and upturned; a bucket of fresh water, covered by a lid, stands ready nearby. I poke through the rest of Kosho's few belongings – vegetables in a bin, writing equipment, candles, matches, a set of glasses which George tells me he used to track the pigeons in their flight. She returns several times to gaze at the made-up cot, sheets and blankets tucked, a flat pillow square at the top, a plain quilt folded across the bottom end.

'I made that quilt myself, Sandy,' Georgina says.

'You, Georgina? I find that hard to believe.' I, too, stare, standing beside her, at the lumpy stitched cotton squares.

'Had to, in school,' she says. It's not the sewing that's difficult for us to take in, but the absolute quality of Kosho's absence.

'When did you last see him?'

'Two days ago. I'd gone out, and by the time I came home my sister had taken the old man away and had the locks on the house changed. When I couldn't get inside, I came here.'

'You sent me a message.'

'I'd seen Dr Love. He told me I had to get you out, and I thought you could help with Kosho. And I needed you, Sandy.' Georgina tips her head so it rests on my shoulder. 'What was wrong with Kosho? Did you ever know?'

I recall what Pete Cooper had told me about Kosho and his terrible crimes. I turn the lying words away. 'Not really, George. Just the usual, I suppose, some bad mistake in love.'

I have to smash several panes of glass in the greenhouse. A flimsy door, easily knocked from its hinges, leads from there on to an unlocked French door at one end, and this door opens into the house proper. The house is cold and damp. I help Georgina light the fires and start the furnace. She heats soup and makes tea in the kitchen. We carry the trays upstairs to one of the bedrooms where we sit in armchairs, wrapped in blankets to get warm. Georgina falls asleep before I do – there's so much on my mind: what I've left, where I am. What's going to happen to me. Her body trembles from time to time, but her face is relaxed and her fists have uncurled and lie open in her lap. I reach over and take her hand.

There's no wind or rain to rattle the windowpanes, so I'm not sure what has wakened me this time. It's still dark out, but there's a suggestion of grey in the stippled plate of water, under clear starlight, that I can see outside. As quietly as I can, I get up and move to the window. Nothing. Yet still . . .

Within a minute, dressed in an old coat of Georgina's father's, I'm back at the little boat and I've upturned the skiff, pulled the oars from under the thwarts and rowed out into the inlet. I feel like I'm in a dream, floating over the cold sea with the scent of seaweed in my nostrils and the bow of the little boat slicing true through the shallow wave crests that mark deep water. I think about the sea serpent and how she rose to meet me, once, from the depths, when I needed her, and how she swam in rapid undulation towards the little island in order to have her pup. I'm almost there, at the northern tip that is really the mountaintop limit of a trench scored through the ancient rock of the ocean floor: a slit that may descend to the core of the planet, and out of which has arisen life in all its forms – diatoms, plankton, spiny fish, molluscs and cephalopods – generations of what look to us like evolutionary impossibilities, and yes, I'm thinking along these lines when there emerges ahead of me – from where it has waited and watched – how long! – the tall black snout of a submarine. I back-paddle furiously, and I hear –

how could I have missed it! – the deep quivering thrumming of its diesel engines and the thrust of its propellers as it nears the surface. Now there's the rest of the conning tower and the black bulk of the wheelhouse, tons of water streaming from its sides – thank God I'm to the rear and not in the way of its massive bows – I crank my head over my shoulder as I frantically row towards the shelter of the island, and hear the deck guns swivel, and then its entire length of several hundred feet lies quiescent on the surface behind me.

Be still, my heart! The bow of my little craft nudges against a rock. I lay the oars across the seats, and reach out to the rock to steady us. The thud of my heart and the rushing of blood in my ears obscures the first sounds, but then I hear quiet voices and the unmistakable splash of a rope as it drops from the deck of the submarine to the sea. From the other side of the rock, like an arrow taking aim at a target, appears the sharp silhouette of a canoe: the figure in it glances over at me, then resolutely turns away. I watch open-mouthed as the canoe quickly reaches the side of the submarine, the figure detaches itself, and begins to climb the rope ladder. Tide and current ease the abandoned canoe away in uneven drifts and slops towards Patricia Bay and I lose sight of it. I hear a few more low murmurs as the figure reaches the deck. Within seconds, it seems, hatches are closed, the engines restarted and the submarine drops below the waves.

You can't stay where you are in a boat, not for long, you can't not participate when you're bobbing on waves. A cramp in my arm makes me let go of the rock, and I have to take up the oars. My mind is full of thought and wonder but I'm strong, I'm Sandy Grey and I've exercised with homemade Indian clubs and I don't stop rowing until I'm back on shore.

The house still sleeps. The whole world.

In the morning I get up, bathe, shave with Georgina's father's toiletries, put on one of the shirts he's left behind and go downstairs. George is already at the breakfast table. A silver teapot nests in a padded stand in front of her, the toast rack is full. She spoons marmalade the colour of summer on to a china-blue plate.

'All right, Sandy?' she says. I nod and smile as if we do this every morning. Georgina unfolds the newspaper beside her plate. The headline reads: 'Attendant Injured, Inmate Burned to Death, Patient Nabbed after Manhunt.'

I read the piece quickly. The farmhouse where Winchell and I had left Pete Cooper had been set on fire and the body of a man identified as me – Sandy Grey! – had been found burned to death in its smoking ruins, *The Storehouse of Thought and Expression* – which must have tumbled from my pack – found lodged beneath him. The 'nabbed patient' had wandered out of a 'mysteriously unlocked door'. There's no mention of Karl or Winchell, nor of the explosions and gunfire.

'Eat your toast,' Georgina says. We wait all day for the police or army or even for Georgina's sister and the lawyers, but no one comes. The long winding driveway remains untrammelled.

Sometimes, even in a life that is less than a third over (all being well) there can still be a happy ending. It is important for people to know that. None of Winchell's bullets hits their mark, no soldiers or policemen died. Winchell made it safely to the truck Bob had left for him at another breach in the wall. Where he is now, I do not know, but he carries with him the letters written for the families of the Russians and if the comrades are any good at all, they'll get him and the letters where they have to go. Karl and Bob are safe as well, although the admiral, who gave me the information, won't tell me more. My country's need for secrecy about the escape of a German and a Communist, and a Japanese act of war on the coast, have worked to my benefit. Who could have guessed it?

Sometimes I think about the dead man who was misidentified as me, and wonder who he could have been, and sometimes, on the bush patrols I fly, in my new identity, for the air force in a Norseman float plane based at Patricia Bay, I see a man walking the hills and fields, with his head down and his hands stuffed into the pockets of his heavy jacket. He's a slight figure, looking neither to left nor right. He walks to keep warm. When this happens and I remember Alan Macaulay and how he'll never fulfil his dreams or have his darling Peggy, and I recall the difficulties I've experienced and the acts of my tormentors, I head out to the open coast and vanquish my troubles in a play of light. Back and over the surge and wash of the ocean, scanning for Japanese subs, I fly low over white sand beaches with an eye out for the sea lions that bask on rocky outcrops and on the whales that follow their own form of necessity as they migrate and mate and feed and play and die; and on the flocks of birds that travel the ancient skyways between their homes. The birds and I, we own the skies together.

So how am I then, overall?

With the wearing out of her grief, Georgina has settled. Now that the house is all hers – the old man having died without changing his will, the sister taking her share in money – Georgina gardens and loves her admiral and looks after Heather – my Heather! – while Heather waits for the birth of her baby. Heather's husband is still missing in action, and one love can't replace another, but I believe that some day, somehow or other, Heather and I will live together and I will bring up that baby as my own.

When I can, I take Heather for walks. The field scents raised by our passage are those that belonged to our childhood: dandelion, buttercup, cow parsley, wild thistle, wild orchid and the blue camas flowers of the bouquet that Heather held when we celebrated our marriage as children. Although I do not speak of this to her, more than once I've slipped from the wedding that was to the one to come: Heather dressed in blue silk to match her eyes, and wearing a blue velvet hat with a veil; there'll be pink champagne for everyone, malt whiskey for the men and gin for Georgina who will understand my happiness and be happy too with her admiral.

The ceremony will take place out of doors during Indian summer, the golden hour of the year, when the veils between worlds are sheer, and all is rich and ripe and outlined in brilliant nimbus: all who wish may attend, both wild creatures and tame, and the good people – Drs Love and Frank and their wives, and Bob and Winchell and Karl and even Ron Signet if he wants to once he thinks things over.

And the ghosts who search for joy beyond their deaths: Alan Macaulay, Georgina's Brentwood, poor Tom who will have recovered his cleverness, all the Russians, and Kosho – alive or dead. For it is clear to me as I help Heather step across a narrow place in the creek that she and I will have happiness to spare and it will flow from us like a river, like the waterways of the world which through flood and drought and war and pestilence are none the less never-ending, and I see a better time coming, when all the world's countries will sit down together and settle their problems and there'll be no more war. For all is held in the perspective of time, and as for me, I crossed out of time the moment I escaped from slavery. Somehow, during the years of my incarceration, and in my nighttime journey across the penin-sula from the asylum, I have stored up a reservoir of good fortune. And if I am to give advice to anyone, it is this: *Never give up, no matter how bad things look* and *Be true to your heart* and *You can always count on love.*

ACKNOWLEDGEMENTS

I would like to thank Shirley MacDonald of Clinical Records, East Lawn, Riverview; Dr Robert Menzies of Simon Fraser University; the National Archives, Ottawa; and the staff of the Royal British Columbia Archives for their assistance with the research aspects of this book. Jody Patterson also provided some important details.

My love and thanks to Michael and Xan and David and Carol for their support; my especial thanks to my cousin Gerry for his story about true love. Thanks as well to Margie and Rooth for telling me of their Cadborosaurus sightings. Other friends – particularly my women writer friends – have kept me going. Paddy Grant gave me valuable feedback, and Ed Carson continues to be an inspiration. I would also like to acknowledge Malaspina University College and my friends and colleagues there. As for the GTBB and our Sunday afternoon concerts – those who were there will understand.

Chapter One of *What it Takes to be Human* was commissioned by CBC Radio's Festival of Fiction. The B.C. Arts Council provided financial assistance during the writing of parts of this work. My thanks to both.

The Storehouse of Thought and Expression is modelled, to some extent, on *Adventures in Thought and Expression*, Albert Blohm and Charles W. Raubicheck, Prentice Hall, New York, 1932.

Merete Morken Andersen OCEANS OF TIME   £8.99   ISBN 1 904559 11 5
A divorced couple confront a family tragedy in the white night of a Norwegian summer.
International book of the year (*TLS*) and nominated for the IMPAC Award 2006.

Michael Arditti A SEA CHANGE   £8.99   ISBN 1 904559 21 2
A mesmerising journey through history, a tale of dreams, betrayal, courage and romance
told through the memories of a 15-year-old, based on the true story of the Jewish refugees
on the SS *St Louis*, who were forced to criss-cross the ocean in search of asylum in 1939.

Michael Arditti GOOD CLEAN FUN   £8.99   ISBN 1 904559 08 5
A dazzling collection of stories provides a witty, compassionate yet uncompromising look at
love and loss, desire and defiance. 'Witheringly funny, painfully acute' (*Literary Review*)

Michael Arditti UNITY   £8.99   ISBN 1 904559 12 3
A groundbreaking novel on the making of a film about Hitler and Unity Mitford, set against
the background of the Red Army Faction terror campaign in 1970s Germany.

**Booktrust London Short Story Competition
UNDERWORDS: THE HIDDEN CITY**   £9.99   ISBN 1 904559 14 X
New writing on the theme of Hidden London, plus stories from Diran Adebayo, Nicola
Barker, Romesh Gunesekera, Sarah Hall, Hanif Kureishi, Andrea Levy, Patrick Neate and Alex
Wheatle

Hélène du Coudray ANOTHER COUNTRY   £7.99   ISBN 1 904559 04 2
A prize-winning novel, first published in 1928, about a passionate affair between a British
ship's officer and a Russian emigrée governess which promises to end in disaster.

Lewis DeSoto A BLADE OF GRASS   £8.99   ISBN 1 904559 07 7
A lyrical and profound novel set in South Africa during the era of apartheid, in which the
recently widowed Märit struggles to run her farm with the help of her black maid, Tembi.
Longlisted for the Man Booker Prize 2004; shortlisted for the Ondaatje Prize 2005.

Olivia Fane THE GLORIOUS FLIGHT OF PERDITA TREE
£8.99   ISBN 1 904559 13 1
Beautiful, vain Perdita Tree is kidnapped in Albania. Freedom is coming to the country where
flared trousers landed you in prison, but are the Albanians ready for it or, indeed, Perdita?

Olivia Fane GOD'S APOLOGY £8.99 ISBN 1 904559 20 7
Patrick German abandons his wife and child, and in his newfound role as a teacher
encounters the mesmerising 10-year-old Joanna. Is she really an angel sent to save him?

Maggie Hamand, ed. UNCUT DIAMONDS £7.99 ISBN 1 904559 03 4
Unusual and challenging, these vibrant, original stories showcase the huge diversity of new
writing talent coming out of contemporary London.

Helen Humphreys WILD DOGS £8.99 ISBN 1 904559 15 8
A pack of lost dogs runs wild, and each evening their bereft former owners gather to call
them home – a remarkable book about the power of human strength, trust and love.

Linda Leatherbarrow ESSENTIAL KIT £8.99 ISBN 1 904559 10 7
The first collection from a short-story prizewinner – lyrical, uplifting, funny and moving,
always pertinent – 'joyously surreal . . . gnomically funny, and touching' (Shena Mackay).

Kolton Lee THE LAST CARD £8.99 ISBN 978 1 904559 25 2
H, a boxer past his prime, is dragged into a multicultural underworld of violence and
extortion. To save himself, he must face his demons and enter the ring one last time.

Sara Maitland ON BECOMING A FAIRY GODMOTHER
£7.99 ISBN 1 904559 00 X
Fifteen new 'fairy stories' by an acclaimed master of the genre breathe new life into old
legends and bring the magic of myth back into modern women's lives.

Maria Peura AT THE EDGE OF LIGHT £8.99 ISBN 978 1 904559 24 5
The story of a girl growing up in the far north of Finland, her first love affair and her
desperation to escape from the restricted life of a remote and extraordinary community.

Danny Rhodes ASBOVILLE £8.99 ISBN 1 904559 22 0
Young JB is served with an ASBO and sent to work by the seaside. He has the chance to
turn his life around, but a storm is coming that threatens to shatter all his hopes.

Dreda Say Mitchell RUNNING HOT £8.99 ISBN 1 904559 09 3
A pacy, blackly comic thriller about Schoolboy and his attempts to go straight in a world of
crime and petty deaths. An exciting debut, winner of the 2005 John Creasey Award.

Anne Redmon IN DENIAL £7.99   ISBN 1 904559 01 8

A chilling novel about the relationship between Harriet, a prison visitor, and Gerry, a serial offender, which explores challenging themes with subtlety and intelligence.

Diane Schoemperlen FORMS OF DEVOTION £9.99   ISBN 1 904559 19 0

Eleven stories with a brilliant interplay between words and images – a creative delight, perfectly formed and rich in wit and irony. Illustrated throughout with line engravings.

Henrietta Seredy LEAVING IMPRINTS £7.99   ISBN 1 904559 02 6

Beautifully written and startlingly original, this unusual and memorable novel explores a destructive, passionate relationship between two damaged people.

Emma Tennant THE FRENCH DANCER'S BASTARD
£8.99   ISBN 1 904559 23 9

Lonely and homesick, little Adèle finds a new secret world in the attic of the forbidding Mr Rochester, but her curiosity will imperil everyone, including her governess Jane Eyre, shatter their happiness and send her fleeing, frightened and alone, back to Paris.

Emma Tennant THE HARP LESSON £8.99   ISBN 1 904559 16 6

With the French Revolution looming, little Pamela Sims is taken from England to live at the French court as the illegitimate daughter of Mme de Genlis. But who is she really?

Emma Tennant PEMBERLEY REVISITED £8.99   ISBN 1 904559 17 4

Elizabeth wins Darcy, and Jane wins Bingley – but do they 'live happily ever after'? Two bestselling sequels to Jane Austen's *Pride and Prejudice*, issued together for the first time.

Norman Thomas THE THOUSAND-PETALLED DAISY
£7.99   ISBN 1 904559 05 0

Love, jealousy and violence play a part in this coming-of-age novel set in India, written with a distinctive, off-beat humour and a delicate but intensely felt spirituality.

Karel Van Loon THE INVISIBLE ONES £8.99   ISBN 1 904559 18 2

A gripping novel about the life of a refugee in Thailand, in which harrowing accounts of Burmese political prisoners blend with Buddhist myth and memories of a carefree childhood.

Adam Zameenzad PEPSI AND MARIA £8.99   ISBN 1 904559 06 9

A highly original novel about two street children in South America whose zest for life carries them through the brutal realities of their daily existence.